ABRAMS AMULET
NEW YORK

RoseBlood

A. G. Howard

Cataloging-in-Publication Data has been applied for
and may be obtained from the Library of Congress.

ISBN: 978-1-4197-1909-7

Printed and bound in U.S.A.
10 9 8 7 6 5 4 3 2

Amulet Books are available at special discounts when purchased
in quantity for premiums and promotions as well as fundraising or
educational use. Special editions can also be created to specification.
For details, contact specialsales@abramsbooks.com or the address below.

ABRAMS The Art of Books
115 West 18th Street, New York, NY 10011
abramsbooks.com

While writing this story, I was struck by how lonely and dark life would be for someone who had to make the journey without friendship. Roman philosopher Marcus Tullius Cicero once said,

"What sweetness is left in life, if you take away friendship? Robbing life of friendship is like robbing the world of the sun."

So, to my two dearest friends, Bethany Crandell and Jessica Nelson, thank you for being my sun—for warming me when the chill of personal tragedy strikes, and for illuminating my footsteps when I take a wrong turn and find myself in the shadows. I love and treasure you both. May we light one another's paths for years to come.

1

OVERTURE

"The opera ghost really existed . . ."
Gaston Leroux, The Phantom of the Opera

At home, I have a poster on my wall of a rose that's bleeding. Its petals are white, and red liquid oozes from its heart, thick and glistening warm. Only, if you look very close, you can see the droplets are coming from above, where a little girl's wrist—camouflaged by a cluster of leaves—has been pricked by thorns as she reached inside to catch a monarch.

I used to wonder why she risked getting sliced up just to touch a butterfly. But now it makes sense: she wanted those wings so she could fly away, because the pain of trying to reach for them was more tolerable than the pain of staying grounded, wherever she was.

Today, I embrace that child's perfect wisdom. What I wouldn't give for a set of wings . . .

On the other side of the limo's window, a gray sky looms above thickly woven trees lining the country road. The clouds heave like living, breathing creatures, and raindrops smack the glass.

Not the ideal Sunday afternoon to be driven along the French countryside, unless I were here for a vacation. Which I'm not, no matter how anyone tries to spin it.

"The opera house has a violent history. No one even knows how the fire started all those years ago. That doesn't bother you?" I mumble the words beneath the hum of the motor so our driver won't hear. They're for Mom's benefit—at the other end of the backseat.

Mom bounces as the tires dip into a deep puddle while turning onto a dilapidated road of mismatched cobblestones and dirt. Mud splashes across the window.

"Rune . . . you're understandably predisposed to hate any building that has suffered a fire. But it's a fear you need to outgrow. The eighteen hundreds were a long, long time ago. Pretty sure by now, all the bad 'karma' is gone."

I stare at the privacy screen separating us from the uniformed man at the steering wheel, watching the wipers slash through the brown muck on the windshield with a muffled screech as they clear a line of vision.

Mom uses the term *karma* like it's a four-letter word. I shouldn't be surprised at her cynicism. She's always had a different view on Dad's heritage than I have. She thinks my anxiety stems from Grandma Liliana's impact on our lives. That my grandmother's actions and accusations compounded the gypsy superstitions my dad had already imprinted on me, and they've affected how I see the world. Mom's partly right. It's hard to escape something so deeply ingrained, especially when I've seen proof of otherworldly things, having been possessed most of my life.

"Six weeks till the end of October," I continue to bait. "And I'll be spending it at a school haunted by a phantom. Things don't get any more Halloween than that."

"A phantom?" A tiny wrinkle bridges Mom's furrowed eyebrows. "Are we on that again? Your life isn't a Broadway musical. This place isn't anything like the one in the story. Leroux's Opéra Populaire was fashioned after the Palais Garnier in the city. You should know that, considering you've read the book at least three times now."

I grip the door panel to brace myself against another dip in the road. If she thinks I'm going to just ignore what I found on the underground RoseBlood forums, she's wrong. It's the whole reason I checked out Gaston Leroux's novel from the library a few weeks before we left in the first place. Although my reading the book so many times had more to do with the story itself—a mysterious composer using his unnatural gift of music to help a girl find the power in her voice.

"You saw the discussion," I say. "The blueprint for Garnier was inspired by a building once owned by an eccentric Parisian emperor in the eighteenth century. A private opera house set out in the country called Le Théâtre Liminaire. AKA: my new school. The Liminaire is rumored to be where the phantom legend first originated." I scroll through my recent searches on my phone, then hold up the screen so Mom can see the text alongside a morbid and lovely illustration of a caped man in a half-mask holding up a bloody rose. "So you're right. I'm not stepping into a musical. It's a horror story. With a side of obsession and gore."

We hit two bumps in a row this time, nearly slamming our heads on the limo's cushioned ceiling. An irritated puff of air escapes Mom's lips, though I'm pretty sure it's directed at me and not the driver. "I told you those forums are nothing more than wannabe students who were turned down by admissions. People say outrageous things when they feel slighted." She opens the school's pamphlet for the twentieth time. "According to the brochure, post-renovation, most of the opera house isn't even the same anymore. Totally different place."

I nibble on the end of my braid. "It just doesn't feel right. Why did it take over a hundred years for anyone to rebuild or inhabit that place again?"

Mom presses the brochure to her thigh, signaling the end of our debate. "Just quit being so negative and focus on the positive. They've had a lot of rain here, so the leaves are changing early. Look out your window and enjoy the beginning of fall. That should remind you of home."

I glance at my lap and make a marked effort *not* to see the jeweled leaves: the browns and oranges, the yellows as bright as the dandelions that overtake my flowers every spring, until I make my way out with a bucket and spade to dig them up. I'd rather not be reminded of what I'm missing at home right now, or of what I'll be missing in six months when warm weather settles in Harmony, Texas, and I'm not there to take care of Dad's garden.

Gardening is one of the two things that reminds me most of him. I inherited his green thumb but also his talent for music. Although I could never master the violin like he did. My instrument is something entirely different, and *it* masters *me*. Which is the real reason I'm being sent away, although Mom won't admit it.

My braid drapes across my left shoulder, the end tapping the belt loops on my jeans in time with the car's movement. I tug the silvery ribbons woven within, relieved I plaited the unruly waves this morning before our shopping spree. Otherwise, I'd have no control over them in this dampness. I pull my handmade knitted cap lower, wishing I could disappear inside.

If I were going anywhere but a music conservatory, I'd be more cooperative. Something happened in Harmony recently . . . something I have reason to run from. Something Mom doesn't even know about.

But to send me to *RoseBlood*? She's so desperate to fix me, she hasn't stopped to consider the hell she's sentencing me to.

"They found a *skeleton* in the deepest basement, floating in the water. A skeleton, Mom. Do I really need another reason to be scared of water? This weather . . . it's an omen."

"Right." Mom scoffs. "Any minute you'll start preaching about auras and visions."

Tension knots in my shoulders. My dad and my grandma spoke of auras a lot, as if they could see them. And since I see rainbows when I sing, I used to think that ability passed on to me. There was a time I was convinced—if I focused hard enough—I could see halos of color around other people's bodies. I made the mistake of telling Mom once. She took me to the eye doctor, and I ended up recanting the claim in order to get out of wearing glasses I knew I didn't need. Now, I've convinced myself to stop looking for them. It's not worth the hassle or the confusion.

"Consider this," Mom continues, "every time you fall back into her way of thinking, you give her power over your life." Mom's voice falters on the obvious effort not to mention my grandma's name. "I know she's working to be a better person, so we'll cut her a little slack. She talked your aunt into paying for your tuition. The least we can do is let her try to make amends since she's dying. Just don't let her get inside your head again."

I press my lips tight. Suffering from congestive heart failure has to be horrible and painful, and I should at least feel something for Grandma Lil. But I remember images of my black hair swirling in dark, deep water as I tried to escape the wooden crate keeping me submerged; I remember her wrinkled, weathered hands on the other side of the planks tightening their grip to hold me under. And because of that, any sympathy eludes me.

I shudder. Yeah, Grandma's got a lot to make amends for, no doubt.

"After all of these years of no contact," Mom continues, "for them to reach out like this because you're having so many problems? It gives me hope we can be a family again. Your dad would've wanted that. It wasn't easy for Lottie to get your transfer moved to the top of the list. She was afraid to show favoritism. But she's doing it as a favor to us. Let's make an effort to show our gratitude when we get there. Okay?"

The famed Aunt Charlotte: retired sixty-something French prima donna and Dad's older sister. I get the feeling this is more of a favor she's doing for her incarcerated mom—so the old woman can save herself from continuing imprisonment postdeath, in purgatory.

I run my palm across the seat, the leather plush and foreign to my hand. Like nearly every woman in Dad's family, Charlotte was a ballerina in the Paris Opera company. As a result, she snagged herself an aristocratic husband. It was love at first sight when he saw her dance. Now that she's a wealthy widow, her generous donations have earned our family a spot among the boarding school's most elite beneficiaries. Which explains my acceptance as a student without the usual three-month consideration period.

Nothing like nepotism to earn you a place in the hearts of your peers.

Hopefully the other students won't know my aunt sent this limo to pick us up at the hotel this morning and drive us around shopping all day; that *she* is paying my tuition for the year; and that she wired Mom nine hundred and fifty euros last week—the equivalent of a thousand dollars, give or take—to help buy my uniforms and dorm accessories at the posh boutiques here.

I've never met her, other than through ten years of spotty, one-sided phone conversations with my mom. Charlotte's never visited America, and I'd never been to Paris until now. According to Mom, she used to call once a month to talk to Dad. Until he got sick enough to land in hospice care; then she stopped. She didn't even come to his funeral, so I can't help but question her motives.

"It said in the brochure they coordinate their calendars with public schools in the states. That means it's already one month in here." I wind my hands together, an attempt to quell the pain in my heart at the thought of Dad's absence—the wound that never heals, even after a decade. "Do you know how hard it is to make friends so close to the end of the first six weeks?" Not that I plan to try . . . but true intentions take a backseat when it comes to guilting Mom.

"It's not unheard of," Mom rebuts. "Lots of people are scrambling to send their kids, even late. Doesn't that say something to the credit of the school? Only two years in, and there's already a wait list. There were at least twenty names in front of yours." Mom looks out her window where the wet trees have thickened to multicolored knots, like an afghan gilded with glitter.

"My point exactly." I tap my fingers to some endless rhythm turning inside of me . . . an operatic aria I heard in an elevator earlier. It's reawakened, and that's not a good sign. The melody will writhe like a snake on fire and burn holes behind my closed eyelids in the shape of musical notes until I sing it out. It's physical torture, like a constant spark in my skull that scorches my spine—vertebra by vertebra. "I'll be winning friends left and right once they hear I jumped the list via my bloodline."

Mom clucks her tongue. "Well, according to you, there's still the phantom. I'm sure he's not too picky about who he hangs out with."

My jaw tightens as I suppress a snort. *Touché.*

I trace the window now curtained by mud, imagining the glass cracking and bursting; imagining myself sprouting wings to fly away through the opening—back to America and my two friends who were tolerant of my strange quirks.

Aching for another glimpse of the sky, I trigger the automatic window to swipe the pane clean, allowing a fresh, cold wind to usher in a spray of mud and rain. I smile as the moisture dots my face and neck, easing the sting of the song in my head. Mom yelps and I send the window up again.

"Rune, *please.*" She tightens her plump, red-tinted lips to a frown. Working her fingers through the dirty droplets in her cropped hair, she digs a Kleenex from her purse.

"Sorry," I whisper, actually meaning it. Using my velvet scarf, I blot my cheeks then sponge the leather seat.

Mom's scrubbing shifts to the taupe crepe jacket and pencil skirt, which hang like tissue paper on her small frame. With each movement, her signature fragrance wafts over me: Lemon Pledge. She cleans other people's houses for a living, and can never seem to shake off the stench of dust solvent and Pine-Sol.

With her delicate bone structure and striking features, she missed her true calling. She did some print modeling back when Dad was alive, but she wasn't tall enough to be on the catwalk. Once he got sick, she needed "job security" to help pay bills. Housekeeping filled that niche, but I know a part of her has always regretted switching professions. And now she's determined to see that I don't lose my shot at something better, something she thinks I was born to do.

Gray light and purple shadows take turns gliding along her high cheekbones as we pass through the trees. People say we could pass for sisters. We share her ivory complexion, the tiny freckles spattered across the bridge of her nose, the wide green eyes inside a framework of thick lashes, and her hair—black as a raven's wings. The only difference is, I inherited my curls from a father whose laughter I still hear when I dance in rain puddles. Whose face I still see in the water's reflections, as if he's beside me.

Without being at home, close to our garden, my only remaining connections to him are the music he loved and his family, each inseparably intertwined with the other. Since Mom's parents passed away before I was even born, she had no one to lean on once Dad got sick. So, Grandma Liliana came from France to live with us in Harmony. She was a lot of help in the beginning, but a few months after Dad died, she left our lives in a blaze of horror, literally. The last time I saw her she showed up at my second-grade Valentine's Day party and purposely started a fire that almost wiped out an entire class of eight-year-olds.

She was carted back to France and has been locked away in the city of Versailles ever since, at a prison for the criminally insane.

Ironic, considering that was her second attempt at killing me. Although I often wonder if I imagined the first . . . if the details got mixed up in my seven-year-old brain because I was fighting so hard for my life. According to what Grandma told Mom, it had all been an accident.

I shiver and rub the scar on my left knee that peeks through the rip in my jeans, a reminder imprinted on my skin. A reminder of the splintering wood I kicked my way through . . . a reminder that, accident or not, I didn't imagine it.

"You have a gift." Mom's statement rakes across the intrusive memory, ripping through the cobwebs and dangling dead hopes in my heart that have settled where a loving and sane grandmother should've been. "This place will help you realize your potential. Be grateful for the opportunity."

Mom doesn't get that I want to be grateful. I miss how singing once made me feel: free, unique, complete.

But what if Grandma was right about me . . . about everything?

The aria I heard earlier in the elevator bumps against my ribs once more, making my breath shallow. From the time they started dating, Dad taught Mom French. He'd done the same for me since birth, and she continued his tutelage after we lost him. Because of that, I know enough to be comfortable here. But the opera piping through the speakers had sounded Russian. I have no idea what the name of it is or what it's about. I don't have to know. Now that the notes are woven within me, the words are imprinted alongside them. Whether or not I can translate what I'm singing, I'll still remember how to form each syllable on my tongue when the time comes to release the song.

It's like I have an auditory photographic memory, although it's not something I can quietly absorb then let sit on the back of my eyelids like an image, hidden from everyone else's view. There's nothing private about my ability.

Dread tightens my throat. I need to ease the tension, to rid myself of the music. But I don't want to lose it in the back of a limo. It's too confined; and then there's the driver . . .

Everyone has experienced the feeling, stepping into a room and the other people stop talking. This happens to me each time I sing. Wall-to-wall silence. If a sweat drop were to fall, you could hear it splatter to the floor. Not an awkward silence. More like an awed hush.

I have no right to be proud because it's nothing I've earned. Up until recently, I'd never had a voice lesson in my life. Yet, ever since I was small, opera has been a living, breathing part of me.

The problem is that as I've grown, it's become more demanding . . . an entity that controls me. Once a song speaks to my subconscious, the notes become a toxin I have to release through my diaphragm, my vocal cords, my tongue.

The only way I can breathe again is through a binge and purge of music. The worst part is what follows—how finishing a performance makes me feel. Stripped naked, cold and exposed. Physically sick. Only hours later, after the symptoms of withdrawal have run their course, can I become myself once more. At least until the next melody possesses me, like the one snaking through me now.

My legs start to jitter, and I clamp my hands on my knees. I cough to suppress the tune that's climbing my throat like bile.

"Rune, are you all right? You're awfully flushed. Is it . . . ?" She takes one look at my face and moans. My flushed cheeks and dilated pupils are her only cue. She's never seen what I see in the mirror . . . what Dad used to see when music burned inside me: my irises brightening to a lighter, almost ethereal hue, like sunlight streaming through green glass. Dad called it an energy surge, but because Mom couldn't see it, she laughed him off.

"Just get it over with," she insists.

Another cough—hard enough to strain my vocal cords. "I can't sing in here." The nagging notes tangle in my throat. "What if I hit a high C and break the windows? Your clothes won't survive that much rain."

She frowns, oblivious to the way my skin prickles under my raincoat, to the sweat beads gathered at my hairline beneath my cap. I dig through the bag at my feet—an oversize tote, with burgundy, mauve, and green beads sewn onto the pearly front to depict roses and leaves—and drag out my newest knitting project.

Mouth closed, I go to work on the cream-colored sweater I started a few weeks ago. With each metal clack of the needles, the fluffy chenille skims lightly through my fingertips. The cold instruments are firm and empowering in my hands. I start the looping and rolling rhythm so the tactile stimulus can distract me—a strategy that sometimes works.

Mom's frowning lips soften to a frustrated straight line. "The one good thing your Grandmother Lil ever taught you, and you use it for a crutch."

Ignoring her, I snap my wrists so the needles loop and roll, twist and twirl. Chenille winds around the shimmery silver metal like strands of cotton candy on a cone.

"The music wouldn't affect you like this if you'd just stop fighting it," Mom presses, trying to stall my hands.

"Why should I have to fight it to begin with, Mom? Is that normal?" I pull free and return to my rhythmic escape.

Mom shakes her head, steadfast in her denial. Secure in her faith in me. If only I could borrow some of it.

I wish I were like those mimes we saw on a street corner when we shopped. If I could pantomime a song's exit from my body—a silent and effective murder of melody—maybe I could once more be grateful for my *gift*, instead of fearing its gradual and violent consumption of me: body, mind, and soul.

2

THE THREADS
THAT BIND US

"Sometimes, the Angel [of Music] leans over the cradle ..."
Gaston Leroux, The Phantom of the Opera

My dad first discovered my "gift" when I was four. I was in the living room with him, building a block tower as he practiced on his treasured Stradivarius violin. Up to that point, he played only concertos, overtures, and sonatas. But he'd decided to try his hand at an operatic accompaniment that day.

I stopped what I was doing, staring up at the stringed instrument. Dad said it was like I was seeing the violin for the first time, although I'd heard him perform since my birth. Knocking down the blocks in my path, I toddled over, placed my hand on his knee, and hummed the opera's tune—the one he'd never played before—in perfect pitch.

When he asked me about it afterward, I answered that his violin sang words to me. They told me how to see a rainbow and follow the colors with my voice . . . he called them auras. He was convinced I was seeing musical scales come to life—that I had a connection to the energized pulses of music. Mom returned from the grocery store in time to catch our discussion. She got annoyed, insisting Dad was being melodramatic. She blamed his superstitious upbringing and overactive imagination, two things that I—according to her—inherited from him. Her father had been a fanatical small-town preacher and had forced religion down her throat for so long, she'd turned her back on anything remotely spiritual or supernatural the minute she was old enough to leave home.

To this day she still shuns all things otherworldly, but her skepticism about my voice died a swift death as she herself sat a few days later, stunned and muted, while Dad played a recording of a Spanish aria sung by a vocalist in accompaniment. I sang along, executing every foreign lyric and note as if *I* were the world-renowned diva. This from a toddler who'd only recently learned to sing her English ABCs.

After that, Dad began accompanying operatic recordings regularly, and many times, I would join in unprompted. One day, as we put on a concert for some close friends, Dad stopped and dropped his bow, listening in reverent silence with everyone else as I finished out the song in perfect German. But without his violin guiding me, something changed. I still carried the song perfectly, until the final pristine note.

At that point, the vivid prismatic colors of the melody dancing around my head bled to a thick red glaze that tinged my vision. I dropped to my knees, trembling and nauseated. I was sick the whole night.

Dad decided it was performance anxiety, that I needed him as an accompanist for support. I became his marionette and he my puppeteer, and I loved every minute of it. At first, he concentrated only on the arias I responded to, and as long as we were bound together by strands of music, his violin's voice leading me, I could sing without incident. Then he taught me new songs. Each one lifted me higher, gave me more confidence. By the age of six, I was invincible. No note was out of range, no composition too complex.

He and Mom agreed I was too young to go public. They wanted me to have a normal childhood, so we didn't seek out formal training, and we kept our rehearsals private.

Dad encouraged my budding talent at every turn—he was my biggest fan—until he was diagnosed with cancer. When he became too weak to accompany me with his violin, I tried to keep singing for him, in hopes to give him the strength he once gave me. But since the musical ties between us had been snipped away, my performances left me exhausted. I ignored the flu-like symptoms and kept pushing myself just to see him smile.

Yet no matter how pristine the clarity of notes, or how genuine and evocative the emotions interpreted through song, I couldn't lift him out of the mire of feeding tubes, catheters, and chemotherapy. I couldn't change his fate.

After he died, my grandmother insisted it was my fault. That my unnatural gift had somehow drained my father of life and killed him.

I can't shake the belief that maybe in some way she's right. How can something so strange and inexplicable be healthy or good? It's not. I know that much. I know it by what happened between me and Ben. Although I'm hoping he'll be okay, I'm also hoping that if he wakes from his coma, he won't remember a thing. He's the only other witness.

My shoulders slump at the thought of last time I saw him, hooked up to IVs and machines in the hospital, just like my dad before he died.

For my part in Dad's death, Grandma Liliana wanted to send me to hell. An old woman terrified of a young child. Whereas Mom was, and is, convinced I'm the one with fears. She's oblivious to the dangers, sees my curse as a talent, and thinks that with practice, I'll get over my stage fright and learn to perform for the public one day.

If only.

It was hard enough feeling normal in Texas. At least there, an operatic aria popping up unexpectedly on the radio was a rare event. I don't know exactly what the trigger is. Although it's always a woman's aria, it's not every single one I hear. Some speak to me, some don't. But once the spark has been ignited, the music eventually wins. And at RoseBlood, I'll be exposed to opera every day, and forced to purge the notes in front of strangers who will see me at my most vulnerable.

No more blending, quiet like a raindrop siphoning into a stream on a windowpane.

Tiny rivulets of water jostle on the limo's window, and I rest the knitting needles in my lap, forehead pressed to the glass. Coolness seeps in to counteract the hot rush rising from my neck to my face. Through the leaves, the sky darkens, as if borrowing from my mood.

"I don't know why you're being so morose today," Mom says, the cadence of her words dancing around me like a taunting chime. "You've always talked about being involved with Broadway or theater. How's opera any different?"

"*Behind* the scenes." I attempt to reason with her. "A costume or makeup designer." In a last-ditch effort to change her mind, I pull out all the stops. "This is so unfair. I never asked for any of it." I start up the knitting needles again, slower this time, and my pulse settles to a calm rhythm. The song recedes into my subconscious, but it's only a temporary reprieve. It will be back.

Mom's suit rustles. She grips firm, warm fingers around my jaw. I set aside my sweater to study her features, each one shadowed with disappointment.

"Oh, you asked for it," she says. "You made poor choices. So now we're going to get your life back on track. And the first step is surrounding you with kids your age." She releases my chin.

And there's where RoseBlood's small populace of fifty students, made up of sixty percent juniors and forty percent seniors, comes in handy. That particular detail from the brochure stood out loud and clear while I was reading on the plane.

I stuff my knitting into the bag and kick myself for the thousandth time for going to that college frat party at the beginning of school. Getting drunk that night had nothing to do with the fact that I feel more comfortable around college kids than my own classmates. But I know better than to admit that to Mom, because were she to know the real reason I took that first sip of beer, she'd turn this limo around and drop me off in Versailles with Grandma Liliana. *Bloodthirsty birds of a feather belong together.*

"It's the only time I've ever touched alcohol," I say over a catch in my throat. "Can't you give me another chance? I made one stupid mistake and you're sending me to prison." It might sound like a barb, but prison is something I probably deserve, which makes it a legitimate fear. "Just admit it. You want me gone so you can play house with your new fiancé without me there."

"RoseBlood is hardly a prison," Mom says. "How many foreign boarding schools offer admittance only to American kids? This is a rare opportunity . . . a taste of French culture in a setting that feels like home."

I suppress the desire to point out that she's quoting the Rose-Blood brochure almost word for word, and instead focus on how she avoided my accusation about her fiancé. A burst of contentment sneaks in unexpectedly. I smirk on the left side of my face. I won't risk the right because she might see it.

I'm so glad she's met someone after all these years of raising me alone. And Ned the Realtor is a really nice guy who treats Mom like a queen and me like a princess. I'm actually glad he moved in. It's nice to have some semblance of a family again. Still, I'm not about to admit any of that since I've found some leverage.

"No Wi-Fi in the place," I say. "That means no Internet access. And we're out in the middle of nowhere with no cell phone service. How am I supposed to stay in touch with you . . . with Trig and Janine . . . anyone on the outside?"

"They do have a landline, Rune. You'll be able to call home." The other half of my smirk has found its way to her mouth. "As for the absence of texting . . . I've got the perfect substitute." She bends over to sift through the shopping bags at her feet, the small ones that were left over after stuffing the trunk full.

I watch, suspicious, as tissue paper crinkles beneath her fingers. We spent the morning driving through the Louvre-Tuileries neighborhood, touring the grand squares, gorgeous gardens, and trendy bistros from the comfort of our limo. We visited several boutiques but were never apart any longer than it took for me to try on my uniforms—three sets comprised of a fitted jacket, vest, long skirt, and ruffled shirt—that look more like Victorian riding habits than any modern dress code. Even the gray, white, and red color scheme is drab and lifeless enough to make us all look like wax museum rejects. Mom stood there and handed me the separate pieces from the other side of the dressing room door. So when did she have time to shop behind my back?

Wrist-deep in a zebra-striped bag fringed with pink feathers, she draws out a rectangle. Tissue paper loosely drapes the gift.

I take it, biting my inner cheeks to contain a smile. She knows how much I like presents. Both getting and giving them. "What did you do?"

She shrugs, the same mom who used to insist we open one Christmas gift a week early every year because she couldn't stand to wait any more than me. I love that side of her.

I feel a prick behind my sternum, as the biggest reason I don't want to attend this foreign school hits me hard and sudden. For the first time since we lost Dad, my mom and I are about to be apart.

An ocean apart.

I force myself not to look at her, afraid I'll break down.

With stiff fingers, I unwrap a fabric-covered box of rich brocade—black and gray striped with red-ribbon embellishments. A hinged lid opens to reveal fancy French stationery. Lacey black scallops trim the edges. The paper is a grayish shade, as soft and translucent as the light filtering through clouds outside. When I hold up a piece and open my hand behind it, I can see the silhouette of my fingers and palm. An embossed ribbon, shimmery red to complement the satin ones on the box, embellishes the stationery's top. Matching envelopes are tucked in the corner next to a black feather quill. The set is exactly what I would've picked for myself.

"So . . . I'm supposed to write to everyone?" I ask, hiding how touched I am. "Kind of archaic, don't you think?"

She tilts her head, smug. "Looks like you won't be in solitary confinement after all."

The smile I've been suppressing pushes its way out. "But I don't have addresses or postage."

"Ah." She digs a roll of global stamps and an address book out of the zebra sack. She must've had them hidden in her overnight bag.

Sneaky. Another thing I've always loved about her.

She points to the red ribbon embossed on the stationery. "Did you really think I'd let you be thousands of miles away from me without a thread to bind us?"

Just that one reference and I'm back at the beginning of first grade, afraid to leave her side until she reached into her purse and retrieved a long red strip of yarn, tying it around my wrist. We'd spent the night before in Dad's hospital room, talking on a toy phone made of empty soup cans and yarn. I'd poured out all of my fears to both of them, and they'd comforted me. When we left the hospital, Mom pulled the yarn from the cans and promised that all of her and Dad's love and protection were woven inside the thread, and as long as I had it with me, they'd be there.

I still have that strip of yarn, marking a passage in my favorite fairy tale picture book that Dad used to read to me: *Les Enfants Perdus*, which translates to "The Lost Children." It's an old-world French version of Hansel and Gretel, a bit more grim, with the devil and his witch-wife holding two lost siblings—Jean and Jeanette—hostage in a forest. Together, the children escape, using their minds and wills to murder and outsmart their dark tormentors before they can be eaten. Although the book's pages are water damaged and crumpled, I've never thrown it away.

I'd been so upset on the plane when I realized I forgot to bring either of those keepsakes to Paris. But Mom found a substitute for the red string.

"Wow, Mom—"

"Oh, and there's this, too . . ." She hands me one other tissue-stuffed bag.

"Hmmm. Maybe I should go off to school more often after all," I tease, dragging out the tissue. My breath catches at the glossy, brand-new *Les Enfants Perdus* staring up at me—as though she's been reading my mind all along.

She shrugs when I turn a questioning glance her way. "It was in a display window at one of the shops this morning. It's a modern edition . . . and the illustrations are different. But it's the same story. Now you have your thread *and* your book to tie us all together."

My eyes sting. "Thank you."

She pats my hand and we share another smile. My lips wobble as I thumb through the pages, remembering Dad's deep, strong voice reading the text to me in flawless French. I miss that so much. Just like I miss him speaking to me with his violin. When he got bad enough that we had to check him into hospice, I took up sleeping with the instrument under my bed every night. It almost seemed like a part of him—maybe because each time he played, he'd cradle it as one would a precious child.

I'd still have it with me to this day, had it not gone missing when Grandma Liliana first arrived in America. Mom suspected she took it, and confronted her. Grandma admitted mailing it back to Paris. Mom was furious, assuming she wanted to sell it due to its value. It was a one-of-a-kind Stradivarius, handcrafted of wood so black and glossy I used to think it had been carved from an oil slick. The scroll curled at the neck's tip like a snail's shell, adding to its uniqueness. But Grandma selling it didn't make sense. The instrument had been a family heirloom since the early 1800s. One of our ancestors, Octavius Germain, had even engraved his initials on the lower bout, just inches from the waist of the instrument. I used to trace my fingers along that *O* and *G,* imagining a man in Victorian finery playing the very instrument my dad loved.

Now, sitting here with this book in my hands, I think maybe we misjudged Grandma's motives. Maybe—just like I needed that piece of red thread to brave being without my parents that day in first grade, and this book to give me courage at a new school—she needed a piece of her son to be waiting at home for her, so when she returned she could survive in a world he no longer occupied.

I glance into the distance and swallow the words I want to say: *Mom, I still miss him. Every day. I don't want to be away from you, too. I don't want to be alone.*

Our limo slows to a crawl as we take a stone bridge over a giant river. I lean into the window, unnerved by how close the water is. Were it to rise just a few more feet, it would overlap the bridge. The river encompasses the academy on all sides, similar to a moat. The only land is the hill where the academy sits, and the eighty-some acres of woods surrounding it. Without any way to cross, it would be like an island unto itself.

I return the stationery box and my book to their bags. Unease roils through my veins in time with the blue-black depths swirling beneath the limo. According to the pamphlet, the water even surges underground beneath the estate's foundation, flooding the third basement.

Water. My least favorite element, second only to fire. And now I'll be surrounded by it. The fact that the rain has finally subsided relaxes me a fraction. Fog settles across the landscape, clinging low to the road as we roll off the bridge. RoseBlood Academy rises up, grim and ominous. The baroque architecture, looming and majestic, looks more like a brooding castle than an opera house in this isolated location.

The auditorium's cupola—a cap of bronze that cuts through the dreary sky like a ghostly crown—descends to a gabled roof where a winged horse stands guard beside Apollo. The god lifts his lyre, as if it were a bow and arrow. In the *Phantom* book, a similar roof played a pivotal and romantic role in the story line. It's where Christine met with Raoul and they claimed their undying love. They were spied upon by the Phantom, who then unleashed a series of events to punish them and make Christine his forever. But the school brochure claims this roof's stairway was sealed off along with the top three floors after the fire.

The driver turns the car onto the long, gravel drive leading up to the opera house. Glistening trees bend over us like sequined actors taking their final bow. As we plunge out from the overhanging limbs, I begin to understand the uniforms. It's as if we've crossed into an alternate time.

Ivy and lichen cling to the huge edifice. The wet façade reflects our headlights so it appears an ethereal white, but as we get closer, the stone's true color comes into view. Time has eroded it to a scaly turquoise green, like a mermaid's tail. Antique street lamps—the kind you would expect to see on a Victorian greeting card—dot the front terrace and cast an eerie yellow glow in the grayish haze. So engrossed in the scenery, I barely hear the bags rattle as Mom puts away the stamps and address book.

The boarding school is flanked on one side by an overgrown garden. The early autumn blooms follow their own call; silvery-green leaves, crimson roses, and frothy white flowers tumble like waves across a wrought-iron fence that at one time held them contained.

Behind the garden, off in the distance, sits a graveyard and a chapel. The abandoned stone building stands tall and proud, despite that it's every bit as old and decrepit as the headstones and statues surrounding it. Busted stained-glass windows glisten like the talons of some violent rainbow creature slashing through the fog. Yet even in its sinister beauty, it seems to cower in fear from the encroaching forest's shadow creeping closer with evening's arrival.

Our limo cruises around to the other side of the academy. Pebbles grind beneath the tires on our coast into a gravel parking area across from the garden. Mom starts digging in her purse, mumbling about lipstick. Out of the corner of my eye, I catch someone half covered by a rosebush that hangs over an iron spike. I angle myself to see him better, nose pressed against the chilled glass.

His tall body turns and watches us, broad shoulders tensed. He grips a cluster of deep red roses—so velvety they're almost black on the edges—and holds a pair of pruning shears in his other hand. The tails of his cape swirl on the wind, stabbing at the fog around his muddy boots. The vintage clothing seems out of place in our century, yet right at home in this setting.

He appears close to my age. The left half of his face stands out beneath the hood: one side of plump lips, one squared angle of a chin. Two coppery-colored eyes look back at me—bright and metallic. The sight makes me do a double take. As far as he is from the car, I shouldn't be able to make out the color, yet they glimmer in the shadow of his cape, like pennies catching a flashlight's glare in a deep well.

I've seen those eyes before—countless times—since the age of seven. But I can't even consider why I recognize them. I can't think beyond what they're broadcasting, loud and clear: He's warning us not to approach him—a part of the sprawling wilderness, neglected yet beautiful and thriving in his solitude.

Transfixed, I don't stop staring until Mom opens the glass panel to speak to the driver. A hot blush creeps up my neck and I glance at my worn Timberland boots, all too aware of the patchwork embroidered vest beneath my jacket and the faded and ripped boot-cut jeans hugging my legs. For the first time since I started sewing and designing, I'm uncomfortable in my bohemian style, even if it is a tribute to Dad's heritage. Here at this castle, faced with the stranger's somber formality, I feel too casual . . . wayward and misplaced.

I'm almost aching to put on that outdated school uniform.

When the limo stops, I brave a glance again, in search of the caped figure and those shimmery eyes. The gardening shears lie abandoned on the ground, and the cluster of red roses he held are now withered, leaving behind a whirl of petals—coal black and crinkled—aflutter on the wind.

An icy sense of foreboding prickles the nerves between my shoulder blades. The gardener's gone without a trace, as if he were never there at all.

3

GHOST WALKER

"The ghosts . . . try to remember the sunlight.
Light has died out of their skies."
Robinson Jeffers, "Apology for Bad Dreams"

He flung off his cape's hood as he glided underground, breathing in the scent of mildew and solitude. Dripping water echoed in the hollowed-out tunnel. The shadows embraced him—a welcoming comfort.

He'd walked as a ghost in the gloomy bowels of this opera house for so long, darkness had become his brother; which was fitting, since his father was the night, and sunlight their forgotten friend.

Jaw tightening, he secured the oars in their rowlocks and stretched his arms to reveal the skin between the cuffs of his sleeves and his leather gloves. The hot rush of vitality still pulsed red light through the veins in his wrists. He'd spent all afternoon in the graveyard.

Being somewhere so devoid of life had drained him and prompted an unplanned visit to the garden.

He should never have risked roaming in such close proximity to the parking lot. Curse his weakness for the hybrid roses; there was no resisting their scent, their flavor, their ripeness.

Shrugging off his annoyance, he began to row once more, water slapping the sides of the cave. He hadn't expected anyone to be on the grounds this early. Not with what was taking place inside the academy. All the students and instructors were preoccupied. The garden should've been safe and isolated.

But there she was—appearing out of nowhere—several hours sooner than he'd expected. *Damn his carelessness.* Thankfully, he'd had the sense to wear his hooded cape; otherwise, she would've seen him unmasked.

Still, all wasn't lost. If he'd learned anything watching the years play out on a stage, it was improvisation. He used the unplanned sighting to his advantage, vanishing and leaving nothing but dead roses in his wake. Though he'd hated siphoning away their life essence, it was a necessary sacrifice. A calling card for her eyes only.

No doubt she was puzzling over the event this very minute.

The boat scraped to a halt on a muddy embankment. He stepped out, alerted by movement in the darkness. His cape swept his ankles as he pivoted sharply at the familiar musical sound—similar to a trumpet yet softer and lower pitched.

He cast one of his gloves into the boat's hull and flourished his bared hand, beckoning the life-force of a thousand larval fireflies along the cave's roof. In reaction, spindly strings coated with orbs lit up and illuminated the surroundings with a tender greenish haze— like strands of glowing pearls strung high overhead. This particular genus wasn't indigenous to this place but had been brought from a foreign land and kept alive over a century through an exchange of energy.

Reflections of rippling water flashed across the smooth stone walls and the curved pilasters supporting the opera house above him. A red swan waddled from the shadows, trumpeting another greeting. She lifted her long, slender neck and clacked her bill, wings spreading as she fluffed herself out, magnificent and fiery-rich—the same depth of the blossoms he'd murdered earlier.

"And hello to you, sweet Ange." He knelt and stroked her silken feathers, fingers leaving trails in the crimson plumes. "Holding vigil for our new arrival, are you?"

She nudged a strand of hair from his temple with her beak. He smiled at her affectionate fussing.

"You shouldn't be this close to the surface," he scolded. "Diable's on the prowl. We wouldn't want the devil to catch our little angel."

The swan nibbled his thumb, as his warning echoed in the cave. His voice magnified—bass and rumbling—an alien sound, as if pebbles filled his vocal cords and ground together with each word. The gruffness made him wince.

"Go on now," he whispered this time and stroked her shimmery neck before standing. "Make yourself scarce."

The red swan watched him with milky blue eyes too perceptive for any ordinary bird, especially one that was going blind. She waddled to the water and skimmed across the surface—afloat and waiting.

He studied her inquisitive pose. "I can't come yet," he answered softly. "You know your way through all the booby traps. Go on home. I'll follow soon enough."

Her head bent on an elegant curl, a nod actually, as if she were royalty and he a peasant who needed her permission to stay. She sailed toward the depths of the tunnel—growing smaller in the distance. He watched until she resembled a velvety rose petal drifting atop a midnight puddle. Plucking his glove from the boat, he slid his fingers back into their sheath of black.

He studied the strands of bioluminescent larvae he'd awakened overhead, lost in thoughts of the girl. He'd never expected *her* to be the one. To step out of the visions he'd had since his childhood into this place and this time. It was all wrong.

Maybe he was mistaken.

His thumb pressed his left temple, rubbing the pounding throb there. But even if she was the one from his visions, it couldn't change things. She was haloed by an aura that fluctuated between white and gray . . . purity and melancholy. She was unsettled at being here. Lost, even. The perfect foil to that other narcissistic and ambitious young prima donna who'd been brought in over a year ago due to her bloodline.

There was depth beneath this new arrival's wounded veneer . . . the essence of light and life in its most raw form: the energy of rhapsody. Music pulsed inside her blood—uncultivated and untamed. He could sense that much.

His mouth watered, hungry to taste those melodies, mocking his struggle to rein in his cravings. He'd never seen the girl's face in their subconscious interactions. It was always covered by her wild, black hair, or submersed in murky water as she fought to break out of the wooden crate that entrapped her. But he'd glimpsed her eyes many times—a bright, electrified green with widened pupils when they were filled with song, reflections of her heart chakra.

He had to see her up close, to be sure; regardless that he didn't know her features, he knew her *soul*.

And if his suspicions were right . . .

What then?

Nothing.

His chest muscles tangled between despair and hope, anger and urgency. Whatever he discovered today, he couldn't forget the reason she was here. She was a means to an end. Payment for an outstanding debt. Nothing more.

He glanced up at the underbelly of the opera house where the tunnel met the foundation. A trapdoor waited there, an entrance to the hidden passages in the building: mirrored walls—the perfect vantage points for viewing the inside of the foyer and classrooms. For him, they were windows, unbeknownst to the academy's occupants. On their side, they simply saw spans of reflective glass.

Trepidation lumped in his throat at the thought of being so close to her. He could pretend the reaction was a byproduct of another time, another place; a dark and cruel past that cloaked and obscured any human interactions he had, like an octopus's ink cloud. But there was more—this newly born possibility he dared not entertain—which threatened all of his resolve.

He slammed a fist against his thigh, using the flash of pain to give him clarity.

There was no room for hesitation.

If she was the one, he would have to get even closer. He would have to prey on her . . . disrupt her daily routine, seduce her curiosity, lure her into the depths of his home. *His hell.*

His fingers twitched in his gloves. There were steps to follow that would ensure success. Calling cards to leave, strange novelties that would drive her to seek out the illumination only darkness could provide. She would find him of her own free will; and she would find herself and her purpose, whether she was prepared or not.

Until then, he'd take no other chances of being seen. Patience was key. He'd already been waiting for what felt like an eternity. What were a few more weeks?

A disturbing mix of anticipation and dread grated along his spine. Mud sucking at his boot soles, he scaled the embankment's slope toward the window.

Let the dance begin.

❦ · I · ❦

Mom and I climb the stone stairs to the entrance. A crow flutters by above us. I hesitate when I hear its cry—a strained mewl, like a kitten in distress. I shake my head. Now I'm not only seeing things, but hearing them, too? My nerves are all over the place.

The scent of wet soil mingles with the perfume of flowers and reels me back in, reminding me of my perennials at home. I won't be there to fight off the weeds so they can bloom. I've always honored Dad's memory by keeping his flower garden alive. Having already lost his violin, I don't want to lose yet another tie to him.

I stall halfway up the stairs and glance again at the overgrown garden where the cluster of dead roses sways in the wind. Is that what the guy was doing earlier? Fighting a battle against weeds? Considering what was left in his wake, it looks more like he's the weed himself, like the phantom in the stories—someone who contaminates his surroundings with death and violence.

An outcast like me . . .

I haven't always affected things around me adversely. I used to be the one Dad would come to when any of his plants were dying.

Maybe that's why I'm here, to find that healing side again . . . to save this garden. Maybe that's why the gardener's glinting eyes appeared so familiar—it was my imagination, trying to revive those precious moments with Dad.

I'm totally losing it. I tap the end of my braid against my lips, nipping at the strands so they crinkle between my teeth.

"Rune, you're chewing your hair, hon." Mom pats my back.

"Did you see him?" I ask.

"Who?" She follows my gaze across to the garden.

"The guy by the roses earlier. He's gone now. I think he works here . . ."

"What did he look like?" she asks.

"I could only see half his face."

She rolls her eyes then looks over my head where the chauffer digs bags out of the limo's trunk. "You're not seriously asking me to believe you just saw the phantom in his half-mask, are you?"

"I didn't say that," I mumble around my wet hair. "Not exactly." But now that I think about it, the side that was hidden from view could've had a mask.

Mom catches my braid and dries the end between her palms. "Sweetie, I understand you're nervous. But I really need you to try. Stop convincing yourself this is going to be a bad experience before you even give it a chance. Okay?"

She kisses my forehead when I nod. I don't dare tell her about the crow and its strange call. It would only validate what she left unsaid: that it's all in my imagination.

As we reach the top step, the double doors—adorned with tarnished brass cherubs—swing open on a foreboding creak. Warm air and the scents of lemon oil and stale candle wax waft over us.

"*Bon après-midi, mon chéri* Emma!" An older woman squeals my mom's name. The opening widens, revealing her height, taller than our average five-foot-six-inch stature by at least two inches.

Long, grayish-white braids dangle over both of her ears and skim her slim waist. A silk chiffon hanky wraps around her head to hold back stray strands. Round, gold-rimmed glasses soften the wrinkles at the edges of her eyes.

She's dressed in a blue button-down short-sleeve shirt and khaki capri pants. Ballet-style slippers hug her feet. Judging by the dingy apron at her hipbones and the dust rag in her pocket, I'm guessing she's with housekeeping.

Mom leaps into her open arms, shattering my hypothesis.

"Lottie," she murmurs into the other woman's swanlike neck. "It's been too long."

So this is Aunt Charlotte. I expected her to be draped in furs and jewels. What is it with the women in my family being housekeepers? Is it a curse they can't escape, even after a run of fame and success? Still, she looks good for sixty. Maybe Ponce de León should've collected feather dusters instead of searching all over Florida for the secret to agelessness.

Giving my mother one last squeeze, the older woman's eyes narrow to slivers beneath her lenses. "Rune?" she asks with a gritty voice, and they both turn to me. My aunt pushes the glasses atop the hanky covering her hair, jangling the chain that connects the earpieces. There's the resemblance: the turned-up nose and soft hazel irises shadowed by short lashes. She favors my grandmother, but I see Dad there, too. Longing snaps inside of me as I imprint his image onto her.

"Yes," Mom answers. "Grown a bit since her christening, hasn't she?"

"She is exquisite." The flavor of France spices my aunt's English but doesn't mask the tremor of emotion in her voice. "Looks so much like you at her age."

Mom and Dad became high school sweethearts when he came from France to America as a foreign exchange student in the twelfth grade. A bitter irony, now that I'm treading his homeland during my senior year and he's no longer in the world.

Aunt Charlotte steps closer, graceful and demure as any ballerina. The woman is oblivious to personal space. "You arrived sooner than expected. We did not anticipate you until later tonight."

"We're experienced shoppers." Mom winks at me.

I teeter on the edge of the threshold, half in and half out, unable to bring myself to cross over like she already has.

"And did you find the drive suitable?" Aunt Charlotte aims the question in my direction. Her breath smells like canned pears and caramel, reminding me of Dad and how we preserved fruit together the last August before he died—something his mom did with him as he was growing up.

"Um, yeah. It was . . . nice. Roomy." I can't even say thank you for all she's done before she whips off my cap, snatches the band out of my hair, and unwinds my braid. The ribbons flutter to the floor. Several droplets leftover from the rain drizzle from the door frame above, sinking cold into my scalp.

"She has his hair," Aunt Charlotte says, and I can't tell if she's sad or happy as she crimps my curls in her fingers. I tighten my grip on my tote.

"Yes, she does," Mom answers. "Thick and unruly, just like Leo's."

My teeth grind. *You mean before he went bald.* I've never understood why Charlotte stayed away when her only brother was dying. And I'm not sure I can forgive her, either.

My aunt wraps one of my curls around her thumb. I might as well be a doll seated deaf upon a shelf, with no personality or opinion. I snatch my cap back and tug it over my head, dragging my waves over my shoulder and away from her scrutiny.

"Ah-ha! She has your *strie têtue*, though." Aunt Charlotte grins at my mom.

She hasn't seen the half of my stubborn streak. Frowning, I pick up my ribbons and tuck them into my jacket pocket.

My aunt twirls my hairband on her finger and tosses back her head with a cackling laugh . . . a sound of pure madness. I bounce a gaze to Mom, who's smiling like a goon, then back to our lunatic relative. Her laughter reverberates on a musical note, echoing in the huge foyer. Upon its final beat, another song comes to life—a muffled surge of instruments—somewhere on the third floor.

I recognize the tune. It's the aria I heard in the elevator this morning.

No. Not that one. Anything but that.

I yank my cap over my ears in hopes to shut it out. "That song . . . ," I whisper, wrestling the instinctual stretch in my vocal cords as they itch to release the suppressed melody.

Aunt Charlotte beams and pulls out her dust rag, waving it. "*Ahh, oui.* The school performs *The Fiery Angel* at year's end. It is our goal to tackle controversial projects. Ones you won't find performed in any high school in the States. The lesser roles have already been assigned to junior participants. Today a handful of senior hopefuls compete for Renata—the heroine. First-tier elimination tryouts always take place on the third floor, in the rehearsal halls. Final auditions will be in the theater the last Sunday of October, once we've reduced to a finite number of candidates for the main roles."

My body tenses as I stare up toward the torrential rain of notes.

Aunt Charlotte narrows her eyes, watching me with thinly veiled suspicion. "This is her confession piece, of her encounters with Madiel, her guardian angel. You are familiar with Prokofiev's opera?"

"Not so much." *And I don't want to be.* I'm dying to find some private place where I can exorcise my musical demons, but Aunt Charlotte has planted herself between me and the way in.

"Well, that shall change soon enough." She's still talking but I'm barely listening.

My gaze darts all around, seeking escape.

"You are to be schooled in vocal pedagogy," she says. "And the history of opera. You will learn. Not soon enough for first-tier competition. Next semester, perhaps. Some of the lesser roles will open up. There are always one or two students who forfeit their parts—be it for grades or nerves. But I expect, in your future, you will have all the lead roles on Broadway. You are your father's daughter . . . born for music."

She exchanges a strange glance with Mom—maybe sadness, maybe dread. Or it could be my own dread I'm sensing, because she's wrong.

I'm nothing like Dad. He was a savant, able to tease out lush, savory sounds that would melt the heart. Music was pleasure for him. He always said, of all the instruments, the violin most resembled the human voice for its ability to express depths of emotion. When played with passion, technique, and vision, the strings would weep words—a tonal persuasion so far-reaching, it could breach the heavens and bring a celestial choir to their knees.

He had already mastered the technique of "voicing" his pieces by the age of fourteen. When he met Mom at seventeen, he'd had his pick of symphonies anywhere in the world, but loving her became his magnum opus, and he chose to be a music professor at our little community college in Harmony, playing only for family and friends.

I shared his passion for music only long enough to know how desperately I miss it, now that singing brings pain and humiliation.

As if triggered by that thought, the aria's mood changes upstairs—a kaleidoscopic shift of strings and winds. The hairs on the back of my neck stand up in response, the melody becoming an electrical pulse under my skin. Prisms of color erupt in my mind's eye as a soloist joins the chaos. Her resonant, booming voice rages in indecipherable Russian against the instruments, teasing me to follow.

Spinning on my heel to retreat outside, I crash into the chauffeur's brick chest. I'd forgotten he was waiting behind us, along with shopping bags and suitcases full of bedding, lamps, uniforms, pajamas, underclothes, and assorted toiletries. His downward stare shakes my already frazzled nerves. I wrinkle my nose at the stench of spray starch and body odor.

"Rune!" Mom yelps. "Apologize."

I mumble, "*Pardon, monsieur*," turn around again, and wind my scarf's fringe between my fingers. My heart hammers my sternum. I'm trapped—a deer in a forest set to flame. Even the air feels thick, as if smoke surrounds me.

At last Aunt Charlotte moves aside with a fanciful turn of the dust rag, but the rest of her body language remains tense.

My boots pound the marble floor on my scramble past my mom. I stop in the middle of the room. My tote slides off my shoulder and I make no attempt to stop it as the enormity of the place steals my breath.

Three giant golden stairways intersect in the middle of a grand hall. The stairs split into columns, each winding like a snake's skeleton to the other six flights where brass balusters enclose circular balconies. Murals of angels and cherubs catch my eye, along with bronze statues set out along the floor. Intricately detailed windows coax in the outside light. Everything glistens, as if made of diamonds. Artwork hangs from the many walls, and the corridors are lined with elegant carved doorways. Uncountable doorways.

The top three flights are sealed off, but that still leaves hundreds of rooms for the school's use. Some are now the private suites that serve as dorms. Others are the lecture and rehearsal halls where I'll be spending the majority of my days for classes.

The chauffer props our bags and suitcases against a marble wall. Aunt Charlotte gives him a tip and he leaves. The double doors slam shut and an echo carries from one end of the foyer to the other, channeling through my ribs and pushing the aria into my throat.

"What do you think, Rune? Isn't it incredible?" Mom's voice is reverent, as if we're standing inside of a church or mausoleum. That last one could be right, considering I might die if I don't purge the song soon. Mom and my aunt discuss the trip here. Chewing on the ends of my hair again, I hum under my breath . . . quiet enough that they won't hear. But the urge to sing aloud escalates until my mouth waters.

On the far right, shimmery mirrors line the entire wall. Thankfully, the only reflections looking back are the three of us. If not for the opera taking place upstairs, I would guess the academy was abandoned.

Hope flutters in my chest. Everyone must be at the audition. If I lose control, the other performance will camouflage my voice.

"Are all of the instructors and students upstairs?" I manage to ask.

"*Oui*. Let us put away the baggage and unpack before the tryouts are *fini*. Would you like to see your accommodations?"

Standing by the wall of mirrors, I ignore the question. Close enough that my nose almost touches the glass, I study my reflection.

It's happening . . . bright, gleaming flecks of green, my pupils dilating with each passing second. The color in my cheeks deepens, too, as if I've been slapped. I always wondered if Grandma was like Dad and could see all of the changes in me—the physical manifestation of music bubbling up inside. That would explain why she thought I was evil. It's eerie, even to me. Almost as weird as the gardener's glowing amber eyes.

The sensation of being watched skitters through my body, then there's movement on the other side of the glass . . . a silhouette.

I blink and it's gone.

Shuddering, I cup my palms over my cheeks to hide the color creeping over them. *It's just the music making me crazy.*

"Rune," my mom calls out from across the foyer. I watch my aunt's reflection as she digs through the things the chauffer left. "Didn't you hear your Aunt Charlotte? Take some of these bags. I don't want to be up all night helping you unpack. My flight leaves early in the morning."

Mom's spending the night to help me get settled. But I don't see how anything about this place could be settling. I don't belong here. Being constantly around this music is going to kill any sanity I have left.

I jitter, itching all over to sing.

"Rune," Mom's voice again, this time with an edge to it. She knows. "Is it—"

"I just need a bathroom," I interrupt, trying to ignore the musical inflection woven into the final word, or how I end it on the same operatic note as the voice upstairs.

"Bien sûr," my aunt answers while struggling with the large pink bag that holds my uniforms. "There's a *salle de bains* underneath the center stairwell. On the other side of the theater, just there."

It doesn't matter that she said under the stairwell; my feet don't listen. The instruments have taken over—a bridge to the soloist's climax. I don't stand a chance against music that powerful.

In spite of Mom and Aunt Charlotte's efforts to call me back, I'm at the top of the second flight of stairs and on the third floor before I even remember taking the first step. I drag my jacket off and drop it behind me.

The music crescendos and the soloist's voice booms over it, not just in my ears, but in my own throat. My song escalates to match the other singer's volume. I'm drawn to a room at the end of the curved balcony as if some entity has attached a ghostly cord to the notes in my throat, tugging each one out like rainbow-colored fish on a line—yet never releasing—pulling my spirit ever closer to the music that possesses me.

The door, slightly ajar, beckons. I shove it open at the climax, sustaining the melody—round and smooth through my stretching larynx. Tall windows line the circular room, alternating with mirrors. A burst of sunset filters through the clouds outside, bouncing apricot light from one reflection to the next. An audience of students and teachers is seated in wooden folding chairs in front of a small stage, nothing more than shadows in the sudden blur of brilliance.

The soloist goes silent. Even the instrumentalists stop. My legs stiffen and my spine is rigid. Every nerve in my body throbs. I'm pinned in place by lyrical thorns, just like the little girl in my poster at home, grasping for those wings so far out of reach, embracing the pain to find the release.

I'm all that's left to carry the tune now, and I do . . . to the very end when the final note, high and full, bursts unrestrained from my throat. The chord reverberates over the silence like a ghostly wail—beautiful and tragic.

Red swirls in my periphery, and my legs give out. A guy leaps from his chair in the front row to catch me. Mortification creeps like poison through my blood as the trance falls away.

I slam my lashes shut, doing the only thing I can to save face. Slumped against my rescuer, I pretend to faint.

4

DEVIL'S TONGUES
AND SKELETON KEYS

*"Men hate the things they fear, and they fear
those things they do not understand."*
Susan Kay, Phantom

I hold my eyes closed as I'm carried downstairs. The guy's muscles strain with each step of our descent. His warm skin radiates a familiar spice: cinnamon and sage infused with male pheromones and body heat. My stomach contracts, an abnormal reaction that makes me nauseous. I fight the sensation along with the terrifying memory of the last time I let a guy get too close.

"*Merçi*, Monsieur Reynolds," Aunt Charlotte mumbles to him. "Take her to *chambre de cinq*." She moves somewhere behind us. "You told me of her stage fright. But this? Is *extrême*, no?" There's a worried edge to her voice.

"She always goes weak in the knees, but she's never passed out before." Mom rubs my shin, comforting. "I think she was just too worked up over everything. She's been researching the place . . . heard that it was tied to *The Phantom of the Opera* book. Then she thought she saw some masked guy outside. She doesn't just have Leo's hair, she has his superstitious nature. You know what it's like to try to reason with someone in that state of mind." Her voice is accusatory, and I wince inwardly. Not just because of the reference to Grandma's crazed fingerprint on our lives, but because I hear a lot of footsteps behind us on the stairs. All I need is for the other students to know about my recent literary obsession.

But Mom's not thinking about that. She's at her wit's end with my "superstitions." She made financial sacrifices the past two years, pouring every spare dime into voice lessons for me. Even though she sought out teachers who played the violin, none of their instruments spoke to me like Dad's. I couldn't perform without becoming ill. Instead of helping, the weekly sessions of operatic techniques and daily three-hour practices seemed to have the adverse effect— pushing my urge to sing to a compulsion.

Mom squeezes my hand, asking me to wake up. Guilt butts against my conscience at the concern in her voice, but the guy's tantalizing heartbeat next to my ear keeps me cocooned in my fake unconsciousness, for his good as much as my own.

I stay limp as I'm laid in a bed. In time, the guy's dangerous warmth and spiced scent fades, replaced by a whiff of chicken soup that ignites a normal hunger.

There's a scatter of movement all around: bags rustling, footsteps shuffling, concerned whispers too soft to decipher. Only when the sounds fade do I dare peek through the strands of hair curtaining my eyes.

A lavender glow illuminates the windowless room. The ceiling stretches high, with dark wooden beams meeting at the epicenter. There's a small closet in the corner, diagonal from where my bed is tucked inside an arched antechamber. On the outer wall overhead, wrought-iron drapery hooks wait to hold the beaded, ginger-colored curtains we bought earlier, to offer added privacy when I sleep. I wish they were already in place so I could hide.

Across the room are a full-length cheval mirror and another antechamber. A dark wooden staircase winds above to a platform with a matching rail, forming a mini-loft. There, a vanity desk and chair are arranged for homework or for making up my face and hair. Beneath the loft, in the snug space where the wall and platform meet, a baroque chaise lounge with a walnut frame and velvet uphol-stery curves to a sitting area. I shove my hair aside and try to make out the blurred silhouette reclining there.

"Mom?" I ask, my vocal cords stretched and tired.

"She went to the kitchen to fetch you some chamomile tea. Said it helps when you're feeling poorly."

I sit up under my covers, caught off guard by the thick Southern accent. "Who are you?"

"I'm Sunflower Summers. But you can call me Sunny. I was assigned as your peer advisor. To help get you oriented."

"So, you're a student?"

She makes a puffing sound. "Let me guess. You're wondering why a hick like me is in a classy place like this."

I stare at her shadowy form, searching for a way to assure her that wasn't what I meant at all, but my tongue lies as stiff, dry, and hot in my mouth as the devil sunbathing in the desert.

"Look, I may be a country girl," she continues, "but I can play a cello like I was born in the orchestra pit of the London Symphony. Ma says I have the mind of a progeny, and the tongue of a heck-o-billy. My uncle's a oil tycoon. He made sure I was taught proper grammar before he'd pay for my tuition, but I sometimes slip off the wagon a smidge."

Great. I've offended her. "I'm sorry. I didn't mean anything . . ."

"Don't give it no nevermind. I'm still your number one fan."

"Huh?"

She pushes off the lounge and steps outside of the antechamber. Her hair is red, but the weird lighting shimmers violet along the shoulder-length ends.

"I never heard anyone sing like that," she says, leaning against the stair rail. "It's like you were trained by Christine Daaé herself."

I try to manage a sarcastic snort, but it comes out as more of a sob. For her to mention the heroine from Gaston Leroux's book, she must have been one of the students following us on the stairway.

"I'm betting Kat's never heard anything like it, neither," Sunny continues before I can come up with an excuse for my mom's claim of a phantom sighting.

"Who . . . ?"

"Katarina. The soloist you threw under the tractor when you came plowing into tryouts."

I cringe. Although I was wrapped within the music, I vaguely remember the gorgeous girl's shocked expression when I stopped to sing beside the stage—her crystal-blue eyes widening, cheeks flushed from peaches-and-cream to a deep plum that almost matched the streak in her long, caramel-blond waves. She appeared simultaneously awed and furious.

I can't believe this is how I made my first impression. Horning in on someone's audition and pretending to be a fainting idiot. A sick shudder rolls through my stomach. Maybe I should take a sip of that chicken soup, after all.

The mug waits on the nightstand along with the lava lamp Mom and I bought. She's already plugged it in, which explains the weird lighting. My bags are piled in a corner beside the closet, and I have the urge again to retrieve my bed curtains and shut myself in.

Instead, I change the subject to something safe. "Are all of the dorms this small?" An attempt to reach for the soup mug reminds me my limbs are still in shock mode. I'm aching all over, as if I were the one thrown under a tractor. I prop my shoulders against the wall behind me and stay burrowed in my cave.

"Yep. They used to be dressing rooms. They tucked the wardrobes and costume trunks in the nooks in the walls to take up less floor space. And that . . ." She points to the second-story demi-balcony. "Since the ceilings were so high, they came up with those teensy lofts. It's a kooky layout. But you get used to it."

I nod, though I'm battling a sense of gloom without the sunset streaming in. I always feel better when I'm basking in outdoor light. Another reason I love to garden.

"The boys and male teachers are on the second flight, and the girls are on the ground level. All except for Headmaster Fabre and his wife. They share a room down here. The third floor is where our classes and rehearsals take place."

In light of this information, and considering the expansiveness of the opera house, the waiting list for the school seems unnecessary. "Why don't they renovate and open up the fourth through sixth floors for more students?"

"Partly 'cause we don't need them as yet. We have seven live-in instructors to the fifty students. Well, fifty-one, counting you. They want to keep the school small till they can hire more teachers."

She moves closer, her barefoot steps silent across the marble tiles. She's about my height but more toned and muscular. Where I look almost too thin, she looks hardy and fit. Faded jeans and a cap-sleeved T hug her frame.

So the students aren't required to be in uniform on the weekends. Good to know.

"But the biggest reason no one's been on the top three flights is 'cause the stairs are boarded up from the fourth level on. There's a mystery benefactor. A rich architect or something. No one's ever seen him, but he drew up the plans for renovation. Every new room was redesigned by him. He owns the land and the castle. So the investors need his permission and keys to open the sealed floors and renovate. And he's refused to give either so far . . . says he wants to keep the rooms for storage."

"But the brochure said there were once over three hundred keys. Do you honestly think all the top rooms are for storage?"

She shrugs. "The extra rooms I've seen down here are. Last year, some gals thought they heard noises. Chains jingling and a baby crying. So I lifted the keys off one of the teachers, and after lights-out at nine thirty, looked in all the empty rooms. I thought I'd never pick through that mess of old props and clothes. It was like I'd stepped into another time. Ya know?"

Her words make me think of the vanishing gardener and his outdated clothes. "You've heard the rumors, right? About the secret lair . . . the bones they found floating in the underground river?"

A snicker bursts from Sunny's lips. "Nothing more than a drowned dog. Our room keys are the only bones still floating around.

You haven't seen yours yet . . . here." She holds up an aged brass key. The shaft is long and ornate, with two jagged teeth on the end. The head looks like a skull.

Although the design is eerie and unsettling, I force a smile. "Gives new meaning to the term 'skeleton key.'"

Sunny grins back. "Right? But the teeth are all different, and the room numbers are engraved on the back. They each open a different door in the academy. So no need to worry about anyone breaking into your dorm."

"Other than someone with a penchant for stealing keys," I tease.

She lifts her palm as if swearing an oath. "I vow to only use my powers for good. So see? Nothing weird going on here. Other than the author basing a few characters on real people, those phantom stories on that forum are all nut-buck. Yeah, there's an underground river, but no one's ever found an entrance to any subterranean house. Not even at that other opera place in the city . . . the one that this building inspired." She's over by my shopping bags now, digging through them. She pulls out my French fairy tale book and stares at it as if mesmerized.

I try to suppress the image in my mind: the gardener with those familiar glimmering eyes, creeping along the halls at night and clanging hundreds of skeleton keys, searching for his stolen bones . . . because I'm not at all convinced they belonged to a dog. "What about the sounds the students heard?"

Sunny diverts her gaze from the book and lays it back in the bag. "Oh, it was just ol' Diable prowling around. He's the resident tomcat. Bug ugly and feral as a fox. He looks like a walking SOS pad. The bells on his collar caused the jingles. And he likes to yowl. It can sound like a baby's tantrum when he really gets going. Don't even know why he stays since he won't let no one touch him. He must've belonged to somebody once . . . his name's written in jewels on his collar. The boys say he's a ghost cat, due to how he sneaks into our rooms even when they're locked."

My eyes widen.

"Sorry," she says, snorting again. "Being so far out in the country, this place can be creepy as a field of devil's tongues. The graveyard out back don't help. Some of us have even seen strange lights coming out of the abandoned chapel at night, but the school has bailiffs who stand guard outside the front and back entrances to enforce the eight o'clock in-house curfew. So there's no sneaking out. But honestly, if anything is haunted, it's the forest." She says it as if it's an afterthought, although her voice is ominous.

"Why do you say that?" I ask, not sure I want to hear anymore.

"Well, I don't get out there much myself, so this is all hearsay." She frowns. "I'm bad allergic to bee stings so the woods are off limits. My ma wouldn't even let me come here without a year's supply of EpiPens." She shrugs. "Anyways, the boys roam out there sometimes. They've gone so far as the cottage. And they've seen things. Or I should say heard things . . . things that ain't right." A chagrined expression crosses her face. "I mean, *aren't* right."

"Like . . . ?"

"A field mouse that croaks like a toad, a lizard that squeals like a wild pig, a fox hooting like an owl. The guys get real inventive when they're trying to scare us girls."

My tongue feels dry again as I remember the mewling crow that I assumed I imagined.

Sunny seems to read the discomfort on my face, because she adjusts her tone. "Aw, just listen to me yammer on. Forget everything I said. They're all made-up stories anyways. And I'm only one door over. Come pounding anytime you get scared."

I mutter, "Thanks," but I won't be getting close to anyone while I'm here. There's no way to pretend I'm even a little normal. Within a few weeks, I'll have a reputation for stealing the limelight that will be impossible to live down, and no one will want to be my friend.

"About Katarina." I wind my hair into a side braid, tying the ends in a knot. "Is she the kind to hold grudges?"

Draped in shadows again, Sunny digs around in her pocket then lifts out what looks like a cigarette. She touches it to her lips, sucks in a breath, and blows out. The end lights up in response, like an LED glow. "You bet she is. And not only did you show her up, you managed a ride in Jackson Reynolds's arms. That's more action than she's seen in the year and a half she's been prowling after him."

Great. Could things get any worse? If only I could tell Katarina she has nothing to worry about. I'm not going to pursue something physical or romantic with anyone. Not after what happened back home with Ben. Just being carried down the stairs by this Jackson guy triggered enough of a reminder to stay true to that promise to myself. But there's no way to bring up something that weird. "Okay . . . so, you're saying I'll be Kat's new scratching post."

"And unlike Diable, her claws are way worse than her hiss."

I groan and scoot down, sliding into the pillows with a palm over my eyes. "How to make enemies in less than sixty seconds flat. I wrote the freaking book."

Sunny chuckles. "Don't worry. It wasn't like you were auditioning for Renata's role. Audrey is her only real competition. But no one's ever been able to beat Kat out. I'd sure like to see that change."

A caramel scent hovers over me, reminding me of my aunt when she stepped into my personal space earlier. I move my hand to find Sunny standing beside the bed with the cigarette perched on her lower lip. Her face is oval with dark freckles spattered across her nose and cheeks in the shape of a harlequin mask. In the low light, her eyes are a striking shade of bluish purple, and her features are elfin. She resembles some wild wood creature, dressed for a masquerade.

She takes another drag on her glowing stick. Her exhalation curls like condensation from a person's mouth in freezing weather. It's not a traditional cigarette. It's an e-cig. She has it clamped in an elegant holder—a smaller version of the slender black one that Audrey Hepburn used in *Breakfast at Tiffany's*.

"Do they know you smoke?" At Mom's insistence, I read the student handbook on the way here. Tobacco is a one-way ticket to expulsion and home. I've kept that little tidbit tucked away on the chance I want to get kicked out of this place. Now I know where I could get a supply. Although that would hurt Mom's budding relationship with Aunt Charlotte, so it would have to be a very last resort.

"Nah. They're oblivious. There's no fire or smoke to give me away. It's vaping. I'm practically exhaling water." She hands the cylinder to me.

I run it under my nose, sniffing the sweet aroma, then hand it back.

"I've got an extra atomizer in my room," Sunny says. "If you want one. I lifted the e-juice refills off your aunt. She orders them in bulk from some place online, so she never misses one or two. I kinda like the clove ones, but the chocolates are best. There weren't any of those in her latest stash, though. Unless they're hid behind the boxes of disposable contacts in her armoire. Speaking of, I hope those aren't just for upcoming costume accessories. She needs to incorporate them into her style. Her glasses look like they're from Ben Franklin's special collection."

I can hardly register Sunny's babbles about my aunt's questionable fashion choices; it's too insignificant compared to her other confession. "Wait. You sneak into her room and *steal* from her?"

"I told you, I use my powers for good. She's been trying to quit smoking since I've been here. I decided to help her along." She wrinkles her freckled nose. "You aren't a snitch, are you? Gonna go running to her because she's your aunt? If she finds out I've been rattling around the teachers' rooms—"

"No. We're not that close." I motion for Sunny to join me inside my bed-cave. Before she sits, she picks up my soup and hands it to me. I nod a thank-you. "To be honest, this is the first time I've met *Mademoiselle Français de fantaisie* in my life."

Sunny barks a laugh that comes from her belly—a cheery and round sound that warms me almost as much as the steaming mug in my hand. "So you caught that, did ya? Your aunt even takes us on field trips sometimes, so we can have a real *expérience* Paris. Still not sure if she's a French diplomat or our dance teacher."

I sip my chicken broth and grin. Maybe I'll make at least one new friend. Sunny's quirky enough to overlook my own eccentricities —like Trig and Janine always did. And her knack for "lifting" things could be useful.

"How about this?" I ask as the soup coats my throat with comfort. "I'll keep quiet about your extraordinary 'talents,' if you can do me a favor in return."

Sunny cocks her head. "A gal who sings like an angel *and* knows how to blur the line between flattery and blackmail." Taking a puff of her e-cig, she smiles. "A kindred spirit. Okay. What's the favor?"

I swallow more soup to soothe my spinning stomach and attempt to appear mildly interested—as opposed to how I really feel inside: desperate for information. "Tell me anything you know about the estate's gardener. You mentioned there's a cottage somewhere in the forest. Is that where he lives?"

My companion chokes on her caramel-flavored vapor. "Haven't you seen the garden? There hadn't been a keeper . . . well, since the whole time I've been here. We have a caretaker—Mister Jippetto—who lives in the cottage in the woods, but he mainly tends the cemetery . . . keeps it tidy. He does a few odds and ends around the school. Pruning the bushes that hang too close to the parking lot, sweeping leaves off the steps, helping us make sets for the stage. Simple maintenance. But he's too old to wrangle all those plants and weeds."

"Too old? I thought he looked like he was our age." I rub my forehead. "Maybe it was one of the students in costume. He was in Victorian clothes, hanging around the garden with a set of pruning shears."

Sunny's eyes meet mine; both honesty and intelligence shine bright inside of them. "I don't know what you think you saw when you got here, but all of us were at auditions. They take role. Attendance is mandatory. There was a time when the garden was beautiful. I've seen black-and-white pictures in the school library upstairs. But that was back in 1925, when a journalist did a spread on the abandoned opera house to celebrate the Palais Garnier's fif-tieth anniversary. The anonymous keeper of that garden would be long dead by now."

My hand spasms and I drop my mug, soaking my jeans and the bed with hot soup.

※·I·※

He arrived at the apartment's secret entrance and found the swan quivering at the bank's edge.

Something was wrong.

"What happened? Why aren't you inside?" he asked, climbing out of the boat and onto the dock that opened into his underground home.

Ange flapped her crimson wings, urging him to hurry. He peeled away his gloves, boots, and cape to prevent trailing mud along the lavishly patterned tiles inside the apartment. The swan warbled low in her throat—a fretful, worried sound. Her webbed feet clacked behind his silent tread in thick woolen socks.

The lanterns along the walls had waned, and being so deep underground meant no windows to invite the last streams of twilight inside. He would've been all but blind had it not been for the glow of his eyes lighting his footsteps. He wove his way through the parlor, past the heavily upholstered furniture, wall tapestries, and garish ornamentation.

He wrestled a familiar niggle of frustration that they still honored the Victorian epoch of antiquity, regardless of how many times he'd tried to bring them into the twenty-first century. The only parts of the house that merited gas lamps or electricity from a generator were the old-fashioned elevator with a gated, cage-style door, the cellar laboratory it led to, and the four-hundred-gallon aquarium that stood on a platform in his bedroom.

The hair on his neck lifted as he passed the birds, animals, and reptiles in shadowy cages and terrariums lining the parlor walls on either side of the pipe organ: a blue jay with a busted wing, a rabbit with a gnawed-off hind leg, a lizard missing one eye—and many other creatures. Some were hurt or orphaned and needed his help; others were patients from procedures he'd done his best to block from his mind, although there was no chance of ever forgetting.

All of them relied on him to stitch them back together with new pieces and parts, and nurse them to health before being returned to the wild. Tonight, they seemed to glare from inside their temporary prisons, judging . . . accusing. It was as if they could see his own brokenness, how he ached to commit a betrayal so self-serving, he should be caged himself.

He swallowed a groan. All this time he'd waited, hoping he might one day connect with the mirror piece of his soul. His *flamme jumelle*.

For the academy's new arrival to be that mirror was a twist of the scalpel. He despised the confusion and conflict she inspired in him, and he despised himself for being drawn to her.

"*Rune*," he muttered in hushed tones. In ancient times, runes were mystical, divine liturgies, powerful enough to cast spells. That explained why he was bewitched by her.

All he could do today was make mistakes. It would have been enough proof to see her eyes from the other side of the mirror, the way they glistened with unspent energy. If he'd only left then, instead of following her through the narrow secret passageways inside the wall to the third floor; instead of watching through the mirrors and hearing her sing . . .

He knew her the moment he saw her soul bared, the instant she released the first note. He'd heard her in visions for years. She had inspired countless compositions upon his violin.

Today, after hearing her in reality, the music rang in his head and burned an imprint behind his eyes. So many colors and emotions, a spectrum of auras—vivid and alive. An abundance of energy so pure, every sensory receptor in his body had reacted. He tasted the music, more luxurious than fresh honeycomb melting on the tongue; he felt the notes on his skin, soothing like raindrops on a hot day.

He'd never experienced anything so healing and sweet.

Yet it nearly broke her to sing.

He tried to be calculating, tried to remind himself that that was as it should be; that it would work to his advantage—the way it pained her to use her gift. She must despise music by now.

Instead, he couldn't stop thinking that if this were another time, another place, nothing would stop him from reaching out. When she fell to her knees, her aura faded to a dark gray too close to black, drained of vitality; it was all he could do to stay hidden. She was so small in stature, so fine-boned and fragile—like the other songbirds he'd healed throughout his life. He understood her pain. Her energies were unbalanced. He had the ability to help her. Her song never broke her in his visions. Instead, her song was her power, because he played for her.

He cut a glance to his Stradivarius, shut within a case in the corner, sugar-coated in dust and fringed with spider webs. He hadn't touched the violin for two years, ever since the academy first opened. He wondered if she'd missed their duets as much as he had.

But today, the melodic energy he'd absorbed from her song shook the silent wail of the violin's strings and rattled the cage of his ribs. A plea so visceral it sucked the core of his heart dry, making it wither and curl like the dead roses he'd left for her to fret over earlier.

How was he going to do what was expected of him now? To have the girl anywhere close to him would only open his veins and bleed him dry.

He would avoid her as much as possible. He had six weeks until Halloween, when they would meet. Until then, the groundwork for bringing her down could be played out behind the scenes . . . all his clues placed without ever having to be face-to-face. During that time, he'd find another outlet to stifle his yearnings—a way to push her voice from his conscious mind. Although there was little he could do for the subconscious.

No matter what, he would not lose sight of his goal. He would lure Rune down, then that would be the end of it for him . . . and the end of life as she knew it for her.

5

BROKEN
SONGBIRDS

*"In order to see birds it is necessary to
become a part of the silence."*
Robert Lynd

He strode past his neglected violin and the pipe organ next to the
dining nook, pausing when he reached the three bedrooms at the
back of his home. The one on the left belonged to him, and the one
on the right was reserved for *her* . . . once she lived again.

But it was the black door in the center where Ange waited that
held his interest now. Even after all these years, the gargoyle door
knocker held him in the thrall of its hideous snarl because what it
guarded within was equally grotesque, powerful, and fascinating.

Choosing not to use the knocker, his knuckles thrummed the
door lightly. "It's Thorn. Are you decent?" He waited for a response.

Eleven years before, at the age of eight, he'd busted inside, eager to show off the ortolan songbird he had rescued from a cat. His guardian was standing at the mirror—bared of the fitted mask that usually hid the top three-quarters of his face.

Thorn had stared in stupefied horror at the exposed reflection: the jaundiced skin, crinkled and waxy . . . stretched so thin that every vein and frayed capillary manifested itself like a gruesome road map, revealing large hematomas, red and pulsing underneath; the cavernous indentions above his eyebrows, making his eyes appear sunken; and most horrifying of all, the bridge of a nose stopping almost before it started, leaving no cartilage to cover the two large, black holes from which he breathed. A missing upper lip opened to a row of teeth, so perfect and straight, that like the strong and flawless chin below, they mocked the jigsaw-puzzle face above.

Thorn had never seen anything like it—a corpse's rotting head atop a man's living form. He'd screamed and clenched his hands in a knee-jerk reaction, crushing the tiny bird cupped between his fingers.

The ortolan's agonized chitters broke through his trancelike state, and he dropped her to the floor. His careless mistreatment of the bird earned him a cuff to the ear from his guardian, a reprimand so sharp and instantaneous, Thorn almost blacked out from the resulting dizziness.

It was the first and last time Father Erik ever struck him. He had other, subtler ways to discipline Thorn, methods far more effective than corporal punishment.

Thorn had struggled to stay standing. The ringing in his ear couldn't drown out the songbird's whistling gasps as she labored to breathe against the broken ribs puncturing her lungs. His guardian bent to pick up the dying bird.

Hot tears streaked Thorn's face. He fixed his gaze on the yellow-and-green clump of feathers inside his father's fine-boned hands, avoiding a second glance at that deformity atop his neck.

After wrapping the bird in a handkerchief, Erik snagged Thorn's chin. Thorn tried to close his eyes, but his guardian simply had to speak.

"Look at me, child."

Thorn's eyelids locked open, unable to resist that hypnotic voice. It was Father Erik's ultimate power. Those vocal cords sparked decadent sensations—so preternaturally persuasive there was no escape. With just a spoken word or a serenade of song, the man had the power to wrap a deadly cobra inside a cocoon of coiled obedience, and bring a cold-hearted murderer to drown in a pool of their own repentant tears. Once the net of his voice was cast, he could capture and manipulate anyone and anything. Sometimes only for seconds, and other times for hours or days or years, depending upon the victim's inner strength and will.

"Embrace your revulsion." Father Erik's resonant, masterful command had cradled Thorn in softness that day, quieting the buzz in his throbbing ear. "But never pity me. *Never.* For pity makes us both victims. Be true to your instinctive horror. Turn it outward and wield it."

Erik held the limp, gasping bird against Thorn's chest. He caught Thorn's hand and urged him to touch his disfigured face . . . to feel the withered flesh that crinkled like moist, decaying leaves under his palm, to rake his thumb at the edge of the spongy craters where a nose should've been. Thorn obeyed, never blinking an eye. Nausea and repellent fear gathered around his heart until it burned. The fiery sensation culminated and passed from him to the bird's feather-encased breast. A shiver of turquoise light flashed through her eyes, then her breathing eased and she fluttered, enlivened.

Cured.

"Did you see the aura's color, Thorn?"

Thorn nodded. He'd experienced such pigments of light in small samplings since he'd been living there, doled out by his guardian, but had yet to learn how to harvest the flashes himself. And he'd never seen such a transfer give life . . . only take it.

"Auras are vibrations of color, signifying the energy around all living matter," Father Erik had said, releasing the songbird from the handkerchief so Thorn could return her to the woods outside. "The colors change with mood . . . a brilliant clarity that only our kind can both see and command. And now you know that one of the most distilled forms of energy is harvested from the depths of dread. The moment you've mastered inspiring fear in others, you will be *their* master. The only thing more potent than the despair of terror is the rapture of music. As you remember, from your own past."

The power of the terror Thorn embraced that day couldn't compare to the remorse he'd felt for bringing shame to the man who had shown him such compassion since the tender age of seven . . . who became his guardian and teacher and friend.

In that one mask-less moment, he had looked upon the only father he'd ever known as a monster. Although now Thorn understood someone's appearance was not the measuring stick for a soul's predisposition toward goodness or evil, he still regretted that instinctual prejudice fueled by immaturity.

Tensing at the memory, Thorn pounded Father Erik's door once more. His chest constricted at the resulting silence. The damp air, a result of being so close to the water, usually soothed him. But today, it clogged his lungs, thick and weighted like a death shroud.

He shoved the door open. The coffin, balanced atop its dais and lined with red velvet, was empty. Just as he'd feared.

Cursing, Thorn stared up at "Dies Irae" painted in lovely black script around the top edge of the room to form a border against the red walls. The verses had never seemed more apropos—a requiem mass as ghastly and rhapsodic as the man who had built this lair over a century ago for his sanctuary: the composer, the alchemist, the architect, the magician, the mastermind.

The Phantom.

But that legendary man had grown weak and sickly of late, and no longer ventured topside alone, neither to the secret passages of the academy that held nothing but bad memories for him, nor to anywhere in Paris. He went only when Thorn accompanied him to provide support.

Or so Thorn thought. There was only one reason Erik would risk going without him today. The same reason he'd lost all his senses a hundred years earlier at an opera house much like this one—before Thorn was even born—and kidnapped the opera's prima donna.

Thorn's gaze shifted to the painting hanging on the wall where Christina Nilsson, Erik's cherished *Christine*, was dressed as Pandora from Greek mythology. A necklace holding a ruby wedding ring hung from a nail beside it.

Thorn growled. Should Erik be seen or captured, their entire way of life—all that his father had worked for and built, along with their ties to the subterranean world—could be exposed.

Turning back toward the darkness of the parlor, Thorn shouted the "Dies Irae," the tension on his vocal cords excruciating: "Day of judgment! Day of wonders! Hark! The trumpet's awful sound; louder than a thousand thunders, shakes the vast creation round!"

Ange answered with her own trumpeting squawk as the elevator made a whining hum, the cables drawing the car up from the cellar. She tottered toward a shadowy figure clambering out of the gated door with a lantern in hand.

"Brava, Thorn!" Erik's deep and dulcet praise floated over to him, stroking him like a loving pat to the head. "Stunning recitation. Although you mustn't strain your voice. And hymns are best delivered in their native tongue. The protestant version holds no torch to the Latin." With a weary grunt, his silhouette slumped to the floor. The swan huddled in his lap and scolded him, her beak tugging at his ear.

Thorn crouched beside the duo, relieved it had only been a case of Ange not knowing where her master was. But that relief sunk to concern when he noticed the sickly gray aura surrounding Father Erik. Thorn fought the usual bout of jealousy that niggled at him, seeing Erik give so much of himself to his cause in the cellar lab. His father was always exhausted on Sundays, after burning all his energy, but this was extreme. "You should be in bed, saving your strength," Thorn said, pushing out the statement from a throat still raw and achy after his panicked tantrum.

"Just as you should be respectful of your own limitations." His father's unsteady fingertip tapped Thorn's Adam's apple in the lantern's soft light, then moved to his face, as if assuring himself all of Thorn's features were in place.

He often compared Thorn's appearance—defined dark brows above piercing, wide-set brown eyes; high cheekbones; a straight nose above plump lips shapely enough to be a woman's; square, cleft chin; and defined musculature—to the heroes in the mythological tomes Thorn liked to read. Thorn, however, preferred the monsters of those tales. Their tragic misbalances and flaws were so much more compelling than any perfection could be.

And so it was with Erik. Having no outer beauty to empower him, he'd honed his inner artistry instead, the things that truly made him unique: mind, talents, voice, and mysticism. Attributes that demanded respect, fear, and awe.

Thorn had watched and learned during the twelve years he'd been under Erik's tutelage. Pretty faces were no more than masks worn to justify laziness and intellectual monotony. Since Erik had been born without one, he'd crafted a myriad of his own—masks that gave the illusion of conformity but could be cast aside whenever he wished to unleash the true, blinding radiance of deviation.

Thorn followed in his guardian's footsteps, made his own masks—some stitched of cloth, some ceramic—to cover the right half of his face in tribute to his mixed bloodline. Although he had nothing physical to hide, a demon lurked inside him, afraid to forge into the light of day. His masks made him feel safe, and as adept as he was at blending into his surroundings, he rarely walked the grounds without wearing one. Today being the exception. A mistake he wouldn't make again.

Erik's palm smelled of formaldehyde and iodine as he patted Thorn's cheek. "How could I rest this evening, my lovely boy? The girl has arrived. I feel it." Thorn could hear Erik smile behind his own chosen mask, shaped of copper and coated with silver. Ange's enthusiastic greeting had knocked the covering askew, blocking his mouth and revealing that sunken crater in his forehead where one of his eyebrows jutted out unnaturally.

When the mask was in place, all that showed was the bottom

quarter of his face—strong chin and full lower lip—making him appear deceptively normal, distinguished. A middle-aged man with a head of black, well-groomed hair and piercing amber eyes that glowed when he was at his most powerful.

With the mask and wig, one wouldn't know he'd been in the world for centuries, or that he was disfigured and had only a scant cluster of hair. With everything in place, one couldn't see the irregular shape of the eye sockets, how they burrowed too deep into his skull. They could only see the expression harbored within those depths: wise, intense, and maniacal beneath the weight of irrepressible genius and tortured memories.

Thorn's palm covered the warm, white swirl of energy from Rune's song, still snuggled under his sternum. He'd been selfish to think, for even a second, that he could keep any of it for himself. That he could feed his latent compositions with the fire of brilliant green that pulsed through her eyes when she performed. Erik needed it so much more than he ever could.

"Yes," Thorn answered at last, helping his father straighten his mask so the synthetic copper nose centered over his absence of one. "It's her. She possesses the gift. Just as was foretold." He gripped Erik's hand and placed it across his glowing chest where his own hand had been. "I hold the proof. Her voice—it's immaculate."

"Seraphic, you mean to say," Father Erik corrected, half-teasing, as his hand began to absorb the power—a tug Thorn felt all the way into his feet.

With a rueful smile, Thorn nodded. "Undeniably. A fine match for yours, or any choir in heaven."

"Despite that she was born to an ensemble of demons," his father answered with that flare for dark, self-deprecating humor.

They shared a laugh, though Thorn didn't feel any joy in his heart as he watched Erik's veins surge with light.

Rune's light. The purest white he'd ever seen . . . incarnate, rare . . . the essence of an angel. Thorn wanted it back, nestled inside his body. Warming him and resurrecting his muse.

"She wishes to be free. I sensed that," Thorn added, more to distract himself from the loss than to justify their heinous plans, although it served the latter purpose well enough.

"Didn't I tell you? Just as the old witch predicted. It will take little convincing for her to give it all up, yes?" The silver-and-gray-striped Milano suit, tailored perfectly to Erik's thin frame, tightened around his shoulders as he tried to stand. He always dressed in his finest clothes on club nights, but today was Sunday. Their weekly sojourns through the underground tunnels and into Paris were reserved for Saturdays. Thorn was surprised to see him in such fine array while working in the lab. He supposed he'd wanted to look his best, in hopes Thorn might've been accompanied by Rune.

Lately, Erik's desperation made him forget his patience. They both knew it wasn't time yet. They had to tease her out with carefully placed crumbs. Once convinced she couldn't trust the students and teachers—on the chance they'd think she was losing her mind—or even herself around them for fear of their safety, she'd venture out on her own, seek the truth within the shadows.

Father Erik had too much to do in his cellar lab in preparation, so it was Thorn's place to lead her down that path. But only *she* could surrender to the darkness—body, mind, and soul.

And once she did, Erik would have everything he needed, at long last.

Thorn looped his father's arm around his neck. Years ago, the man's six-foot-two frame had towered over him. Now, Thorn overshadowed him by two inches. Using his thigh muscles, Thorn lifted them both to standing. Only fitting, after all the times Erik had carried him in his childhood.

"You must take me to her once night falls," his father pressed, admiring the glow at his chest, beneath his lavender tie and navy shirt, where Rune's aria fed his heart with a burst of strength. "Let me see the little pigeon for myself. Her aura will be most visible as she sleeps."

Thorn seated Erik on the chaise lounge and propped his hip against the curved arm on the other end. A refusal flared at the base of his larynx. He didn't want to spy on her while she was so vulnerable.

The absurd thought extinguished as quickly as it sparked. How laughable, that such a thing would occur to him.

Their kind was descended from hunters . . . renowned for infiltrating darkened bedrooms and wearing the breath of sleeping women like precious pearls upon their flesh, hijacking their dreams and seducing their bodies and spirits—feeding off their passion, need, and fear.

Even if Thorn tried to argue, Father Erik would convince him all was perfect and proper with a hypnotic purr of those celestial and hedonistic vocal cords.

Over the years, Thorn had become acutely aware of his guardian's manipulations. When he was that eight-year-old boy, Thorn had delivered the ortolan back to the forest that afternoon after being "healed" by Erik. Then he watched as the bird tried to fly but instead floundered on the ground, gasping for breath. Erik had *convinced* the songbird she was healed . . . but her ribs still pricked through her lungs, and she died just the same.

Nothing could live forever. At least, nothing of the natural world.

Thorn often wondered if he had the strength to refuse his father's will, now that he knew. But this had evolved to something beyond Erik's web of persuasion. Thorn owed him his life and purpose, and would do most anything to hear pride and praise on the strains of Erik's beautiful voice—no matter how maniacal or horrific the request. He wanted to be the son Erik needed.

The man behind the masks was his father in all the ways that counted. And family counted above all else.

So, of course Thorn would take him to Rune, as soon as Erik had digested her song's energy and could make the trip. They would be silent in their observance; she'd never know they were there. A slight detour from their relaxed Sunday routine of resting in their rooms wouldn't hurt.

Thorn told himself this, in hopes to stifle the truth: that he himself wanted to see her again, and that later, when he and Father returned home, he would pick up his violin. After two years of sleep, his muse had reawakened.

Tonight, he would serenade Rune in her dreams once more.

❈·I·❈

It's his eyes that call to me first—coppery and glimmering. I squint, unsure if they're real.

Then I hear the music, and there's no denying the reality, or that I'm meant to be in this place. Meant to see, hear, and feel everything. It's the only way I'll be complete and comfortable in my own skin.

I stumble into the pitch-black tunnel without hesitation, following the heart-rending chords of the violin. *Literally* following the notes. Each pitch dances along the stony wall—a different color— like a laser-light show. My hand traces them, drawn to the tactile delicacies they offer: blistering reds, temperate greens, sun-warmed yellows, and blues as cool and variable as the ocean depths, where cerulean and navy glisten like sapphires on the tails of monstrously fanged fish.

In the distance, I see him: my maestro, draped in shadows. His eyes flash again—two pennies at the bottom of a wishing well. Can he make my wishes come true? Can he help me sing without pain?

A heavy mist seeps down from above and separates us.

A dripping sound echoes, and my feet splash through cold, rising water. I'm momentarily brave, but my courage wanes when the liquid turns black and swallows me up to my neck.

I shiver in the icy waves. My throat constricts. I panic . . . struggle to keep my head exposed. It's not a tunnel; it's a box. A box filling with water that reeks of rotting fish and stagnant mud.

I'm drowning.

My skin freezes, my lungs burn; my mind grows dizzy, numb. I kick against the wooden walls, but I'm too weak, too small, too scared to break through.

Unconsciousness ebbs.

The violin revives me. It becomes more than music. It becomes a voice.

My maestro speaks through it, coaxing me to fight my way to freedom. I grit my teeth and kick again. Everything I do is in slow motion, until finally, my left knee bursts through, leaving a gaping gash in my skin. It will be a scar one day.

But all that matters right now is I'm free.

The box bursts open and I swim to the surface. Overhead the night sky greets me, blanketed in stars. The musical laser-light show becomes planets in chaotic disarray. I drift upward until I've joined them, in the middle, at the epicenter of the Milky Way, where it's warm and comforting like a velvet throw.

My own song breaks free to join the violin, a duet both celestial and powerful. The spaces resonate in my head, lining up behind my mouth and nose and transitioning to my upper register. My voice lifts—a high C so pristine it forms a golden glow—a bubble made of glittering energy. It matches my maestro's sparkling eyes.

The planets and stars in the galaxy float around us, aligning, riding upon the melody the violinist and I now carry as one.

Two halves united.

With the heavens aligned, all is right with the world. Music and love and happiness. Also, peace.

The universe belongs to us. Together, we own it.

Together, we won.

"Rune."

The whisper warms my ear. I curl up and pull the covers over my head, reluctant to leave the private haven of REM sleep.

"Come on, hon. They're serving breakfast in the atrium. You need to eat so you can get to class on time. How are you feeling today?"

The concern in Mom's voice shatters my utopia, but I already know the details of that dream by heart. It's the same one I started having shortly after Dad died. The dream that pulled me through the darkest and most terrifying event of my life, when my grandma tried to drown me. When I was falling unconscious, his music roused me and gave me the power to save myself.

Even after that, my maestro continued to keep my subconscious company for a long time during nightmares of the event, until I suddenly stopped dreaming of him two years ago. I've missed our duets in my sleep. It felt so good to finally be in that place of comfort again.

All this time, I'd always assumed Dad's spirit was the one play-ing the violin . . . my deliverer of music. And that his eyes shifted from hazel to flashing coppery-gold to serve as my beacons in the darkness.

But yesterday, I saw those eyes shining inside the gardener's hood. And now I'm having my dreams again.

What does that mean?

I shiver, only partly because Mom drags off my covers to expose my skin to the chilly room. I squint at her. She's holding the bed curtains open, and soft lavender light filters into my comfortable cave from the lava lamp. It still looks like midnight in my tiny room. Her stance is blocking my digital clock.

"What time is it?" I ask.

"Seven thirty a.m."

The answer shocks me enough to sit up, so fast I almost bump the top of my head on the antechamber's low, arched ceiling. "You're supposed to be at the airport by eight! Why didn't you wake me up earlier? I wanted time to say good-bye." I feel like a little girl again, needing that red thread around my wrist so I can let her go.

Mom pats my hand. "It's okay. I called and got my flight changed. I'm going to stay till the end of the week, to catch up with Lottie and to do a little sightseeing on my own. I can buy a few outfits to wear while I'm here. Maybe I'll even find the perfect wedding dress, yeah?"

"Mom . . . you should be back home with Ned, planning the wedding." Newly engaged, and he's all alone at our house instead of spending quality time with his fiancée.

She shakes her head. "You're my priority, Rune. I just don't feel good about leaving yet. Your spell was . . . different this time."

Her unspoken *I'm worried you might be going completely bat-monkeys like Grandma Lil* echoes in the silence. The lava lamp makes a soft burbling sound and the fluorescent light casts everything in eerie shadows. Mom looks like half of her face is gone.

I cringe and roll my shoulders to alleviate the sense of dread and confusion rising around me like the freezing water in my dream, adding to the guilt I'm already wrestling with over so many things—including making Mom stay longer, all because I faked fainting yesterday.

Not only did she have to call the airport, she had to notify her boss at the house-cleaning service, too. Now she's using up vacation days that should be saved for her honeymoon. She must be really upset to disrupt her life like that.

And to think, she doesn't even realize how screwed up I am.

"Let's get a move on." She nudges my left knee with her palm, almost touching the scar that's exposed by my lace-trimmed shorty pajamas. "The seniors have last breakfast while the juniors start their classes. It's the perfect time to meet the kids you'll be graduating with."

I cringe. After the "fainting" incident yesterday, I stayed in my room the rest of the evening and was able to avoid meeting any of the students other than Sunny. However, most of the teachers breezed through for introductions.

Professor Diamond Tomlin—the youngest of the staff at age twenty-five, and instructor of all things theatric and scientific—came in, having just returned from a weekend gig in Paris with his alternative punk band. Other than his tweed jacket and pleated pants, he looked the part of a drummer, with his dark beard and wiry build. But his hair sticking up in thick, brown waves all over his head and the sharpness of his inquisitive blue eyes gave him more of a young, rebellious Einstein vibe, which fit with what Sunny had told me: that he likes to perform science experiments in his dorm after lights-out, resulting in strange orange flashes beneath his door.

Principal Norrington came in behind the professor and shook my hand, saying he looked forward to having me in his financial-literacy and career-planning classes second semester. With his accent and weathered good looks, I was convinced there was a British spy hidden behind his stuffy sweaters and wire-rimmed glasses. Confirmation came when he unintentionally bumped into Madame Harris—school librarian, classical lit teacher, and counselor in a curvy, blond-haired, gray-eyed package—on the way out of my room. As he helped her pick up the papers she'd dropped, their eyes locked, and a 007/Miss Moneypenny vibe passed between them.

Their romantic moment shattered when Madame Bouchard—instructor of historical musicology, vocal pedagogy, and all around scariest staff member at the academy—appeared. Bouchard fit perfectly inside this gloomy, haunting place with her stiff-as-iron poise, thin-lipped, heavily painted face, and straight white hair bleeding to a hot-pink dye job before falling to her waist. She was something fresh out of *Bride of Frankenstein*. Yet from what Sunny told me, Bouchard is more mad scientist than monster. Her favorite pastime is taxidermy. She's even transformed one of the empty dressing rooms on the second floor into her workshop and personal exhibition hall.

Her gruesome reputation precedes her, judging by how the other three teachers scattered as Bouchard started to grill me about my training: who my instructor was in the States, how many times I've performed in public, and how long I've "been such a little songbird because you must have practiced Renata's aria from *The Fiery Angel* for months on end to master it so well." Aunt Charlotte adjusted her glasses and insisted I'd had a stressful enough day and wasn't to be interviewed.

The two ladies began arguing. My mom and I sat, dumbfounded, until Headmaster Fabre arrived and told Bouchard to save her questions for another time. He had a kind, handsome face and a French accent; but his thick white hair and burly beard were more reminiscent of a distinguished seafaring captain than a Frenchman. Bouchard didn't dare back talk to the man who hired and fired the staff. She glared at Aunt Charlotte, then left in a fluster of stutters and snarls. After rescuing me like he did, the headmaster would've been my choice for teacher of the year, if not for his subjects being world geography and social studies, my least favorites. He complimented my singing at the audition, then apologized that his wife, the costume designer and health teacher, was away in Paris at a fashion show.

She is the teacher I've most wanted to meet, and I've already decided to look for her today. I'm hoping to offer assistance with costumes. If I'm going to be stuck here, sewing and designing are the best shots I have at staying sane.

"Where are those uniforms we borrowed?" Mom interrupts my thoughts, digging through my closet where we shoved my things last night before we settled in to sleep—me in my comfortable curtained-in cave and she on the chaise lounge. I'll offer her the bed tonight. It's unfair for her to have to curl up on a couch that's four inches too short just because of my dishonesty. Besides, I'm curious to know whether she'll hear the same things I heard coming from the vent above my bed . . . rustling and breathing. Maybe those are the kinds of sounds a hundred-year-old building makes. But I'll feel better knowing it wasn't all in my head, like everything else seems to be.

Mom drags some clothes from the closet. The pink bag that held my uniforms went missing yesterday between my unplanned operatic performance and our attempt to unpack and pretend everything was normal. Aunt Charlotte had to sift through old uniforms donated by last year's seniors to give me temporary substitutes.

I wrinkle my nose, remembering how awkward and big they looked last night when I tried them on. "Why can't I just wear street clothes until they show up? These are extenuating circumstances, right?"

Mom chews her lip. "Rules are rules. Lottie's already bent enough for you. She has to draw the line at academics. It affects your grade if you go to class out of uniform. These will have to do until we find the ones we bought. I'm sure they'll turn up by the end of the day."

I nod, not mentioning how violating it feels, having your clothes stolen, wondering why anyone would take something so personal in the first place.

Unless it was for revenge because I interrupted the tryouts . . .

My unruly hair cascades around my shoulders, several strands sticking to my suddenly overwarm cheeks. I use the brush Mom hands me to rake the waves from my face until they pop with static. Snuggling a knitted headband into place, I swing my feet over the bed's edge and yawn.

As I'm pouring my sleepy limbs into the gray jacket, long skirt, and white ruffled shirt that make up the riding habit wannabe, the scent of bacon and something cinnamon blends with rich notes of coffee and wafts under my door. My stomach rumbles. Last night, after I showered to clean the sticky soup from my skin, I refused to eat anything else. I said I wasn't hungry; but the truth was, I was too freaked out.

How is it possible that I saw a guy in Victorian clothing who no one else knows about, who can vanish and drain the life from roses with just a touch? Whose eyes have been in my dreams for years, alongside violin music I thought belonged to my father?

I force the unsettling thoughts deep down inside. I have enough to worry about today in the real world. Cinching the borrowed skirt's waist with a belt only causes the excess fabric to pleat and bulge in weird places. At least the red necktie fits. After applying light strokes of blush and peach-tinted lip balm without risking a peek in the cheval mirror, I follow Mom toward the door, resigned to my fate.

I won't be able to get out of this until I prove myself capable of performing without breaking down. Yesterday's fiasco brought this truth to light, and it's been confirmed by Mom's determination to stay at my side until she feels I'm strong enough to be here without her. For years, Mom has put her life on hold to deal with my lack of one.

It's time to figure out why this overpowering ability to sing—that once brought me so much satisfaction—is gnawing away at me like a sickness. I need to know why I'm broken, so I can fix myself. One way or another. Maybe this place can help me do that, and then I can finally look forward to my future. Because I'm starting to realize there's something worse than stepping up and facing your fears—and that's living as if you're already dead.

6

PERFORMANCE ART

"Thinking will not overcome fear, but action will."
W. Clement Stone

Abandoning my claustrophobic dorm room for the vast opulence of the grand foyer, Mom and I squint against the sudden brightness. Morning filters through tall, cut-glass windows, casting dappled imprints of diamonds, squares, and stars along marble floors, bronze statues, and the mirrored wall.

I focus on my reflection, and that eerie sense of being watched shivers through me. In Leroux's lore, the phantom often observed his prey through mirrors, even used them as doorways to lure Christine into his underground world.

An icy gust whisks over me and teases my hair. Startled, I glance upward at the vents, breathing a sigh of relief to find the air conditioner kicking on.

I start to relax, basking in the dissonance of the warm sun dancing with the chilled air. There's always been something about being in natural light that invigorates me, and makes me feel capable and strong. It's almost as if I absorb its power somehow. Dad would've said I was basking in its aura. And Mom would've laughed at him. But it doesn't matter whether she believes or not. I know what I feel.

I step directly into a ray of sun and my blood responds, sparks of stamina bursting through my limbs and muscles. The energizing sensation feeds my courage. As Mom and I take the winding stairs, following the scents of food to find the atrium, I convince myself I can do this. This is a school founded on theatrics. I can act confident. I can face the other students, apologize for interrupting the auditions, and win them all over.

My optimism wavers as we arrive at the atrium on the third floor, partly due to the quiet chatter seeping out through the dark, arched entrance, but even more because of the song being piped in softly through speakers. I recognize the rich nuances of the language— marked with aggressive and hard consonants—as Russian. It's from the opera the students were auditioning for yesterday; although this piece belongs to one of the male performers, which explains why the orchestral rainbow blooming in my mind isn't consuming me. Only female arias seem to have that effect.

I hesitate at the threshold, hoping that if another of Renata's songs comes on today, it won't speak to me . . . or if it does, that the low volume will subdue my itch to purge. I'd like a day or two to recoup before facing another bout of humiliation.

Mom crosses the threshold and gives me a nod of encouragement. Nibbling the ends of my hair to taste the sweet orange and vanilla of my shampoo, I follow behind her, and step into character.

I expected the spacious cafeteria—made of three lecture halls with the walls knocked out from between them—to be well lit, with windows at every turn to let in the outdoor light. That's what atriums are, right? Big, bright, and sun-filled, burgeoning with plants and flowers like a rain forest?

Not this one. I'm not even sure why they call it an atrium. There's not a plant in sight and it's as dreary as our dorm rooms. Round mirrors were substituted for the windows when the layout was redesigned. The reflective surfaces—splotchy and black in places where the silver-backing was rubbed off to appear fashionably distressed—resemble the portholes on a ghostly, sunken ship.

Driven by that unshakeable feeling of something on the other side of the reflections, I pick up my pace. The glossy floor, a deep red-and-black-striped design, glides soundlessly under my Mary Jane loafers. Square red-and-black tiles continue the color scheme up to the ceiling. The long room is divided lengthwise. Shiny red chairs and matching candlelit tables, most of them filled with students draped in shadows, hug the far walls.

This half—the entry side—is open and provides a path to the buffet located around the corner at the far right end of the room. A gothic-style chandelier dangles from the low, red ceiling above us, like twelve-inch-long black and gold taper candles turned upside down. Multiple glowing tips, the size and shape of tiny flames, light the walkway with a subtle yellow haze.

As we follow the illuminated path, staying close to the wall, I tense my shoulders . . . waiting for the whispers to begin. After a few steps, I gaze sidelong at the diners and find everyone preoccupied by eating, deep in their own conversations, or writing notes in spirals or journals, apparently about the opera taking place on the two big-screen TVs suspended at the ends of the room to offer a clear view from all directions.

Now I get why the cafeteria is so dimly lit. The songs streaming from the speakers are synchronized with the picture in movie theater style. The student handbook stressed that we would be immersed in the world of opera, especially pertaining to the end-of-the-year program. Not only were we to learn the music, we were to master the theatrics behind each performance: embrace both the visual and aural aspects. And what better way than to play each act over and over on TV as opposed to popular or classic movies, reality shows, or other teenage programming?

It's obvious by the number of students concentrating and jotting notes that some sort of assignment was given over the operatic performance taking place. On the giant screens, a blue-lit stage lined with a crowd of young nuns in different poses comes into view. A Catholic cardinal seduces one of the sisters who's half-dressed. Her expression can only be described as impassioned terror, as if the unlawful desire they share will combust and end the world in a holocaust of pain and rapture. An audience of strange men leer at the duo and cheer them on, their faces painted like grotesque clowns. The spectacle is equal parts sensual and disturbing.

Mom and I step around the corner into the well-lit alcove where the slick floor surrenders to black-and-gold-checked carpet surrounding a buffet counter. A digital menu board juts down from overhead, filled with both American and Parisian cuisine, along with a list of prices. Mom hands me my student meal ticket—prepaid by

Aunt Charlotte—and readies her credit card, waiting for the two girls in front of us to decide on their choices.

Five students—decked out in uniforms under khaki aprons—keep busy behind the long, black marble surface, taking orders and replenishing the fare: cinnamon rolls, assorted baguettes, croissants, and muffins inside glass cases, then eggs, pancakes, and bacon in steaming stainless steel tubs on the other end.

One student polishes silverware, straightens the mugs, and keeps the coffee pots running. There's also a fruit-and-cheese station. There, a guy with twinkling blue eyes and pale blond hair—almost glimmering white in the fluorescent lighting—dishes some watermelon from a stainless-steel bowl half buried in ice. A pretty Hispanic girl reaches up for the serving. She can't be more than five foot one.

Towering over her at six foot two or so, he draws back the bowl so she can't quite reach it, then finally hands it off with a teasing grin. She shakes her long, dark ponytail, gives him a playful scowl, and says something in Spanish. He smirks as she walks away. Apparently, he knows the language and thinks he scored some points. He catches me looking and flashes a flirty grin. I put up the necessary barricades and avert my eyes to a chalkboard on an easel that blocks part of the wall beside the cash register.

The school has four live-in chefs, but students are in charge of helping in the kitchen and at the counter, along with cleaning up. It's partly to save money, but more to teach them responsibility. That's why they're also charged with mopping the floors, cleaning the bathrooms and showers, keeping the dorm rooms straightened, and dusting the many banisters, along with any other manual upkeep for the opera house.

Students are charged with these things, meaning me, too. As part of our grade, we're each required to take a weekly assignment. The chalkboard serves as the duty roster, where everyone writes in their work schedule for the week. The teachers lead the volunteers and take turns helping out. Which is why, when I first met Aunt Charlotte, she was wielding a dust cloth and wearing an apron.

I scan the chalkboard, trying to find Sunny's name. She suggested I piggyback on her assignment—insisting that most incoming students follow that protocol with their peer advisors, to help with the adjustment period. But I've decided I'm going to find a task of my own—and look for the mystery gardener in the process. I discussed my idea with Aunt Charlotte last night . . . that I'd like to volunteer for a job that no one else has done in years. She gave me the okay, although it took some persuasion.

Lifting the chalk from the easel's tray, I scribble the number 51 to start a final row in the second column of names. Then I write: *Gardening duty—Rune Germain*, while trying not to think about the forest or the cemetery on the other side of the garden.

I've barely had time to rub the chalk dust from my fingers when Mom and I are called up to the cash register. I request a bowl of fruit, a pumpernickel muffin, and an almond cappuccino. The woman taking orders introduces herself as Headmistress Fabre, the very teacher I've been hoping to meet.

My heart dances a beat—nervous and excited.

She's in her upper forties and is thin and leggy like a model, with flawless skin one shade lighter than the rich, brown bread she retrieves from the glass case and wraps in a paper liner. She relays my fruit order to the boy with the white-blond hair, her perfectly arched eyebrows framing fawn-soft brown eyes. Her hair—spirals of ebony glossed with streaks of bluish gray—fringes her shoulders as she reaches out to take my meal ticket over the counter. From what I can tell of her clothes under the apron, they're every bit as stylish and chic as the lady wearing them.

I search for some way to bring up the costumes for the opera, and am just about to find my tongue when she speaks.

"My husband told me about your performance yesterday." Her voice is silky, like her palm brushing mine as she hands me back my ticket. She delivers each word in perfect English with no French accent. I'm curious as to her personal story—how she met her foreign husband and ended up here. "He's not one for being at a loss for words, but he said I'd have to hear you to believe it. He said there was nothing to compare it to. How long have you been practicing?"

Practice? I've never had to. My face flares to the pitch of a bonfire. Mom clears her throat nervously. Before I can concoct a believable lie to save us both, a familiar Southern accent bursts over my shoulder.

"There you are!" Sunny steps up to the counter beside me, her welcoming grin so wide I can see two crooked teeth on her lower jaw that I didn't notice yesterday. Her freckles clump together with the strain of her facial muscles, heightening that harlequin mask effect. She's plaited her hair into a messy side braid. A spray of fake velour flowers weave in and out, the same red as our matching clip-on ties.

"Madame Fabre, you gals have something in common." Sunny takes the muffin the teacher holds, crinkling the paper lining as she hands it to me after pinching off a piece to stuff in her mouth. "She's a fashionista. I saw patterns and such in her baggage."

I smirk. Last night, I mentioned to Sunny how much I'd like to be a part of costume design. And now she's provided the perfect introduction. I'm bursting with a thank-you that has no chance to slip out before Headmistress Fabre takes over again.

"Is that so? Well, I could use the opinion of another seamstress. Did you see the scene that was playing on the TVs? The nuns?"

"I saw most of it," I answer, eager to finally showcase a talent I actually had to work at to master.

"I need to decide on a fabric that's inexpensive but versatile and durable. There's a comic relief scene in act four that takes place at a tavern. We use the same actresses for both settings, so that means two times the costumes—nun habits and tavern wench uniforms. If I'm not careful, we won't have enough money left over in our budget for the lead roles' costumes."

I furrow my brow. The last look I got at the TV, the nuns were hopping around the stage, their eyes huge and wild, as if possessed. "It needs to be comfortable enough they can move around . . . lightweight so they won't get overheated under the stage lights. But it should *look* sturdy and heavy—like authentic nun habits. Right?"

Madame Fabre nods. "Exactly . . ."

Blocking out the clang of silverware being dumped into a divider, I track a glance over Sunny's hair again and the tiny velveteen flowers—how the fluorescent light gilds certain petals, making them shinier than others, depending on the direction they lay. "You need a fabric that has a nap. Like velour. Cut it on the bias, then finish all the seams with a serger so the robes are reversible. When the light shines on the front for the nuns' robes, it will be matted and dark. On the reverse side, it will be a different shade and texture—shinier and brighter. Convert the wimples the nuns wear on their necks and heads to bonnets and aprons that can cinch the waists on the wenches' uniforms, holding up the robes' hems after they've been folded at the knees for short, poufy dresses. Same pattern, same accessories, totally different look. And you'll only have to buy enough fabric for one set."

Headmistress Fabre smiles—a spread of white teeth behind plump lips. "That's brilliant." She offers me an extra muffin. "On the house, for your help."

I nod a thank-you but the muffin on her palm stalls across the counter as she rethinks.

"Say, how would you feel about helping me out after classes? I'm going to start taking measurements tomorrow so that once the elimination and final auditions are over, we can jump right into cutting out the patterns. And we can start on the costumes for the supporting roles immediately, since they've already been chosen. We'll be sewing from four until dinnertime at least two or three nights a week. It'll earn you extra credit."

Sunny elbows me. I glance at her, then at Mom who's taking a cup of coffee from one of the students behind the counter. "That sounds great," I answer. Grinning, I pass Sunny the muffin she's already sampled, and take the other.

"Perfect." Madame Fabre gives me a cappuccino for my free hand. "It's about time we get a student who knows a thing or two about a needle and thread."

Smiling, Mom pats my arm. "Look at that. Behind the scenes, just like you wanted. But keep your grades up in all your classes."

"I personally guarantee no health homework," Madame Fabre says. "And I have some influence with the social studies professor, so we'll see that you get time in class to finish work in there." She winks.

"Mrs. Fabre is a gal of many hats." Sunny slips in the remark, smirking as she stuffs another bit of muffin into her cheek.

The teacher laughs. "And that's Sunny's not-so-subtle plea to borrow one of my hats for the outing this coming weekend." She purses her mouth in thought. "I'm thinking my floppy fedora . . . with the daisy on the side."

Sunny beams. "The one that just so happens to match my daisy tights?"

"Pure coincidence, right?"

"I'll drop by your room on Saturday morning, before we head out." With a nod of her head, Sunny tugs me toward the guy at the fruit bar, who's now dishing up the apples and cherries I ordered.

Mom motions me on so she can stay and chat with Madame Fabre.

"So, what outing are you going on this Saturday?" I ask Sunny as we head to the fruit bar.

"Shhh. We'll discuss that shortly. But first, you meet the man of Katarina's dreams."

I put the brakes on behind her, the carpet popping with static under my soles as she tries to drag me. "You mean the guy who—"

"Carted you down two flights of stairs? Yep. In the fine flesh." Sunny plants me in front of the twinkling blue eyes that caught me watching earlier.

That smirk has returned to his face. Not exactly a snide expression, just perceptive, as if he knows more about me than he should. It's the same way he looked at the ponytail girl. He has a surplus of self-confidence—suave, playful, and a little arrogant. The typical rich boy one would expect to meet at an elite academy like this one. His attractiveness makes him dangerous . . . someone I should avoid.

"Rune, this is Jackson Reynolds," Sunny says. "Your knight in shining armor from yesterday."

He places my fruit on the edge of the counter within reach. The scent of his spiced cologne lingers—taunting me with the memory of his heartbeat next to my jawline, teasing out the flutter of nausea I've been fighting.

"The name's Jax," he croons in a rich baritone as he tips his head to me. "And stop giving her hell, Sunny."

"I won't never give her hell. She's my hero. Did you hear her sing?"

"Yeah, and so did you-know-who." He gestures with his chin toward the other side of the counter. "So keep your voice down."

I turn to see Katarina beside the chalkboard, waiting for a chance to order at the cash register where Headmistress Fabre is still talking with my mom. The snarl twisting Kat's flawless features is intimidating, but it's her blue eyes that bore into me. Her stare could melt diamonds . . . or mirrors, like the one behind her on the wall, a few feet from the easel.

I didn't notice it earlier with the chalkboard in my way. From this angle, I can see movement on the other side—a filmy silhouette—similar to what I saw yesterday in the foyer. This time, two coppery gleams flash, like eyes blinking. A half-mask takes shape, white and ghastly. I yelp and clasp my hand over my mouth.

Kat narrows her eyes, obviously misreading my body language to mean I'm faking being scared of her looks. I shake my head, but she turns away when a girl with chic, cropped hair the color of Jackson's, grabs her elbow and points to the chalkboard. When I look again at the mirror, the silhouette is gone.

Returning my attention to Sunny and Jax, I tell myself I imagined it. That there's no one behind the mirror.

No one but the phantom. I saw the mask this time.

It's not possible. Even if some poor disfigured soul had actually inhabited this opera house and inspired Leroux's book, he wouldn't still be alive today, over a hundred years later.

"—a little compassion that I'm stuck in the middle . . . that's all I'm asking," Jax says to Sunny, pulling me out of my dark meditations. He turns to the Asian boy behind him. "Li, I'm going on break." The boy nods.

Coming around to our side of the counter, Jax unties his apron, revealing taut muscles beneath his long-sleeve polo shirt and gray dress pants. He must lift weights because RoseBlood doesn't have a fitness program—other than dance and choreography classes.

I scold myself for noticing, and follow his gaze as it flicks again to the platinum-blond girl over by the register. I force myself not to look at the mirror.

"My sister hasn't shut up about how unfair it is that Kat has to audition for first eliminations a second time." Jax shrugs into his uniform jacket.

"Psssshhh." Sunny rolls her eyes. "Roxie and Kat can hiss and holler all they want. You and me both know Audrey was born to play Renata. Her sister begged her not to visit in New Mexico last summer . . . to stay here and get tutoring, because she wants Audrey to nab that part. That's a big deal. It ain't fair that Kat always gets the leads just 'cause her great-great-grand-something was a member of the Royal Swedish Academy of Music."

"*Isn't* fair," Jax corrects, a comical glint in his eye.

"Blah, blah." Sunny scowls. "Now that first-tier eliminations have been postponed until Wednesday, Audrey has extra time to master that final note she's so scared of. And with any luck, Kat'll trip over the cadenza that was giving her fits a while ago. Can't believe she managed to nail it earlier. Here's hoping it was a one-time thing."

Sunny's statement grounds me to the present. "Wait. They're redoing the first-elimination tryouts because of what I did?"

Sunny plucks another chunk from her muffin and pops it in her mouth. "Yep. The teachers voted . . . decided you should have a chance to try out for the part, too, since you obviously know the opera."

I shake my head. "No, I don't want . . . I don't know the part. It was all a—" I stop myself short of saying *fluke*. How would I explain that? "I can't believe they're making everyone have do-overs because of me." No wonder I'm on Kat's hit list. There were five other girls who were in those auditions. They might be frustrated, too, but at least—other than Audrey—they hadn't sung yet. I interrupted Kat's flawless rendition of the aria, and now she has to go through it again, and possibly mess up this time. My throat tightens in sympathy at how nervous she must be. "I should apologize."

Sunny looks mortified at the suggestion.

"Not a good idea," Jax adds, and flashes a pleading glance to his sister who's now facing our direction.

Her pretty features are so much like his, they must be twins. The only noticeable differences are her brown eyes to his blue, her carefully applied makeup, and her delicate build beneath our more feminine version of the boys' uniforms, along with the sequined headband in her hair. She grimaces back at him, unforgiving.

"See?" Jax mumbles. "There's no reasoning with them. Kat would claw you to shreds, and my sis turns feral at the scent of blood."

Sunny almost coughs up her bite of muffin. "Ha. Right? Rune, no more feeling guilty. You did us all a favor. In our rendition of *The*

Fiery Angel, the roles of Madiel and Otterheim are played by one performer. Jax is going out for the parts, so he can be Renata's guardian angel and bad-boy love interest, all in hopes of being Audrey's guardian angel in real life. Considering who he's up against, the roles are as good as his. But . . . Audrey still has to snag Renata for the plan to work."

A flush rushes through Jackson's ears. "Did Quan tell you that? Could you strap a feedbag to his mouth or something?"

"How about a muzzle?" Sunny offers. "He's already in the doghouse. Made me miss the Clint Eastwood marathon last weekend on our day trip, all 'cause he got caught up at the arcade."

Jax rolls his eyes and turns back to me. "I only went out for the parts in the opera because there's no football or soccer to occupy my time here." He tosses his apron across the counter behind him as we move out of the way for other students to pick up their orders.

Sunny snorts. "Sure ya did, Jax. Who needs contact sports when you have kissy scenes with a pretty gal, right?"

"Can it, Sunny." Jax frowns, his entire face red now.

I can't keep from smiling. First, because it's such a relief to know he isn't a rich-boy player at all; he's a grand performer, trying to hide the fact that he's crushing on a girl who doesn't seem to know how smitten he is. Second, because I've never seen a high school guy blush. It's endearing.

I misjudged him and am so glad I did.

"By the way," he continues, frowning at Sunny, "you really suck at this peer advisor thing." Pretending to be preoccupied by my lack of an extra hand, Jax offers to carry my bowl of fruit to the table for me. "Trays are beside the register. Sunny should've grabbed you one but she's too busy being obnoxious to be *responsible*."

"It's all right," I say.

"No, it's not. But no worries. I'll be her backup if you ever need anything." His flirty sideways grin doesn't intimidate me this time. "I'll help you learn the routine."

I shrug. "So long as it doesn't get in the way of you earning your guardian angel wings." I bite my lip, shocked I teased him like that. His and Sunny's easy rapport has lulled me. For a second, I almost felt like I was hanging out with Trig and Janine.

"Nice one, Rune!" Sunny high-fives me, smirking. Jax responds with laughter. I let myself smile, relieved I didn't offend him. Maybe being here won't be so bad after all . . . as long as I can avoid the music, the bloodthirsty diva duo, and the phantom's shadow lurking around every corner.

7

FACING
THE MUSIC

"Only when you drink from the river
of silence shall you indeed sing."
Khalil Gibran

Sunny, Jax, and I step into the main dining area's dimly lit expanse. Thankfully, the pictures on the TVs have faded to a blank screen, and the music's no longer piping through the speakers. This leaves the candles popping in the background, students chatting quietly, and silverware scraping plates as the only sounds.

The three of us make our way to a seven-seater table wedged into the farthest corner. Two students wait there, faces flashing in the soft candlelight. I take a place on the empty side, positioning myself so I can wave Mom over if she decides to come out of the buffet area and join us.

"Rune, *this* is Audrey Mirlo," Sunny says, motioning to the girl with the ponytail who Jax was flirting with earlier.

"Also known as our little blackbird." Grinning, Jax flips around a chair at the head of the table to sit on it backward, arms wrapped around the frame. Now it's crystal clear why he wanted to help me carry my food over. How can she not see it, with the way he looks at her?

Audrey gives him a scolding side glare. Then she nods hello. I nod back, sensing tension. I concentrate on the hearty flavor of the pumpernickel and wash it down with a hot sip of nutty cappuccino, trying not to wonder whether she considers me a lucky charm or a rival.

"Howdy there, Sunspot," teases the boy on the other side of Audrey, his sloped, almond eyes locked on Sunny. "Saved a seat for ya, ma'am." The fake Texas accent coaxes my pensive lips to smile.

"Thanks but no thanks, *Moonpie*." Sunny takes the place beside me instead, across from him, making a show of avoiding the chair next to him that he's pushed out with his foot.

He snorts. "Still mad at me, huh?"

"She's not the only one, big-mouthed guppy." Jax reaches behind Audrey to smack who I now realize must be the aforementioned *Quan* in the back of the head.

"Hey!" Quan rubs his fuzzy scalp while sporting a mischievous grin. I'm guessing he always looks mischievous. His thick black hair sprouts up in every direction on top. It looks like an unkempt front lawn when compared to the buzzed sides and back. One eye's slightly higher than the other and his boyish lips are at a constant upward tilt on the left side—asymmetrical quirks that make him uniquely adorable. Sunny must agree, considering she's now playing footsy with him under the table.

As the others crack jokes and tease, Audrey watches in silence, smiling shyly in intervals. Her irises—the color of shimmery mahogany—are deep seated within a fringe of mascaraed lashes so long they reach to her dark eyebrows. This girl has perfected the smoky-eye makeup trick.

The flickering candlelight brings out streaks of auburn in her hair. There's a burgundy tattoo of a flying bird—the size of one of the caraway seeds on my muffin—just below her left eye that draws attention to her shapely mouth, painted almost the same shade.

Chewing ripe, sweet cherries and crisp apples, I listen as my peers carry the conversation. I learn that Sunny and Quan have been a couple since last year, when they sat next to each other in orchestra during the showcase of *Faust* and connected over their appreciation for spaghetti Westerns and any movie featuring Clint Eastwood. I also find out that Quan's last name is Moon-soo, which is how the nickname Moonpie came to be, much like Audrey's nickname was inspired by her surname, Mirlo, which in Spanish means blackbird.

I make the mistake of asking Audrey if that's why she got the bird tattoo, and the whole table goes quiet. There's a story there, but she's obviously too uncomfortable with me to share it.

If only I could assure her that I'm not here to steal her limelight; but I can't keep that promise. I have zero control over whether or not I'll interrupt when it's her turn to audition. And since all the students are expected to be present as part of their grade, I can't just not show up.

I'm about to drop my muffin on the floor so I can crawl under the table and escape the awkwardness when Sunny saves the day with a reference to the outing Headmistress Fabre mentioned earlier. Every Saturday, the teachers and students make a day trip to Paris.

This weekend, the students will be going to the Eiffel Tower, and afterward the seniors plan to take a water bus to a riverfront shopping mall that has a ten-screen cinema and a huge selection of restaurants.

"Since Halloween's a little over a month away," Sunny explains, "we're gonna see if we can snag some decorations to spruce up this place for October. Last year all we had were old props from the storerooms. And after shopping, we might catch a movie. They'll be showing *Casablanca* in French subtitles. You're in, right?"

I hesitate, tapping my cappuccino's mug with a fingernail. So far, everyone in the group seems genuinely nice. But will that change after a full week of classes and uncountable impromptu serenades?

"Come on," Sunny presses. "You have to go."

Before I can answer, Kat and Roxie step up to our table.

"Aw, not sure that's in the cards, Sunny." Roxie horns in, reaching across Sunny's shoulder to grab the last bite of her muffin. "You have to earn outing passes by finishing your tasks for a full week. Remember how that works?"

"But maybe not in Rune's case." Kat practically purrs as she leans between me and Jax, her thick, caramel waves draping his left bicep. He shifts his chair closer to Audrey, leaving Kat's hair hanging. Her jasmine-laced perfume settles over me. "Seems like our new soprano is exempt from all the rules. Considering how she got into the school without being evaluated . . . and how she penciled in her own job instead of getting her hands dirty with the ones we've always had to do . . . oh, and how she gets to audition for roles without ever having gone to rehearsals. She has an unfair advantage really, seeing as she was trained by the phantom himself. She brought him with her. Did you guys know that?"

My tongue dries. Looks like Kat was one of the students following us down the stairs yesterday when Mom mentioned my sighting. *Great.*

Sunny glares at Kat, but before she can say a word, Kat's up and running again. "What do you think, Audrey? Looks like I finally have some real competition. Did you hear how Rune nailed that final note? It's still ringing in the halls, pristine and clear as a bell."

Audrey looks down at her plate, turning almost green. Without a word, she pushes her chair back and leaves.

Sunny's cheeks puff as if she's a blowfish about to pop, but Quan grabs her hand and gestures to Jax, who stands up to face his sister.

"What is your problem?" Jax snarls.

Roxanne pats some imaginary dust from his jacket lapel. "Come on, Jackio. Why should anyone get special treatment just because of who their aunt is?"

He squints. "Are you kidding me? Kat's always getting breaks because she's distantly related to Christina Nilsson. Did any of the other first-year students receive a formal invitation from that anonymous benefactor to enroll here last year?"

Both Kat and Roxie look at each other blankly, as if struck mute by his truth.

"Yeah, that's right. Kat's the queen of nepotism. Audrey's the only one who's ever actually had to work for this. Working two jobs. Fundraisers. Babysitting. No inheritance to throw away like the rest of us. So why don't you just lay off her for once? Both of you."

With that he turns and follows the trail Audrey took into the corridor, leaving me to stumble over his words as I stare openmouthed at Katarina.

Christina Nilsson. I ran across the name during my Phantom research online. That was the stage name for the real-life Swedish soprano—Kristina Jonasdotter—rumored to have inspired Gaston Leroux's heroine. So that means Kat is practically related to Christina's fictionalized counterpart, Christine Daaé. And she was invited here because of that relation, by a mysterious benefactor who no one has ever seen, but who redesigned this opera house. A reclusive architect, just like the phantom from the books.

Paired with all I've seen since I've been here, this can't be a coincidence, and there's no longer any doubt in my mind.

I *am* in a horror story.

�·1·❦

Thorn adjusted his half-mask, hidden behind the mirrored wall that led to the grand foyer. The furred silhouette of gray at his feet rubbed his ankles—collar jingling softly—impatient to get the task underway.

The subtle droning of lectures drifted down from the third floor, where the juniors attended classes, and the scent of coffee, cinnamon, and buttery croissants indicated the seniors were still breakfasting in the atrium. All the teachers were preoccupied, as was Rune's mother, which should've left the first floor abandoned and ripe for the plucking. But two students had just wandered down.

Audrey and Jackson. She was crying next to her dorm room door, and the boy was comforting her. Thorn had watched their dance long enough over the past year to know how deep their feelings ran. Long enough to know he envied them . . .

What would it have been like, to have such typical problems growing up? To have people your age to learn with, argue with, talk with?

Thorn sighed and bent down to pet Diable. The cat was a good friend, no question, but it wasn't the same. It also wasn't only Erik's lifestyle to blame for Thorn's isolation. Honestly, in the beginning, Thorn had been too fragile to be around anyone but the clandestine man who'd saved him.

During their first two years together, Erik taught him how music could heal a broken soul. He taught Thorn to play through his pain on an Andrea Amati violin. He showed him how the instrument could speak to the heart, like Thorn's own voice once had, before his vocal cords were damaged. How it could replace what was taken from him, and make him whole again.

So grateful and eager to find a new outlet for his songs, Thorn had practiced twelve hours each day. Then, on his ninth birthday, Erik rewarded him with two gifts. It had been a surprise, to have the event remembered at all. Erik wasn't fond of birthdays, having never had anyone celebrate his. Erik's own mother despised the date he was born because of his deformity, and her disdain grew with each passing year.

So when Erik had Thorn take a seat in the underground parlor and offered the gift-wrapped boxes, Thorn knew it was a special occasion. And special it was, for it was the only birthday he and his guardian would ever celebrate.

Thorn had started to open the bigger present first, small fingers eagerly plucking at the paper and ribbons, but his guardian took it back and handed over the littler gift. "Open this one first."

Thorn did, and was struck mute at the shiny medical instruments that rested on a sheet of cotton inside the box.

"They're scalpels." The lower half of Erik's face brightened on a smile. "You're always bringing home wounded animals. You've shown great compassion. It's time I taught you how to be a proper doctor to them. Would you like that?"

Thorn's chest swelled with pride. "Yes! Oh, Father, I will make you proud!"

"Of that I have no doubt." Erik tilted his head, offering the bigger gift once more. He held it between them when Thorn reached for it. "I've given you back your songs, just as I promised. Have I not?" The eyes behind his mask glittered with emotion.

Thorn nodded. "Yes, Father Erik."

"Then one day soon, you will return my generosity, and help me acquire the songs I need, just as you promised."

"I will."

Erik's gaze drifted to the cellar lab, then back to Thorn. "All right then. Open the gift."

Inside the box was a violin wrapped in red velvet: a black Stradivarius, as elegant as any lady, and formed of wood as glossy and fathomless as ink. Thorn's heart soared at the beauty of it, and he itched to play. "Thank you," he said, trying to sound as grateful as he felt. "But, there's no bow . . ."

Erik stepped back until he was on the far side of the room, his fingers burrowed into the folds of the dressing jacket he had draped over his thin shoulders. "Ah, but there is. Just hold out your hand."

Setting down the instrument, Thorn did as he was told, palm turned upward. A light flashed inside Erik's jacket, then illuminated Thorn's fingertips—a transfer of warm energy that seeped through his veins and lit them up in response. As the heat and glow diminished, the coolness of a long, graceful bow replaced them, balanced atop Thorn's palm as if put there by Erik himself, although he was still across the parlor.

Thorn's mouth gaped. "Show me, please. Show me how to do the magic trick!"

Erik laughed—a beautiful resonance that echoed through their home, wrapping Thorn in happiness until he laughed, too.

"In time, child, I will show you." Erik crossed the room and took a seat beside Thorn on the chaise lounge. "You're very special. We all are. We have the ability to manipulate matter via energy. However, this specific trick can work only among others of our kind. It's a symbiotic exchange. I have many magical things to show you. But right now, I'd like to tell you a story."

Then Erik closed his eyes behind his mask, and let down his barriers, opening up about the role the Stradivarius had played in his history.

He had stolen the instrument when he was ten years old. There was even a picture of him holding it, dated 1840, taken shortly after he'd escaped the gypsy carnival that served as his home after leaving his mother. With only the violin to his name, Erik found solace with a kind architect, and mastered the instrument while he learned about crafting blueprints and building structures. He was forced to leave six years later when the old architect died. Erik left there a young man, still honing his musical talent, while he discovered the cruelty within the wide world and himself: first running with circuses as an attraction, then becoming a masterful assassin. When at last he found his way back to Paris at age twenty-six, the Strad was as much a part of Erik as an arm or a leg. It was the violin he used to seduce Christina Nilsson—the girl who would become his beloved Christine—and to unleash her otherworldly voice.

During his time with her, Erik engraved the initials *O.G.* on the lower bout, close to the waist of the instrument. The letters stood for *Opera Ghost*, the faceless and ominous identity he embraced so he might haunt the catwalks and basements of the Théâtre Lyrique during Christina's odyssey from a chorus girl to a diva. Erik only had to hear her sing one time to know she was his twin flame. He took her under his wing, convincing the young and naïve chorus girl that he was an angel, sent to train her voice. He watched his prima donna rise for three years, all the way to a London tour, then lost her to another: a Parisian financier with a flawless face, who she'd known from her childhood.

What a cruel dice destiny had rolled, to present him with his twin flame only to snuff out all of his hope. But that wasn't the end of their journey . . . they met up again later, as mirror souls will do. Many more tragic layers were added to their star-crossed history, before it ended with Erik serenading his beloved Christine on her deathbed, playing the same violin that had first tied them together.

Upon hearing the close to Erik's story, Thorn's heart ached with sadness. "Father, I can't. I can't take this from you."

He held out the instrument, but Erik shook his head.

"Remember what I taught you about pity, child. That violin was crafted by an artisan witch. It holds its own special magic. A magic I want to share with you, my son. If you wish to honor me, you will play it often, and with your whole heart."

Thorn's entire body lit up, not with pulsing energy this time, but with the splendor of a father's love, for Erik had called him his son. From that day on, Thorn did just as his father asked. He honored him by playing the violin every chance he had. Ironically, the first time he played it, he experienced his first dream-vision with his own *flamme jumelle,* Rune—and saved her from drowning. Thereafter he decided *that* must be the magic the instrument held: the ability to bring two souls together when they needed each other the most.

Diable mewled quietly, shaking Thorn out of his thoughts. Audrey and Jackson were climbing the stairs, headed back to the atrium. Thorn waited until they were out of sight, then opened the mirrored doorway, stepping across the marble floor. He and Diable took the route beneath the stairs, avoiding strands of sunlight and staying close to the walls. The cat was here to offer distraction, in case Thorn needed to make a quick escape into one of the many secret passages. It would be safer were there trapdoors in each of the dorm rooms so he wouldn't have to risk a trek in the open. But since the school's investors had overseen the domestic renovations for safety standards—both the living quarters and bathrooms—Father Erik left anything suspicious out of the designs. No two-way mirrored walls, no hidden entrances. But he did arrange for vents in each dorm room, which allowed for eavesdropping. A fact they took advantage of last night.

Thorn had turned away when they'd stepped into the hidden passage to spy on Rune through the slats in the wall above her bed. He couldn't cite nobility for the act. It wasn't as if he'd never infiltrated a lady's room in the past—claimed his drowsing prey.

The point was he and his father didn't follow that practice anymore. Most of their kind didn't. Both males and females had found other means to appease their appetites. Which meant Rune wasn't their prey. How could she be, since she was one of them herself?

Which was why Erik needed so much more from her than to feed. As did Thorn, although he could never admit what he needed.

Arriving on the girls' side, Thorn slipped the keys from his pocket and paused at Rune's closed door. Diable looked up at him with lime-green eyes and slitted pupils, glaring with annoyance at the detour.

"Just give me one second," Thorn whispered, amused by the cat's assuming air. "You go on . . . get the other girl's door open for me."

With a haughty sneeze, Diable sauntered ahead, rubbing along the line of doors as he went. Thorn had seen the cat unlock countless rooms in the opera house while hanging from the knob with one foreleg like a monkey and using the other paw—claws extended—to dig into the keyhole and release the mechanism. The trick would keep him occupied for the next few minutes.

Thorn turned to Rune's room, his gloved palm cradling the door's handle. The imprint of her energy lingered there, electrifying him through the leather. She had seen him in the mirror twice now. By her reaction, there was no question . . . yesterday when she first arrived, and this morning as she met her peers for breakfast. He suspected she could hear him, too.

He'd haunted this school since it first opened; haunted it for ten years before that, when it was abandoned and nothing but the occasional transient or tourist dared to venture inside. All that time he'd slipped silently through the mirror passages, no one detecting him. Yet she was tuned into him without even trying. A sense of fulfillment warmed him on that thought. Twin flames could find one another from across the universe. He and Rune had already proven that, sharing duets and escaping into their own world ever since they were children. So it was no surprise she could sense him on the other side of a thin pane of glass.

He leaned the bared side of his face against the door's cool wooden surface. What good did it do to celebrate their singularity? To take pleasure in the knowledge that he'd found her at last? He couldn't tell her. He couldn't act on it—or break out of this solitude.

Unlike the two students standing here moments earlier, fighting their feelings while having all the time in the world to find their way, he and Rune would never have that luxury. Clenching his jaw, Thorn wrestled the urge to open her door, just to step inside for a moment. But he had to stay away so he could follow through with all he'd promised to do.

He cursed Erik for being blind to what was already in front of him . . . for always regressing to the past. Thorn was alive and devoted, yet his father clung to sad and empty hopes that were only half-living, subsisting on borrowed time and unsung songs.

Five doors down, Diable had managed to unlock and open Katerina's room. The tip of his wiry gray tail disappeared inside. Thorn followed, resolved to complete today's mission. It was time the diva earned her place here. Time she contributed to the plan.

❧ · I · ❧

My first three days at RoseBlood fly by.

I don't have time to chase a phantom's ghost, imagined or otherwise. Daylight hours are devoted to classes and attending rehearsals, afternoons to my chosen daily task, and my evenings to homework. Although I haven't had a chance to get out to the garden once yet, due to afternoon storms. The downside to this is I won't be eligible for the outing on Saturday. That was the penalty of writing in my own job; I chose something dependent on the weather but am still held to the same standards of completing them daily, as is everyone else.

It wouldn't be so bad if I weren't going stir-crazy. Behind every wall and every mirror and every vent, I hear sounds: breathing, rustling, footsteps, and murmurs. I try to tell myself it's just mice making their nests behind the barriers, but since when do rodents whisper?

Still, there is one bright side to the dark and eerie setting: Sunny and my new group of friends. They save my spot at our cafeteria table in the atrium's far corner at every meal except for dinners—which I eat with Mom and Aunt Charlotte—and I'm lucky enough to have at least one of them in each class, sometimes three. Each day, they're more funny, open, and friendly than the day before, even when I screw up and burst into song.

I have, however, learned how to outsmart the arias piped in via the TV screens during meals. I've found, if I concentrate hard enough on my friends' comical banter, I'm able to suppress the itch until I get back to my room, where I can sing within the safety of my walls.

Any windows of spare time during the afternoon are spent helping Madame Fabre take measurements for costumes and cinching in the seams of my borrowed uniforms, since my new ones still haven't turned up. Wednesday, when we finally get some quiet moments to sew without students coming in for measurements, she tells me she and her husband are taphophiles—aficionados of all things graveyard. Their favorite pastime is reading epitaphs, gravestone rubbing, taking pictures of tombs, and learning the history of people's deaths. I haven't been a fan of cemeteries ever since my dad's funeral. Seeing his full name, Leopold Saint Germain, engraved upon a stone left an indelible and morbid impression. But since Madame Fabre and her husband have been here for almost two years with their own personal boneyard to explore, I feign interest in the hobby, hoping maybe the guy I've been seeing might have ties to an unmarked grave. The phantom didn't have loved ones, so it makes sense; if he had a headstone at all it might be isolated and devoid of sentiments.

My teacher assures me that the cemetery was reserved for the royal family who owned the opera house, and the only unmarked grave belonged to a baby. However tragic that is, it doesn't explain sightings of a guy who wears outdated fashions and hides half his face.

Later that night, while I'm on the chaise lounge watching Mom sleep with the bed curtains open, I wonder if she's heard any rustling inside the vent this week. I try to stifle my phantom superstitions by looking at things from her cynical perspective. Maybe it was the elderly caretaker in the garden that first day, after all. I haven't met him yet, so I don't know what he looks like. Maybe the mist, along with my nerves, made me imagine him as someone younger. And maybe that supposed sighting fueled my imagination to feverish heights, until I thought I was seeing him in the mirrors. It's possible this whole time I'd been catching people's reflections behind me and blew it out of proportion.

Of course my superstitions conjured him. I want with all my heart for my fantasy maestro to be real—even if by some impossible twist he's the phantom—because if anyone could help me defeat my song sickness, it's him. On that thought, I close my eyes and find my dreams. He's already there with the violin, waiting to take away my pain.

8

OMENS

"She failed to see a shadow which followed her like her own shadow,
which stopped when she stopped, which started again when she did and
which made no more noise than a well-conducted shadow should."
Gaston Leroux, The Phantom of the Opera

On Thursday morning, it finally looks like I might have a chance to get out in the garden later in the day. But the rain has already started again as Quan and I walk from breakfast to our shared first-period class.

Professor Tomlin's science room is everything you'd expect from an ecologically minded rock-star Einsteinian who dabbles in theatrics. There's a genuine skeleton in one corner dressed in a Shakespeare costume, spindly legs spray-painted blue in lieu of tights to match its velvet tunic and hat. A sign hangs under its fake beard that says: RESPECT THE BARD. Test tubes line several shelves, each filled with water and seeds, some already blossoming into plants. A picture of a wrecked motorcycle in a standup frame occupies one corner of the professor's desk, seated beside a deeply dented helmet. Tomlin hit a brick wall a few years back at high speed and was thrown off his bike, yet he survived. Rumor has it he uses that story to demonstrate Newton's law of inertia. Macabre, but memorable.

The students' table surfaces are slick whiteboard, and each of us has our own set of dry-erase markers to work out formulas and theories, then erase them once we've jotted down our answers, to prevent the need for scrap paper.

Tomlin always schedules labs on Thursday, and this morning's is on how "external force can alter the energy of a given system." He's separated everyone into groups of four and sent us to our tables where a steel-hooked weight sits beside a two-foot plank of wood balanced atop some books in the center. The idea is to make a ramp and alter the number of books beneath for different heights. Then we'll drag the hooked weight up and down to measure force.

It has to be some kind of sick joke that he paired Quan and me with Kat and Roxie. There's no love lost between Quan and the diva duo, considering how they treated both Sunny and Audrey last year. And they certainly haven't welcomed me with open arms. A genius professor can't be that clueless, can he?

Things are even worse ever since first-tier auditions for Renata's role yesterday afternoon. Of course I couldn't stop myself from leaping up and singing her aria, and despite that I fell back into my chair fatigued the instant I delivered the last note, my rendition was pristine enough it won me one of the three spots for final Renata tryouts, alongside Audrey and Kat, should I so choose. I'm already planning to develop infectious laryngitis that week and be quarantined to my room. But Kat and Roxie don't know that tidbit.

"In your lab journals, copy down and record your data for these questions," Tomlin says with his back turned, scribbling on the chalkboard. A few of the students have their gazes trained to his tight buns. I'll admit he's the hottest teacher at the school, even in a nerdy, two-piece wool suit. "And be sure to include the incline variations of your ramp from each run-through."

As we wait to transfer Tomlin's questions to our journals, Quan and I play tic-tac-toe on our half of the dry-erase table. It's the only way I can keep myself from staring at the mirrored wall on the north side of the room.

The scent of chalk dust and chemicals irritates my nose, though it's pleasant compared to Kat's overpowering perfume and the stench of dry-erase markers saturating the air. Roxie, the resident artist, draws sketches of me on their half of the white surface. She puts an impressive likeness on a cross made of musical scores, my hands and feet nailed in place by quarter notes and whole notes, my eyes blocked out with treble clefs. It's an obvious reference to the idiot I've made of myself during rehearsals and auditions over the past three days, and my cheeks grow hot when both girls start snickering.

Quan fakes a body-jolting sneeze. Eraser in hand, he swipes it through Roxie's masterpiece as he drags his arm back across the table. I mime thank-you and he tips an imaginary hat, snubbing Roxie's dagger glare.

By the time Tomlin reaches us to drop off our remaining lab materials, we've wiped our entire table clean.

"Each group needs to check the screw top on their spring scale," our teacher stresses. "Make sure it's calibrated to line up with the capital N. It takes a specific amount of force to stretch that spring.

You want to be sure you're measuring the stretch accurately when recording your newtons."

Just as he hands off the final scale, there's a knock at the door. He opens up enough to step out but ducks his head back in. "Everyone get started. Mister Jippetto's here to discuss theater props. I'll be out in the hall if anyone has questions." Then the door shuts behind him.

The class erupts in whispers and the sounds of books being shuffled, wooden planks being adjusted, and journal pages being flipped.

"Well, shoot." Kat pouts her lips. "Our scale is broken." She holds up the tool that I could've sworn wasn't missing the top piece earlier when Tomlin placed it next to her. "This would be a good opportunity for Rune to see the walk-in closet where the Prof keeps all the extra supplies, don't you think, Roxie?"

The girls exchange twin smirks, devious enough to light up a warning inside me like a fiery red flare.

Roxie offers to show me the way, but Quan stands up instead. "I'll take her," he says.

We walk side by side toward the back of the room where a door waits. I don't have to try to ignore our classmates watching us. My mind is preoccupied with the movement I'm catching in the mirrors via my peripheral vision, as if something or someone's following alongside me. A reflection . . . a shift in the atmosphere . . . an omen, maybe.

I won't let myself go there, remembering my logic from the night before. It was the caretaker that I saw the day I arrived. The one who's standing in the hall right now talking to Tomlin. As soon as I meet him in person, it will be confirmed.

We arrive at the closet and Quan tugs the door open. The light switch doesn't work, so neither of us can see inside. He shrugs. "Let me get a flashlight."

I nod and opt to wait at the threshold while he heads to Tomlin's desk. My eyes adjust to the shelves along the left wall. There's a box labeled: TUBULAR SPRING SCALES. I step inside to dig through it.

A shiver races through me when something rakes the top of my head. Lifting my hand, I feel the outline of a shoe tugging my hair. I look up in the same instant Quan arrives and flips on the flashlight, revealing a body swaying above me on a noose tied to the light fixture.

Icy terror freezes me in place. I scream, my vocal cords strained to near breaking and my bones shaking as if they'll shatter.

Quan drags me out and props me against the wall. The world seems to move in slow motion. "Rune, you okay? It was a dummy. Someone played a sick joke." His eyes narrow to angry slits as he looks over his shoulder to our table, where Kat and Roxie are doubled over, snorting with laughter.

My heart pounds in my chest, trying to speed things up again. Trying to hammer me back together.

Puzzled classmates join with the laughter—a timid chain reaction —first confusion, then relief that they weren't on the receiving end of the prank. Tomlin rushes in with the caretaker at his side. The man is tiny, comparable to Audrey's petite height, but portly. Still trying to catch my breath, I concentrate on him. His white beard and flannel shirt paired with a handkerchief cinched around his neck are a cross between a pint-size lumberjack and Santa Claus. He lifts a silver charm hanging under his handkerchief and blows it. The class silences as the sound of birdsong fills the room.

I'd been told he was a mute and communicated via written notes and gestures, but I knew nothing about a whistle. After pointing an accusatory finger at Kat and Roxie, the caretaker shuffles over to the closet where Quan helps him drag down what I can now see is a mannequin. Before becoming the resident caretaker, Jippetto used to make them for shops in Paris, and he still has a collection. Those woodworking skills are the reason he's the go-to for sets and props at the academy.

I slide down the wall and curl my arms around my knees, barring the shell shock from all sides. Not only did Kat manage to shake my foundations, but there's no way Mister Jippetto could possibly be the guy I saw half hiding in the garden on my arrival.

I can't do this anymore. Someone very real is shadowing my every move, and I need to know who.

I shift my gaze to the mirrors and for an instant I see it, clear as day: a gloved hand pressed to the opposite side of the glass, as if to tell me I'm right, or maybe to offer support. Then it's gone.

Once I'm on my feet again, Tomlin gets the class back on schedule without skipping a beat and everyone manages to finish their labs. Two minutes before the dismissal bell rings, the professor tells our table to stay put. After everyone's left, he closes the door and gives the four of us a speech about how we're all in the opera together, which means being supportive and being a team. That the reason he paired us for the lab in the first place was in hopes we might learn to work together.

"You guys really need to end it here. Headmaster Fabre and Principal Norrington aren't taking Rune's missing uniforms as lightly as you might think. Student perks are in danger—"

"Uh, wait a second," Kat interrupts. "We had nothing to do with the uniforms! This mannequin thing was to teach Rune and her kleptomaniac pal Sunflower Sunshine a lesson about sneaking into my room and stealing my brush."

"Summers," I correct, annoyed by her subtle dig on Sunny. "And why would either of us want anything that has your DNA on it?"

"It was a *Mason Pearson* boar-bristle hairbrush," Kat says, her perfect forehead furrowed, as if she can't fathom my ignorance. "Worth more money than Sunny's cheap dye job."

"Sunny's hair is naturally red," Quan interjects. "And she doesn't steal."

For the most part, anyway, I think, and by the gaze Quan shoots me, I can tell we're sharing brainwaves.

Roxie stands up at the table. It's unsettling to see such a hard expression on a face that matches Jax's, who's almost always smiling or cracking a joke. "Awfully coincidental how it went missing the first full day you were here. Kat hasn't seen it since Monday morning before breakfast."

Tomlin pounds the table, getting our attention back on him. "Here's my one-time offer. I don't care who did what. I won't report any of this conversation, or what happened today in my room, but only if these pranks stop now. Because were anyone to go to the headmaster with even one more thing, you guys can forget about having any fun activities for a while. That includes Saturday outings and the masquerade being canceled. Do you hear what I'm saying, ladies?"

The three of us nod.

He turns to Quan. "Okay, dude, I'm appointing you as referee. See that everyone gets along so you and Sunny can win the title of best costume couple again this year."

Quan gives the professor one of his lopsided smiles along with a thumbs-up. "You got it, Prof."

The four of us head out. I'm last, and just as I step into the hall, Tomlin stops me. We move to the wall beside the door, out of the wave of students rushing to class.

His intense blue eyes study me. "How's your voice? Did you hurt it screaming?"

I tamp down the panic his question inspires, feeling eyes on me from inside the walls, too. My voice is the least of my worries. "Um, no."

"That's good."

He starts back inside when I mumble, "I wish I had."

He turns on his heel and rubs his beard. "Look, you know about my accident, right?"

"Yeah." I cinch my arms around my books and strain to hear him over the passing students.

"Before that, my parents used to pressure me to be a doctor because I was so good at science and biology. To appease them, I was going to medical school, even though I didn't want it. I wanted my music. And I wanted to make science and theater fun for kids," he says. "After the crash, I realized how much time I'd wasted trying to be what someone else thought I should be. So, believe me, I get it. Just because you're good at something, doesn't mean you want to do it forever. Or at all. I made my choice and never looked back. Someday, Rune, you'll get to make your choice and be free to do what you want. Just take care of yourself until then, okay?"

His kindness touches me, even though he has no clue. My issues have nothing to do with any choice on my part. I see Sunny wave at the other end of the corridor where we always meet up before second period and offer a nod. "Thanks, Professor Tomlin."

He flashes his teeth in a grin that makes him look way too close to our age, even with the facial hair. "Call me Prof. And give it time. Things will get easier for you soon."

He's wrong again. They don't.

While having dinner with Aunt Charlotte and Mom that night, I find out Mom won't return to Ned or her job until she's sure I'm safe. The missing uniforms are eating away at her more than she originally let on. It would be so easy to admit that I suspect Kat took them, considering the macabre hanging in science class. But that would screw up every extracurricular escape the students look forward to, including my new friends. So I fake a confession: that I hid them myself in the beginning because I was so scared to face my stage fright, but now they've gone missing for real. I apologize profusely, and promise to get my act together. Mom pats my hand, saying she's proud of me for being honest, and is relieved. Aunt Charlotte watches us quietly while chewing her veal cutlet. I get the distinct impression she sees right through me, yet she doesn't say a word.

On Friday at breakfast, I tell Sunny, Jax, Quan, and Audrey the truth: that I've no idea what happened to my uniforms, but that lying is the only way to send Mom back to Texas so she can live the life she's worked so hard for. Quan tells everyone the other reason I'm doing it—to save us all from losing privileges.

However, pretending to have a severe case of stage-fright-turned-neurosis doesn't earn me any points with Kat. She croons soprano in full vibrato when I pass her in the hall then drops to the floor, flailing as if she's having convulsions. I decide not to hold it against her; she doesn't know how seeing a person in a convulsive state affects me. She isn't aware of my experience at the frat party.

All I can do is turn and walk away, wishing quietly that I could sever and discard the musical entity that lives inside me, and finally be normal. But even then, I still wouldn't be. Because although this academy is full of interesting and quirky personalities, I'm pretty sure I'm the only one who's left a guy comatose in a hospital across the ocean.

My loyalty to my friends pays off in other ways. During fourth-period historical musicology, Audrey passes me a note that explains the meaning behind her tattoo, and why her future career is so important she can't let herself get distracted by a romantic relationship. Her ballerina sister was the victim of a hit-and-run in New Mexico, and was left a paraplegic. Her name is Ravyn, and since she "can never fly again," as Ravyn herself puts it, she wants to ride vicariously on Audrey's operatic wings. So Audrey got the tattoo in honor of that sentiment. Their beautiful bond echoes my memories of Dad, and from that moment on I, too, want to see her reach all of her goals, not only for her, but for her sister.

Unfortunately, Bouchard catches us whispering and makes me stay ten minutes after class, carving time out of my lunch period. Audrey argues that she is to blame, too, but I shut her down. I've come to realize Bouchard's a fangirl of Katarina, and since I tromped over her star pupil during tryouts and various rehearsals, the vocal instructions and musical studies on my schedule have been even more painful than I already anticipated. There's no reason Audrey should suffer for that.

As soon as I'm released, I find Sunny in the hall waiting for me. She says I deserve vindication and sneaks me in to see Bouchard's room of deceased pets on the second floor—complete with the mounted heads of a beloved parakeet, a pampered chinchilla, and a plaque showcasing three field mice with real butterfly wings stitched meticulously to their backs. The scent of something medicinal blends with animal dander and stale bones, creating a sinister and clinical combination that knots my stomach.

"I've heard her talk to them," Sunny murmurs.

"To the dead things?" I ask as we both stare up in petrified wonder.

"Yeah, sometimes when she's in here with the door closed. Or maybe she's talking for them. Maybe she's one of those . . . what do they call that again?"

"Ventriloquists?"

She nods. "Yeah. And they're her marionettes."

"Or maybe she's theirs," I half joke, eyeing a white rabbit head still attached to its front torso and forelegs. Bouchard has carved a window in the rabbit's chest where it's hung flat against the wall, embedded an oval wooden frame within, and inserted an image of her holding the prized bunny years earlier, when it was still alive. She's younger with no wrinkles, without that trademark layer of French powder and rouge. A white lab jacket covers a casual button-up shirt. It's unsettling how happy she looked back then. Not even a trace of the stern bitterness I've come to dread each time I'm in her class.

"She flunked out of veterinarian school," Sunny whispers. "That picture was taken before. She obviously didn't ever get over having a scalpel in her hand or her love for the scent of blood."

I cringe. Neither one of us notices that the Bride of Frankenstein herself has stepped up behind until she shouts: "Get out!"

We both yelp in surprise and spin around.

Her eyes are glossy and glaring, like pointy blue beads. She might as well have pulled them out of one of her projects. She wields a frighteningly sharp pair of scissors as she backs us into the hall. "How did you get in?"

Sunny stammers, vowing the door was already ajar. Only I catch the implication of her hand tucked inside her skirt pocket where she earlier dropped the key she'd lifted.

Headmaster Fabre appears at the top of the staircase. "Is there a problem, Miss Bouchard?" His commanding presence ignites a blush through Bouchard's rouged cheeks—coloring them the same shade as the dye in her hair.

"Whatever it may be," the headmaster continues, "I think we could solve it without physically threatening our students."

Bouchard slaps the scissor handles against her palm. "The *problem* is a deplorable lack of respect for other people's belongings and privacy. In my experience, the best way to make an impression on the uncivilized is by giving them a taste of their own barbarism." She stomps back into the room, mumbling in French about shoving marble eyes into a hedgehog. The door slams shut.

Sunny repeats her excuse for us getting into the room. Unable to prove otherwise, Headmaster Fabre sends us to the last fifteen minutes of lunch with only a warning.

Friday comes to an abrupt end when Mom leaves for the airport. We stand out in the foyer, saying our good-byes while everyone else is at dinner. I make a marked effort not to look at the mirrors . . . not to let in that uneasy sense of being watched. The chauffeur gathers Mom's bags and offers to wait outside with the limo. As he opens the door, the scent of wet roses and foliage drifts in and the room brightens with the sunset's soft blush. In the parking lot and the foyer, the academy lights are set on timers to conserve energy—from six thirty until nine thirty every evening.

Mom tucks an unruly wave behind my ear. I admire how pretty she is in the pink haze, and think of the gauzy, romantic dress she found at a chic Parisian shop this week. She's planning to wear it for her wedding in December, when I'll be home for Christmas break. A smile inches across my lips. Her fiancé is picking her up from the airport when she lands tomorrow. "Ned's got to be dying to see you."

She smiles and shrugs. "Nah. Only mildly eager. You know his true passions are en suite bathrooms and hand-carved mahogany millwork."

I laugh at her realty humor, but it's forced. I'm going to miss her. I've become accustomed to sharing my dorm room. She hadn't been willing to take the bed every night, so we'd alternated, but her presence was the one thing—other than my dreams—that made me feel safe.

"I'll call you on the landline," I say, in lieu of what I want to say: *Please don't go.*

"Not if I call you first," she teases.

I grin. Then, against everything telling me not to, I ask, "So, when you slept in my bed this week . . . did you hear anything weird?" Granted, I'd only heard the sounds in the vent that first night, but maybe she'd heard them since.

She frowns, looking pale as the lights in the foyer switch on. "No, sweetie. Like what?"

Startled by the worry clouding her eyes, I change tactics before she decides to stay another week. "Oh, nothing. Just . . . the air filtering through the vent. It's noisy. Maybe I'll ask Aunt Charlotte if maintenance can look at it. It might be stuffed with lint or something."

"Okay." She grins and her cheeks warm again with a healthy

flush. "It's been so nice having this extra time with Lottie. I'm glad you'll finally be getting to know her, too. She sees so much of your father in you." Mom's eyes tear up a little. "He'd be so proud of you. How you're facing your stage fright. And how you're making friends."

I manage a bright smile by thinking only of my new friends and blocking out all things operatic or phantasmic. Ever since yesterday morning, I haven't seen any movement within the mirrors; but I don't think my shadow's gone. Not for a second.

Mom wraps a lock of my hair around her thumb. "I know you're disappointed that you can't make the trip to Paris tomorrow. Lottie says you can go with her to Versailles instead. She's really set against you staying here alone for the day. In fact, she keeps asking if I'm sure you're up for staying at the school at all. I assured her you are. That you're doing it in honor of your dad."

I nod, because I'd do anything for him.

"But since you're family," Mom continues, "Lottie said you can skate around the weekly task rules if you're with her. It'll get you out of this building for a few hours, you know?"

Thoughts of Grandma Liliana in the prison infirmary gnaw at my already-frayed edges. "There's only one reason Aunt Charlotte would go to Versailles."

Mom's lips purse. "Yes. She visits her mother once a week. But . . . Grandma Lil seems to be sorry. She arranged all of this for you. Maybe soon she'll even confess where she hid Dad's violin, or why she started that fire. Maybe then we can try to forgive her before it's too late." Mom shrugs because in her heart, she knows there's almost zero chance of that ever happening. I frown, because it's possible Grandma Liliana was only trying to rid the world of a plague, and

Mom could one day be stepping inside Aunt Charlotte's doeskin ballet shoes to visit *me* in a penitentiary.

"Pretty sure the other students wouldn't consider a day trip to Versailles as a family outing," I say. "I've already received enough favors." My tongue stiffens, barricading what wants to escape: that even though I have a few new friends, I'm not going to be class favorite anytime soon. That someone hates me enough to have left a dead crow on my chair at lunch earlier today.

I noticed it only seconds before I sat down. As if the sight of its black, greasy feathers wasn't enough to make me lose any appetite for the cordon bleu chicken rolls on my plate, it also triggered a vivid memory of the meowing crow I saw the day I first arrived.

Quan picked up the corpse with a napkin and covertly threw it away while Jax tried to reason that the resident ghost cat, Diable, had struck again. It was obvious Jax was trying to keep Sunny from attacking the diva duo, her number one suspects. But a part of me doubts they did it, because they don't want to lose privileges any more than the rest of us.

"Mom"—I sidestep the bird confession with another, more obvious one—"I don't think I'm ready to make that trip to see Grandma."

She squeezes my shoulder. "Oh, honey, Lottie wouldn't expect you to go with her to visit your grandma. There's a library within walking distance of the prison with computers. Lottie goes there to check the school's email each week. So she'd drop you there so you can get on the Internet, check your emails, do some Facebooking. And you'll have access to cell towers, so you can make phone calls and text."

I sigh. Regardless that I won't be expected to visit Grandma, I don't even want to be in the same vicinity. "I really need to start on the garden. The weather is finally supposed to clear tomorrow."

Mom nods, then scans her watch. "Just make sure you get out of your dorm for a while. I don't want you staying cooped up for too long. It can mess with your mind."

Tell me about it.

Pulling me into her arms, she whispers in my ear, "You have the potential to be something . . . amazing. Please, Rune. I don't want you to spend your life with other people's dust and soap scum under your fingernails. Your father wanted so much more for you than that."

She kisses my temple. Then she's out the door and in the limo, disappearing across the bridge and into the sunset, as every fear, flaw, and insecurity wraps tight around my shoulders—a chilling foil to the warmth of her good-bye hug.

9

THE DEAD AND
THE BELOVED

"Do you know what it means to have Death know your name?"
Anne Rice, Interview with the Vampire

Thorn crouched beside an array of overgrown chrysanthemums. When morning first dawned, the garden had been pristine. Sun drenched and sparkling with dew. Now, several hours later, clouds filled the sky.

He coiled the shredded remains of a gray stocking around the bright-yellow blossoms. A honeyed scent drifted up from the petals and settled on his tongue—sweet and heady.

He'd stumbled upon Rune's school uniforms behind the stage in the ballet rehearsal hall the night she arrived. Each piece had been clipped with scissors, ripped at the seams. The one responsible played a dangerous game. But she'd warranted a reprieve, since the maneuver had provided the perfect means to lead Rune through his maze of horrors today.

He hated to put her through more trauma after what that obnoxious diva and her sidekick had done with the mannequin. But he could reason it was necessary; he and Erik were going to lead Rune to the truth she'd been craving. It's just the way they were going about it wasn't at all gentle or kind.

Sickened by what lay ahead, Thorn waved away a fog of gnats and fished a tattered vest from the pink shopping bag. In the distance, a territorial squirrel argued with a song thrush perched on a blackberry bramble. It would be a typical nature scene, if not for the squirrel quacking like a duck. Unable to bear the deviant sound, Thorn tossed a rock to break up the fight, careful not to hit either of them.

The squirrel scampered away and the bird took flight, lifting Thorn's attention to the sky, where greenish-gray clouds hooded the midmorning sun. The entire plan would be compromised if Rune didn't complete the maze before the rain, and judging by the dampness on the wind it would be within the hour. Ideally, the storm would hit the moment she found the final clue and would chase her into the chapel.

She'd need to venture out soon. If she didn't on her own, he would lure her out. When he'd looked in on her earlier, she was seated on the first-tier steps inside the foyer, penning a note on a piece of stationery as translucent as the dress she wore. Had it not been for her sweater and leggings, he could've admired that expanse of skin, the way it glowed milky soft and radiant with energy. He wanted to do more than watch from afar. He wanted to stir the music inside her, to drink the pure, white light pulsing through her veins.

He fought the craving, thinking instead on the beauty of the frilly, sculpted paper beneath her feather quill—an illusion of lace and ribbon. An illusion like Rune. She might resemble an angel, but there was a ravenous demon waiting to be roused within. If he were to cinch that dark, silken cord of rhapsody hanging loose between them, he could help her wake it . . . and together, they could tame it.

But that delectable task did not belong to him. Although it should. It was written in the stars. He squeezed his gloved hands and stood.

Damn the stars and their ill-wrought timing.

His boots shuffled through a carpet of mushrooms and decaying plants as he dropped articles of damaged clothing across nasturtiums, dahlias, roses, mums, and asters—each bloom flashing their last jeweled bursts of color before the chill of winter came to tarnish them. Even with all the beauty at his feet, his gaze kept straying to the distance, past the ornate wrought-iron gates and fence separating the cemetery from the forest's thick canopy of leaves—in greens, oranges, and golds. He suspected that must be how Rune's eyes looked when they brimmed with freshly absorbed energy. He'd see for himself, soon enough.

Yesterday he'd visited the cafeteria. He watched from behind the mirror while the senior students had lunch. A clandestine drama erupted between Rune and her new circle of friends. He knew who had planted the dead crow. Just as when she stole and vandalized Rune's uniforms, her aura had glowed a stubborn, dogmatic brown. Her motivation was transparent. But things were already in motion, and there was no changing them. She would have to accept that fate had chosen Rune for this role, just as Thorn himself had to.

After the atrium cleared, and all the aromatic foods had been wheeled away on carts into the service elevators, Thorn had slipped through the hidden door and searched for Rune's name on the chalkboard.

When he saw that she'd chosen gardening duty and hadn't completed it for the week, it was as if heaven itself had opened up and delivered her. It gave him the chance to lay out the crumbs and coax her into the garden, across the footbridge, and to the edge of the cemetery while everyone was gone for the day. Of course she would be frightened, but her curiosity would make her brave. He knew that much about her, from their shared visions.

Personally, Thorn never felt afraid amongst the graves and statues. They had been his playground as a child. Ironic that he was most at home on a field of death. After watching the teens at the academy over the last year and a half, how their lives paralleled the plays they enacted on stage—rich with relationships and morals and romance—he understood how strange and different that made him.

In some ways, he craved their simplistic interactions and carefree lives. But he wasn't like them. He didn't belong outside this place, in a world filled with travels, and activities, and families and love.

He'd turned his back on any chance of that years ago. He'd been raised by a phantom who slept underground in a coffin, and he would no doubt do the same himself one day—to keep his past at bay.

Father Erik wasn't insane. His past had molded him . . . warped him. Before he came to understand the power his deformity could wield, he'd feared it. At age six, after being on the run for weeks—trying to escape his mother's hatred and abuse—Erik had snuck into a gypsy camp and was caught stealing food. They allowed him to live, but he had to earn his keep, taking off his mask and shirt, and posing behind bars as a child's living corpse to terrorize onlookers for money. It took little imagination to convince customers he was a skeleton wrapped in a sheath of decomposing flesh.

His fame grew quickly, and crowds would come, prepped with rotten eggs and spoiled fruits and vegetables to cast at his feet as offerings of food—as if a beast such as himself deserved nothing more than pig slop for sustenance.

It was the first time he'd been unmasked and vulnerable to anyone. His own mother had made him wear his mask both awake and asleep. The shame and revulsion he faced when bared pecked away at any semblance of self-worth he had left. The horrified screams of other children, of their parents, bled into his nightmares and replayed mirror images of his own horrific face in vivid colors to haunt him.

At last, one night, after having insomnia for months, Erik took refuge inside his cage, slipping into the prop coffin used as part of his act. He closed the lid and slept soundly until morning, shutting out the terrified wails, depraved cries, and images of the monstrous deformity that always followed him in his waking hours.

The one way he could feel completely safe while at his most vulnerable—to assure no one would see him and scream in horror —was to be locked within a casket. So that came to be his eternal refuge.

Thorn understood his father's need to shut out the past, as others never would. He'd lived in a cage himself, three harrowing months before Erik found and rescued him.

Father Erik's eccentricities were by-products of his past, as were Thorn's. As were anyone's. Even the mundane staff that populated the academy had their own peculiarities and secrets. Thorn knew them all. He'd been observing from the shadows and taking notes.

Such knowledge could prove useful, should he ever need to capitalize on it.

A chilled gust blew across him, tugging at his cape. He let the hood fall away as he positioned the last piece of clothing from the pink bag. His ceramic mask covered one side of his face, the shimmery white of bleached bones, and there was no chance of being seen by anyone anyway. Other than Madame Bouchard and Rune, the occupants of the academy were out all day.

Bouchard would be oblivious, preoccupied with her gruesome hobby—making amends to animals even in their death, via stitches, stuffing, and glassy eyes. An eccentricity the old woman shared on some level with Father Erik, to Thorn's grim dismay.

He tensed, following the path across the footbridge and to the graves. Dirt clods crunched under his boots and his shoulders drooped, heavy beneath the vile obligation he'd been waiting a lifetime to fulfill.

❈ · I · ❈

Standing by a window, I position my third attempt at a letter to Trig and Janine where the dreary gray light filters in, so I can read the closing one last time:

> *Well, I should go. I had to stay behind while everyone else went to Paris for a day trip. Not happy about being stuck here, but I'm going to make good use of the time. I want to get out to the garden before it rains.*
>
> *Oh . . . and one more thing, could you tell me if there's any news on Ben? Is he better? Is he talking? The last I heard, he'd been showing signs of waking. Do the doctors still think it was*

a seizure from a head injury? Four weeks is a long time to be in
a coma, right? I should've never come on to him after his poor
cranium stopped my fall off that ledge. I should've insisted he get
checked by a doctor right then.

Please, write back. You're my only link to all things Ameri-
cana. Even the food here makes me miss home.

Viva la hot dogs and hamburgers!
Rune
P.S. I miss your faces.
P.P.S. I took some pics of the academy with my phone. I'll text
them once I get to Paris where there's service. No kidding, it's like
living in a primeval forest here.

Satisfied that this note won't have to join the others in the trash,
I fold the paper, slide it into the matching stamped envelope already
addressed to Trig, and drop it into the outgoing mail slot in the box
next to the main entry door.

I'm so tired of acting oblivious about Ben, but as much as I trust
Janine and Trig—who've always accepted my operatic outbursts
without judging me—I can't tell them what really happened at that
frat party.

When I met my two pals in theater during my sophomore year
at school, they were both seniors. In spite of our age differences, I
was drawn to them because they were outcasts like me. We live in
an ultraconservative town. You can't be a boy who likes boys and
designs ladies' fashions, or a bulimic ballerina whose mom raised
money for her college tuition by being an exotic dancer, without

the majority of people looking at you through lenses tinged with discomfort and judgment.

Still, the truth of that night is something even my two best friends wouldn't understand. Yes, they know *why* I was drinking at the party . . . that while some of the guests wandered about the deck or splashed in the pool (I'd dressed the part—bikini and swimsuit cover—but hadn't been brave enough to venture into anything deeper than a wading pool since the age of seven), the college junior who was hosting led others of us to his basement to show off his vintage record player.

I was fine, listening to big bands from the forties and rock 'n' roll from the fifties. It was when he dragged out a vinyl of *Rigoletto* that my world came crashing down. I sprinted for the stairs just as the heroine's aria erupted, and my fate was sealed.

Janine was my ride, but I couldn't find her anywhere. So I drank. A lot. I figured if I drowned the notes in alcohol, I'd be able to prevent them from breathing . . . from surfacing. Unfortunately, I had even less control with three beers in my system. Seated precariously on the second-story balcony's railing, I slapped my hands to my mouth to keep the song subdued and lost my balance. A hot college guy on the pool deck below broke my fall when I landed on his head.

He helped me stand. He'd been swimming, and his upper torso sparkled in the twinkling white lights strung around the deck. His auburn hair was wet and mussed, and his blue eyes—slightly glazed as if having trouble focusing—trailed along my bared legs where they stuck out from my cover-up. I recognized the expression. Like I was a piece of meat and he was starving. He staggered a little, but it wasn't from my crash landing. He was even more wasted than me.

I'd noticed him once or twice while visiting Janine on campus during her summer session. I knew his name was Ben, and that he didn't have a girlfriend. I also knew he was a player. But the aria pressed against my sternum and crept into my throat, climbing like bile toward my mouth. So instead of listening to the voice of caution, I threw myself at him to silence my itching vocal cords, to suppress the music burning behind my eyelids in myriad colors.

I poured all of the emotions boiling in me—all the fear, mortification, passion, and longing—into a hard, demanding kiss that tasted of bitter hops, sweet malt, and musky pheromones.

It wasn't my first kiss. I'd gone to junior prom with a sweet, nerdy guy named Tate. We shared a benign closed-mouth peck at my door, when he dropped me home. But it never amounted to anything else.

My kiss with Ben was different—mouths opening, tongues seeking. I was the instigator, lifting my arms around his neck to push the aria down. Ben groaned—deep, masculine gratification—and his lips felt as if they caught fire. His tongue scalded as it wrestled mine. He dragged me hard against him. The film of chlorinated water between our skin seemed to sizzle, and his chest burned my collarbone.

We ignored the rap song blaring from the speakers on the balcony, ignored the snickering guests who opened a path so Ben could back us into the empty pool house and slam the door shut. He lowered me onto a pile of damp and musty beach towels on the cement floor—his heavy body straddling me.

His hands were everywhere. There was nothing sweet or tender driving either of us. It was spontaneous, harsh, lusty, and degrading. I hated how fast we were moving, how out of control we were, and for an instant, I hesitated, until the notes resurfaced. In that muddled, hysterical state, I convinced myself that the humiliation of an impromptu vocal solo would somehow be worse than letting things go too far with a boy I didn't even know.

Those are the facts I shared with Janine and Trig.

What I *didn't* share was that just as my cover-up came off, as the kisses grew intense and gasping, Ben's flavor changed to something singed, sweet, and unnatural—like roasted autumn leaves, sulfur, and copper wrapped in toffee. I devoured the taste, starving for more.

A fiery sensation soldered Ben's chest to mine, like someone had poured a pint of gasoline on us and followed it with a lit match. A bright grayish-yellow glow buzzed and ignited at the point of contact, where my bikini-wrapped breasts were flush to his pecs.

I was so wasted—I can't be sure I retained every detail. All I do remember—vividly—is that the glow jumped from Ben's sternum to mine, catching flame to my blood while turning his cold and paling his face to a deathly white. I remember how he gasped for air as he rolled onto his back atop the heap of towels . . . how he clawed at this throat, trying to breathe. I remember screaming when his lips started to turn blue, when the veins in his temples and wrists seemed to sink into his skin, as if being hollowed out from within.

Forgetting the odd glow within my chest, I stumbled from the pool house and shouted for help. By the time the EMTs arrived, Ben was convulsing, and the heat behind my sternum had snuffed out. But even before it stopped burning, no one had seemed to notice the strange light at my sternum. A few kids did, however, comment on my glowing contacts. I didn't dare tell them I wasn't wearing any.

Instead, I stared at the ground until the warm tingling behind my irises subsided, scared and worried for Ben, yet horrified for myself. *Of* myself. When the paramedics arrived, no one mentioned anything about my eyes being abnormal. A kind EMT assured me what happened wasn't my fault, that Ben was having a seizure and I'd just been in the wrong place at the wrong time. I let them believe it, but I knew it was my fault. Because when we were kissing, when he began to thrash for life, I felt stronger and more alive than I ever had. I fed off his lust, and then his terror. And I wanted to keep feeding . . . but somehow, I came back to myself when I saw those blue lips. It was me who broke our connection in that instant.

If I hadn't, he'd be dead today.

Over the past few weeks I've tried to convince myself I imagined everything. But I can't explain away glowing eyes any more than I can the sprained wrist I suffered from the fall—something I was too drunk to notice at the time. If not for me being rushed to the ER alongside Ben in the ambulance, Mom wouldn't have found out about the party, or my drinking, or my indiscretions with some guy I barely knew.

And it wasn't even worth it. In the end, the alcohol didn't make a dent in my musical compulsions—because it didn't change who I was. It didn't *fix* me. Before Mom arrived to pick me up from the hospital, I'd already serenaded the staff with the aria. After they'd recovered from their awe-struck shock, they applauded then hooked me up to an IV, mistaking my post-performance malaise for dehydration.

How could they have known I wasn't thirsty anymore? That I felt satiated and full of life. All because I'd almost drained Ben of his.

Even worse, how could I not wonder if I was cursed like Grandma had said all along, and that I'd done the same thing to my father years earlier with my demonic gift of song?

❦ · I · ❦

Refusing to wallow in pity—for Ben, Dad, or myself—I go seeking redemption instead. If I can find a tangle of weeds overtaking some flowers and revive their beauty and purity, I can restore my self-worth on some level, and maybe investigate the location of that first gardener sighting almost a week ago.

I slip into a pair of parchment-thin leather gloves from my winter clothes' supply, and make my way outside, armed with a stainless-steel food tub, a large spoon and fork, and a serrated pie server from the cafeteria—temporary substitutes for a bucket, shovel, rake, and trowel.

This morning at breakfast, Aunt Charlotte convinced me to wait until tomorrow, since that's when Mister Jippetto promised to bring the gardening tools I'd requested last time we spoke. Although her real goal was to convince me to go with her to Versailles. Fortunately, Bouchard ended up staying, which seemed to make Aunt Charlotte feel better about leaving me behind. But I've changed my mind about waiting to explore the garden. I have to do this today.

My tank top, leggings, and a flowing chiffon floral rust-print dress, followed with a navy raglan-sleeved cardigan that I knitted a few months ago for autumns in Texas, are more suited for the day trip my classmates took. Still, with the way the sky looks, I can't waste any time changing, other than my shoes.

I trudge through the parking lot, careful not to slip on the gravel rolling under my cowboy boots—their soles so worn they've lost all traction. When I was small, Dad and I weeded barefoot to keep from crushing the tender plants underneath. As I got older, and had to do things without him, these became my gardening shoes, because the smooth soles protected the leaves and stems.

Several birds flutter overhead, and I'm relieved to hear them trilling and chirping. I take it as a good omen. Once I reach the yellowed, grassy outskirts of the garden, I'm in awe. At home, my plot of perennials and vegetables is manicured and tamed. There, I'm the conductor.

Here, I'm the audience.

Nature provides the performers—spicing every inhalation with floral perfumes, rotted wood, moldy leaves, and soil. Everything from shrubs and brambles to vines and weeds encompasses the sprawling landscape, as high as my knees on either side of the cobblestone path. In the distance, crimson rose bushes that rise to my chest bow to the rhythm of rain-scented gusts, like actors answering an encore. Fall flowers burst up from the graves of dead summer blooms, reluctant to shed their costumes of purples, oranges, golds, and blues, in spite of how garish they are against the withering landscape.

Clouds swirl in a grayish mass, dimming the light. A thin film of fog clings to the plants and to my face like ethereal cobwebs. The sun has always restored me when I'm tired, sad, or unsettled. I could've used some of that positivity today.

Due to the ominous sky, I earlier clipped an LED book light—the one Mom bought for us to use on the ten-hour flight here—onto my sweater lapel. After I pull up weeds and break up clods with the fork from the cafeteria, I'll have to remove any roots left in the loosened soil. A little extra illumination will help me find them. Some weeds, like elder, bindweed, and couch grass, will regrow if any chopped roots remain. They're regenerative, like salamander tails, earthworms . . .

And phantoms.

I veer my gaze to the roses far to my right, those left for dead at the touch of a man's hand last Sunday. The way they sway on their stems, heavy and black, proves I didn't imagine it at all. My chest tightens and my footsteps falter as I notice a piece of gray cloth, strung across a cluster of golden flowers right beneath the thorny bush. I move closer. Partly because the fabric looks familiar, but more because it's so out of place in this untouched wilderness.

Swallowing the knot in my throat, I crouch to tug the cloth free, recognizing it as one of the stockings Mom and I bought—part of my missing uniforms. The side seam gapes open, frayed but systematic, as if someone sliced it with scissors.

A sense of violation rattles through me, jarring. I stand on weak legs, catching movement everywhere now—other articles fluttering like flags on various flowers and plants, all along the path.

All this time, I'd assumed Kat and Roxie stole them, despite what they said to Tomlin. But when would they have had a chance to lay out a trail like this?

My windpipe narrows until the damp air seems to burn. I venture into the overgrowth, because no matter who's responsible, I'm not going to give them the benefit of chasing me away.

Gathering up the damaged vests, stockings, and skirts, I place them in the tub I'd intended to use for gutted weeds and dead flowers.

The trail of damaged articles is like a macabre Easter egg hunt. Around every winding turn of the path, I find another ragged or frayed piece, all of them torn but possibly salvageable for someone who knows how to use a needle and thread.

Finally, I see the last article—a white ruffled shirt cuff hanging over an oddly shaped statue I can't quite make out—on the other side of the footbridge where the garden ends and the cemetery begins.

I make my way over the water, trying not to look down into the depths, careful not to slide off the curved, cobblestone surface. Several yards away, the chapel casts muted shadows across the graves. The jeweled glint of the broken stained-glass windows frames the darkness within—a disorienting contrast that spurs the feeling of being watched again.

I step off the footbridge. Unlike the garden, the cemetery is easy to navigate. Ankle-high yellowing grass fringes a spongy, green carpet of moss between headstones. Stray, fallen leaves scatter across the ground on the wind. I stop at the tomb where my shirt cuff flaps, fighting the uneasy crimp in my stomach.

It's an antique statue of a baby's cradle with a canopy—the stone molded and etched to look like wicker. This must be the unnamed infant's grave Madame Fabre mentioned. There's only a year carved into the surface: 1883. Not even a month or a day.

Inside the stony cradle, my shirt covers the opening where a baby would be. The cloth puffs out, and red spots, resembling spatters of blood, tinge the white color. Ice-cold dread clenches my neck, makes my breath tight and whistling. After all the time I spent in Dad's hospital room, observing him being poked and prodded with needles, watching his veins drained for test after test, blood is the one thing I'm squeamish about . . .

I shake my head, willing myself not to lose it. This is fake blood. At an academy like this, everyone has access to theatrical makeup. Gusts of wind tug at the shirt's ruffles, creating the illusion of something moving underneath.

Goose bumps prickle my skin. I fist my free hand at my side, long enough to remind myself it's all a prank. A cruel joke meant to scare me and send me running back to the states. Opening my fingers, I gingerly lift away the shirt. A bouquet of white roses waits underneath in place of the zombie baby my wild imagination had conjured.

I choke out a laugh, but it's short-lived once I realize how the red stains got onto my shirt. From within the spirals of petals seeps a running, dripping, liquid trail—as if the roses are bleeding from their hearts.

Thunder growls in the sky and a stray droplet of rain hits my face. I shiver, though it's not the impending storm that chills me to the bone; it's how the flow of blood creeps into the stone's cracks and crevices beside the thorny stems, forming letters, as if Death himself is penning the scraggy, cursive words before my very eyes:

B-e-l-o-v-e-d R-u-n-e.

10

ALONG CAME
A SPIDER

"A spider spins its web strand by strand."
Author Unknown

My name, written in blood, chains me in place.

The wind picks up—cold and brutal. It slaps my face with dampening locks of hair and tugs at the shirt in my hands like the insistent ploys of a ghostly toddler. When the downpour of cold rain hits—drenching all the way to my scalp and through my clothes—I still can't move. Not until I see the white rose petals cleansed, the red script smearing into streams, the words erasing, yet leaving me nauseous in their absence . . . violated and confused.

Lightning breaks—dangerous veins of electricity ripping the sky. In the forest, a tree sparks with glowing embers, its branches shorted-out circuits falling to the ground. Three seconds later, thunder shakes all around me.

The storm is too close. I need to find cover, and the academy is all the way across the footbridge and on the other side of the garden.

My only option is the chapel. I scoop up my bloody shirt and the white roses, because I'm convinced they're a stage prop with a mechanism in their stems that pumps out red ink through the petals, like we once used in a play during my sophomore year. As I lift them, I realize that each petal's edge is fringed with deep red to form a duotone bouquet. Even when I scrape the edges, the contrast remains. It's the natural color scheme. I once saw roses like this at a plant nursery in Texas. They're called Fire and Ice. I must have been too panicked earlier to notice their uniqueness.

After placing them atop my uniforms in the tub, I slosh through shallow puddles and mud-slicked moss toward the ominous building.

The sky darkens to a bruise that resembles evening more than noon. Intermittent bursts of lightning shift the landscape around me—fractured images of decaying gravestones, a sagging garden, and blowing leaves. I clamber up the crumbled steps to the chapel. My gloved fingers reach for the door, then jerk back as the serpent-shaped latch seems to slither and writhe away from my hand. I struggle to catch my breath.

It's made of tarnished brass . . . it just appeared to move because of the crawling shadows generated by the lightning.

My attempts at logic are the only thing keeping my courage afloat. I can't let myself consider that underneath the howling wind and scraping leaves, I heard a hiss when the sky lit and the latch moved; or that even with a mechanism inside their stems, how could the roses manage to bleed a legible rendering of my name?

My heart pounds in my chest, competing with the thunder, as I study the latch. Having spent time with my dad outdoors, I have no phobia of rodents, reptiles, or insects. What's freaking me out is the fact that *metal* shouldn't move like a living thing. Gnawing on my lower lip, I grip the brass serpent to open the door. The rusty, wet hinges give slowly, like old bones, creaking and grinding as I force them open. I thrust the stainless-steel tub inside. It hits the floor with a metallic clang, prompting another hiss like the one I heard earlier.

A dangerous scatter of lighting forces my feet forward. The wind shuts the door behind me. I inhale, acutely aware of the stifling darkness.

Shoulder blades pressed to the wooden frame, I stand in place— the black surroundings heavy as a blanket on my head. The sounds outside dull to near silence: muted raindrops and muffled wind. My clothes drip onto the stone floor in a disturbing rhythm.

The scent of dank stone, wet roses, and dust permeates my nostrils. Lightning blinks through the jagged stained-glass windows, painting prisms of color along the walls. Something shuffles in the shadows, and a jingle follows—like the tiniest bell.

Gooseflesh spreads over me again. I scoot away from the doorframe, flush to the wall, until the sensation of vines weaving in and out of the stone juts through my sweater between my shoulder blades.

"Hello?" I attempt, my voice a shrill echo.

The jingling erupts again, then stops just as fast, as if it's driven by movement.

"Who's there?" I shout this time.

I regain enough presence of mind to search for the book light clipped to my sweater. The gloves make my fingers stiff, so I peel them off to flip on the dime-size bulb. I rotate the long, skinny neck so it casts a spindle of light twelve inches in front of me. My eyes begin to adjust. The room takes on a dusky haze, everything blurred to indiscernible outlines beneath the beam at my lapel.

I'm about to brave walking around when something attacks my feet. Yelping, I snag my fingers in some ivy on the wall to stay upright. A vine slices the inner bend of a knuckle, prompting a sting tantamount to a paper cut. I pop my finger in my mouth to ease the throb, tasting blood, but I'm unable to think beyond whatever is still wrapped around my ankles. Every muscle tensed, I jerk my left leg and nudge it loose.

A bundle of nappy, grayish fur shoots out from the tangle of my boots and skirt, and into the splay of LED light.

"Diable?" I ask tentatively, almost breathless. The cat jingles as he backs up and snarls. His ears—disproportionately large, like a bat's—spread low on his head.

I lean forward, elbows pressed to my knees, and laugh, relieved to find the cat's as real as me, and not a ghost at all.

Diable responds with a deep, throaty yowl, his yellow-green eyes locked on me. He's obviously not as impressed to be sharing the space. His tail twitches. It's a strange, hooked shape—as if it was broken at one time and never healed right—so thin it resembles a coat hanger wrapped in fraying felt.

"Wow. You really do look like an SOS pad," I tease and hold out my hand for a peace offering.

He sniffs a breath across me, and sneezes on my palm, as if to assure me he might look like a soured dish sponge, but I smell like one.

I grin. He's probably right. I've been overwarm ever since stressing in the cemetery, and being in here makes it worse. The air is too close—claustrophobic. Moving the book light to the bodice of my dress, I peel out of my soggy sweater and drape it across the roses in the tub to distance myself from what happened at the grave—at least for the moment. Next, I tug off my headband and use it to bind my wet hair into a ponytail, leaving only a few ringlets plastered to my temples and the nape of my neck.

Diable loses interest and trots out of my beam's radius.

I kneel and move the book light's neck to search for what the cat was playing with at my feet when he tripped me. A clear plastic wristband, like people wear in a hospital, scrapes beneath the toe of my boot. I shift, and something else rolls beneath my heel: a flexible, transparent plastic cord, about six inches long. Droplets of red liquid cling to the inside. It reminds me of IV tubing, fresh off a patient. My stomach turns.

These items are so intimate . . . reminders of Ben and Dad. It's too timely, after having thought of them both today. Maybe I'm losing my mind to guilt.

I prod the tubing with a fingertip, proving to myself it's real, and another theory takes shape. Maybe whoever pulled the prank on me used this chapel for preparations. This could be from the roses that were bleeding—part of the mechanism within their stems. Determined to make my case, I retrieve both items and drop them into the tub alongside everything else.

I'm itching to leave and hole up in my dorm room where I can piece together the events in the garden and cemetery, but the lightning continues to torch the surroundings in intervals. I have to wait out the storm.

Diable's confident jingling in the shadows gives me comfort. He's not the least bit unsettled, so there can't be anything dangerous here. Resituating the light on my bodice, I move the neck around to scope out any more clues.

There aren't any hiding places. No benches . . . no prayer altar and no pulpit. Nothing one would expect to find in a traditional house of worship—just a spacious, empty room with an air of gloom and loneliness drifting with the dust particles from the cathedral roof. Along the left half—the back of the chapel—the floor has caved in over time, sloping downward. A thick ground cover coats it like carpet.

Following Diable's jingles, I inch closer to the right side—the front—where nature's progression has been slower. Weeds have pushed their way up from cracks in the foundation, just like the vines across the walls, but in sporadic intervals. I take small steps as my slick boots skate atop a gritty film of dirt on the stony surface.

The cat's silhouette leaps up to perch on what was once a baptismal. I join him at the oval basin. The brick edge hits me mid-thigh. A pool of murky water glitters inside—some nine feet in diameter— reminding me of a well. It seems unusually wide and deep. The scar on my knee throbs, and I'm reliving the dreaded memory . . . kicking my way out of a wooden crate that held me underwater.

I shake off the uneasiness; let it run down my spine like droplets of melting ice.

There's nothing to fear here. It's a baptismal. People stood in it. The water can't be very deep. It's an illusion created by the darkness. The beam attached to my dress shimmers along the glassy surface. Its bright reflection moves in ripples as something stirs inside.

Diable notices the ripples, too. He seems intrigued. His long, pointed ears tilt forward and he balances on the basin's lip, tapping the water with a paw and emitting a long, low mewl that starts deep in his throat and ends with a sharp-toothed snarl.

The water bulges as though something is surfacing. My skin goes cold and clammy.

It's got to be a fish . . . or a frog.

I back up a step, because I'm lying to myself. Whatever is causing the water to churn is too big to be either. I read once that rats are good swimmers. With their aquatic ability and flexible bodies, they can make their way up from city sewers into toilets. I ease back another two steps, my pride the only anchor keeping me from bounding away in fear.

"Hey kitty . . ." I gulp. "Did you trap a rat in there?" Diable's eyes stay pinned on the eddying currents, leaving my words to hang in midair, taunting my raging imagination.

I'm not a skittish girl. Last summer, I was the one who took the biology class pet home. No one else volunteered to take care of our Mexican red-knee tarantula for three months. But Sister Scarlett and I got along famously. Especially at feeding time. For some reason, I was intrigued by the way she trapped her prey against the wall of the terrarium, by the way she danced around the hopping cricket until it was so entranced with terror and fascination, it froze in place and practically begged for her to eat it.

That was before Ben.

Nausea sweeps through me at the thought. After our encounter, I realized why I was enchanted by the spider's feeding rituals, that there was something in my gypsy blood—something tainted and wrong . . . just like Grandma said.

The water in the baptismal surges again. If it is a rat, it's the biggest one I've ever seen. The bulge pressing up from underneath is now the size of a basketball.

I try to adjust my light, but my trembling fingers knock the neck off-kilter so the beam shifts to my toes. Before I can fix it, a wave rises, sloshing water across me, the cat, and the floor.

Feathers and wings emerge in sync with a cavalcade of lightning. A long, graceful neck unfurls into the most beautiful swan I've ever seen—as red, bright, and vivid as the blood seeping from the roses earlier.

Thunder rolls, and Diable lunges at the bird. He loses balance, plopping into the water belly first.

The swan releases a trumpeting croak then flaps its wings. I dodge its webbed feet as it swoops over my head on a gust before landing safely in the shadows at the back of the chapel, out of sight. The bird grows silent, to the point I wonder if it's still there.

Yowling and sputtering, Diable snatches my attention. His battle against the water has propelled him into the middle of the baptismal. I try to reach him, but even when my thighs hit the basin's edge, my arms aren't long enough.

My throat lumps. I hesitate, telling myself this isn't like the time when I was little and my *Les Enfants Perdus* fairy tale book fell into the river . . . the water isn't deep enough to cover my head. My grandma's not seated on the dock beside me, waiting to push me over the edge and trap me under a crate when I try to retrieve the one thing left of Daddy.

In my book light's beam, I watch the cat's head disappear.

Fingers digging into the bricks, I pull up onto the edge and balance my right hip there. I lean sideways, anchoring myself with my legs bent over the outside lip, and dunk my arm in. After stirring the cold water around, I snag the flailing ball of fur by his collar.

"You know, a dishrag would have the decency to lie still," I scold him as he fights against me until chilly water coats both my arms. My book light falls off during our wrestling match, submerging in a shimmery trail.

Our surroundings grow dim again, broken by sporadic slashes of lightning. I tug the cat close enough to the edge so he can climb out. Startled by a clap of thunder, his front paws latch onto my knee with razor-sharp barbs. Yelping, I writhe to free myself. We break apart, him tumbling to safety and me teetering headfirst into the water, swallowed up by frigid, liquid shadows.

I capsize, unable to right my body, clawing my ponytail loose in the struggle. The book light descends below in slow motion—like a hazy yellow star orbiting farther and farther off in the distance— illuminating the bubbles and swirling currents caused by my violent entry. The depths seem to be unending.

My body seizes in fear, as brittle and dysfunctional as a cricket's empty exoskeleton after being drained by a hungry spider. My dead-weight limbs drag me down, suspended in a web of dread, and it all comes rushing back . . . the squeeze of my lungs begging me to breathe, the tear of my fingernails against splintering wood, the swirl of my hair tangling around my neck.

Grandma, why?

An arm binds my waist from behind, stopping my descent with a jolt. Somewhere beyond the muffled swish of water filling my subconscious, that familiar violin song pricks at my eardrums— poignant, pure, and enticing—my maestro commanding me to fight. A spark, hot and charged, like a shock from an outlet, leaps from my rescuer's body to mine, and I revive enough to start kicking again.

I'm dragged out and over the edge like a piece of luggage, hacking up the flavor of bile and soured water. My feet squish inside my waterlogged boots as I try to stand. The soles slide out from under me and I miss busting my head on the brick basin by inches when a pair of gloved hands catches me. They settle me to sit on the floor beside the well, raking away the slimy hair glued across my eyes before tilting my chin back as if inspecting me for bruises.

Coughing again, I jerk free and look up in the dimness, half expecting to see Grandma in my fevered state, half expecting her to finally offer some explanation for trying to drown me.

Instead, the looming silhouette takes a different shape: broad shoulders and a masculine build inside dark clothes. So intent on him, I barely notice that the rain has let up—that the clouds have started to thin and a gauzy gray light gilds the room. The figure standing over me comes into sharp focus before I'm even aware of it.

Thick curls of dark hair cascade across his forehead and drip water along the nose of his porcelain, white half-mask. Rivulets stream down the naked side of his face—some real, from the bath he encountered while fishing me out of the well, and others impressions, from the drizzling rain and jagged colors stamped onto his skin by light filtered through the stained-glass windows. I choke back a gasp of recognition.

It's the gardener . . . *the Phantom.*

I haven't been imagining things at all. They're one and the same.

The description of his deformity from every incarnation of the story, what hides beneath the cover-up, taunts me: rotting yellow skin . . . no nose or upper lip . . . sunken forehead and eye. But my attention strays to the left side, and the features both symmetrical and sensuous. He's his own foil—two polar opposites, squashed into place like mismatched halves of clay onto one man's immaculate form.

"I knew it . . . ," I mumble, my pulse shaking the words in my throat. "You're *real*." I'm not sure if I'm referring to him being the Phantom, or the maestro from my dreams.

The bared half of his full lips twitches, as if debating whether to respond.

"It was you all along," I accuse. "The bleeding roses, the torn uniforms, the dead bird." It's my voice, but someone else must be talking through me, because where would I find the courage with so much fear pounding inside my chest? I don't have the presence of mind to demand the reason he did those things . . . maybe to lead me here, so I'd find him. But why?

Then it hits me . . . the only reason he could want me to find him. And I want it, too. I want it so much, my blood burns.

"Please tell me you're here to teach me. To help me release my song, like you did for Christine." I realize too late that I say her name wrong. It slips out before I can stop it, before I can even hear how insane I sound. How insane this moment is. I'm not blind to the irony: that my need to feel normal has driven me to seek the counsel of the *abnormal*.

I stare up at him, waiting. His silence reaches as high as the cathedral ceiling, interminable. In spite of his impressive size, he folds himself effortlessly, crouching to stretch out an upturned hand. I flinch, horror-struck, my pulse thundering a warning through my ears.

An expression of sympathy and supplication deepens his brown, hawkish eyes, before they fluctuate to that shimmery, coppery gaze

I saw in the garden upon my arrival. The gaze that's always there to drag me from the water in my dreams, and now in my reality.

Drawn by their magnetic pull, I become the cricket, entranced by her eight-legged captor. Despite every instinct telling me to leap away as fast I can, I take his gloved palm and push myself up with his support, my hips propped against the basin's edge so my face is level with his sternum.

My eyes drift up to his—my other senses attuned to every aspect of his realness: The strength of his leather-bound fingers wrapped around my palm, the steady rhythm of his breath only inches from my forehead . . . the scent of his warm skin, wet and earthy, like moss on a forest floor, bathed in sunlight and dew.

Dread and hope grapple for control inside my heart, threatening to implode the organ. As though absorbing my inner turmoil, a faint glimmer of light spreads at his sternum, beneath his dark clothes, reminiscent of how I glowed when I devoured Ben's anxiety.

"What are you?" I murmur.

The naked side of his face changes, softening to an expression so open and ethereal he looks almost angelic. "What are *we*, you mean to say." His response reverberates around the chapel, deep and gruff—English words framed within a French accent. He winces at the rumbling echo, like it hurts to hear the hoarseness of his own voice.

To see him vulnerable, even for an instant, awakens that morbid hunger in me—a lust I don't understand and can't control. With my free hand, I touch his chest to reabsorb the glow he stole, not even hesitating. His gaze shifts down at our point of contact. The air seems to close in around us, pushing us closer together, although neither of us moves. The light behind his sternum deepens to green and seeps into my fingertips, then sluices through my veins, hot and intoxicating. My body wakes up, energized.

His jaw clenches and with a charged buzz, a green light ignites in my own chest. It snaps through my veins to my fingertips, then into him. The loss leaves me famished. Frowning, I concentrate, coaxing the glow toward me again, but it slips into the darkness between us. The light bounces back and forth as we wrestle for dominance.

Unable to choose, it stalls in midair—a sizzling, green ball—then bursts into a thousand pieces and floats upward, like luminous dandelion seeds, carrying away my insatiable appetite. All I feel beneath my fingertips now is his heartbeat, steady and strong. It matches my own, satisfied and controlled. It's like coming back to a place I've been before, a place I've been trying to find again for years—maybe for my whole life.

Home.

That sense of peace and comfort swells to a rush of adrenaline, as hand in hand, I mentally climb with my partner onto some ancient, omniscient plateau, view our likenesses from the summit, and tread to the edge, prepared to swan dive with him into the cosmos.

Wait . . . what am I doing? I waver, afraid of the dizzying heights, anchored only by my palm, so small, wrapped within his.

Baring the straight, white teeth not covered by his half-mask, he bites the glove on his free hand, peeling the leather away. With his thumb, he touches my temple and silences the doubts within.

A throb ignites where he presses. A current, musical and pure, passes from my skull to my spine to my feet. I'm a quivering thing—the plucked string of a neglected violin, shaking off the dust of disuse until harmony resonates between me and my maestro, pure, sad, and sweet.

"Yes, we'll conquer them, *Rune*." I feel his grinding voice through my palm at his chest. The tenderness he attributes to my name, delivered on such a pained rasp, swipes through the chalky residue coating my brain. "The arias that haunt you." His thumb caresses the hairline above my ear, and he leans so close I feel his warm whisper only inches from my lips. "I'm here. In your mind. Listen for my violin's voice from your dreams. Shut out everything but me. Together, we already own the notes . . . *every last one*."

Watching me intently, he drops his hands and steps back. My palm falls to my side and the musical current tethering us breaks. With a swish of fabric, he flourishes the cape to hide himself. A puff of glittery smoke, pungent with sulfur and ash, forms a wall. Once it clears, he's gone, as if he vanished into the floor.

Without his eyes or touch to hold me, I rouse from my dazed state, rattled and raw, but at the same time, enlightened.

All that's left of the Phantom are puddles shaped like his shoeprints and a discarded black glove. Diable saunters over, plops his haunches down, and scowls at me while licking his wooly, wet fur. He yawns, as if bored . . . as if the monumental encounter never took place.

My body knows better, my tongue still savoring the flavor of the Phantom's heartbeat—a delectable, caustic burn like an electrical charge.

Frowning, I grab the glove and inch toward the door—my focus never straying from the spot where he stood. I slip twice before I gather the tub and plunge back into the cemetery, no longer running from bloody roses, operatic arias, or a guilt-ridden past.

For the first time in years, I'm running *toward* something . . . toward the girl in my dreams who has taken her place among the planets and stars, beside a pair of glimmering, coppery eyes.

11

THE TEMPORARY NATURE OF PRECIOUS THINGS

"Of all possessions a friend is the most precious."
Herodotus

I stumble into the grand foyer, my body cold and wet, but my mind set aflame. The door thuds behind me, echoing through the spacious, white marble hollows. In the poststorm light, I glance around. My clothes drip, forming puddles—a rhythmic pitter-pat to accompany the images clicking through my mind: glimpses of a masked man with a shattered voice and strong hand.

Every bronze statue stares back—all-knowing and familial, as if they're linked to the Phantom, too—welcoming me into their secret brotherhood with carved gazes and immortal expressions.

How is it possible? That he's the maestro who's been in my dreams all these years? It can't be. But his glittering eyes said otherwise, as did his knowledge of the music we've shared in those dreams.

A tingling thrill scrambles through me at the thought of how many times he's helped me escape my drowning nightmares, again and again and again. And then today, he came to my rescue when I fell into the baptism font in reality.

He shouldn't have been there in the first place. The fictional character died at the end of the book. Alone, without the woman he had loved and obsessed over until madness became inextricably entwined with his genius. In the end, he had no one but a police chief he'd met in a foreign country at his side as he closed his eyes in death.

How much of that story is true for Leroux's inspiration? He must be a ghost. How else could he still be in this world and look so close to my age after over a century? But *I'm* not a ghost, so that doesn't make sense.

"What are you?" I'd asked.

"What are we, you mean to say." His taunting response scrolls through me, the credits to a horror movie I've lived without ever knowing I was an extra.

I still can't imagine the answer . . . what *are* we?

What am I?

Something dark and hungry. I have an appetite. It scratches at some place deep inside me . . . the same place that thrived on Ben's lust and fear. It's a morbid instinct I share with the Phantom, something he understands and can satisfy just by holding my gaze and my hand, by drawing light from my heart and joining it to his own. The heat of that connection still nestles beneath my sternum—feeding me.

Grandma Liliana was right. I'm a curse, a monster. Or a murderer.

My throat tightens, as if talons clamp over it. *Daddy . . . did I kill you somehow, like I almost killed Ben?*

A sob bubbles inside my mouth. Tears prick my eyes.

The solitude of the foyer magnifies the remorse rolling over me in waves. My hands tremble, no matter how I try to still them. Blinking my eyes to clear the tears and raindrops from my lashes, I peel off my boots and leave them by the door along with the tubful of torn uniforms, a haunted bouquet of roses, and other cryptic items I'll need to examine later. But right now, before everyone comes back from Paris, I have to let my experience play out. The answers are there, if I can process them.

I lift the black glove out of the tub and pull it on. It's too big, yet the weight of it is comforting.

There are things that don't add up, that contradict the stories. The beauty of the Phantom's voice was his ultimate weapon—an acoustic quicksand that could consume and hold any prey. But in the chapel, his voice was a raw, damaged sound. It was his touch and the pleading depth of his eyes that captured me.

Then there was the red swan. I've never seen one that color. I didn't know they existed. The bird was preternatural. The way it disappeared into the shadows just before the Phantom materialized to save me, I would think they were one and the same. Yet there's another possibility: in lore, otherworldly creatures, like witches and vampires, have familiars that do the master's bidding. Is that the bird's role in his life?

Life. If the Phantom is some bloodsucking, hex-casting being, he can't truly be alive.

Yet, he was undeniably real. Real enough for me to feel his flesh against mine, to taste his breath only inches from my lips. He hadn't intended to touch me . . . he had planned to stay hidden. I sensed that. He fought slipping out of the shadows, but finally gave in because he had to, to save me.

That place above my ear, where he traced my hair and skin, still thrums with music—a visceral, tonal reminder that we exchanged heartbeats, then walked together in our minds as he showcased our likenesses.

Everything seems different now, deciphered through *his* eyes. My senses buzz to heightened awareness, and my emotions twist and tangle with his. I can make out his silhouette as I stand next to him, hiding behind the mirrors along the walls. They're actually windows on the other side, and he looks in—watching students come and go, sometimes dressed in velvet, laces, suits . . . dripping with jewels, furs, and entitlements as they take their places on stage. He longs to be in the audience . . . to be a part of the glitz and glamor, to sit with friends and laugh about the common and mundane until the curtains rise and feature a world of romance, acceptance, and magnanimity the likes of which he's never known.

Next, I follow him deep beneath the ground, but not here—not the opera house. It's an earlier, hazier time. He shares a cage with other children I can't quite see; I'm blind to his face still, maybe because now I'm looking through his eyes. They're treated like animals, but it's different for him, because *he's* different. His appearance forces his tormentors to isolate him, and to steal away something so precious, it leaves him incomplete, humiliated, and lost. To the point he wants to die.

My heart sinks inside my chest—an anchor dredging the depths of his despair. I break free and surface within another memory. A warmer time, before his loss. I can feel his intense hunger; he goes without food often. Seated at a dusty table, he asks an innocent question, and I hear a Frenchwoman's sweet voice, chiding him. It's his mother. "You don't want that kind of love," she says. "It isn't love at all. It's dark, and it's evil. Just like the devil and the witch in your favorite story, who treated Jean and Jeanette like possessions, to be eaten like fatted calves. But children are powerful, and clever. They should be treated as gifts from the heavens."

A devil and a witch . . . Jean and Jeanette . . . the fairy tale from my childhood: *Les Enfants Perdus.* His mother used to tell him the same fable that my dad read to me.

In that blink of recognition, the vision slips away. I'm in the foyer, standing inside the academy in my soggy clothes and wearing a man's glove. That's where the intuition stops.

I need more. I need the Phantom's history. I need *everything.* Because somehow, my present, and even parts of my past, are interwoven with his.

I walk, fingers wiggling in his oversize leather glove, led by spectral footprints I can sense but not see. I wind my way through the corridors toward the renovated theater—the Phantom's deadly playground. My wet, stockinged feet grow colder with each step. Other than my dripping clothes, the journey is quiet. It's the absence of sound that leads me onward . . . a silence that breathes and beckons.

As I shove open the heavy, elaborate double doors, my breath catches, lungs stuffed with sawdust, fresh paint, and the sterility of furniture polish. I prop the doors open, allowing light from the corridor to seep across uncountable tiers of seats like a dusky nebula.

It's the first time I've been here. I'm not sure where any of the power switches are, so sparse illumination is all I have.

I consider the plays and operas that were performed here centuries earlier, before the top three floors caught fire, before smoke and soot forced the designers to stain the wooden décor black. Tainting the edges of those moments are the murders the Phantom was rumored to have committed in an opera house much like this one. I wonder if anyone ever really knew what happened. Anyone other than the object of his obsession.

He seemed sincere when he said he would help me. Maybe that's what he wanted with Christine . . . *Christina* . . . in the beginning: to be her friend. To help her. Until he fell hopelessly in love with his own creation.

If the stories are true, he's dangerous. But what if they're embellished, or completely wrong?

I descend the slanted aisle. Mister Jippetto's half-finished props sit on canvas tarps, in preparation for the upcoming opera. They clutter my path and I edge around them. On the night of the performance, all it will take is a flick of the wrists, and prismatic spotlights will line the rafters, mirroring the rainbow palette I see when I sing—the one that always ends up staining my mind with splashes of bloody red in that moment when the last note is ripped from my soul.

The dark, gaping maw of the stage waits below. One side of the red velvet curtains folds open—the tongue of a rabid wolf, slavering to devour my song and leave me gutted and drained.

For so long music has bled me dry, but today, something changed. When the Phantom touched me, when his eyes held mine, I felt it. And I still feel it now.

There's a new compulsion burning inside. Not a serpentine aria coiling around my heart and squeezing, demanding to be purged so the toxin can strike me down. Determination and confidence are driving me now.

I want to sing Renata's aria, while everyone's out, to prove to myself I can perform it to the end without getting sick, but also on the chance my maestro is in the farthest corners of this theater, up in box five, waiting . . . expectant. I lift his glove to my nose, inhaling the leathery scent. I want to please him, because it would bring pleasure to me. We're mirror images, somehow. My desires are his.

My gaze flicks from the pitch-black balcony to the highest point in the ceiling where a gargantuan chandelier glistens in the dim light: thousands of miniature crystals, eager to reflect my humiliation or triumph.

Climbing the steps to the stage, I pause as something rustles in the orchestra pit, followed by a soft thump and a clack. I glance down at the impenetrable velvet darkness. Silence overtakes again, and I continue up the stairs. What do I have to fear? The Phantom is in every corner of this opera house. He won't let anything get in my way.

He wants to hear me sing . . . to hear me *triumph*.

Up close, the curtains no longer appear ravenous or threatening. Instead, they welcome me.

I turn to face the rows of seats, straighten my posture at center stage, and take a breath. Opening my throat to widen the space in the back of my mouth, I release the first note. The room begins to spin, but there's no pain, only the faint lament of a violin—the one from my dreams—as it adapts to my song, rearranging the whine of its strings, shifting its rhythm and melody until it slips across the aria to fit it, like the glove cradling my hand. I shut my eyes and study the violin's silhouette in my mind, watching those feminine curves grow and sway until they take my maestro's masculine form. My plain floral dress transforms into a red opera gown, flowing and lush. He latches his fingers to mine and draws my chest against his, my cheek nestled between his sternum and collarbone. His free hand skims my lower back, and we fold into each other like rose petals, so close we move as one. We dance. The violin becomes his voice, serenading me as I serenade him back. The music brightens our synchronized steps, as warm and honey yellow as the sun, flooding our surroundings, relaxing me until there's no strain anywhere on my body. Though the aria rages from my throat in a powerful crescendo of color—the mood dark, mad, and melancholy—I'm unaffected. Bubbles of serenity encapsulate every staccato, trill, and glissando, then lift them from my vocal cords and roll them off my lips, effortlessly. My partner spins away and sets me free the moment I release the last golden note—in complete control.

The finale stretches, silken and luxurious, before falling in an audible drizzle that coats every wall, rafter, and seat with tremulous emotion.

The room stops spinning, and I'm left standing, strong, powerful . . . victorious. For the first time in ten years, I conquered the music. *I did it.*

"I did it!" I shout, spinning in place on the stage, my wet floral dress opening like a parasol and sprinkling water everywhere. I haven't felt like this for so long . . . elated, like when Dad would accompany me, when together we carried the songs.

That unanswered guilt at his absence flutters through my heart again, but can't find a place to perch. My chest is too full of happiness; it feels effulgent, as if it's glowing from within. I look down to find it is, and can't help but wonder if somewhere above me, the Phantom's chest is glowing, too.

I glance up at the box seats and project my voice, smiling. "Thank you!"

The soft wail of that familiar violin answers, not in my mind, not from the balcony, but from the orchestra pit. One murmuring, sensual note that winds around me like a caress. My cheeks tingle and I press my palms to them, only to realize the black glove is gone from my hand, as if he took it back during our dance. As if he really held me in his arms . . .

Before the magnitude of that discovery can register, the lights burst on overhead, blinding. I shade my eyes.

"Have you lost your mind?" Madame Bouchard's booming voice bounces around the auditorium.

The minute my eyes adjust, I study the orchestra pit. A glistening pair of yellow-green irises looks back at me. *Diable.* Other than rows of chairs, nothing else is there. No instrument . . . no Phantom . . . no glove. Since when has a cat been able to sound like a violin?

"Well, what do you have to say for yourself?" Bouchard's question slices through my bewilderment.

She's standing inside the doors I left propped open, one hand on her hip. Her thin lips are stretched in a snarl—a glaring expression even across the span of the enormous room. She has her hair pulled into a tight bun. With the duo-color job, white at the scalp and fuchsia at the nape, she looks like a grumpy powder puff. It would be almost comical, were it not for her latex gloves and the blood smeared across her white apron's bib. I must have interrupted her while she was working on her latest project. Sunny said there's a rumor that when she runs out of deceased pets, she sets traps for animals in the forest. The way she looks now, crazed and blood-thirsty, I'm guessing she's demented enough to peel roadkill from the country road that leads to RoseBlood.

I cringe.

At first, I wonder if she heard me singing . . . if she's angry again because she thinks I'm trying to horn in on her star pupil and steal the lead role of *The Fiery Angel*. Then I realize what I've done . . . the line of muddy water I've tracked across the auditorium's plush red carpet, as well as the pool surrounding me on stage. I can't even imagine how bad the white marble in the foyer and corridors must be.

"I—I'm sorry. I wasn't thinking."

"Apparently not. Have you any idea, *oiseau chanteur,* the extent of damage standing water can cause to marble, wood, and carpet?"

My lips freeze together. *Oiseau chanteur . . .* songbird.

She did hear me.

"There's a mop and carpet cleaner there, behind the curtains. Fix your mess before everyone returns and tracks it all over the school. Understood?"

I nod.

With haughty disdain, she looks down her nose at me—an unnecessarily exaggerated gesture given the fact that I'm standing in the midst of a sunken stage.

As she turns to leave, she casts a half glance over her shoulder, showing only her severe profile. "It doesn't matter if you've mas-tered bel canto. You don't have the stamina to be our prima donna. Renata has to sing over two-thirds of the opera. There's not any angel, fiery or otherwise, who can prepare you for that kind of role. So you managed one aria at last, here in the darkness with no one watching. A momentary victory, already fading. Any attempt at the entire repertoire before an audience, and your stage fright would kill you. Abandon the music and go back home to the States. That's the best choice for everyone, don't you agree?"

I stare at her, slack-jawed.

Without another word, she leaves, shutting the doors behind her with a vicious thud.

※ · I · ※

Seated inside his room, with only the soft blue glow of his aquarium to guide him, Thorn lost himself to his music—a dark and gloomy nocturne movement by Shostakovich.

He cradled the neck of his violin, the chin rest tucked under his jaw like a mother's loving hand, and let the strings speak, coaxing out notes with a mastered repositioning of his left fingers and the liquid glide of the bow. They shared a familiar dance, founded on trust and sensation, perfected after hours, days, and years of performing together. Just like the spiritual dance he'd shared with Rune in the theater only an hour ago, while his body hid within the darkness of the orchestra pit.

His gaze caught on the black glove at his feet, remembering how it felt to hold her soft curves against him, how her sweet orange-vanilla scent embodied the purity of her magnificent voice . . . how gravely he'd betrayed Father Erik.

It was a miracle he'd avoided exposing the glow in his chest when he returned home after Rune's triumph. *Their* triumph. It belonged to him, too. Now that he and Rune had connected, physically as well as spiritually, her strongest emotions and most potent energy surges would feed his own, and vice versa, once she learned to control the power.

When she'd conquered the music, her radiant happiness had filled him to the brim. It had been so long since he'd felt such joy; he thought he'd forgotten how to form a genuine smile.

Thankfully, his father was so engrossed in his personal side of the planning, he didn't even spare Thorn a passing glance upon his return. Erik had been in too much of a hurry, headed to the cellar lab, to ask about progress.

But it was only a matter of time. Soon, he would come seeking news about his "pigeon," and the truth wouldn't be well received.

Tightening his chin, Thorn brought the violin's voice to a wailing fervor, an appeal for forgiveness, altering the instrument's center of balance and the bow pressure, angling his body forward in a humble pose. The piece was no longer Shostakovich's. It was his . . . a newly inspired piece born of guilt . . . a prayer for absolution.

Bringing the song to a heartrending close, he laid his violin in its case gently. His fingers traced the lines, the perfect imitation of a woman's curves, then moved to the scroll at the fingerboard's tip, which arced like the graceful spiral of a seashell.

The Stradivarius was the most precious gift he'd ever received from Erik, worth even more than his freedom. For this violin was his and Rune's beginning, and now, since they'd at last made physical contact, she would be able to conjure those visions while awake just as he could; she no longer had to rely on her subconscious to make his spirit manifest as a reality. They could touch each other, taste each other, hear each other on some level, regardless of the distance between them.

Thorn hadn't yet decided whether to be thrilled or grief stricken over this turn of events.

"You have indeed mastered the voice." Erik's statement from the doorway shook Thorn from his thoughts. "No one else could own that instrument now. It is an extension of you."

"Thank you, Father." He closed the violin's case. "Maybe later this evening, you can harmonize with me on the pipe organ." He relayed the request in an effort to quiet his inner qualms. He used to live for their duets, but Erik had become so distracted once the academy opened that he'd abandoned all other pursuits.

"I've missed playing," Erik admitted, his timbre quavering with a poignant din of longing. "But only when she's at last with us, fully complete, can I resurrect our music once more." He was pencil thin in an untucked white shirt, gray slacks, and flesh-colored mask. So deceptively frail to the untrained eye, but his mind was a lethal trap for anyone who dared judge him by appearance alone.

Still, it was unsettling to see him in disarray. All the years Thorn had lived here, Erik was never less than meticulous with his clothes and surroundings. Lately, he'd been letting such things go, too preoccupied to notice.

"After such a long silence, to hear you composing again this past week has been divine." Erik's smile bloomed at the lower edge of his mask—wide and perfect. Many had fallen prey to the stunning charm of that partially hidden expression; even Thorn couldn't resist feeling soothed, in spite of his storm-tossed mood.

Erik padded across the black marble that stretched from end to end and up the walls. Ange waddled at his feet. Dust dulled her feathers, an indication she'd been in the laboratory, too. The swan rarely left his side, and was only with Thorn earlier because she'd followed when he'd slipped from the apartment—activated the trapdoor in the baptismal with her bill and swam her way into the chapel.

Being Erik's familiar, she was able to sense when Thorn was doing something to help him reach his goal. She'd trailed Thorn to assure he didn't mess things up. And then he had after all, except she and Diable had a hand in that . . . or more like a wing and a paw.

He was lucky the bird couldn't talk, or Erik would already know.

Thorn pulled a gray, long-sleeve shirt into place over his arms and shoulders and fastened the buttons. The soft fabric absorbed residual droplets of water from his shower. He'd come into his room still dripping and dropped directly into his chair to play without putting on anything more than pants. When he was younger, he'd often be overtaken by his muse in such a way, stopping to compose half-naked, barefoot and shirtless. Erik would tease that he couldn't escape his upbringing, that he was a peasant violinist if ever there was one.

Erik took a seat at the edge of Thorn's four-poster bed and slumped, elbows on knees. His eyes looked dull behind the mask . . . drained. He'd spent too much energy in the lab. Thorn knew it couldn't go on much longer. Erik was practically committing suicide, spending all of the extra life he'd obtained through bloodshed and butchery. Thorn had been the one to convince him to stop his murderous ways, years ago, although he had blood on his hands, too. Now he'd thrown a wrench into everything, and would have only himself to blame should the killing start again.

He strode to his fish tank and settled on the far side so he could face his father with the glass and water between them. He sprinkled flakes of food atop the surface. The bluish glow tinged Erik's gaunt, bony outline, and the ripples in the water created waves in his image, causing him to resemble the ghost all the rumors made him out to be.

"Busy caring for your pets and animal patients as usual." Erik batted Ange's bill playfully. "But have *you* eaten today?" He'd always been diligent about seeing to Thorn's physical needs: clothing, food, shelter. It was as if he was trying to make up for all Thorn lacked as a child before he found him . . . or possibly, all he'd lacked himself.

"Before I showered," Thorn answered, battling even more guilt for his father's kind concern. "I had some dried beef. Some figs and cheese. And wine."

"So, your body is fed. Then why this discontent I sense? It's been some time since you've written new music, but from what I remember, your compositions were never so insatiate or bleak."

"I came face-to-face with her in the chapel." Thorn leaned against the cool glass, his arms propped in place at the top. His fingertip tapped the temperate water, bringing the fish to tickle his skin with eager, puffy-lipped kisses.

Erik stiffened, sitting straighter, his golden eyes fixed on Thorn.

"I was wearing a half-mask. She thinks I'm you. The phantom from the stories." Ange tottered over and pecked Thorn's toes with her bill, as if prompting him to confess everything. He frowned and nudged her away with his foot.

Erik's flawless chin twitched—a tick that always made Thorn uneasy, as it indicated a shift in mood. "You were wise to wear a mask. Surely *she's* wise enough not to tell anyone. Our spy within the academy has informed me that the staff now thinks she hid her own uniforms. No one would believe her, were she to claim she saw a fictional character from a book. But you sparked her curiosity, yes? Offered the clues that would bring her to me for answers."

Thorn silently relived what he'd shared with Rune. How he'd

allowed her to look upon the reflection of his identity. She knew she was like him. Now all she needed was to discover what *he* was.

"I led her to the grave and the roses," Thorn answered, wary of how much he disclosed. "She saw the message. The storm chased her into the chapel, where I'd planted the wristband and the tubing of blood."

Erik nodded, calling Ange over with a flick of his fingers so Thorn could finish feeding his fish without distraction. "All of that was in keeping with the plan. So, you improvised, as any good performer. I am curious how the sighting happened. You're not usually that careless."

"Ange filled the baptismal with water. Rune fell in and panicked. She was going to drown."

Watching her sink, like a deadweight, had shaken him to the core. It was too similar to their nightly interactions. He'd always wondered what horrible event had spawned such torments in her dreams. Earlier, when he shared his memories with her—a connection only possible with two pieces of one soul—he'd taken some of her own. After all this time, he'd finally seen the old woman who had tried to drown her. He was shocked to have recognized her. She was the same one who Erik had visited in a Versailles prison three years ago, and several times since. Thorn always accompanied him, but stood back in the shadows, and could only hear what Erik said as they spoke through telephones with a glass partition between them. Now he was even more curious. The old woman had been instrumental in bringing Rune to them. What was her angle . . . why did she wish to harm Rune, her own granddaughter?

"Then you were right to step in and save her." Father Erik's observation dragged Thorn back to his bedroom and their dark conspiring, against his will. "A corpse would do us little good."

Thorn almost groaned at the irony of the words, considering what was in their cellar.

"How did seeing you affect her?" There was an undertone of almost desperate interest in Erik's question. Although the urgency wasn't for Rune, but for someone else, someone Erik had obsessed over and put above every other aspect of his life for more than a century. Every aspect including Thorn.

Thorn grimaced against the acid sting of that knowledge. "She was afraid." *Until I revealed myself as her maestro. After that* . . . Thorn's jaw twitched. "Once she realized I'd helped her, she trusted me."

Erik huffed. "Trust. A weak and visionary concept, for the lonely and the lost. We're going to fix her . . . make her *better*. For that, she'll only need trust herself." He reached into his shirt pocket and dragged out two crumpled pieces of paper. "She's in the perfect frame of mind now. Isolated and miserable, trying to live in a world where she doesn't fit. These unfinished notes were in the trash in the foyer. She left some boy in a coma back home and somehow feels responsible."

Thorn's heartbeat stumbled. "You've been visiting the academy? I thought we agreed you shouldn't venture there without me."

Erik shrugged. "Just a quick trip up. I was careful to go while most everyone was away."

Thorn didn't respond. Erik was stronger than he'd been led to believe, if he could venture into the halls of his tainted past alone.

"The point I was making," his father said, "is Rune has had her awakening, and lost control in the process. When she comes to us at the club, she will lose control again. And then, when she's fraught with torment, I'll offer her comfort and understanding. I'll become what she's been seeking for so many years: a father. You've already set the stage by earning her gratitude. In my full mask, I can easily step into your shoes without her ever knowing."

"Our voices sound different . . . she'll know," Thorn asserted without thinking.

Erik's lower lip curled on a scowl. "You *spoke* to her? What did you say?"

Thorn measured his answer. "I said that she and I are the same."

Erik chuckled, a lyrical vibration that at first trickled like sweet rain, then bristled the hair along Thorn's nape as the beauty soured to silence. "Making the first incision with the razor's edge of sincerity. Well done. I'm apt at mimicry. I can sound enough like you to fool her. Although, I could simply erase you from her mind. She'll forget ever hearing your voice once she hears mine."

Thorn's ears grew hot as that irrefutable truth ignited a flash of envy, no doubt visible to Erik's discerning eye through the auras he was so adept at reading. Thorn struggled to compose himself.

"So what else is there?" Erik stroked the swan's velvety red feathers, raking off the dust. "Why do you still seem so shaken?"

Because I've shared dream-visions with her for ten years. Because your pigeon is my mirror soul, but I didn't know until she arrived. Because I touched her. As hard as I tried not to, I couldn't resist. Our heart chakras have connected, and I'm helping her master her songs, against everything you asked me to do. I'm making her stronger instead of weaker.

The truth sat immovable in Thorn's chest, and he couldn't decide if it was fear, rebellion, or something else entirely motivating his silence. Under the scrutiny of Erik's studious gaze, he felt his insides quake.

"I was ashamed to tell you how I'd failed," Thorn answered at last, to ease the tension between them. "I know you wanted to be the first to make contact." The excuse drizzled from his tongue like honey, sticky enough to make a mess but sweet enough to soothe the ache.

"I will still be the one to lead her to her identity and purpose. To free her of her cancerous songs. You merely interacted for a moment. You did what you had to do." Erik stood, tucking his shirt into his pants. His fingers crept toward his mask and trailed the edge that covered his missing upper lip. "Unless there's more."

The accusation resonated on silvery notes, rising like a creature with wings, fluttering gracefully over to Thorn and tugging with its audible beak at the secrets he held caged behind his ribs. Thorn cringed at the tension in his chest, as if his breastbone actually shifted from the strain. He told himself it wasn't real . . . buried his secrets deeper to keep them contained.

He'd learned hypnotism from Erik, although he couldn't utilize his shattered voice for it. His talent was with his eyes and his touch. Yet, knowing how to wield such a weapon didn't make one immune to it. Resistance was a skill that took all of his will and concentration.

"You're not hiding anything from me, are you." It wasn't a question, it was a dare, and it didn't come from Erik's lips. It gargled up from Ange's bill, a dark, trumpeting croak . . . it burst out of the bubbles on the surface of the fish tank . . . it hummed from the strings of Thorn's violin housed within its case on his floor.

The barrage of disembodied voices was disorienting, even knowing his father was behind it. The first time Thorn experienced Erik's ventriloquist wizardry, he was a child and it was entertaining and silly fun. Thorn practiced on his own so he could throw his voice, too, but never became as adept as Erik. Over time, seeing his guardian utilize the trick as a weapon to torture victims until they bent to his dark whims, Thorn lost interest in it altogether.

Just as bad as watching someone else be a recipient of the technique was being one himself. Ange squawked and waddled at his feet, sharing his discomfort.

Her ruffled reaction shook Erik out of the perverse and savage game—his default when he felt threatened. As if waking from a fugue, he blinked behind his mask, then glanced from Ange to Thorn. "Forgive me."

Thorn wasn't sure if the apology was directed to him or the swan.

"I can sympathize with what you're feeling," Erik continued, clarifying. He bent to pick up Thorn's violin case. "This girl's rhapsody and beauty have reawakened your muse. But know this: it's temporary. Inspiration is a fickle and vicious mistress." Bitterness laced his words as he tossed the case atop Thorn's bed. "Rune was born for one purpose and only one, and she will accept this. If she doesn't come to us, I will capture her myself. I know every catwalk, maze, and trapdoor. I redesigned the damn opera house to make it so. If your way doesn't work, we take her by force."

"Like what you did the first time?" Thorn suppressed a snarl. "You've seen the consequences of those actions. The witch told you it wouldn't be successful unless the girl agrees to the sacrifice. Don't let desperation cloud your judgment. Don't let impatience endanger what you've waited so long for. She'll come to us as planned. On the night of the masquerade. I'll see to it myself." Thorn strove for sincerity, all the while his mind scrambled to find an answer to satisfy everyone in this jumbled and hopeless equation.

Impatience glittered within the depths of the mask's eyeholes. "If your plan fails"—Erik held his mouth tightly closed, again throwing his voice—"I'll burn the whole opera house to the ground this time." His answer drifted through the door, rising from the cages in the parlor. A flutter of feathers, growls, and chatters followed—discontentment and confusion rippling through Thorn's animals.

Thorn cursed under his breath and strode across the threshold to settle them. "Don't my patients already bear trauma enough?"

Erik followed, but stopped in Thorn's doorway, a menacing imprint against the calming blue that radiated from the aquarium behind him. "You're right, of course. It was not my intent to upset them." He used his own mouth now, all tenderness and humility. "Remember our pact . . . made in the sewers of Paris all those years ago. Everything I've ever asked of you has a purpose. And you've earned your place as my son by doing them. But this is different than our work with the animals. It involves a mortal soul. The witch said it has to be done on a night of liminality . . . when the boundary between the dead and living can be crossed. We need Rune in my laboratory by All Hallows' Eve to complete the circle. Only when she's with us at last, will our family be complete. A family that can endure forever."

12

L'HORREUR, L'ENLÈVEMENT, LE FANTÔME

"It is better to be feared than loved, if you cannot be both."
Niccolò Machiavelli

Thorn shut himself in his room.

A family that can endure forever.

He wasn't sure he liked the sound of that. If they accomplished what Erik wanted, was he going to resume stealing life from his victims again, so he'd never die? He hadn't mentioned that as part of the plan.

The temporary nature of living was what made it invaluable. Life was to be respected, even the lives of people who had made bad choices, for there was always a chance for redemption. Thorn wouldn't forget the woman who taught him this.

Mother . . . warmth . . . peace.

He lifted his violin from its case, caressing the silky black wood.

Drawing out his bow, he poured every emotion into the instrument—letting it speak in ways his damaged vocal cords couldn't. Every soulful vibration purled from the strings to his jawline, and sank into his throat, setting him adrift upon a sea of turmoil.

He'd never needed an anchor more than he needed one now.

"Maman," he whispered. She'd been his moral compass, as ironic as that was. What would she think of the monster he'd become? Or had she expected as much from him, all along?

Thorn hadn't been a typical child. He'd learned to talk at a very young age, and could sing songs so beautifully and affectingly, he could move people to tears, force them to face things they had hidden from themselves and the world. He was only four years old when the full ramifications of this power was revealed.

That was another time and place, when he was Etalon Laurent. When he and his mother lived in a small shack just outside of Bobigny, a suburb of Paris. They eked by without electricity, gas, or modern comforts, surviving on bread, water, dried meat (mostly from pigeons, rabbits, and the occasional squirrel), and the rare bruised and squishy tomato or plum—whatever damaged items fell from produce carts without the grocers being aware.

Back then, Etalon was too young to understand the sacrifices his mother made to keep him clothed and fed. He knew only that each night, she poured herself into skimpy dresses, then waited on their porch in a cloud of noxious perfume, her face caked in powder and lipstick, for a black car to drive her away until morning.

She would leave him in the care of a neighbor in their slum—an old hag named Batilde who did nothing but complain and recount stories of a better life, when she had a television, four-course meals, and money, before her husband left her for a younger woman.

Etalon's mother gave Batilde food in exchange for her help, though the two women often had shouting matches over why Etalon was there at all.

"You should've given that bastard child away, Nadine. Sold him when Arnaund first made the offer months ago," Batilde spat one morning after spending a sleepless night with a feverish Etalon crying for his mother. "We would both be out of this pig swill and living in the city."

"Swallow your tongue," Maman scolded, her freshly washed olive skin darkening as she shielded Etalon's ears. "Never call him that. He is an angel born of dreams. And you! You are lower than a serpent's belly to suggest something so debase! I would never have even left Ettie last night had I known he was ill."

"Children get fevers." Batilde bared her teeth—all four of them. "And when they aren't sick with snots and vomits, they eat you up, house and home. Parasites they are."

"You're the parasite! Get out!" Maman screeched, pushing Batilde toward the shack's paper-thin door.

Batilde pushed back, almost losing the moth-eaten shawl on her narrow shoulders. "One day you will see! You'll tire of men's pawing hands, their slimy tongues, and diseased lusts. We can leave the filth behind. Have working lights, hot baths, new clothes, restaurants . . . all the things we once had. The offer stands. Never has he seen a child so beautiful, Arnaund says of your Etalon." The old woman lifted her hands to punctuate her point. The flab hanging on the underside of her arms shook like a chicken's waddle. "This from a man who deals in children every day."

"And those *dealings* are the very reason Arnie is the devil himself. Leave and never come back!" Maman tossed a plastic-wrapped brick of cheese onto the muddy ground, shoving Batilde out alongside it.

Etalon wiggled atop the pile of books that made him tall in his chair at the kitchen table. His body ached and shivered from fever as he drew circles with a dried bread crust in the surface of thick dust. He'd seen other children in the slum playing with real toys—stuffed animals, tiny metal cars and airplanes, music boxes. Some even had plastic walkie-talkies that worked with batteries. But he used his imagination. His toys were just as good as theirs.

"What are you drawing, little Ettie?" His mother asked as she kissed his temple, testing his temperature. "Are you practicing your letters?"

"Musical notes, Maman," he answered. "See the colors?" He often made up tunes in his head when he was frightened or upset. The songs would come alive in his mind, a rainbow that sparkled like the jewel-colored candied fruits at market—the ones Maman loved but could never afford. One day, he would buy them and fill the cupboards and pantries as fat as treasure chests. And Maman would never be sad or hungry again.

As Batilde stood outside their door screaming obscenities, Etalon heard that word once more.

"What's a bastard, Maman?" he asked.

"A filthy lie that has nothing to do with you," she said, raking his hair from his face with a hand that smelled of tobacco, stale men's cologne, and something he didn't quite know—a soured bleach stench fraught with regret and desperation. "Now, you just draw your music. Don't listen to that wretch. I will get a washrag to cool your face."

She puttered about the tiny kitchen, and as she opened the cupboard to find a tattered cloth, Etalon munched on the dust-caked crust, craving the cheese she'd tossed out for Batilde's payment. His stomach sucked into itself on a growl so deep, it pulled all the way to his feet. For a distraction, he wiggled his toes until they poked out of the holes in his stockings. Earlier, he'd drawn eyes, noses, smiles, and frowns upon each one with a piece of charcoal. Though they chilled in the cool air, he giggled at them, his piggy puppet friends.

"Maman, Batilde's a mean old witch," he said, making his voice high and silly, pretending his toes' mouths were speaking. "Take me with you next time."

His mother's sad brown eyes met his. "No, Ettie. You will never go with me. Do you understand? Never follow me, either. Do you hear? The place where I go . . . it's no place for a child."

"But Batilde said it is. She said Arnie likes me most of all the children. He loves me."

His mother paled as she pumped water from the spigot, holding the rag under the brownish flow. "You shouldn't even know that demon's name. And you don't want that kind of love. It isn't love at all. It's dark, and it's evil. Just like the devil and the witch in your favorite story, who treated Jean and Jeanette like possessions, to be eaten like fatted calves. But children are powerful, and clever. They should be treated as gifts from the heavens. Remember what happens?"

"They ax the witch and outrun the devil!" Etalon shouted, laughing.

"Yes." Maman pointed her finger at him in praise. "But that's the only time killing is all right . . . when it's to save a child's precious life. Do you hear me, Ettie? Now, enough of this gloomy talk. Sing for me. Make my heart full."

Etalon started humming then, following the colored notes written in the layers of dust. Maybe it was the fever, or maybe it was the suffocating worry as Maman spoke of the fairy tale, but something was different this time. The colors conjured by his voice didn't stay in their place at the table. They rose and drifted to his mother beside the sink, spinning around her then capturing her wrists and linking together—a rainbow of chains. She closed her eyes, and tears streamed down her cheeks. Soon, she'd fallen to her knees with a loud thud.

The melody was simple, yet somehow it weighed heavily enough to drag her to the floor. Her eyes opened, and sunlight streamed from the window, shadowing every wrinkle and line within her once-pretty face. Her mouth gaped, and like the spigot spouting tainted water, she confessed the ugly truth: why Etalon never knew his father. That she didn't even know who the man was, but he was too beautiful to be real; he'd come to her in a dream and then was gone. She believed the devil himself had seduced her. She believed it the penalty for the life she lived. For she was a whore, and Etalon her baseborn child.

After that day, his mother loved him even more fiercely, but she also feared him. As he grew over the next two years, she watched with cautious, sidelong glances. Each time he became agitated or sad, he would sing instead of cry, and level her emotions until she confessed something else from her past. Something she'd never told anyone.

Their positions had shifted, and Etalon was in charge. He demanded she not leave in the car anymore at night. Although, at age six, he didn't quite understand what a whore was, he knew it hurt her. He wanted her safe.

Maman found a new job as a laundress, to appease him. He was wiser than most children his age, and she left him alone on the days she took the bus to collect and deliver laundry, knowing he would stay inside and care for himself. She was afraid for anyone else to watch him.

She told him he'd been sent to the earth to expose men's evil ways, that God himself formed his vocal cords of truth serum. Because his songs not only brought his listeners to tears, it sliced their hearts open and forced them to look upon their vilest secrets—sins they'd blotted out with the ink of repression in hopes never to remember.

She insisted he would not be safe if anyone knew, and begged him to stop singing. But Etalon couldn't, for by then he understood that music gave him power. One autumn afternoon, Batilde came to prey upon Etalon while his mother delivered laundry. The hag threatened that Nadine would be punished if she failed to fulfill her contract with Arnaund, but that Etalon could fulfill it for her and save his mother's life.

Her words scared Etalon, and birthed the most powerful song he'd ever sung. The poignant melody forced Batilde to confess the affair she'd had with her sister's husband, that it was the real reason her husband left her. And that she was to blame for her poverty-stricken state. After her confession, Batilde scooted out of their house on her hands and knees, like a whipped dog.

She stayed away after that, and each time Maman would hang laundry outside with Etalon handing her the clothespins, Batilde would slam all her shutters and doors closed.

On the eve of his seventh birthday, Etalon's mother didn't return from delivering laundry to her patrons in Bobigny. By morning, news had reached their hovel that she'd been killed by Arnaund.

Etalon stood on his porch with the basket of clothespins cradled to his chest. It was his fault. He hadn't traded places with her; he could've given himself for Maman. Now she was gone, as far out of reach as the invisible father he'd never know.

Etalon crumpled on the concrete step, remembering Maman's hand when it patted him to sleep after a nightmare . . . the way they danced through the sheets that flapped on the lines during sunny afternoons, playing hide and seek. All of it was gone, just like his chance to buy her the things her heart longed for, so he could see her smile.

No song could appease the ripping sensation in his heart. So he remained quiet as tears crept along his cheeks and lips.

Batilde slithered out from her house and wrapped her arms around him, lulling Etalon within her familiar, sweaty, onion-scented embrace. He didn't see the burlap sack until it came down, binding his head and arms. By then he was sobbing too hard to save himself.

Strangling on snot and gasping for breath inside the scratchy cloth, Etalon passed out. He woke up deep in the catacombs—a windowless, loveless world with walls made of skulls and bones— imprisoned with other children, who like him, had no family or place to go. His cell smelled of urine and the same desperate sour stench his Maman had worn like a second skin while working as a whore.

Batilde had sold him to Arnaund, and it was too late for escape. Being without Maman, haunted by his part in her death, Etalon's music stayed locked inside.

Three months passed without a glimpse of sky or sunlight. Etalon watched other children suffer unspeakable acts at the hands of Arnaund's henchmen, being "taught" the skills they'd need to make themselves worthy of a good price. His heart ached for them—some younger than his seven years and gaunt as skeletons with paper-thin flesh that showcased blue veins. Etalon felt guilty for being spared. So he asked a guard why . . .

The ugly man smiled, his teeth stained by tobacco, and his eyes vacant of any emotion. "Why? Why are ya spared?" He snorted. "Feeling neglected, hmmm?" He ruffled Etalon's unruly waves, which now reached past his shoulders. Etalon winced and stepped back, leaving the man's filthy hand in midair. The man laughed. "I'd like to help ya out, but Arnaund has marked ya untouchable. Your beauty makes ya worth a fortune already without all the . . . lessons." The guard leaned in and slid a calloused finger down Etalon's neck and chest, barely covered by the fraying rags draped over him. A nauseous chill raced through Etalon's body. "Your innocence, well, that just makes ya extra special."

The way he slurred the word *special,* the way his breath cloaked Etalon's face like sticky, whiskey-scented fog as his gaze traversed him from head to toe—triggered a white flash of hatred, and Etalon found his song once more. His melody brought the henchman to his belly on the floor like the snake he was.

The man wailed, bemoaning his weakness for gambling, followed by a boisterous account of how much money he'd skimmed from Arnaund's profits. Several other guards overheard the confession echoing through the cell, and by morning, the embezzler was dead at Arnaund's own hand.

No one knew Etalon had caused the event. They assumed the henchman had been drunk, which loosened his tongue. Etalon kept the secret, until his cellmates were ready to be auctioned. Several patrons came to the catacombs early, to consider which child they wanted to bid on for cheap labor or sick sadistic pleasures. As they stopped to study Etalon's friends, he wielded his song like a sword, slashing them all until they moaned and wept.

The patrons stumbled out, one by one, faced with their own depravity. They refused to return, or to buy any other child from the lot. Instead, they spread the word about the avenging angel locked in the catacombs, who sang with such fierce sweetness and critical accuracy, it made a soul beg for the release of eternal damnation.

Furious that Etalon was costing him money, Arnaund bound and gagged him. There was talk of cutting out his tongue, but it would compromise his worth. Patrons wanted their merchandise intact. Besides, it wasn't the words Etalon sang; it was the quality, richness, and purity of his voice.

So Arnaund and his henchmen force-fed Etalon lye—diluted enough to keep him alive, while caustic enough to blister and damage his vocal cords beyond repair. After hours of strangling on the hot, acidic vomit he was forced to swallow due to Arnaund's fear of damaging his lips or face, Etalon lost what made him unique, and the ability to defend himself or the other children.

Etalon prayed for death, but instead fell into a deeper level of hell. A week later, a man contacted Arnaund, specifying he wanted the little songbird whose tale had been entertaining and horrifying the dregs of society. Up until then, Etalon's outrageous price tag had kept him safe.

On the day of the sale, the guards dragged Etalon into a small room with a lone lightbulb strung from the ceiling, casting snatches of light on the dirty, webbed skulls embedded into three of the stone walls. The fourth wall was bare, and they cuffed him there. Once Arnaund arrived, the guards left and shut the door. Etalon stood across from his mother's murderer. The man had a bucket and sponge in hand. Etalon shivered, his body bared, all but for a pair of pants too short to reach his ankles, bloody and disheveled after fighting the guards.

"What a mess you are," Arnaund grumbled. "A perfectly calculated mess. Every bit as wily and stubborn as Nadine was. But what did her fire get her, hmmm? Got her snuffed out, it did." He splashed Etalon with the bucket's frigid contents. Etalon coughed, inhaling the sudsy water. Soap slime oozed down his nasal passages and clogged his windpipe. He choked for breath.

At the mention of his mother, flames lit inside his heart. His song burned to be born and bring Arnaund to his knees. Colorful notes that would never have the chance to rise from his useless throat.

Arnaund sponged Etalon's face and chest, making him squirm. "Your efforts were wasted. This particular patron has unusual appetites. No one knows his name, and no one's ever seen his face. He's simply known as a phantom of the night. It is said he scuttles in the shadows, like a scorpion."

Etalon shivered again, terrified of the imagery.

"And believe me . . ." Arnaund chortled, gleefully. "One such as that has developed a taste for dirt and grime. You're too pretty to pass up. Messy or no. Lovely as a milk bone to a half-starved dog."

Refusing to look into Arnaund's beetle-black eyes and harsh round face, Etalon studied his cold, mucky feet—remembering a time when his toes were clean and poked from his socks like playful puppets. It seemed so long ago.

"Can't tell you what a pleasure it will be to see you carted off, *little Ettie*," Arnaund spat. "Nearly leveled my business to dust. I've been far too easy on you. Maybe I'll cut out that tongue of yours after all, and wear it as a necklace. I doubt your new owner would have the presence of mind to notice before—"

"Better you not underestimate my observational prowess, *Monsieur.*" Neither Arnaund or Etalon realized they had company until the man's baritone swelled inside the room—poised over them, above them, around them—as magnificent and threatening as a tidal wave. Had Etalon not been pinned to the wall by his aching wrists, his knees would've buckled under the weight of the dulcet, hypnotic sound.

"Being as I'm a scorpion"—the melodious voice swelled higher, louder—"who scuttles in the shadows undetected, I'm inclined to see and hear *everything.*"

Arnaund teetered in place, as affected by the sound as Etalon. They both looked to the doorway. A white, satiny mask covered the buyer's entire face, with a small slit for the mouth. The artificial lines of a perfect nose and cheekbones were molded into the fabric— hauntingly distinguished alongside his pressed black suit and cape, both of which appeared to be from another century.

Arnaund offered a bumbling bow. "Might I see the payment?" He braved the question as soon as the stranger's words stopped echoing through the room—the tidal wave leveling to a peaceful, lapping lull.

The buyer's gaze glinted an otherworldly gold inside the black depths of the mask's eyeholes. Etalon whimpered as a leather-clad hand flashed a bagful of silver coins—more than he'd ever seen in his short life—then tucked it away before Arnaund's eager fingers could grab it.

The Phantom was tall and rail thin, but he didn't need meat on his bones. He radiated power, something beyond the physical—a feral confidence that crackled from him, like an electrical pulse on the air. He nudged Arnaund aside and crouched in front of Etalon, who withered at the cool, slick touch of the glove cupping his chin.

The Phantom looked him over twice, clucked his tongue, and released Etalon's face. He stood, took off his cape on a swish of dark fabric, and wrapped Etalon's shivering half-naked form in its warmth, an empathetic gesture Etalon never expected from a creature that frequented the haunts of bugs and serpents. A scent of something alkaline and burnt lingered in the velvety fabric, stinging Etalon's nose.

"This?" The Phantom gestured to Etalon. "This is the avenging angel feared by all the tittering rats of Paris?"

"Yes," Arnaund said. "Is there a problem? Does he not exceed any and all hopes you had?"

A hiss seeped from under the mask. "The problem," the Phantom's mesmerizing voice growled, "is that this is a *boy*. I was led to believe otherwise." He stepped toward Arnaund with the grace of a black panther, and stopped short of standing on his toes.

Arnaund eased two paces back, his forehead beading up with sweat—a physical transformation so spontaneous and swift that it appeared his skin was melting under the flickering light. Etalon wished he *would* melt . . . all of him. Melt to a puddle of bile and blood on the floor to be licked up by the vermin that overran this hell hole.

"Y-yes, a boy," Arnaund stuttered in answer to the Phantom's observation. "But . . . look at him. He's lovely enough to be serviceable to any preference. And a boy can offer the same pleasures as a girl—more in fact. Once they're properly taught. That will be your privilege. He is untouched."

The buyer glanced over his shoulder. Etalon's throat went dry, dread squeezing it tight, as he saw curiosity in those glinting eyes—as though the masked creature was reconsidering. "Sing for me, little one. I want to hear this life-altering voice. *Force me to face my most unforgivable sins.*"

Etalon froze, as did Arnaund. The only sound in the room was the buzz of the lightbulb.

The Phantom's gaze flashed like currents of heat under the mask. "I said sing, child. Sing, and live to see another day."

His voice drifted toward Etalon—an alluring and irresistible summons, despite the threat it carried—and shook his vocal cords, as if to wake them. Etalon opened his mouth and released his broken song, more grating than a screeching rabbit thrown into a boiling stew. He winced simultaneously with the masked man.

The Phantom spun on his heel to face Arnaund. "Is this your idea of a trick, flesh peddler? Bringing me the wrong child?"

Etalon sobbed, unable to contain his loss and shame another minute. "I was the angel. They took my voice." He strained against the cuffs that ate into his wrists. "They took my voice . . ."

Arnaund grunted, growing impatient. "The little freak wouldn't *shut up*. What does it matter? We didn't break anything of import. Do you want him, or no? I'm sure there are others far more wealthy and discerning than you who will see his worth—busted vocal cords notwithstanding."

Arnaund's ultimatum hung in the air—the last words he would ever speak. In a subtle move, less than a twitch, The Phantom snapped a long, thin cord from beneath his right glove where one end had been wrapped around his wrist. An egg-size ball of lead rolled from his sleeve and swung at the other end. He flung out his hand before Arnaund could even react. The cord released a high-pitched whine, like a dog whistle. The lead ball wrapped the strand around Arnaund's neck, three times, until slamming violently into his Adam's apple, crushing it. A strangled gasp escaped his mouth.

The Phantom tightened the noose with a sharp tug. "Plead for your life, swine. Plead, and I vow to let you live."

Etalon watched in awed silence as Arnaund gripped the hairline wire at his neck—face bulging and purpling, unable to release even a whimper.

"Ah-ha," The Phantom crooned. "Perhaps now *you* can be discerning enough to appreciate the value of working vocal cords, and how life-altering it is for them to be taken at the hands of another." He gave a harsh twist and brought Arnaund to kneel on the stone floor. "There you are, little one," The Phantom's rapturous voice purred to Etalon. "You have brought him to his knees even without your song. Vindication is sweet, no?"

Alongside his terror, Etalon secretly savored watching his mother's murderer captured and suffering.

"Shall I spare him?" the Phantom asked, fixated on his squirming victim.

Etalon grimaced at the skulls and bones lining the walls. Killing was wrong. Maman always said so. But she also said it was right . . . when it was to save a child's life. Thinking of his friends who had already suffered at Arnaund's hand, of those who would soon be sold as possessions, Etalon croaked his answer: "You should spare none of his kind."

The Phantom's eyes met his, and an unspoken alliance passed between them—so earnest yet so vicious, Etalon knew there would be no redemption from this sin.

The Phantom lifted one side of his mask and leaned over Arnaund, too deep in the shadows for Etalon to see what he revealed. Arnaund flailed, his expression filled with fear and revulsion. A pulse of grayish-yellow light jumped from Arnaund's wide-eyed gaze and sunk into the Phantom's chest, illuminating his sternum from behind his shirt and suit jacket.

Stunned speechless, Etalon watched the Phantom's neck where it was bared above his shirt collar. The veins grew luminous beneath his skin, as if siphoning from the glow in his chest. In contrast, Arnaund's coloring drained to a deathly white and he stopped moving.

The Phantom flipped the lifeless body over. "Thank you for sharing the remaining years of your life, *Monsieur*. And in return, I've given you your necklace. Wear it in good health." He tightened the cord around his victim's neck until a pool of blood spread like a dark, seeping hole along the floor. With a flick of his wrist, he retrieved his deadly weapon.

Without speaking, the Phantom freed Etalon's wrists, offering him the boots off Arnaund's feet. They were too big, but with ripped bits of cloth stuffed in the toes, they sufficed.

"Most of the guards are either drunk or sleeping at their posts," the Phantom said, yellow eyes aglow. "I will be swift and cut them down in silence, one by one. You free the other children. But I must not be seen, for I would haunt their dreams."

Together, they made their way through every level of the catacombs, quiet and deadly as scorpions. As promised, the Phantom killed the guards, coaxing that strange grayish-yellow light from each of their bodies before ducking into the shadows. Only then would Etalon unlock the cells, so the masked silhouette remained nothing but a ghost—blending into the background, sensed, yet never seen.

Death was everywhere, juxtaposed with hope for new life. Etalon slipped in puddles of blood and stepped over the Phantom's victims. Heaps of carnage became stair steps to freedom as he opened the doors and released his peers. Chaos reigned—a frenzied race to escape the cells and congregate in the corridors. In the narrow spaces, children clung to one another, weeping and afraid. After everyone was freed, Etalon kept to the darkest passages, out of their sight, in search of the Phantom. He found him hidden in the depths of the catacombs, his hands bloodied, his suit torn, and his veins and eyes effulgent with that supernatural glow.

"Will you help them find their way out?" Etalon asked, understanding on some level that to ask any other question would put him in mortal danger.

"No," the Phantom answered without pause, smearing blood from his hand across one of the thousands of skulls stacked along the wall. "They have food and lanterns from the storage surplus; they have one another. The weak will die, and the strong will survive and be stronger for it. That's the nature of things. Those who find the surface have the gendarmerie. Let law enforcement step in for once. Let them fill an orphanage with their abandoned souls. Even alone, those children have better parentage than I ever did."

He started to leave, but Etalon caught the skilled hand that had slaughtered over thirty men with a singular cord of string, his own fingers too small to wrap around the blood-slicked palm. He gasped as some of the illumination from the Phantom's veins siphoned into his own, lighting beneath his skin.

The Phantom narrowed his eyes then pried himself free. "I

suspected as much, the moment I heard about you." He drew out a handkerchief and cleaned his hands before offering it to Etalon for the same purpose. "You are an anomaly of nature . . . a brilliant miscreation. No doubt you've known this for some time, even before you were imprisoned."

Etalon nodded, handing back the soiled handkerchief.

The Phantom tugged gloves onto his hands and looked toward the cave's roof, the muscles in his neck corded with tension. "It doesn't matter that you're a demon's spawn. You could still have a normal life. Your perfect face, flawless features . . . they'll earn you a place of respect and power in that world. You can blend in, even rule, where I never could."

"I don't want to blend," Etalon whispered. "I want to belong."

The Phantom's head tilted. "To follow me is to make a pact with darkness and solitude. No more sunlight. No more sky. No more friends or relatives. What I can offer you, in exchange, is a way to reclaim your songs. And I'll give you an education, training, and protection."

"You will show me how to wield the wire garrote and strangle those who would harm me?" Etalon asked eagerly.

A bubble of laughter erupted within his savior's chest. "It is in fact a violin string. Catgut makes an excellent Punjab lasso. At least, my version of one. But I don't believe I'll share that particular skill. I must keep some form of leverage. I'll educate you with other ways to defend yourself. I acquired many such useful talents in my past lives. Many useful talents." Then, in silence, the Phantom guided him through a secret entrance into one of the sewage tunnels deep beneath Paris.

They walked, led only by a pinhole of light far in the distance and the fading glimmer beneath their own skin. Etalon tuned out the dripping water, their sloshing feet, and the stench soaking into the hem of the cape draped across his shoulders—so many sizes too big, yet something he aspired to one day grow into.

"Why did you wish to buy me?" he asked on a raspy murmur, half dreading the response, yet desperate to hear his rescuer's melodic voice again.

"I thought you were someone else." The answer broke beneath the mask, muffled and wracked with so much longing it bordered on agony.

"Who, sir? Who are you seeking?" Etalon pressed. "It will be my life's work to help you find them."

His savior stalled, those golden irises flickering in the recesses of the dark eyeholes, cauterizing Etalon's heart like lit torches. "Your question will be answered in time, and I will hold you to that promise. Also, you are to address me as Erik."

Etalon nodded. "And my name is—"

"Don't even speak it." Erik placed a glove on Etalon's head, quieting him. In the blackness, the lower half of his mask made a scraping sound, as if a smile shifted the fabric. "Today, you become someone new. From this moment on, you belong to the underworld, from which you were born. You are something monstrous, but beautiful. Something fierce, yet fragile. You are Thorn. The part of the rose that is unloved . . . that everyone fears for its ability to bring a soul to bleed. That was your gift, and shall now be your identity, to honor what was taken from you by vile and treacherous men. It is a falsity, that monsters are the instigators of all the evil in the world. Our kind is capable of acceptance and mercy where *mankind* is not. For we see beyond the surface, as we live beneath it."

Etalon leaned into the leather rested upon his head. He believed every word; this was the kindest, safest touch he'd felt in months. And it was at the hand of a monster. "Will you be my papa?"

Erik's palm dropped away, and he turned his back, shoulders hunched as if the question pained him. "In time, perhaps. For now, the blood shed at our hands binds us. We will never again speak of our actions this day, unless I precipitate the conversation. Your secrets are mine to keep, and mine are yours. You will hide nothing from me. Swear to that, or turn away and leave me now."

❈ · I · ❈

Thorn ended his violin's song with a gradual slide of the bow, letting the note carry on a mournful wail through his underground home—the place he'd lived since he'd vowed his loyalty and devotion to the Phantom twelve years ago, a pact sealed by the blood of evil men.

Thorn had never spoken of that day, or of the children they saved and abandoned. In that, he'd been faithful. But he'd kept his visions of a twin flame silent for years, and harbored quiet, unspoken goals that he now knew went against everything Erik needed . . . everything he had waited over a century to possess.

Apprehension crept through Thorn's blood, chilling him all the way to his bones. He rubbed his forehead, hard enough to pinch the skin—trying to erase his traitorous thoughts of Rune. Should he continue on this path, he would betray the only father he'd ever known. He would lose the accepting and merciful side of that heroic monster he met so long ago, and face the wrath of the scorpion with the Punjab-lasso tail.

13

SONG TO
THE MOON

"You are the night, and the night alone
understands you and enfolds you in its arms . . ."
Anne Rice, Interview with the Vampire

By the time I've changed into a dry sweater and jeans, mopped all
the puddles, and spot-cleaned the carpet, it's five till five. The curfew
for Saturdays is ten o'clock, with lights-out by eleven, but everyone
planned to be back from Paris today by six. I need to look through
my findings at the cemetery before they return.

The musical rush I experienced in the theater hasn't left my system. It's numbing me to things I should fear . . . to things I should
reevaluate. It made me brash enough to hide a note for my maestro
in the orchestra pit, asking to see him again. There are so many
questions that need answers. I also want to look into his eyes and
thank him for giving me power over Renata's aria. Not the coppery

eyes from my dreams, but the deep, brown, soulful ones I saw in the chapel for an instant. The ones that held so much vulnerability. . . so much longing for humanity. The eyes I looked through in memories that are somehow now mine.

I even went so far as to retrieve the book from my nightstand, the one my mom bought to remind me of Dad. I couldn't stop thinking of how long it had been since the Phantom heard *Les Enfants Perdus*, our shared fairy tale. I couldn't stop empathizing with how much he missed his mother. Since the story made him feel closer to her, I wanted him to have it. So I left it in the orchestra pit, too.

Only now, when I'm starting to come back to myself, do I realize that's another detail that doesn't fit with the phantom from the novel. His mother hated him.

I stop at the kitchen to grab a plate of crackers, a chunk of cheese, a knife, and a bottled water, still plagued by the intense hunger I sensed in the Phantom as a child. A shiver of bells bounces behind me and I turn to find Diable at my ankles, looking up at my plate. He's tagged along since I left the theater. He still won't let me pet him, but seems determined to stay by my side. I get the distinct impression he's either guarding me, or stalking me.

I pour some milk into a bowl for my jingling shadow, then together we retreat to my room. I place the cat's treat close to the stairs leading up to the mini-loft.

His lapping tongue and rolling purr drown out the gurgle of my lava lamp as I use the lavender glow to help me slice cheese and make cracker sandwiches, while sifting through the items in the steel tub.

Keeping busy is the best way to block Madame Bouchard's cruel insinuations from my mind. Considering the impression I made from the very beginning—crashing an audition, stealing the limelight from students who'd been practicing for months, then fainting like a histrionic heroine from some outdated romance novel—it's no surprise the school's distinguished voice teacher wouldn't want me for her lead role. But I would never try out for that part. I want Audrey to have it, more than anything.

Bouchard just doesn't understand . . . I had something to prove to *myself* today. Otherwise, I wouldn't have been singing on stage in the dark. It certainly wasn't for my love of music.

Or was it?

My face flushes, remembering how it felt to be one with the song again. So accomplished, so alive . . . so *complete*.

And I have the Phantom to thank for it.

My skin grows warmer at the memory of our fantastical dance on stage. Besides the fact that somehow he took his glove back, my senses say it was anything but pretend: the heat of his body, the scent of him, the press of his muscles moving against me, and his violin's voice in my ear—seductive and empowering. I can see how Christina was drawn to him. In that moment, while sharing in the glory of music, wrapped up in the essence of his genius, the deformity he hides under his mask no longer mattered.

Lifting one of my uniform vests from the tub, I debate how best to fix the torn lapel, trying to get him off my mind. I shouldn't be drawn to someone who's over a century old, or to someone I don't know enough to trust. Yet on some level, it makes sense that I am.

On Tuesday, Madame Bouchard gave us a project in our historical musicology class. Since some operas are considered "lyric fairy tales," she assigned each of us a performance to research that encapsulates the construct of that narrative. By mid-November, we're to have journal articles, a biography of our composer, a list of the roles, and photocopies of a traditional fairy tale similar to our production. After Thanksgiving break, we're to turn in an essay focusing on how the words and music contribute to the fantasy atmosphere.

I was assigned a Czech opera called *Rusalka*, by Antonín Dvořák. As I was researching in the academy's library with Audrey and Sunny, I found the plot similar to *The Little Mermaid* by Hans Christian Andersen. A Water-Goblin's daughter falls in love with a mortal man, and even though her father and water-nymph friends tell her it's a mistake, Rusalka takes a potion so she can be human, at the expense of losing her beautiful voice forever. She sings one final song to the moon, begging its silvery light to carry her message of love to the human prince. They meet, he falls for her, but then betrays her. By the opera's end, the prince is dead, and Rusalka is imprisoned in the river as a demon of death. The moral "it's safer to stay with your own kind" rings in my ears as if meant for me alone.

Was Christina my kind—whatever I am? Was she like the Phantom?

I drop the vest back into the tub and glance over my shoulder. Diable stretches out on the chaise lounge as if he owns it, having finished his milk. He mewls at me, his big eyes blinking contentedly. White droplets coat his whiskers, and I can't help but smile as he licks his paws and cleans his face. I'm hoping he might stay until morning. I had a hard time sleeping last night without Mom, and I expect tonight to be even worse, considering all that's happened.

Spreading an empty garbage bag over my bed to protect the covers, I lay the damp pieces of my uniforms atop the plastic. The skirts' front panels gape, ripped open to the thigh. My fingers trace the frayed fabric. Madame Fabre has a box of scrap fabric from old costumes. All I need are lace ruffles and netting to mend the skirts and shirts. Zigzag stitches, along with trims—like lacy strings of butterflies or satiny roses sewn onto strands of ribbon—can patch the stockings' side seams.

The only piece I can't save is the shirt that covered the bleeding roses. I doubt even bleach can take out those stains. I wander to the corner of my room where I earlier piled my wet dress, leggings, and tank top, stuffing the soiled shirt beneath them.

I'm not sure how I'm going to explain the state of my uniforms to Madame Fabre. Since everyone already thinks I misplaced them on purpose, what's to keep them from thinking I ruined them, too?

That would be the last straw. They'll send me back home for sure. Now that I'm so close to understanding things that have haunted me for years, I can't leave.

I don't understand why the Phantom took such measures. If he was trying to lead me to him so he could train my voice, why do something so destructive as part of the plan? I would've followed the trail of clothes, even if they'd been whole. And what purpose did the dead bird on my chair serve?

A shiver shuttles through my bones without warning. I debate going to the theater and taking back the note and my fairy tale book before he finds them. There's a dangerous side to my maestro. The Phantom in the original novel occupied the shadows, and had little respect for human laws and morals. This one seems to share those characteristics. So is it really safe for me to be alone with him?

Memories of Ben resurface, reminding me it's not safe for anyone to be alone with me.

Nibbling on the ends of my hair, I kneel once more on the floor next to the steel tub and turn my attention to the two-toned roses. I pull one out. Taking the knife I've been using to slice off wedges of cheese, I sever the stem, careful to avoid the thorns. Even before it snaps in half—releasing the grassy scent of chlorophyll—I already know the truth. These flowers are real. There's no trick valve to pump out blood, and the stems are too narrow to be hollowed out to make room for one. These roses literally bled, just like the ones in the garden died at his touch.

What kind of creature has the power to manipulate nature like this? The stories claimed he was an accomplished magician. That explains how he vanished into the floor in the chapel behind the puff of smoke. Most likely he has trapdoors there, just like here in the opera house. But there's still something preternatural at play. Something that keeps him from aging and gives him the power to step into my mind not only in dreams, but in a reality that straddles the physical and the spiritual.

Desperate to find a loophole, I tear apart each rosebud until my floor is a pile of fragrant, red-edged white petals and broken, thorny stems. The cloying scent seeps into my head, making me dizzy. I jump along with Diable when someone knocks at my door.

I glance at the digital clock: 5:40.

Still fuzzy, I stumble to the threshold and pull it open.

The Phantom faces me from the other side: Red Death costume, skull mask, dark hair, red suit, and cape. "Here's lookin' at you, kid."

Clapping a palm over my mouth to stifle a scream, I stumble backward before realizing the voice belongs to Sunny—that the phrase is from the movie *Casablanca*.

I trip over Diable, who's hissing at my heels, and plummet into the stack of petals and thorns. Little droplets of blood ooze through my sweater sleeves at my elbows where I catch myself. The sting from the punctures clears my head enough to recognize the "Phantom" is a life-size 3-D cutout from the movie.

Jax curses and shoves aside the cardboard outline. Quan and Audrey rush into the room behind Sunny, and Diable darts between their legs to make his escape.

"Bless your heart!" Sunny helps Jax lift me out of the mire of vicious potpourri. "Quan, go fetch some bandages."

Rolling his eyes, Quan steps out again.

"What's he in a grind about?" Sunny asks no one in particular as she helps me straighten my clothes.

"Probably that we all told you it was a stupid idea to wave that thing in her face," Jax scolds as he and Audrey pluck stems from my now crimson-dotted sweater.

Sunny sighs. "I was hoping to impress you with my resourcefulness, Rune. Last night you said you wanted your own Angel of Music to help with your songs. Remember? I didn't mean to scare you. I'm sorry." She hands me a bag filled with Halloween candy that fits the Red Death motif. Her mournful expression looks like a fairy who misplaced her wings.

I force a grin. "It's all right." The truth lumps in my throat: that I managed to find the real angel of music all on my own. "I've had a weird day. Otherwise, I would've been impressed. He's actually pretty hot." I gesture to the phantom's back, a flat brown-paper shadow on the floor, although he holds no candle to the real man I met earlier. There was an undeniable sensuality and grace in every move he made.

"Darn right he is." Sunny nods at her cardboard boyfriend. "So, about this weird day . . . do we get deets?" She drags her boot's toe through the petals. "Let's start with the roses. Are you making a rug?"

"Maybe that's how they garden in Texas," Jax teases. "Bringing the great outdoors *indoors*. Kind of like Bouchard does, with her hobby." He grins at me, releasing my arm and dropping the last stem to the floor.

I smirk conspiratorially—a façade to hide my jittery insides.

"Where'd you find these?" Audrey interrupts, her soft voice barely audible as she picks up a two-toned petal. "I've never seen any roses like this in the garden here."

Before I can fabricate a response, Sunny's blurting another question. "What happened to your clothes?" She's halfway over to the muddy dress and tank top in the corner. I'm fidgeting—worried she'll find my bloody shirt—when she pauses beside my bed. "Oh my gosh, your uniforms! What happened to *them*?"

My brain spins like a top over all the questions flung my way.

"Sunny's a little amped up. We let her have too many espressos on the outing." Jax mimes taking a drink.

Sunny scowls at him over her shoulder, lifting up a stocking. "Shut your pie hole, Jax. If that were true, I'd have the backdoor trots. Caffeine tears up my tummy." Eyes narrowed, she turns to me. "We all know who did this. If it weren't for our pact with Tomlin, she'd get expelled for sure. Then Audrey would have Renata cinched tight."

Audrey paces over to my chaise lounge and sits down, a strange expression on her face. "Did you any find proof it was Kat?" Her question is directed to me, but her smoky-eyed gaze bounces between the rose petal in her hand and the stocking flapping out of the top of Sunny's fist.

"Who else is devious enough to do it?" Sunny retorts.

Jax snaps his fingers. "I got it. It's Jippetto. Pretty sure he secretly wants to be in the spotlight."

Quan chuckles from the doorway. "Well, there's a week's worth of nightmares. Old Jip in a ball gown on stage, twittering soprano with his bird whistle while his mannequins dance in tutus around him." He lifts to his tiptoes and pretends to dance ballet.

It's a disturbing image. I know firsthand after the closet scare that Jippetto's mannequins are old-world and exquisite—made of soft white pine and painted to realistic perfection. Jax and Quan, along with some of the other senior guys, once spied on the old man in his forest cottage and swear he has a shed filled with naked pieces of the eerily lifelike figures—arms, legs, torsos with red hearts imbedded in their white chests, and heads—caked in spider webs.

Strangest of all, he had three completed, fully dressed mannequins—the ones that often accompany him around the school—posed inside his house around the kitchen table. He sat having tea with them, as if he believed they were real. The idea is unsettling, but more than that, sad. He must be so lonely out there.

In spite of those melancholy thoughts, Quan's clumsy pirouettes spark laughter from all five of us. He leaps across the threshold and tosses me a box of Band-Aids.

I shake my head, still grinning. "Thanks." Sitting down next to Audrey, I roll up my sleeves. She takes a few and together we stick them into place over my seeping wounds.

Sunny methodically sifts through my uniforms. "Rune, you never answered what happened to the clothes you were wearing earlier. Did you get caught in the rain?"

Quan crouches beside Jax who's scooping up rose petals and dropping them back into the tub.

I bite my lip. Where did I get the Fire and Ice roses? Why are they torn up? And the same questions for my clothes and uniforms . . . It's hard to decide what's safe to answer. The one thing I've learned over the years while trying to hide my secrets: The most believable lie has remnants of the truth.

I preoccupy myself with one of the Band-Aids hanging off my elbow—only half stuck to my skin—pressing it into place as the four of them watch me expectantly, their faces lacquered with purplish light. "When I was gardening today, a storm hit. I went inside the chapel for cover. That's where I found my uniforms and the roses."

"Then why are they so wet?" Sunny asks, picking up a vest that drizzles water. "If they were in the chapel, they should still be dry, right?"

I grimace at her powers of observance. Where's an e-cig when you need one? The things are like pacifiers to her. "The clothes were tied up in the plastic bag, floating around in the baptismal."

Jax stops picking up the stems. "Wait, what? That baptismal has been bone dry since the school opened. I've never seen water in it."

No. That can't be. I almost drowned in those depths . . . I can't even process the implications before Quan practically dives into the tub, his eyebrows almost reaching his unkempt hairline.

He yanks out the hospital wrist band and the IV tubing, holding them to the lamplight. "Were these in the chapel, too?"

Audrey almost topples the chaise as she scrambles over to see. Everyone gathers around the items now placed on my nightstand under the lava lamp. I step into the ring of bodies to study the tiny letters and numbers I didn't notice earlier, neatly written on the plastic label:

Rune Germain
1986 boulevard du Pernelle
passage à la Bouche de L'enfer
10-29 / 18:30

Dread ices my veins and frosts my heart.

Even though this time my name's not taking shape before my eyes, it's a reminder of the bleeding roses, and just as intimate and unnerving as before, because it's on a hospital wristband where the third line of the address translates to . . .

"Passage to the Mouth of Hell," I whisper.

Audrey and Jax exchange a glance. Quan and Sunny do the same. Then everyone turns to me.

"What?" I ask. "Do you know the place? Is it a hospital?"

"Try a morgue," Quan answers as Sunny pries the wristband from his hand. "An abandoned morgue."

"*Dios mío.*" Audrey drags a rosary from inside her shirt, kisses it, and crosses her chest. Then she touches the crucifix to the bird tattoo on her face and shivers.

"Don't think of it like that, Blackbird." Jax wraps an arm around her, pulling her petite body against his tall, powerful one and hugging her tight. The room grows quiet, all of us sympathizing as Audrey is dragged back to that horrific day when her sister almost died. After Jax whispers something in her ear, she nods and swipes some tears from her cheeks, breaking out of his embrace but keeping her fingers laced through his.

He slants his blue eyes my way. "*The Mouth of Hell.* That morgue is rumored to be the entrance to a rave club, but none of us have ever been able to pinpoint exactly where it is. It's just the name of it, floating around online. They say if you get tagged, you wait at the address on the instructions and a car will come for you. But the pickup locale is different every time. And you're forced to wear a blindfold, so you can't see the way to the final destination. It's also rumored, since the morgue once housed the dead, that creatures of the underworld can emerge and mingle with mankind there. That's why the parties are so wild. People lose consciousness . . . don't wake up until days later and find themselves out on the street with puncture marks on their arms and ankles. It's got to be some kind of drug or something, because along with the needle tracks, they all have amnesia and don't know how they got there. No one can ever find the place again either, unless they get tagged a second time. It's some crazy stuff."

"Yeah. We all decided it was an urban legend, since no one we know has ever actually found any proof of the place." Quan takes over, still eyeing the IV tube. "Yet here's something used to drain corpses during the embalming process, and there's an address staring back at us."

Sunny offers the wristband to me. "More than an address. Rune's name is on that dang thing. And there's a time and date. A month from now . . . two days before Halloween. This isn't no hospital identity bracelet. It's an invitation for a pickup. You've been tagged." She presses my fingers around the plastic band, then slips out of our circle wearing an expression that wavers between concern and curiosity.

Every muscle in my body tenses as I glance at the clear tubing now dangling from Quan's hand, unable to look away from the red droplets clinging to the inside.

My name bleeding across an infant's grave, and now written on an invitation to a morgue.

What's it mean? That I'm tagged for death? My blood runs cold.

I study the cardboard cutout that Quan kicked out of the way so he could shut the door when he came back earlier. The Phantom would've already taken me if he wanted to harm me, right? And he wouldn't be helping me with my music if he had bad intentions, would he?

In the chapel, we connected on some indescribable level. He showed me his memories; he felt like *home.*

Audrey touches my elbow. I flinch.

"Hey, you okay?" she asks. "You're as white as a ghost."

"She has reason to be scared." Sunny's standing next to my pile of dirty clothes, holding up my bloody shirt. "Rune, it's time you're straight with us. What really happened today?"

I'm rescued by a knock at the door and Bouchard's voice, rounding everyone up for dinner in the atrium.

14

ROMANCING THE ABYSS

"If you gaze long enough into an abyss,
the abyss will gaze back into you."
Friedrich Nietzsche

At dinner, I sit with my friends, since my aunt hasn't yet returned from Versailles. I tell them enough to give them the illusion that they're my confidants, but not enough to put them in danger. I can only imagine how it would go if I confessed: "I might be a monster, though I'm not sure what kind." Or, "I might be under a gypsy curse, and that's why my grandma tried to kill me." Or, the best one of all: "The Phantom is real, and he's helping me master the music that has possessed me since I was four years old."

Yeah, none of that would get me sent home for a psych evaluation.

This whole thing has become too unfathomable, like the premise to a horror movie. So once again, I elaborate on the truth: that I suspect I'm being pranked—the torn uniforms and cut-up roses (their blood remains my secret), the dead bird, and the wristband—but I have no proof who's behind it, and until I do, the teachers will think I'm lying after my earlier confession. I convince my friends to support my claim that the cat found my bag of uniforms and tore up my clothes.

They agree, but only once I promise I'm not going to use the wristband. They reiterate that the rave scene is known for drugs, and they've all sworn off getting high out of respect for what happened to Audrey's sister.

Sunny, however, still wants us to go to the pickup address and see who comes. She won't let it drop until I finally pretend to toss the wristband into the trash in the atrium at breakfast on Sunday; unbeknownst to any of them, it was a sleight of hand trick, and I still have the band.

I can't throw away the opportunity without thinking things through. As far as being seduced by the rave club world, it would appear I already have the upper hand in seduction . . . just ask Ben, if he ever wakes up.

While everyone heads back to their rooms to do homework, I search the orchestra pit and find that the message and book I left for the Phantom the prior day are gone. My reaction fluctuates between apprehension and anticipation. The rest of Sunday afternoon, I hole up in my dorm with a borrowed sewing machine, piecing together my uniforms with embellishments and scraps until they look more bohemian chic than Victorian. All the while I wonder if the Phantom will contact me—if it was a mistake to reach out to him.

I don't have to wait long to find out. That night, with Diable curled at my feet, my maestro's violin music drifts down from the vent over my bed. I take comfort that the metal slats are on a downward slant. No one could see me anywhere else in the room other than when I'm lying in bed. Maybe that knowledge shouldn't make me feel safer, yet when combined with the ballad he's playing on that familiar violin, it soothes me to sleep.

Each consecutive day over the next four weeks, I stand at the edge of the abyss and stare it down, unfazed by my growing attachment to him, seeing myself come alive within his provocative shadow. During rehearsals, and while the opera plays in the cafeteria on the big screens, I never once lose control. The moment any of Renata's solos light my mind on fire, all I have to do is surrender to my maestro's violin, reimagine it from my dreams—see his shadow inside the mirrors around me—and he douses my operatic compulsion in a cerebral flourish of strings and steam.

Every night, he's back behind the vents, playing whatever song plagued me that day, and because I fall asleep humming the melody alongside him, it satisfies any need to purge the music when I wake up. At last, I'm in control and at peace, other than the desire to see him face-to-face, and not just as a pair of flashing copper eyes in my dreams.

Even when we share our fantasy dances—like the one onstage—spinning together in the center of my room, I can't see anything but his silhouette. But, I can smell his scent as I nuzzle his clothes, hear his raspy humming next to my ear, feel the calluses on his fingers—traits of an accomplished violinist that remind me of my dad—as he holds my right hand in his left. And I have to wonder if he's smiling like me.

Those nightly interludes always end with a Fire and Ice rose cradled in my fingers, materializing out of thin air in the instant his hand fades from my clasp. I place each flower in the vase beside my bed with the others I've accumulated. Then, my chest aglow, I close my eyes to embrace whatever new insights the Phantom imprinted upon me when our spirits touched: A mother who adored him and played piggies with his toes to warm them when they were cold; dolls made of the simplest things, such as twigs, leaves, and empty spools; a black car settling like a cloud over his childhood, taking his mother away forever, and leaving him orphaned.

The car is yet another layer to his ever-evolving mystique. If he's a centuries-old creature, he wouldn't have seen cars in his childhood. And his name was Etalon then, not Erik, as he's known in the stories.

I'm beginning to have my doubts if anything in the literary version is correct. If I could only see his disfigured face, I would know. But I never do, because in every instance, I'm watching his past through his eyes.

Which leaves me curious . . . as his memories become my own, do mine become his? Is it possible he knows all my secrets, all my childhood experiences, hopes, and wishes?

Not once, when we're together, does he mention the note I left in the orchestra pit, or the gift I gave him. But there's no question he received it, because when he does speak aloud—in that broken, raw voice that is more achingly poignant than anything I've ever heard—it's to deliver quiet excerpts in perfect French from our fairy tale.

Those moments are the most peaceful of all, for both of us. I sense the quiet calm inside him with every word. It's that serene bubble encapsulating us that prevents me from asking the questions I've been plagued by: Why did you cut up my uniforms? Why did you place the dead bird in my chair? Why is Diable my shadow now? How old are you? *What are we?*

One night, while I'm snuggled beneath my covers in bed, listening to him read, the ache to have him sitting beside me in reality grows too intense and I can't keep from bursting through the bubble.

"Etalon."

There's a sharp intake of air and he grows silent, as if my speaking his childhood name shocks him.

I roll over, facing the vent in the wall, stretch my arm, and push my pinky between the slats. The warmth of his fingertip touches mine back. I gasp as a spark passes between us, shocking in spite of how slight the pressure.

Riding the wave of sensation, I find my voice. "Tell me something about you in the present. I only know you from your memories. Do you have a hobby?" It feels strange, asking such a simple question to someone who might've been alive for centuries.

His fingertip drops from mine. A few minutes pass. He becomes so quiet, I'm afraid he's left. But then his clothes rustle, and he answers. "I tend the animals of the forest. I suppose you could say I'm their . . . doctor."

I smile in the darkness, envisioning him caring for the wild creatures no one else would ever give a passing thought to. It makes perfect sense for such a quiet soul. He's so much like them, hidden away and asking nothing from anyone but to let him survive. Like me, with the plants and flowers I love. "I think that's beautiful," I whisper.

A soft grunt breaks the following hush and there's sadness in it.

Scooting closer to the vent, I brave asking another question. "You said we're the same. I think I knew that before you even told me. But I still don't know what we are . . . or how I got this way."

"You were born into it. It's in your bloodline. Look back through your family's history."

I grow silent, frustrated that his answers are always so cryptic. Why can't he just give me details? I'm not ready to let him off that easy. "Why did you give me an invitation to the club? Will you be there? Can we finally see each other if I go?" If I can just be with him, face-to-face, I can get the answers to everything I've been dying to ask.

His breath seems labored. He's torn . . . aching to be sitting beside me, too, wanting to be forthcoming, but something is holding him back. Instead of him answering me, his violin whispers through the vent—a hypnotic melody. And although I try to fight it, the song lulls me to sleep.

I want to be angry when I wake up and find him gone in the morning, but the mental intimacies we share, however unusual, always leave me stronger, always help me find my footing. Because of him, I no longer have to worry about bulldozing over anyone at the final auditions that are on the horizon.

So I choose to be grateful for whatever moments he can offer.

During our daily rehearsals, Madame Bouchard seems as annoyed by my newfound silence as she was by my unplanned outbursts. At times, she even tries to goad me into breaking down by cranking Renata's arias full blast in the background. When I don't react, it seems to unsettle her. Then, when she forces me to sing for a grade, and I manage the songs without fading or weakening, she's just as upset. It's as if no matter what I do, it's not what she expects or wants.

I don't let it get to me, because my control has given Audrey the confidence she was lacking. And with my own growing abilities, I'm able to offer her tips for reaching that final note with a more consistent flow of air and forward consonant delivery. Almost four weeks have passed since the chapel incident, and now Audrey's nailing her part like a pro. All she lacks is the intensity and hysteria that the role demands, which Kat hasn't quite mastered herself. This puts them on level ground, and Audrey has a real chance of claiming the lead at the upcoming final audition on Sunday.

Even though I've chosen not to try out for any roles, the fact that I'm helping Audrey with her technique lands me back in Kat and Roxie's bad graces.

Thursday, during lunch break, they decide teasing me about my "homespun uniforms" isn't enough for them anymore.

Kat steps into the bathroom as I'm washing my hands. She opens her purse on the counter, digging through her makeup.

I try to hurry, not because it's her, but because I'm uncomfortable being alone with anyone now. Even on our day trips to Paris the previous three weekends, I was careful to always be with the group, or by myself—like when I left everyone long enough to purchase gray and black yarn and emoticon appliques for my newest knitting project.

I'm making toe socks for the Phantom, in honor of how he used to draw faces on his toes and play puppets when he was little to distract himself from holey stockings and lack of friends. Maybe it's a silly gift for a guy, but I want his toes to never be cold again. I want him to never feel alone again. I'll do whatever I can to thank him for giving me my power back. Because of his help, I'm in control of the music and can appear normal.

The downside, though, is now I know without a doubt that I'm the furthest thing from it. I'm different. Understanding I'm not the only one like me makes it easier to swallow, but I have to take precautions to keep others safe until I can make sense of who I am. *What* I am.

Kat clears her throat while applying strokes of silvery eye shadow that brighten her icy-blue irises. "So, rumor has it you and the

Phantom are hooking up every night," she says, her voice laced with innuendo.

I pause—soggy, apricot-scented soapsuds dripping from my hands onto the sink's edge. The accusation levels me. Although it's obviously a dig at the "supposed" sighting I had upon my arrival, and my virtue or lack thereof, she's hitting too close to the truth for comfort. I tug a paper towel from the dispenser, buying myself a second to compose. *Be ambiguous . . . ignore the paranormal crack; that's what a normal person who isn't singing duets every night with a phantom would do.*

"As if there's time for hooking up with anyone around here," I manage. My voice comes out steadier than I feel—a side effect of the sarcasm I inject into the response.

"Methinks Rune doth protest too boisterously." Roxie surprises me, stepping out of a stall behind us.

I glare at both of them in the mirror's reflection, slightly relieved I'm not alone with Kat, but unwilling to let them see anything that could be construed as weakness. I toss the paper towel in the trash. Conquering my musical demons has given me a new perspective. If the diva duo is going to stop tormenting me and my friends, I can't play victim anymore.

"Should've known this was a tag-team event," I accuse.

"Aw, come on," Roxie says, brushing past me to flip on a faucet. "We just figured you must've found a very special voice coach, considering . . ."

"Considering . . . ," I repeat like a ventriloquist dummy.

"How you suddenly seem to have control over your 'stage fright.' Unless maybe it's the kitty giving you voice lessons," Katarina adds, a wicked grin on her pouty mouth. "That would explain the gift you left him. Payment, right?" She fluffs up her honey tresses, tucking a red barrette into one side to bring out the color of the tie at her collar.

Everyone has noticed Diable's recent devotion to me; he even sits at my feet during class, in the instances when the teachers are chill enough to accommodate him. So there's nothing new there. No, Kat's referring to something else entirely.

I turn on my heel and prop my hip against the counter to face her. The sudsy water I spilled earlier seeps into the ruffles stitched along the side seam of my uniform, chilling my skin. An ice-cold splash of fear rushes through my spine, as if following in the water's wake. What if she and Roxie saw my note and gift for the Phantom in the orchestra pit before he found them?

Roxie rubs her hands under the faucet's stream. "Then again, maybe it wasn't his payment. Maybe Rune was saving it for dessert. Crow brulee is the perfect complement to chicken rolls." I flinch as she flutters her wet hands in my face like wings, an obvious allusion to the dead bird on my chair in the cafeteria a month ago.

It's a relief they didn't stumble upon my secret, but why bring up the bird now, so many weeks after the fact? I swipe droplets of water from my forehead, wondering how they know about that event at all. Unless . . .

"Jackson confronted me the other day," Roxie says before the suspicion fully forms in my mind. She pumps soap into her palm. "Asked if I was the one who put the crow in your chair. If I made coleslaw of your uniforms and gave you some fake invitation to the morgue club. Imagine that. My own twin, having so little faith in me. Because I guarantee, if I wanted to scare you, I'd come up with something way more creative. As you already know." She rinses and dries her hands.

I scoff, tempted to tell her that the mannequin prank is nothing compared to what I've encountered since, or to what I've done myself before I came here. Instead, I dole out more sarcasm. "Yep. Definitely fraternal. There's no way you and Jax are from the same egg."

At the mirror, Kat coughs a laugh, nearly smearing the coating of gloss she's brushing on her lips. She turns all her attention to Roxie, wearing a strange expression. "She's got ya there, Rox. As much as you and your bro look alike, you could never be identical . . . not in the ways that really count. Too bad for us, huh?" The eight-minute warning bell rings and she leaves without a backward glance.

I consider her parting jab at her friend—how it seemed to drip with double meaning.

Roxie stares herself down in the mirror, raking a hand through her shimmery platinum crop. Her brown eyes flash inside their black liner and mascara . . . or maybe they're tearing up.

Ever since I've been spending time with the Phantom, I've been letting myself notice the colored halos around my classmates' heads and bodies. The ones I used to force myself not to see. And after researching auras on my phone during a couple of the Paris trips, I have a sense of what emotions the colors portray.

While I'm studying Roxie in the mirror, her halo shifts from a feminine, affectionate pink to a depressed and gloomy gray, and a hypothesis starts to form.

I stand there awkwardly, battling a bout of unexpected sympathy. "Does Kat know how you feel?"

"How I feel about what?" Roxie slides her harsh gaze to mine in the mirror.

"Never mind." Obviously this girl and I aren't tight enough to ever share any secrets. "Look, we don't have to be enemies. I want to get along with both of you. But you're making it personal."

"You made it personal," she seethes. "You had to go and help Audrey. If Kat ends up as the understudy, she'll walk away from the entire opera and sign up for sets. She has too much pride to play second fiddle to anyone."

"That's her ego trip, and her issue," I say.

Roxie grinds her teeth. "You know what your problem is? You're from Podunk Texas and you've never lived in the entertainment world. Kat has grown up saturated in opera and is expected to be the next"—her fingers form air quotes for emphasis—"'*Christina: world-renowned prodigy.*' That's a lot of pressure from her family. A talent scout is coming to our performance at the end of the year . . . they're planning to offer two scholarships for la Schola Cantorum Conservatory in Paris. One girl and one boy recipient. This is something she's been working for since she was in grade school. Then you come in without any training . . . all freaky savant who wants to upstage everyone. Yeah, as Kat's bestie, I'm gonna get in your face. Unlike my brother, who claims to be crazy about Audrey but doesn't care if you crash her hopes and dreams, I'm loyal to the ones I lo—" She stops herself short, her delicate features flashing bright red.

Clamping her mouth shut, she slams her paper towel into the trash and walks out.

The five-minute bell rings, but I don't move. Finally, their animosity makes sense. Kat thinks I'm going to steal her shot at a scholarship. Whereas Audrey needs it more than any of us. And Roxie . . . she's crushing on her best friend, who keeps her on the side as a plaything, but is ultimately in lust with her twin brother.

This place isn't just an opera house, it's an *opera:* unrequited love, jealous rivals, eccentric personalities, stalkers, sabotage, and vandalism.

And last but not least: mortals pitted against monsters.

Taking one last look at myself in the mirror—black, wild hair that ties me to Dad like my possessed musical performances once did; eyes the same color as Mom's but that see things no one else can; cursed, gypsy blood like Grandma's—I have to wonder: on which side do I belong?

There's only one way to know for sure.

To earn this week's Saturday trip to Paris with my classmates, I've been diligent with my gardening duties during the two-hour span between helping Madame Fabre with the costumes for the lesser roles and dinner. I haven't missed a single day, despite that the weather has decided to be fickle again.

Friday after classes, I talk to Mom on the landline for a few minutes and finish reading a letter I received from Trig and Janine. Then I make my way out to do some weeding, trying not to think about Ben. He's fully conscious now, but has amnesia. I chide myself for finding peace in that.

It rained most of the morning, and soggy leaves drip water softly around me. The wet scent of foliage tastes refreshing on the back of my tongue. Invigorating, in spite of the clouds. My dark mood lifts as I weave my way across the parking lot and find the dead roses left in the Phantom's wake staring back at me.

Ever since I first saw them drained of life, I've been tempted to touch them, as if the ailing blooms and shrinking stems were calling to me, but my insecurities always stopped me. Today, I notice halos of blackish-gray light surrounding them.

Dad used to say all organic things have auras . . . even plants and animals. But I thought these roses were dead. Somehow, they're still giving off life energy. So, maybe they're only dormant.

I glance over my shoulder, assuring I'm out of view of the academy . . . hidden behind brambles and vines. I take off my gardening gloves and wrap my fingers around a rose's crinkled, soggy head. At first, the bud feels cold and empty. A lifeless hull. Then, a thrumming sensation shakes through the petals, originating from the roots in the ground and trembling under my boot soles.

Instinctually, I start to hum, drawing off an ability I've suppressed for years, ever since Dad died and music became a parasite. I hum like I used to when we gardened together. I hum like I do each night now, when it's just my maestro and me alone in my room, calming and hypnotic. My song coaxes the earth's heartbeat into the rosebush; my vocal cords become tributaries, channeling the life beneath the soil into the roots, stems, and leaves.

By the time the final note leaves my vocal cords, a deep red, edged with burgundy so velvety it's almost black, bleeds into the petals as they soften inside my hand. The spiky leaves unfurl from their coiled and withered stasis, plumping to a vivid green, as if a rush of chlorophyll races through them. The stems stand tall, and the scent shifts in one breath, from musty and decayed to a fresh perfume.

I step back, staring in disbelief as every rose lifts its head and displays a halo of crimson light, the entire bush in full bloom. A memory comes back to me, quiet and soft: Dad bringing me outside when I was six, showing me how to use my music to revive the wilted places in our garden.

He knew . . . *he knew I was different and he cultivated it.*

In a daze, I gather my gardening tools and head for the footbridge, drawn by an irresistible compulsion to search for my maestro in the chapel, to get the answers he has—no more waiting. Each time I've attempted to find him there over the past few weeks, Mister Jippetto has been in the cemetery, repairing tombstones that were damaged during the storms, raking leaves, and pulling up weeds. A few times I heard him trilling that bird whistle, and down came several wrens. It seems to work like a dog whistle, because every time I see him outside, he has flocks of his feathered friends following him.

Even when I couldn't see or hear him, a couple of his mannequins were always propped against the side of the chapel with his wheelbarrow, as if standing guard. Their presence prevented me from venturing past the footbridge and kept me on the garden side, on the chance he'd return.

But today, I'm more determined than ever. And since he's nowhere in sight, and neither are his mannequins, I slip into the chapel unnoticed. Sunlight slants through the jagged stained glass, painting the walls. I shut the door behind me. There's enough of a dim haze to see I'm alone. A niggle of disappointment winds through me, but I continue toward the baptismal, led by Jax's claim that it's always been bone dry.

When I lean over the edge to study the basin, it's exactly as he said. Even more confusing, the bottom stops at around four feet. Not consistent with my experience in the endless depths of water.

As uneasy as that makes me, it could be chalked up to one of the Phantom's architectural illusions. He's famous in the stories for crafting escape hatches and hideaway places. If he could construct an entire palace in Persia with sophisticated traps and torture devices, he could make a false bottom in a well that would open, and once triggered, fill with water.

Still rocking on the restless waves of my discovery about Dad and myself, I'm about to turn and leave when I see something on the floor where shadows drape the other side of the baptismal. It's cardboard, the size of a shirt box, and wrapped with violin string. Using my gardening sheers to pry free the strands, I pop off the lid.

Phosphorescent blue light greets my eyes and brightens the chapel, pulsating. It's fabric. Lifting out and opening the silky folds reveals a sleeveless, knee-length fitted dress made of shear stretchy mesh—the color of my skin. On the bodice, fiber-optic panels—like galaxies of tiny blinking blue stars—crisscross in the shape of a corset, then plunge down to the hem in the front and lower back, covering all of the appropriate places and leaving the sides and upper back see-through.

The flashing panels remind me of Professor Diamond Tomlin's room . . . on those nights when an eerie orange glimmer throbs beneath his door, when he's doing his science experiments.

Confused about the gift, I search inside the box. A Fire and Ice rose waits within, and an envelope secured with a red wax skull resembling its metal counterpart on our dorm keys. Snapping off the seal, I pull out a note, written in the same tiny, neat script as the address on the wristband invitation:

Dearest Rune,

Thank you for the fairy tale. You brought my maman back to me when I needed her most. I want to do the same for you, with the father who taught you to sing and garden when you were a child. Follow the invitation's instructions and meet me at the club tomorrow night. Wear this dress, and I will find you.

O.G. (Opera Ghost)

A thrilling rush of butterflies fills my stomach as I imagine my maestro's raspy, deep voice speaking those words in his French accent . . . his calloused fingertips and strong hands folding the dress and wrapping the package for me.

He called himself O.G.

Opera Ghost.

Maybe he no longer uses his given name, Etalon, because it stirs up too many painful childhood experiences. Recently, in one of his memories, I learned that his vocal cords were cruelly damaged when he was young, and that's why his voice is broken.

Somewhere, another epiphany wants to struggle loose about the initials "O.G." and what they stand for—but I'm too preoccupied with his words about my father to give anything else my attention. I return the glowing fabric to its box and walk back to the academy, my mind spinning at the depth of our connection, now confirmed. Just as my maestro's memories are on a frequency I can now some-how reach, the same is true of mine for him. He knows that I lost my dad at a young age, and that I've always wished we'd had more time together. But even as powerful as the Phantom seems, how can he ever give Dad back to me?

It doesn't matter. The slightest possibility is enough to warm my heart with hope. I'm going to that rave club . . . even if it means deceiving my friends and all the teachers, even if it means meet-ing the Phantom alone inside a morgue full of demonic creatures mingling with mankind.

I can no longer fight the dark intuition that I'll fit right in . . . that it's where I've belonged from the very beginning.

15

MIRRORS

"No one has more thirst for earth, for blood . . .
than the creatures who inhabit cold mirrors."
Alejandra Pizarnik

This morning, when everyone left RoseBlood, I told my friends I'd decided to spend the day with Aunt Charlotte in Versailles. Two reasons: One, I wanted to use the Internet at the library across from the prison for research. The Phantom's cryptic answer when I asked what I am and how I got that way keeps haunting me:

"You were born into it. It's in your bloodline. Look back through your family's history."

And the second reason I wanted to come with Aunt Charlotte?

I have a plan for sneaking away to that rave club tonight, and it hinges on my friends thinking I'm with my aunt, and her thinking I'm with them in Paris. But the latter part of my plan has to wait until I can make sense of what I'm seeing on the glowing computer screen in front of me.

All it took was searching the Internet with three key words: *Germain + France + strange power*. So many entries popped up, each one touting the weird and inexplicable immortal life of Comte de Saint-Germain. I knew I was onto something immediately, because Dad's middle name was Saint, to honor the original hyphenated surname from generations earlier. It's a family tradition, passed down through the years, for each firstborn son to have the designation.

The clicking of keyboards and shuffle of pages around me become nothing but white noise as I choose an entry and read. Hand gripped around the mouse, I scroll down, afraid to miss anything: *Saint-Germain traversed France in the 1700s, and had a reputation for never aging. He adored wine . . . but was only vaguely interested in food. He had a fascination with mirrors . . . insisted they were the portals to other worlds. He knew twelve languages. Managed to out-philosophize the philosopher Voltaire, whom he befriended. He also developed sleight-of-hand tricks beyond what most magicians would even dare conceive to try. And he had the uncanny ability to impress his desires upon people, without them being the wiser. With this talent, he befriended dukes and kings. His closest friend was a Parisian emperor who built and owned the opera house Le Théâtre Liminaire. Saint-Germain spent many an evening there, socializing with royalty.*

My breath catches on that last detail, locking the scent of carpet and old books inside me. *Liminaire* . . . the building where I attend classes every day. Where I *live*. My ancestor used to frequent Rose-Blood's halls when it was an opera house long ago.

I look around the room in search of Aunt Charlotte. She was on the other side of the table earlier, checking the school's email.

I don't see her now, but my gaze veers back to the computer of its own accord.

Saint-Germain used his many connections to accrue great wealth in the form of gems and jewels. He stashed it away, keeping only what he needed to travel. His life was an unending quest for knowledge. He imbibed it, as if it gave him the energy to stay youthful and sharp-minded. It was said he died in 1784, but there were alleged sightings of him still alive and youthful all the way into the 1900s.

"Rune." Aunt Charlotte's voice breaks the silence behind me. I let out a startled yelp and click the *X* to close the page. I turn and try to hide my trembling hands by tucking them into my tunic's pockets.

"*Pardon!* I didn't mean to frighten you." She pats the white bun at her nape and nods an apology to the librarian in the corner who's now glaring at us. "What were you looking at so intently?" Her hazel eyes scan my face, as if they're digging into my soul.

I swallow hard and study her with equal intensity. "Nothing, really."

She squints beneath her glasses. "I hope you know, *ma douce,* you can talk to me about anything. About the music that has plagued you . . . about how it no longer seems to hold you in its thrall. It is wonderful, the strides you've made since you've been here. But if you are still having trouble, with anything, you can tell me. Or any questions to ask? You can trust me."

Can I? Where was she when my dad was sick? She didn't even take the time to come to the States when we buried him. And now, she's dragged me to Paris to appease her insane and homicidal mother's dying wishes. So, no. I don't really think I can trust her.

What could she possibly know that would help anyway? Compared to the other teachers here, Aunt Charlotte is so normal she borders on boring. I've been eating dinner with her three nights a week since Mom left. Our conversations range from my grade-point average to if I'm sleeping well at night and waking up refreshed. *Refreshed.* Who even says that? Stilted, awkward conversations that go nowhere. If there is some strange affliction I've inherited from our ancestor, Comte de Saint-Germain, it passed my aunt by. There's no glow to her eyes. There never has been. I've also never seen anything strange about her auras. But then again, I am new at reading them . . .

My cell phone vibrates inside my beaded tote. I drag it out, careful not to let my aunt see the clothes and makeup I have stashed inside. I open the text. It's Sunny responding to my message. I told her I had to escape Aunt Charlotte . . . that my aunt was being a helicopter and I wanted time alone to check out the Palace of Versailles. So I needed to lie and say I'd be with my friends, then asked if she'd cover for me.

Curfew is ten o'clock. I promised Sunny I'd get back before that, early enough that she can watch for my arrival and sneak me in. I wanted to be sure no one at RoseBlood will pay for my dishonesty, including Aunt Charlotte.

I bite my lip, pretending to read a long message that's nothing more than a thumbs-up emoticon from Sunny. I stand. "Look, Aunt Charlotte . . . I hate to ditch you, but I know you're going to visit Grandma Lil anyway."

She frowns and nods for me to continue.

"Sunny and a few classmates want me to meet them in Paris to buy our Halloween costumes for the masquerade on Monday. We'll hang out the rest of the day in the city." It's an outright lie. Unbeknownst to my aunt, we bought our costumes two weekends ago. My friends would go ballistic if they knew what I was really planning, even more so if they knew I used them to do it. "It's just, it feels weird, to be so close to the prison. The memories of the fire . . . it's like I can smell the smoke from here."

Aunt Charlotte winces, and I know I've hit a nerve. It's deplorable, to use her shame over Grandma Liliana's crimes to my advantage . . . to make it impossible for her to refuse me. Yet it doesn't stop me from asking for her Paris metro pass so I'll have unlimited access to the city, or leaving her to buy herself a new ticket so she can get back to the academy later this evening.

My stomach churns, the guilt overwhelming as she digs in her bag for the pass and also pulls out seventy euros. "This should be enough for lunch, dinner, and the costume." As I start to take it, she holds the money between us, like a bridge she's reluctant to break. "I need you to assure me you will stay with a group of friends the entire time. Do not venture anywhere alone. It's dangerous." Her whitish-gray eyebrows furrow. "Your mother would never forgive me, were you to end up in trouble."

I make the promise, although I know it's a lie.

❄·l·❄

It's 6:05 p.m., and I'm in Paris on a deserted street corner, waiting for some nameless car to escort me blindfolded to an undisclosed location.

I have to wonder how many missing persons reports start with this premise.

The sunset hangs low and the air chills, scented with mildewing mortar. Lavender and apricot hues soften the glimpses of sky between buildings. Stagnant puddles glimmer in inky spills at every curb.

The wristband itches on my arm like poison ivy, as if to demonstrate that I've chosen the toxic path. I can't shake the image of the taxi driver's disapproving face when he dropped me here alone a few minutes ago, an obvious inference that he knew I was in over my head.

What am I doing?

An icy tremor radiates from my spine to my limbs in answer. I should have sense enough to call back the taxi; I should get myself out of this situation before it turns into a full-blown mistake with irreparable consequences. I would, if my plan hadn't fallen into place so seamlessly—like a cosmic sign I'm doing the right thing.

My tote's strap eats into my shoulder. I cinch it higher, trying not to think about the jeans and tunic tucked inside, the fiber-optic dress I'm wearing in their place now hidden under my hooded gray trench coat and clinging to my every curve, or the nude underthings I'm glad I brought from Texas—being the only ones that don't show through the shear fabric.

In any other situation, these surroundings would be a tourist's haven: the damp brick streets and abandoned buildings surrounding a cathedral-style church—pillars emblazoned with carved ornamentation and drainage pipes topped with gargoyles frowning down at me. I feel as if I've fallen into the pages of Victor Hugo's romantic gothic novel, *The Hunchback of Notre-Dame*.

I glance again at the clock on my phone. Twenty more minutes, and my ride will be here for the 6:30 pickup.

I shudder and draw my hood tighter around my face. Logic tells me I should be afraid. But I can't stop thinking about all the hours I've spent with my maestro, how I no longer fear what he hides beneath his mask. How I've seen his soul written upon the pages of his past, and it's beautiful.

He wants me at that club enough that he gave me a starlit dress, and I'm going to be there. I'll be there so he can tell me what he knows of *my* past—and my father. So he can fill in that missing piece to the puzzle of my identity.

Since the age of four, I've been singing as if possessed. I've waited thirteen years to understand. I'm ready to face everything. *Anything.* As long as it's the truth.

That courageous thought shrinks to a cowardly whimper in my throat at the glimpse of headlights rounding the corner on the north side of the cathedral. It's too far to make out the car color or model. If this is my ride, why's the driver fifteen minutes early?

An urge to run sends a jolt all the way to my legs, but I think better of it. I wouldn't get far in my stiletto ankle boots—the only fashionable, pewter-toned footwear I could find earlier on my shopping spree to complement the shear fabric of my dress and the pearly surface of my tote.

The surroundings have dimmed enough for streetlamps to blink on, illuminating halos of amber dust around the bulbs. I roll up my trench coat's cuff to showcase my wristband, proof that I should be here. The closer the car gets, the more details come into view. My feet twitch on the cobblestone . . . debating whether to start walking the opposite direction, or leap in as soon as the door opens.

It's a taxi, and it stops in front of the church, some twenty feet away. I engage in a stare down with the windshield, hoping to see who's driving before deciding my next move, but the beaming headlights make it impossible.

Going to the rave via public transportation doesn't make sense, if the location is to be kept secret. Cautiously, I start toward the car, only to stall as both back doors open. Sunny and Quan step out from the right side, and Jax from the other.

My throat drains of moisture. Jax leans in and pays the driver, then they all start toward me—dressed in bright and glowing clothes.

Rave wear.

"You can't be serious," I mumble, loud enough to snap Sunny's eyes to mine as Quan helps her step up onto the sidewalk in her furry, platform neon-green boots.

"Dang right we're serious," she growls.

Within moments they're all beside me on the cobblestone, glancing over their shoulders as the driver disappears around the corner.

Jax's features pulse from shadowy to bright, an effect of the LED green alien head on his shirt fading and appearing with his movements, keeping time with the light-up soles on his black tennis shoes.

"Well, there's no going back now," Quan says, somewhere between a sigh and a groan. Beneath the fluorescent-orange cowboy hat perched crookedly at his brow, his face looks as pensive and uncomfortable as Jax's. It's obvious who's behind this raid.

Sunny has me in her sights again, but my gaze keeps flitting unintentionally to the top of her head. A fiber-optic wig covers her hair and vacillates between colors for a rainbow effect—the perfect match to her sexy minidress, adorned with strands of glow-in-the-dark fabric paint swirling along the contours of her body.

I inhale a shallow breath, drowning in the combination of her cherry blossom body spray and the guys' mix of colognes. Before I can think of anything to say, Sunny unties my coat's belt and whips the flaps open, slipping off my hood in the process.

I cup my hands over my hair, an attempt to hide my upswept curls. They took a quarter of an hour to pin in place after I heightened my makeup to nightclub proportions in a posh boutique's dressing room.

Sunny forces my hands down so I have nowhere to hide.

"Whoa," both boys say in unison, as my dress's fiber-optic panels reflect off their stunned expressions in blue flashes.

"Dayum. You clean up *nice*, Rune." Jax offers an approving whistle, reminding me how tempting his flirty nature is when it comes out to play—a perilous observation I shouldn't be making. "What I want to know is, who are you cleaning up fo—"

"I told ya." Sunny interrupts, thankfully. "You both thought I imagined the glowing dress in the box. Now who's pecking at gravel in the chicken feed?"

The guys exchange chagrined glances.

Frowning, I cinch the trench coat in place over my dress, retying the belt. "How . . . *what are you doing here?*"

Sunny's freckles seem to darken, that masklike visage apparent even beneath the thick coating of makeup on her face. "Ain't no way in hell we were gonna let you do this all alone."

Jax sighs. "She lifted your key when you weren't looking last night and took a picture of your wristband in your room. She made us replicas with leftover props from last year's fall performance of *One Flew Over the Cuckoo's Nest*. Some of the juniors played mental patients."

They hold out their right arms, displaying matching wristbands, a similar translucent style to mine. Every written word on the labels mimics the words I've already memorized, other than the name. Instead, each bracelet is individualized to them, making it appear they've all been tagged like me. Sunny did a masterful job of forging the handwriting.

"So . . . you were onto me?" I direct the question to Sunny's smug grin. "When I faked throwing it away?" I don't even give her the chance to answer because everything starts falling into place. "Wait. That's where you were during dinner last night. When you got stuck in the bathroom for ten minutes with a wardrobe malfunction. You were actually in my *room*." Heat blooms in my cheeks. I want to lash out. She violated my privacy. But it was out of concern for me.

"Well, the wardrobe part wasn't a complete lie," Sunny corrects, humility softening her voice, proving she knows she crossed a line. "While I was looking for the wristband, I saw the box you carried back after gardening yesterday, so I peeked under the lid. I'm guessing you found that in the chapel, too, along with those dozen roses in that vase on your nightstand. Because we all know those roses aren't anywhere here at RoseBlood. Am I right?"

I have no answer. At least I'd hidden the Phantom's note. This girl is way more resourceful and devious than I ever gave her credit for. A burst of affection warms me against the cool air.

How could I have thought leaving home and coming to France would mean never having friends again? Sunny and her crew have had my back from the day I arrived almost six weeks ago. I care about each one of them. Which is why I won't let them do this.

"You can't come with me . . ." I attempt.

"Sure we can," Sunny responds, unfazed. "We got the bracelets and spent half the day getting the clothes, thanks to Jax's Master-Card. So why can't we?"

"So many reasons." *The biggest one being I don't know what kind of monsters might be there. What kind of monster I am, myself. Saint-Germain was definitely not human.* "I—I can't protect you," I blurt before thinking.

"Protect us?" Quan responds, tugging at the brim of his cowboy hat. "Kind of think that's mine and Jax's job, little lady," he drawls.

"Unless you two are scairt now and want to change your minds?" His dark, puppy eyes, exaggerated Texas accent, and slightly off-kilter smile are adorable. I'm not sure how Sunny manages to resist him, though I suspect he wins his fair share, considering how often I've caught them making out in the ballet room behind the stage.

Jax snorts. "Fat chance of changing this one's mind." He tilts his head toward Sunny. "Audrey was tough enough." His attention settles on me. "She wanted to come along if we went through with it. Despite what her private trainer said about staying indoors at night to preserve her voice."

I chew my inner cheek, remembering this morning when I witnessed the end of an argument between Audrey and Sunny just before we left. Audrey had already told us that she'd be going back to the academy early with some of the juniors who had finals and needed to study. She didn't want to stay out past late afternoon . . . that's how dedicated she is to landing Renata's role tomorrow at the audition.

To think she'd planned to sacrifice that for me makes me feel even worse. The muscles in my neck knot with tension.

Sunny glares at Jax. "You wouldn't have let Audrey come anyway, Mr. Guardian Angel," she scoffs, adjusting the magenta, orange, and black-checked flannel shirt half covering Quan's purple tank. A bluish-white angler fish is airbrushed across the dark knit. Neither the over-shirt nor the tank's designs glow like the rest of our clothes, but they'll definitely stand out under black lights.

"I don't *own* her . . . but I wouldn't have liked it," Jax answers Sunny while glaring at me, his bright-blue eyes accusatory. "And I don't like Rune going, either. Or the rest of us. This is all too weird and risky."

You don't know the half of it.

"What is it with you guys?" Sunny snuggles up to Quan, coaxing his arms around her. "Come on, Moonpie. We always wanted to see if this place is real."

"That was last year, when we were idiot juniors," he counters without pulling away, obviously enjoying her attention but not willing to give up the fight. "What about the puncture marks on people's wrists and ankles?" He traces the freckles on her face. "Are you so curious, you're willing to break our promise to Audrey about steering clear of drugs?"

"Aw, come on. There isn't any proof that those are needle tracks," Sunny answers with a pout. "If there even are puncture marks. Other than a few flaky pictures online, there's nothing legit, like police or doctor reports. I get the feeling all of it's nut-buck. But if it makes you feel better, I brought bottled water and granola bars in my bag. We won't eat or drink nothing there. I've got this covered."

The nervous kinks in my neck spread to my shoulders, my concern metastasizing by the second. I attempt to focus on Sunny's face instead of her wig's fiber-optic acrobatics. "Look, what makes you think the driver will take all of us? He probably has a passenger manifest or something . . . some way to know how many people he's supposed to pick up. As good as you are at snooping, I doubt you're the first one to ever come up with this trick."

"She's got ya there, Sunspot." Quan steps back and takes out his phone, punching the keypad on his screen. "Let's call another taxi and get the heck out of Dodge."

Sunny grabs his phone and drops it in her purse next to her stolen e-cig atomizer. "No. It's time we get to the bottom of this. Someone's been creeping on Rune. And they want her at that party so much they got her a dress. If they want her that bad, they'll take us, too. We're a package deal. I'm gonna make that real clear."

"Well, I guess we're about to find out how convincing you can be," Jax murmurs, a car's approaching headlights brightening his worried face.

With a trembling finger, I activate my phone's screen: 6:30 . . . on the dot.

My companions and I share a collective gasp as a charcoal-gray hearse coasts to a stop at the curb next to us. Long, black-tinted windows reflect our astonished expressions like mirrors.

The driver—a pudgy man with gopher-like features and a red velvet suit that belongs on a circus ringmaster—steps out and asks to see our wristbands in a nasally voice. He studies my friends' fake invites longer than I like, spurring a hammering sensation at my pulse points. Trying to look nonchalant, I concentrate on our reflections in the window. An amber ring glints inside my green irises and my cheeks are flushed—like when music is burbling inside me. But that's impossible. I don't feel the need to sing. I do, however, feel *hungry.*

The auras around Quan's and Jax's heads draw my attention— that same grayish-yellow glow Ben had before I nearly sucked the life from him. I stifle a moan. Is it possible? Is my appetite triggered by their anxiety? Repulsed, I break the connection by shifting my gaze to the ground.

Whipping out a cell phone, the driver walks to the other side of the hearse and makes a call, mumbling in French.

I can only translate snippets:

"Yes, she's here . . . unquestionably ours . . . three others—all underage . . . no, not any indication of . . . sure, sure . . . more for everyone. Understood . . . I'll keep them together. Yes, sir . . . will do."

The driver tucks his phone away, and without another word, indicates a shoe box of blindfolds and terry cloth headbands in the passenger seat. Instead of running like any sane person would, we meet one another's gazes as the driver has us turn our backs to him so he can secure our wrists with the headbands, winding them around until we're handcuffed.

"So you don't get the bright idea of peeking while I'm driving," he explains in English frothed by a thick French accent.

Next, he ties a blindfold in place on each of us, then rests a gloved palm atop our heads so we don't graze our scalps on the doorframe as we tumble like a line of dominoes into the backseat. After a chain reaction of car doors closing, the motor shudders to life, humming through our bones. The car freshener—a stale mix of pine and cinnamon—chokes me as I sit, hands tied behind my back and sandwiched between Sunny and Jax, headed to a party that will either be the beginning . . . or the end—of everything.

16

AN EXQUISITE
NIGHTMARE

*"There is no exquisite beauty without
some strangeness in the proportion."*
Edgar Allan Poe

Thorn had spent many years in this sitting room, one story above the club's main floor, but he'd never felt so alien here.

The lavender sectional couch—paired with the ceiling cloaked in inverted parasols that looked like a field of giant mushrooms—reflected off the mirrored floor and painted the room in the soft pinkish-purple hue. Even the pillars supporting the ceiling shared the color scheme. Peaceful, serene, and thought-provoking. Yet after speaking to Rune's driver, there would be no peace tonight. Things weren't going at all as he'd planned.

"Stop looking so distraught." Erik's voice cast a silken web, wrapping Thorn in luxurious tendrils of melody. His father sat on the other side of the couch, holding a snifter of brandy. He sipped the drink where his three-quarter mask—a silver skull, with eyeholes edged in black velvet—bared his chin and lower lip. "Telling Jon Paul to bring Rune's stowaway friends was a stroke of pure genius."

Thorn scowled. He'd had little choice to tell the driver anything else, with Erik seated across from him.

"The entire point is to make her feel like a monster," Erik continued. "Convince her that her songs are tied to her insatiable hunger. That to give up the music will cure her."

Lie to her, in other words. Thorn's frown deepened.

Erik held up his brandy, admiring its color in the light. "Back in the States our precious little pigeon attacked a stranger, and it has haunted her. But to feed off someone she actually cares for . . . it will *break* her. Render her incapable of forming relationships or functioning in that world. And that's exactly what we want. So, take pride in a card well played."

Thorn tightened his grip on his wine goblet and swirled the deep, burgundy liquid, watching it slosh the tall, clear edges—a sea of tainted blood seeking to escape the crystalline fortress too pristine to contain it. He wished he could look into Rune's memory and see the night she attacked the boy, Ben, to know what really happened. But only childhood moments were strong enough to survive transfer. Once innocence was gone, once a person started keeping too many secrets, memories frayed, became impossible to pass on without disintegrating into threads.

"You need to stay up here tonight," Erik interrupted his grousing thoughts, blotting the upper lip of his mask where driblets of golden brandy dotted the tooth-shaped edges. "Your black moods make you unpredictable. Watch from your ringside seat, or go home. But do not show your face on the dance floor."

Thorn managed a cynical smirk. "I wouldn't dream of showing my face, Father. Grand unveilings are your modus operandi, not mine. *À votre santé!*" He raised his wine for a toast. "To the Exquisite Nightmare."

Erik leaned in and clinked his glass against Thorn's goblet, releasing a flat-pitched, high ping—strangely at odds with the deep, melodic laugh that drifted from the skeletal mask. "Honored, as always, to be the main attraction." There was a sad underpinning to the quip—a genius and once gentle soul enslaved by the vile shadow of his own monstrosity.

Thorn battled an unwanted wave of admiration as he watched his father his drink, then, wrapped in a hooded monk's cloak—a striking contrast to his metallic mask—leave the room without a backward glance.

Erik had designed this establishment five years ago, when Thorn was fourteen. Back then, Erik was still testing the waters, to see if such a ruse would work to lure in people and harvest their energy. To see if they could keep the place secret from the outside world. He wouldn't allow Thorn to join him and his demonic compatriots for another year after that.

He was protective, like any father. So Thorn would take solace up here, settling atop the lavender couch. Chin digging into the cushioned back, he'd stare out through walls made of windows on this side, and mirrors on the other, watching their victims arrive in Erik's fleet of hearses. The cars were different than the ones that used to carry his mother to her reprehensible job—but every bit as ominous and sinful. Erik's hearses brought unwary prey: bodies to provide entertainment and sustenance that would later be discarded in the streets of Paris. And after being injected with forgetting serum—a form of midazolam that Erik had altered in his lab—they would awake in a weakened, half-amnesiac state, alone and confused as to where they had been or what had taken place.

Thorn agreed it was more humane than how things were once done. There was no lurking in bedrooms, preying upon the vulnerable as they slept, or seducing them in their dreams. The victims came to them of their own free will, seeking a night filled with music, dancing, and uninhibited revelry. And their desires were met . . . although that pleasure came at a price.

Thorn needed the energy supplements, just as all psychic vampires did. And Erik needed them even more than most, being constantly drained to keep his one hope alive.

Although they were from different bloodlines, he and Erik were one and the same. Thorn had been born of a dream, just as Maman used to tell him. His incubus father—a creature Thorn never wished to know—had seduced his human mother as she slept, drained her of energy, but left her alive and with child.

Using his connections in the subterranean domain, Erik had traced Thorn's preternatural lineage to a prosperous clan who lived in an underground mirrored city in Canada. When Thorn turned fourteen, Erik offered him the opportunity to go to them. But Thorn chose to stay. By then, he hated his real father for abandoning his mother, resulting in her death and Thorn's orphaned childhood.

More important, by that time, Thorn already loved Erik as family.

That's what drove him to lie to Rune in the note yesterday. A half-lie. He was going to give her a father tonight. Just not the one she was expecting.

If only he could forget the sound of her gentle voice from the last evening they were together, when she said the word: *Etalon*. How long had it been since he'd heard his true name spoken by anyone?

Each time he closed his eyes, he imagined Rune's lips curved to a smile and pressing that name against his mouth, imagined stealing a kiss, drinking of that pure white light—her celestial essence that cradled and calmed him like nothing ever had in his life. Spending time with Rune gave him true serenity. She inspired him, yet at the same time, left him teetering at the brink of desolation. It was overwhelming, to be so close to being united, after being separate for so long.

Erik had once told Thorn how rare it was for twin flames to be incarnated on the earth at the same time—for them to be close enough in age and proximity to find each other. "How precious and fragile the bond," he'd said. "It can be heaven or utter hell."

If either or both of the twin flames were incomplete people, if they were still learning who they were themselves, the relationship would be fraught with pain and misfortune. At the time, Erik had been referencing his own experience with Christina. But it appeared Thorn was cursed to repeat that tragic performance.

Rune was his soul's mirror. Each time he looked at her, he saw himself. Her strengths paralleled his: a seamstress, with the talent for taking scraps and making masterpieces, just as he did with broken animals; a kinship with flowers and plants—the quiet, lovely parts of the world that asked nothing from anyone other than to be admired, respected, and appreciated; and a deep, introspective curiosity that sought out powers too strange or frightening for typical people to embrace.

She even shared his flaws, the things he struggled not to despise about himself: the inability to sing without pain, the isolation from being born different, a deep distrust of everyone but himself.

But he had managed to bypass her distrust; he'd healed her pain, by speaking to her with his violin—a violin that he now knew, after experiencing her childhood memories, had a deeper tie to her blood than she could possibly fathom.

He was having trouble reconciling that detail himself, how the instrument had come into his possession at all. No wonder their connection was so strong.

It had been easy to justify taking advantage of their spiritual bond. To tell himself he was helping her on some level. But all he'd really done was make things more difficult for everyone. She came here hating her gift. And he'd opened the door for her to love it.

If she truly had come to love it, how could she possibly give it up when the time came? She had only two days left until Halloween and her imminent appointment with fate in Erik's cellar lab.

The thought of his father's plan coming to fruition sliced through Thorn's gut like the brambly clawed vines that waited downstairs to capture their unsuspecting victims.

He stared at the floor. All it would take was a flip of a switch, and the mirrors would slide open, revealing the club below—his ringside seat. The guests would still see a domed, reflective ceiling from their side. They'd never know he was spying upon them, or siphoning off their terror through black, energy-absorbing tubes that connected the club to this room.

It was an art form, the way Father Erik could enchant an audience, cushion them with billowing chords of operatic splendor, then send them plummeting into the depths of revulsion and dread before they even realized the trapdoors of their subconscious had been triggered.

Thorn ground his teeth, envisioning Rune alone, trapped by an instinct she didn't yet understand or control, in that surging fray of victims and harrowing energy. He slammed his wine goblet to the table. No way in hell was he going to watch from here.

But he'd promised Erik not to show his face tonight. That much he would honor.

※ · I · ※

On the drive here, we passed what felt like a half hour in dead silence, other than the sound of the hearse's motor, our breaths, and the wind streaming through the slightly cracked windows. The dampness of evening sifted in and a slight breeze rustled the loose curls at my neck—an odd, unsettling tickle like the one inside my head, warning me: *turn back, turn back, turn back.*

Our ride has now come to a stop. The car doors open. No words are exchanged as someone helps me and my friends out and removes the headbands from our wrists. It's not the driver. Whoever loosens my "cuffs" isn't wearing gloves. The blindfolds stay in place but my coat is coaxed off my shoulders and tossed into the backseat. Cool night air chills my skin as we're herded like sheep away from the hearse. The one thing that keeps me from changing my mind is the bone-deep knowledge that my maestro is here, waiting for me. I can *feel* his anticipation. It matches my own.

"Hey, what about our bags?" Sunny pipes up, causing our escorts to pause. "I got money in there!"

"You have wristbands." The driver's nasally French accent answers from behind us. "That's all the currency you need inside. I'll keep your personal effects locked in your car. They'll be here for the trip back to the city."

Back to the city . . . where exactly *are* we? Goose bumps erupt on my bare arms, an acutely vulnerable sensation when paired with my blindness.

"Just want to reiterate"—Jax grumbles at my left as we're nudged forward again—"how stupid this whole plan was, in case it's the last thing I ever say."

Sunny snorts from my right, and Quan moans from her other side.

The clomp of several sets of feet keep time with my stiletto heels as, arm in arm, my group is guided along a rough surface that feels like cement. Our direction shifts and we follow a gritty, descending incline, enveloped by a musty odor. Every sound echoes, as if we're moving through a tunnel.

The unmistakable ping of an elevator greets us and we're steered into the small space, the air thick with carpet cleaner and foreign colognes. The hum of a motor under our cushioned feet carries us down. As the elevator doors sweep open at our stop, an unrecognizable subgenre of dance music shuttles through my body and hammers my ears. It's like chamber music meets underground techno rock. My heart pounds in time with the frantic beats.

We're led out, instantly slammed with a fusion of perfume, sweat, and the faint sting of sulfur—reminiscent of summers on Fourth of July with my friends. That thought sends me spiraling back to Trig and Janine, and how crazy they'd say I was for doing this. Just like I was crazy when I went to that frat party.

Poor Ben . . .

Jax tightens his arm through mine. "You okay?"

"Yeah," I lie. If he knew what I'd left in my wake in Texas, he'd already be running in the other direction. So would Sunny and Quan. But I'm not going to let them out of my sight. I'm the only protection they have here. I can't allow anything to happen to them tonight. Tensing my arms through Jax's and Sunny's, I link the four of us tight as an escort removes our blindfolds.

It takes a minute for my eyes to adjust to the contrast of darkness and throbbing, neon lasers. From our bird's-eye view on the narrow balcony, a pulsating surge of reflective, brightly colored clothes makes the floor appear to shiver under the black lights.

"Holy goat balls of fire," Sunny says as she looks over the waist-high railings. The shimmers across her face blink in time with the rainbow lights on her wig. "Are you seeing this, Rune?" The question sounds like a whisper under the growing swell as the band onstage at the back wall begins a new techno-dance number.

I home in on the architecture and décor.

"Incredible," I mumble. I'd know this place anywhere, thanks to all the Phantom research I did online. The infamous opera house. But it's a grand deception . . . an intricate design crafted upon the walls by skillful strokes of fluorescent paint. Instead of a flat and false representation, the glowing 3-D scene looks as if you could walk straight into it . . . become a part of its baroque resplendence: interweaving corridors, winding stairs, bronze statues of Greek mythos, alcoves and landings, and row upon row of velvety seats. The cleverly executed optical illusion gives the stadium-size space the appearance of stretching on for miles, while accommodating the frenzied movement of ravers who would otherwise trip over any real stairwells, seats, or statues.

In place of the infamous crystal chandelier, a massive, black wrought-iron replica spins at the center of the domed, mirrored ceiling. The scrolling tentacle arms seem to multiply with each rotation like a larger-than-life mutating octopus. Thorns, the size of sewing needles, jut out along the lengths instead of suction cups. At the tips of the tentacles, candle sleeves with black-light luminaries drape the room in phosphorescent splendor.

"It's a mirror image of the Palais Garnier, gothic-glammed," I answer at last, talking over the music.

"Exactly my thought," Sunny answers. "Things just got weird."

"*Just* got weird?" Jax shouts to be heard over the music. "Pretty sure I've been saying things were weird since we put these overpriced circus rags on my dad's credit card!"

The volume of the song escalates, as if trying to drown out Jax's complaints. Electronic keyboards and cymbals swarm my eardrums like audible bees, muffling Quan's ensuing comments. Beneath the buzz in my head, I hear my maestro's raspy voice. He's somewhere in this room. His magnetic force lures me to lean over the balcony's edge. The compulsion to dive into the sea of bodies and swim until I find him is overwhelming.

I teeter there, tethered in place by my friends' arms. A nudge between my shoulder blades urges me toward the long, winding stairs that lead to the lower level. I glance over my shoulder, finally getting a look at the escorts who brought us here. The three of them turn and walk back to the elevator. I can't tell if they're male or female. All I see are hooded vests—aglow with flashing pinpricks of blue light like my dress's panels. The fabric appears to be floating without a body, then a laser show ignites, illuminating our platform and their black pants and shirts before dimming once more. At the elevator, the escorts step inside and face me. I can't make out anything under the obscurity of their hoods, other than glimmering eyes, similar to the Phantom's.

His words at the chapel revisit: *What are we, you mean to say.*

These employees are like him . . . like *me.*

"Wait!" I start forward, but too late. The doors slide shut.

Sunny grips my elbow and forces me to look below. The band has left the stage, and all the dancing bodies freeze in response. A drastic hush falls over the room, coating everything with a chilled muffle, like a fall of snow-encrusted feathers.

The walls on the lower level transform, snapping free and taking on strange shapes—a puzzle being pulled apart and rearranged into something new. The 3-D paintings of stairwells, auditorium seating, and statues interlock, forming grotesque creatures: nymphs and cherubs cracking apart at the torso, so rib cages made of stair steps can fill their hollowness. Red velvet auditorium seats shift upward and rip through the statues' mouths to mimic bloody tongues. They're gargoyles now—a convergence of beauty and horror unfolding before our eyes.

The floor rotates, the guests wavering to keep balance, making way for the stage to revolve until it stops in the center. A sign drops down from above with tiny white lights around the borders—a vintage carnival poster, spotlighting a freak-show attraction. Glittery red letters spell out the words: BEHOLD: THE EXQUISITE NIGHTMARE.

"Oh, we gotta see this." Sunny breaks free from our chain of arms and starts down the stairs. Quan adjusts his hat and hustles to catch up.

"Sunny!" I shout. "Be careful." What I want to say is: *Here there be monsters.* Before I take my first step, Jax clutches my fingers in his. I glance upward at his concerned features.

"Don't get any ideas about going off on your own," he says, as if reading my mind. "We're staying together, right guys?"

Quan and Sunny send nods over their shoulders and continue their descent.

Hand in hand, Jax and I stay close behind on the winding staircase, all the while watching the transformation still taking place around us. Lanky figures in skintight, blinking costumes plummet graceful and quiet from the ceiling, twirling on gleaming ribbons in a spectrum of colors. The acrobats swing toward one another and join hands. They form a chain around the revolving chandelier, like luminescent jellyfish worshiping an octopus in the depths of an ocean. Giant brass bells drop down beside them, pealing loud and deep. Silver confetti descends from the mirrored dome, glittering under the black lights. Before the shimmery rain touches our heads, the swirls of paper come to life, fluttering up and up like metallic butterflies, hovering around the trapeze artists and bells.

The instant Jax's feet and mine meet the floor behind Quan's and Sunny's, the bells stop pealing. In the wake of the fading gong, a haunting assemblage of acapella voices drifts from the acrobats—male and female alike—chants worthy of monks in a gothic cathedral.

The eerie hymns nudge that place inside of me . . . those dormant depths I can't let awaken.

Rune . . . I'm here. Stay in control.

My maestro's hoarse command, in my head. I stop and turn, searching. It feels as if he's standing right next to me, but I can't find him in the multitude of shadowy faces. Trepidation twists in my throat, forming a knot that burns.

"Stay close." Jax's insistent hold on my hand drags me closer to Sunny and Quan. The four of us wind through heated, sweaty bodies and ultraviolet adornments: fiber-optic dress shells that look like glowing baskets, animated shirts and shoes like Jax's, suits made of an electrified fabric that sprays fizzing light into the air, like lit sparklers. Some ravers sport luminescent lipstick and eye shadow or LED jewelry. Others have fiber-optic dreadlocks along with neon body paint curling around their faces, arms, and legs in tribal designs. A woman with flashing orange fingernails moves aside so we can push through.

As we pass, I notice another source of light, something that has nothing to do with rave fashion. Luminous halos appear around each person's shadowy head, the colors vivid in the darkness: reds, oranges, blues, and greens. Pinks and grays and browns. The frantic dancing of earlier must have burnished their auras to a new level of electric brilliance.

The sight makes my feet drag, as if my boot soles keep sticking in tar.

"Rune." Jax pulls me close. "Come on, we have to keep up."

His warm breath lingers on my temple, teasing and tempting. Scenting the primal stir of pheromones beneath his cologne, my nostrils quiver and my mouth waters.

Stay in control.

Beads of sweat tickle my hairline. Hoping to escape Jax's allure, I put as much distance between us as possible while still holding his hand. A few steps ahead, Sunny and Quan join a cluster of ravers standing midway to the stage where glowing-vested employees gather to keep order. Jax and I are almost there when streams of multicolored smoke gush from metal nozzles lining the ceiling, forming a sulfur-scented cloud between us and our friends.

The Gregorian chants rise above the hissing smoke. The metallic butterflies flutter through the audience and graze our skin and hair, spurring a collective gasp.

The smoke fades to a translucent fog. Returning to the stage, the band members wait by their instruments, each one dressed in a flashing orange costume. They stand at the ready, while the drummer accompanies the chanting with a deep, hypnotic beat. There's something about him . . . something in his movements that is familiar now that we're closer. Before I can put my thumb on it, the crowd shuffles in anticipation as the fog parts on center stage and a dais rises from a trapdoor, lifting a coffin into view.

The lid opens. A beam shines down to spotlight a man in a monk's robe sitting inside. Giant white canvas panels unfurl down the walls. Somewhere a camera clicks on, projecting an enormous view of the coffin's occupant. His silvery skeletal mask—covering all of his face but his chin and lower lip—fills every screen. I'm struck by minute differences from how I remembered him in his half-mask in the chapel. Yet behind the velvety eyeholes, his flaming yellow irises call to me.

My heartbeat kicks against my sternum.

Etalon?

He seems thinner somehow. During our fantasy dances in the dark, I've become familiar with his tall, sculpted body and the strength of his arms. Maybe it's the distortion caused by fog, or the rave wear shimmering in my peripheral sight, or even the large robe—a grim parallel to the spiritual reverence that's overtaken the room. Everyone around us begins to sway as the chanting acrobats lower their melodious voices to a hum.

Jax squeezes my hand to get my attention. "I don't see Quan and Sunny anymore."

I lift to my toes and spot Quan's hat in the sea of swaying people.

He's arguing with one of the employees, who, other than his glowing hooded vest, is half hidden by the crowd. Quan shoves at the guy's chest. The employee—at least a good three inches taller than Quan—takes both of my friends by their arms to escort them out.

Jax curses. "We have to get over there."

My face burns with shame. How could I have let them out of my sight after promising to watch over them? "Let's go."

Jax and I push through, me leading the way this time. My gaze keeps straying to the stage, drawn to the man who taught me to tame my songs, waiting for something momentous, a current to reach from him to me and close the space between us. I'll be back, after I see to my friends' safety.

I find an opening in the crowd and start to sprint. Jax hangs tighter to my hand to keep up with me. I refuse to slow my footsteps, torn between the need to protect my friends and the compulsion to get as near to the Phantom as possible.

We're almost where we last saw Sunny and Quan, prepared to follow in their tracks, when the Phantom's giant image onscreen repositions, stopping us. He's standing inside the coffin now. His looming form hovers there for a few seconds before levitating gracefully onto the stage. He opens his mouth, and one pristine note escapes, so pure, lyrical, and heartrending, it's like the marriage of every harp, violin, cello, flute, piano, and bell that has ever been played.

Everything falls away. All I can see, hear, and feel is the performance unfolding before me.

The Phantom spreads his arms and casts a song from his throat in a rain of operatic ornamentation. It floods through me and reaches inside with liquid fingers, plucking at the strands of my heart as if *I* were his instrument. This is different than when he guides me with his violin. This is intrusive, seductive, frightening—yet at the same time, inevitable.

The notes sluice through the nucleus of my being, invading every pore, bringing the music I've dammed within my depths to rise in my throat on a surge of anguish, but I fight releasing it.

I'm drowning and gasp for breath, edging closer to take the lifeline the Phantom's voice offers. Jax follows, his eyes on the stage, mesmerized like me. Like everyone.

Nausea churns through my stomach. The music has trapped me, my enemy once more. I'm a marionette, but this time, it's the Phantom's beguiling voice pulling at my strings. I want to ask him why he betrayed me; why he promised to bring my father to me, only to make me a victim; I want to know why he helped fix what was wrong, just to break me again. But if I open my mouth, I'll be incapacitated once I purge the song.

I can't be vulnerable like that, not here.

Beneath my confusion and the Phantom's serenade, another voice breaks through: *Rune, turn away. Do not sing for him.*

Then I remember the boy from my dreams. The Phantom onstage doesn't sound like my maestro, he isn't humble and gentle like Etalon. This man is powerful, majestic, and menacing.

Somehow, they're not the same person at all.

In that moment of clarity, the music gurgling in my throat sinks into my chest until I'm in control once more. The danger of the situation hits hard and fast: Quan and Sunny are missing, and Jax is standing beside me in the darkness, hand in mine, still entranced, both of us overshadowed by the other ravers leaving us behind on their journey to reach the stage.

Holding tighter to Jax, I back us up, headed for the stairs we descended earlier. He tries to pull away and join the forward-moving crowd, but I overpower him, taking advantage of his weakened, song-induced stupor.

Like the others, he doesn't hear what I hear: the Phantom's serenade is no longer beautiful . . . it's raging and violent. All the instruments have resumed: electronic keyboards, cymbals, and drum lines, throbbing into the roots of my teeth and knocking against my bones and marrow. Jax doesn't see what I see: the chandelier's black tentacles curling down like living, thorny vines, stretching closer and closer to the crowd; the acrobats with eyes aglow, floating like spiders on anchor lines, creeping ever closer to their prey; the employees surrounding the stage in their flashing vests, offering a distraction to keep everyone from looking above.

Oblivious, the ravers march around me and Jax—an ultraviolet line of ants avoiding two strands of grass on their journey to get closer to their source of nourishment: the Phantom and his rapturous, brutal song.

I whimper upon seeing one of the employees in pursuit of us. Jax and I scramble up the stairs to escape. Once we make it to the balcony, I've lost sight of our stalker's flashing, hooded vest.

It gives me some small relief that Sunny and Quan were escorted out before all the mayhem began. The surge of ravers has reached the edge of the stage. They stretch their hands high, some crying, others moaning as if in pain, each one surrounded by an aura of purple and crimson—offering up their spirits and loyalty to their tormentor.

As the music reaches its crescendo, a fluctuation on the giant screens snags my attention. The Phantom lifts a black glove and rips off his mask, exposing a horrific distortion of crinkly, waxen flesh, hanging askew on a gnarled, misshapen skull. His eyes—those eyes I thought I knew—burrow under his bulbous forehead, and his nose is gone, as if it were a candle that melted away. I don't know who's been visiting me each night, because this is the true Phantom. He doesn't even have half a face.

A sob lodges in my throat. I peel my gaze away, unable to watch another second. It's not the deformity that makes it unbearable. It's the unquenchable agony inside those glimmering deep-set eyes— over a century's worth of dejection, sorrow, and rage.

Pandemonium breaks loose below. The thorny vines whip down and wrap around each raver's ankles and wrists, so they can't hide their eyes or run, forcing them to look at the screens. Their auras pique to a grayish yellow—the color of pure terror. Somehow, the light from their halos bleeds into the vines, filling them with illumination all the way into the chandelier's base in the ceiling. Screaming, fainting, and wailing hammer my ears. The glowing-vested employees gather around their quarry—joining with the acrobats who leap upon the imprisoned ravers, feeding off what's left of their light. The victims gyrate as if convulsing.

A flavor awakens on my tongue, a memory of an essence I've only savored once but want to taste again.

Jax whimpers beside me, reminding me he's there. He covers his eyes, trying not to view the screens and the Phantom's tragic face still singing the final, mournful notes of his song.

I turn Jax around so he's facing me and the elevator at my back. "It's okay, Jax." I shake his shoulders gently. "Just look at me."

He blinks, his glazed expression clearing. "Rune?" He steps back. "Your eyes. They're glowing. Like . . . *his*." Horror strains his features.

I try not to notice how my mouth is watering . . . try not to remember that Ben's face looked the same when I was feeding on his terror . . . try to forget that heady flavor of power. But I can't think anymore. All I can do is act.

Lifting to my toes, I wrap my arms around Jax's neck and force him against me, pressing our lips together. Groaning into my mouth, he pulls me closer, deepening the kiss, both of us riding waves of music, passion, and dread.

I attempt to drag myself away when he drops to his knees, losing his breath. But his desperation only feeds my gluttony. He tastes like Ben: singed, sugary, and unnatural—roasted autumn, sulfur, and copper wrapped in sweet, dark candy. I'm too weak to resist; I go to the floor with him, still siphoning that delicious pulsation of life.

The ping of the elevator registers behind me. I ignore it, locking Jax's jaw in my fingers so he can't escape.

Strong hands grip my shoulders and break us apart. Jax hunkers on the balcony floor, gasping for air as I growl and kick to escape the set of arms holding my spine immobile against a solid wall of chest muscles.

"Don't be greedy." Etalon's deep rasp is muffled, his breath filtering out in a stream that warms my neck. "Learn to know when you've had enough."

I stop struggling, though my tongue still stings with electric scintillation. He drags me across the balcony and deposits me, slumped, inside the elevator. I roll over to watch his broad back as he activates the brake and steps out again. He's wearing an employee's uniform—hooded, glowing vest with black pants and shirt. He retrieves Jax's unconscious body and settles it next to mine on the carpet then releases the brake.

As the elevator doors shut us in and the motor carries us down,

Etalon drops his hood, revealing thick, dark, disheveled curls that graze his shirt collar. He studies me from behind a full black satin mask, then kneels, those expressive brown eyes shifting to Jax. Fishing a syringe from his fiber-optic vest, he aims the needle at my friend's bared arm.

I struggle to sit up. "Please, don't hurt him." I attempt to push him away.

Etalon stops my wrist with his bare hand. A jolt passes between our skin and lights up our veins in synchrony, hot and rejuvenating. In that moment, deep inside, I know without question he's not going to hurt Jax. He's trying to help. I jerk free, shocked by the potency of our connection. Etalon's silence stretches out like a shadow—leaving me bewildered and astonished.

Eyes glinting like copper coins, he looks away and injects Jax with the syringe before straightening my friend's rumpled clothes and covering the top of his face with a blindfold. When Etalon holds up a blindfold to me, I shake my head.

"It's for your own safety, Rune," he speaks at last, his accent dusting each gravelly word with French decadence. "I've been lying to you and don't deserve your trust. But you're going to have to give it to me one more time. It's the only way to get you out of here before the Phantom realizes you're gone and unleashes his wrath on us all."

17

THE ARTIFICE
OF PRETENDING

"We are what we pretend to be,
so we must be careful what we pretend . . ."
Kurt Vonnegut

"All right, Miss Nilsson, *les charges de poo!*" The glee in Madame Bouchard's call from the stage curdles inside me like heartburn; her every syllable and consonant echo with bravado along the rafters of the theater as she awaits her star pupil.

Kat steps from her row but stops to grimace at the right side of the auditorium, where, triggered by Bouchard's "loads of poo" expression, snickers erupt among the junior-year students. They still can't rein in their juvenile reactions, even after being taught the meaning behind the saying. Back in earlier times, audiences took carriages to the opera house or theater. The bigger the attendance, the more horses—each one fully stocked with a supply of manure.

So to convey success to the performers, what could be more appropriate than wishing them a full house, i.e., loads of poo?

"*Chut!*" Bouchard claps her hands, silencing the laughter so effectively that the jingle of Diable's collar at my feet draws the attention of several students from the two rows surrounding ours.

Bouchard aims one of her infamous snarls at the juniors. "You can rest assured I've taken note from whence the laughter originated, and you will each be in detention tomorrow. A full hour after classes, reorganizing and cleaning my art studio and supplies."

A collective moan arises but fades just as quickly, as if the students fear an even worse fate should they offend her again. I don't blame them, considering the "art studio and supplies" are in fact the tools of her trade: bloodied and gut-gooped taxidermist equipment and the stuffed heads of animals waiting to be mounted on plaques.

I nudge Diable affectionately with the toe of my cowboy boot. He wraps his front claws around the worn leather, gnawing it with sharp little teeth. He sits up with a start. His large ears perk tall. Paired with his flicking whiskers and tail, it's a sure sign he either hears Etalon in the walls, or a mouse or rat somewhere. I really hope it's Etalon. I haven't heard from him since I left the club last night. Even my dreams were devoid of his songs.

Not giving me a second glance, Diable's off, disappearing into the shadows. I wish I could escape as easily. The final dancing auditions took longer than expected. We started at two o'clock, and now it's four. But the most important singing audition still remains. Only Kat and Audrey made it to the finals, since I bowed out. After today, one will become Renata, and the other will be understudy. Or, if Kat ends up with the lesser role, we'll have no understudy at all.

"Now, Miss Nilsson, if you please."

Kat resumes her walk down the aisle and ascends the steps to the stage. Sunny grunts, keeping the volume low enough that the teachers seated at the back of the theater can't hear her. It's all for Audrey's benefit.

Her turn will be after Kat's, and I've never seen her this nervous before singing. She was back early enough from Paris yesterday to practice five more times without a single mistake, and she was already nailing the aria days before that. Yet something's shaken her up, to the point she won't even look at me when I try to help.

Maybe it's because several of the juniors stopped my group after lunch this afternoon and asked if I planned to try out. Apparently, since Kat and Roxie are no longer giving me hell over my stage fright, some of our peers have decided I'm worth a second thought.

But a role in an opera is the last thing on my mind. For one, I would never step all over Audrey and her hard work, not to mention betray our friendship. I won't do it. And two, the stage is a reminder of the performance and ensuing events at the club last night, and that I'm a dangerous liability. I'm a ticking time bomb of energy-sucking savagery. Just look what I almost did to Jax and Ben. *What I'm hoping I didn't do to my dad.*

I'm lucky Jax, Quan, and Sunny remember very little about our weird outing, but that doesn't make me any less guilty.

As incredible as it felt a little over a month ago, singing in this theater when it was just me and my fantasy partner, that kind of temporal joy seems so far out of reach now. Everything is tinged by what happened almost twenty hours earlier—and the questions that were answered only to birth a thousand more.

Why was Etalon pretending to be the Phantom? What does his face look like under the mask—is he damaged, too? And who is the real Phantom? What am I to him . . . how does my family fit into all of this?

My stomach bunches tight as I burrow deeper in the velvety seat, sandwiched between Sunny and Quan on one side and Audrey and Jax on the other. Audrey's upset with Jax, Sunny's upset with Quan. And they're all acting weird toward me. It must be nerves getting the best of everyone. Maybe it's some side effect of the stuff Etalon injected into their veins, another thing no one remembers but me.

The musicians in the orchestra pit begin to play and Kat joins in on cue, her voice powerful, her Russian flawless. Attempting not to listen, I focus on the knitting project I brought—my one chance for sanity. I left my hair down earlier so it hangs around my face on either side like thick, wavy curtains, offering privacy. I'm weary of catching glimpses of people's auras in my periphery. They seem brighter and more noticeable today than ever before. Either that, or I'm hyperaware because I'm curious about the flavor each different emotion might contain.

I brought my wooden knitting needles since they're quieter than the metal ones. They swirl silently, eating up the tangled mass of gray yarn. Loop, knot, and pull . . . loop, knot, and pull—I cast my stitches, linking and locking. The needles swing, ferocious in their speed, giving me something to concentrate on other than these long hours I have to get through before I can see Etalon tonight.

I'm not sure why I'm still knitting socks for him. Maybe because the yarn cost money, as did the emoticon appliques I'm stitching onto the individual toes to represent the faces he used to draw as a child.

Although deep down, I know it's more. It's because, even though he tricked me, I can't forget that there are unknown, torturous details of his past that connect him to the dark world I experienced last night. For some reason, I've never been able to see past the moment his voice was damaged. Yet somehow, even after those cruelties he suffered, he still had enough goodness in his heart to save me and my friends.

Hopefully not at his own expense.

The thought of him in danger makes my mouth dry and stickery, like I've been chewing on thistles. I take a slow breath, surrounded by the scent of the club. Even though I showered twice in hopes of washing away every horrific memory hanging onto me via my senses, there's still a hint of sulfur and stale perfume in my tunnel of hair.

Kat's vocals escalate, but I shut her out, my needles slowing to a rhythmic, calming lull. Filtering through wavy strands of hair, the soft purple spotlight relaxes me further, reminding me of the lava lamp in my room.

I imagine myself curled up under my covers with the vent at my back, Etalon's music playing, me humming along, and both of us adrift on currents of peace. Despite how angry I am about his lies, I still feel connected to him. For one, because he shares a very powerful and scary side of me; but even more because we've been a part of each other since I was seven. His music saved me from drowning that day my grandmother dunked me. I haven't told him that yet. Maybe he already knows. How do you hate someone who pulled you from the brink of death, not once, but twice?

If only it could return to the way things were just two nights ago. When I hadn't almost sucked all the life from Jax, one of the sweetest and funniest guys I've ever met. When Etalon was still the Phantom. When I knew him, and trusted him.

Trusting a phantom. I slam my eyes shut on the stupidity of that thought.

Last night was stupid, too. I know that. I knew it even when I went to that club, when I was letting myself believe . . . but it's hard to abandon the chance to know yourself, or to redeem yourself for years of guilt.

My fingers move mechanically now, knitting on autopilot.

Those last few minutes I had with Etalon roll over me in waves, whisking me back to the elevator. While helping with my blindfold, he explained that we were in a den of psychic vampires—vampires that feed off energy instead of blood—modern descendants of old-world incubi and succubi who had evolved to utilize all varieties of emotional energy, beyond just lust. He warned that although they were our kind, they were more dangerous than either of us.

All these years I believed the mythology, that incubi and succubi were creatures who fed off sleeping victims. But they can attack anytime, anywhere.

We can attack.

"I'm a vampire," I'd whispered. I grew woozy in the elevator, trying to wrap my head around that terrifying revelation.

Etalon steadied me. "You already suspected," he said. "You just needed someone to make you face it. It's in your lineage, on your father's side. I saw the memories . . . how he took you into the garden and showed you." I tried to turn around, but he held me in place, still working on the blindfold. "Hold still. I don't want to pull your hair and hurt you."

The elevator doors opened before I could respond.

"You must have a thousand questions," he continued in that familiar husky voice that had been reading bedtime stories to me for weeks now. "I'll answer them soon. But for tonight, you need to pretend to be in a trance if you want to keep your friends safe."

He grunted, hefting Jax up to carry him while guiding me by my forearm back to the hearse we arrived in.

Thankfully, everyone else was preoccupied in the club, either feasting, or being feasted upon, so we had no interruptions. Etalon said nothing until the driver spoke.

"So, you found our last stowaway." The nasally man chuckled from the other side of my blindfold.

"I did," Etalon answered. "We'll put him in the car with the others. They've all learned a valuable lesson tonight. Too bad they won't remember it tomorrow."

I heard the hearse's door pop open, then a rustle of clothing as both men scooted Jax into the seat.

"And the girl?" the driver asked.

Etalon's hand cupped my elbow. I recognized the violinist's calluses on his fingertips. My arms grew warm as something was pulled into place over them then settled onto my shoulders. My coat . . .

Etalon tugged a fallen curl free from my collar. His finger grazed my neck, sending a delicious bolt of friction through me before he rested a palm on my lower back.

"She's to be left awake and uncuffed." His deep voice ground out the command. "She's fed. And I've hypnotized her not to remove the blindfold. She poses no threat."

"Understood."

"I'd like a minute alone with her, to ensure she stays under until you drop them off. I'll help her into the car once I'm done."

"Of course, sir." A car door opened and shut, indicating the driver taking his place inside.

I was led some feet away. I clenched my teeth, barricading the thousands of accusations and questions wanting to leap out—furious in my blindness.

"You have every right to be angry." Etalon's patronizing tone stung like hot oil.

"Meaningless words from someone who's always hiding," I seethed. "I should at least get to look into your eyes when you explain why you set me up."

"And you will," he answered, his voice so raw in its sincerity, it made me remember the little boy he once was whose beautiful songs were stolen away with the flavor of lye and bile. A jagged line of sympathy sliced through my heart.

I caught a breath as something cold and metallic tickled my chest a few inches beneath the dip at my collarbones. Etalon spun me slowly until my back faced him, clasping a delicate chain at the nape of my neck.

"*Vous êtes si belle.*" His gruff whisper gilded my earlobe in a sliver of heat—somehow even more sensual for its confinement behind the mask.

You're so beautiful . . . My skin hummed, both from his proximity and the compliment, but I refused to let him see. A sarcastic retort formed on my tongue and I tried to spin around to unleash it.

"No, no. Not yet." He held me in place, one arm crossing me from behind—a provocative weight edging my rib cage—and the other hand clutching the front of the necklace. "You're in a trance, remember? Any emotional outburst would shatter that illusion." With each shallow breath I risked, his knuckles brushed my skin at the dress's neckline, releasing sparks of sensation that made my pulse spike.

"What did you put on my neck," I whispered, less of a question than a distraction technique so my heart would stop racing.

"A key to RoseBlood's roof," he explained, his own respirations uneven, proving he was equally leveled by our physical contact after so many days and nights being separated by walls, and so many years separated by space and time. "If you'll wave it in front of Diable—let him get a good sniff—he'll lead you through the secret passage." He released me and the necklace, helping me turn without slipping on my stilettos.

"He's your familiar, isn't he?" I traced the key at my chest like a person reading braille. It was a metallic skull with jagged teeth, like the ones every student and teacher used to unlock their dorm rooms.

"You could say that." The fidgeting scrape of Etalon's soles on the ground indicated either discomfort with the subject, or a desire to hurry the conversation along. "Although no one is his master. He's my companion and accomplice, when he chooses to be."

"And the collar is to make him appear to be a normal pet."

"The collar is for Ange's benefit. She's half-blind . . . needs the advantage of the bells to warn her of his whereabouts."

"Ange?"

"The swan."

"Oh, her." *The red one from the chapel.* "So, whose familiar is she?"

Etalon didn't answer, as if he'd already said too much.

"Why have you had Diable following me?" I asked, trying to pull him back so I wouldn't be alone in the darkness.

"That was his decision. You earned his trust and respect, because you tried to rescue him. Is that so hard to believe? Isn't that what our friendship has been based on—from both sides—for the last few weeks, and for years before in our dream-visions?"

I curled my lips over my teeth and bit down.

"He may be a cat," Etalon continued, "but he has the nose of a bloodhound. He'll know what door that key opens, and will lead you there. Meet me tomorrow night after lights-out."

I fisted my hands, frustrated by the limitations imposed upon me, both the blindfold and the fake trance. "Why *then*? Why not tonight? I need answers now. You owe me that after what I almost did to my friend."

"I owe you more than that. But, your friend will be all right. They all will. They'll only recall the moments that were safe. Every harmful memory will be blocked. The drug has that effect. Tonight, you need to get back before curfew. And I have to do damage control here, if I'm to protect you *and* your friends. Meet me tomorrow. I promised you your father, and I can give you that much."

I huffed through my nose, though the apathy was forced. "More bait to lure me into another trap?"

Etalon made an exasperated sound. If I could see his dark-lashed eyes, they'd no doubt be narrowed in tempered frustration. How strange that I would know such a detail. It's because I know *him*—on some level that defies explanation.

"I have his Stradivarius, Rune," he answered, snuffing out my astonished introspections. "Black as oil, with the initials O.G. carved into it. I've been playing the instrument for you since you were seven and I was nine."

Any response died on my tongue. My grandma said she mailed Dad's violin back to her own address here in Paris ten years ago, when he became too weak to play it. So how did Etalon come into possession of it?

I couldn't voice the question; his confession had left me mute and numb.

After leading me to the hearse, Etalon drew my coat flaps together to hide the necklace. As he knotted the belt, I caught his hands and held them at my waist, craving that electric charge of contact one last time.

The moment spun out, breathless and silent.

Tomorrow night. With only those words spoken to my mind, he cupped my elbow and helped me into the car, then sent me away with my friends.

Upon our arrival, the driver took off our blindfolds and deposited us on the same street where we'd been picked up. I pulled out my phone. First, I used it as a mirror to study my eyes. No light reflected back. Like my experience with Ben, the glow had passed. Relieved, I activated the screen and checked the time: *8:30 p.m.*

Somehow, only two hours had gone by, even though it felt like an eternity. I called a taxi and watched over my friends until they started rousing.

When our ride pulled up, we all squeezed into the backseat, whispering about the night's events. Just like Etalon promised, they each had partial amnesia. Quan and Sunny remembered being on the dance floor and getting approached by a tall, well-built employee with a raspy voice, asking to see their wristbands. He accused them of forging their invitations, and escorted them to the elevator. After that, nothing . . .

As for Jax, he remembered more: chasing Quan and Sunny, then stopping to watch an "out of this world" show put on by a masked opera singer. But he couldn't remember how the performance ended. Everything faded to black until he woke up on the curb.

The relief that he didn't recall my attack made it easier to suppress the guilt, and pretend that I, too, remembered nothing of consequence.

But, today, here in the theater, surrounded by the scents of the club locked within my hair, the indelible memories refuse to relent.

Kat's audition ends on a pristine note. She still hasn't mastered Renata's madness and range of emotion, but she's perfected all the gesturing and poses, and technically, she did everything right. Almost every student in the auditorium applauds as she steps off the stage.

Bouchard calls on Audrey next. Our friend turns our way, her smoky-eyed gaze bouncing from each of us, as if absorbing support and confidence. When she stops at my face, pain flickers behind her expression.

My jaw tightens. I can't imagine what I've done to offend her.

Jax tries to touch her hand as she steps into the aisle, but she brushes him off. He casts a stormy scowl over to Quan on the other side of Sunny.

I stuff my knitting and yarn into the tote on my lap as Sunny motions for Jax to take Audrey's empty seat next to me. He eases over, keeping his head low. The spotlight blinks on, illuminating Audrey and casting the auditorium in darkness.

"All right. What's going on, guys?" I whisper to my three rave accomplices as the instruments begin the intricate piece.

Slapping a hand over his face, Jax hunches in the seat. "I told Quan about what happened between us. I . . . wanted to know if anything weird happened with him and Sunny. I thought maybe there was a mood enhancer in the smoke during the performance or something. But Quan can't keep his fat mouth shut and leaked it to Sunny. Audrey overheard them talking."

Sunny punches Quan's arm. He glares at her and a whispering argument sparks between them, leaving me and Jax uncomfortably close in our seats. A sense of dread grows within me, mirroring Audrey's haunted vocals as they swell over the instruments and float to the crystal chandelier.

Gathering up my courage, I turn to Jax to find him studying my face intently in the dimness. So, he's remembered more than he admitted yesterday. But he's not acting scared, which means he still hasn't remembered that I almost killed him.

My pulse pounds in my wrists. "What are you talking about . . . what happened between us?" I blurt, a lame attempt at playing dumb.

Jax squeezes his thighs with his fingers, his blue eyes—bright even in the shadows—fixing on mine. "Our kiss." He squints. "Rune, don't you remember? We were crazy. I didn't want to stop. I'm blanking on what led up to it—if you initiated it, or if I did. Or what happened after. But I remember *that*. I've never felt so much so fast. Intense . . . uninhibited."

His breath, scented with cinnamon gum, warms my face. I shift my gaze to the stage and watch Audrey, biting the inside of my cheek until I taste blood.

"I hate myself for hurting her," Jax continues, intent now on the performance. "All she asked was that I didn't distract her for a little longer. Give her space to get that scholarship and secure her future. Then, finally, we were going to go out this summer." He moans then looks again at me. "I haven't forgotten how worth the wait she is. But I can't stop thinking about that kiss, either. Come on, you gotta remember. Right?"

Sunny and Quan are watching us with bated breath, waiting for my response.

My windpipe feels stuffed and cold, like a straw stuck in a milkshake. I struggle to inhale. "I—I'm sorry. I don't remember any of that." I'm such a jerk, and as good of a liar as Etalon. It must be habitual for our kind. "Are you sure it wasn't a dream?" The irony of such a question from a succubus would make me laugh, if I weren't still struggling to accept what I am to begin with.

Jax licks his lips. "No. I remember how it tasted. Like nectar, spiked with a thousand volts of electricity. I don't dream that vividly, Rune. We need to talk about this."

I pry my attention from his attractive features, afraid of the intrigue there, of how it's juxtaposed with shame and confusion. *What's to talk about? We're both attracted to other people. You were entranced by an incubus's song. I was driven by instinct to siphon away your energy while you were vulnerable. No other explanation necessary.*

These are the things he doesn't remember, and the things I can never share.

Sunny touches my knee and gestures to the stage. Instead of portraying madness, Audrey's voice and body movements—not to mention her glowing aura—vacillate between betrayal and regret, completely out of character for the solo. Still, her notes are flawless, until the final cadenza, where she cracks while swallowing back a sob. She stops and the instruments follow her lead, silencing.

Her petite form slumps like a fragile doll. "I'm . . . I'm sorry!" She half shouts, half moans in a wretched attempt to save face. Then she runs backstage behind the curtains before the tremor in her voice stops echoing.

The houselights click on, washing us all in unforgiving light.

Mumbles burble up all around.

Roxie and Kat bump fists.

Bouchard struts across the stage. "Well, it would seem we have our prestigious lead role. The part of Renata goes to—"

"Wait!" I shout, standing up so fast my tote sluffs to the floor like a dead thing. Hair hangs across my eyes, graciously blurring the fifty-some students shifted in their seats to gawk at me. Audrey has lost her chance to let her paraplegic sister live vicariously through her. She's lost that one shot at a scholarship and the future she can't afford otherwise. And she and Jax are on the outs before they ever got to reach the supercouple status I know they're capable of. Because of me.

Unless . . .

There's one thing I can do to make Jax forget he ever liked kissing me, and to see that Audrey still gets her chance to shine in front of that talent scout, but my entire body quakes just considering it.

A lump of dread strangles me. I clear my throat. "I—I haven't had my turn yet." My statement to Madame Bouchard sounds stronger than I feel. I swallow against the lump making another appearance. "I *know* I can do better than those two amateurs." The cruel insult shatters loose, jagged and cold as broken glass, cutting both my heart and my tongue.

I sense my friends' stares of disbelief, but can't bring myself to look their way.

Kat and Roxie are turned full around in their seats to glare at me, so I focus on them. I'll use everything Etalon has taught me. If I can master Renata's song once more and knock Kat down to understudy, she'll walk away from the opera completely, leaving Audrey next in line.

I glance at the row of teachers behind me. Everyone is there but Professor Tomlin, who often spends weekends in Paris to play with his band. But I don't need him to sway the vote.

"You told me I could try out if I wanted, right?" I ask.

Aunt Charlotte drags her glasses off her face and considers for an instant, as if worried I'm not ready. Or maybe she's ashamed that I slammed Audrey so heartlessly, someone who's supposed to be my friend. Finally she nods—her forced enthusiasm spreading through the others.

Headmaster Fabre pipes up: "Madame Bouchard, it would appear we have one last prospect to consider."

In spite of the Bride of Frankenstein's obvious disapproval, she nods me forward, jowls clenched to razor-sharp angles.

I wriggle past Jax, whose face reflects the same disgusted shock as Sunny's and Quan's. Without offering any explanation, I step into the aisle to land the biggest role I never wanted.

18

NATURE'S MORATORIUM

"Merciless is the law of nature, and rapidly
and irresistibly we are drawn to our doom."
Nikola Tesla

Two hours until lights-out. Thorn had to find a way to escape this prison.

Something had happened with Rune today. He sensed the surge in her spirit when she'd performed. She was wonderful and she triumphed, but it upset her. He wanted to know every detail. If it meant what he suspected, if she'd won the most prestigious role in the opera by conquering the music on her own at last, yet still felt no satisfaction, maybe Erik's plans had merit after all.

There'd been a mental disconnect between Thorn and Rune since last night at the club. Her anger erected a barrier to any spiritual visitations in her dreams . . . a wall that he couldn't tear down unless he could find a way out to see her, and win her trust again.

He closed the latch on a cage, then stood and straightened his half-mask and cloak. He had a strategy planned, although it was dangerous. Possibly lethal.

Last night, Erik had activated all the pitfalls and torture devices that surrounded the underground apartment, shutting him and Thorn in together. In his youth, Thorn had been taught how to maneuver safely through most of the booby traps, but he knew the Phantom well enough to anticipate a few had been kept concealed. Erik never fully trusted anyone but himself.

Yet there was one passage, via the cellar—a secure escape route Erik had designed, in case their underground home were ever flooded by the river surrounding it. Erik had in fact dammed the tributaries himself, and crafted a latch in the cellar that would open the dams and flood the apartment within a sixty-second destruction sequence, in case he ever needed to obliterate any and all traces of the Phantom.

But the escape route could be used independent of the destruct sequence. It was an airtight chamber that jettisoned through a water-filled tunnel leading into the baptismal. The very route Ange had hijacked the day Rune was in the chapel, causing the basin to fill with water.

That would be Thorn's safe exit tonight.

Should he try leaving any other way, he would risk tripping devices Erik had kept secret. Each trapdoor led to cubicles containing their own horrors: plants hiding tiny poisonous dart frogs; bats trained to chase and disorient their prey until their hearts gave out; heat-seeking missiles that released swarms of wasps and hornets upon detonation; shrinking quicksand floors surrounded by walls crawling with assassin bugs that would slowly eat their compressed victims alive . . . not to mention the boxes of scorpions connected to trip wires lining every corridor.

The Phantom had honed the art of persecution in Persia while serving as an assassin for the shah over a century ago, long before motion sensors, laser beams, or computer electronics ever came into the world. At the time, he made do with booby traps, secret lairs, and concealed poisons. His twisted intelligence, paired with the elegant destructiveness of insects, had proven unsurpassable. Nature's arsenal roused an instinctive fear in mankind. To torture someone utilizing that fear rendered them psychologically broken.

Erik, in his brilliant paranoia, had installed a labyrinth to protect his home from enemies, but also so he could keep prey trapped inside. Thorn had never been considered an enemy, or prey. Now he was both.

Gripping the two large cages he'd prepared, Thorn stepped into the gated elevator leading to the cellar lab, shut himself in, and pressed the button, hoping his father would be in his coffin resting. Thorn already had his violin hidden beneath the false bottom of one cage where he usually stored feed. He didn't want to resort to any more lies.

The car rattled and groaned on its descent, spurring the three birds and five reptiles within the cages to rustle restlessly behind their bars and screens.

Thorn had thought he'd executed the perfect deception last night: leading Rune's friends out of the club while disguised as an employee. No one had recognized him. And after hypnotizing the driver upon his return from dropping off Rune and her crew, he'd covered all his tracks.

What he failed to remember was that the Phantom had eyes everywhere, beyond the surveillance cameras that Thorn had taken care to avoid. There were the living spies, those who had been manipulated and tormented until Erik's will became their own.

Thorn had run into one such operative inside the club's elevator on his way back up to the lavender room, where he'd planned to discard the employee vest and mask, then feign sleeping before Erik returned upstairs. From behind his orange flashing costume, the man had commented on the blindfold in Thorn's hand.

Thorn shouldn't have taken it from the driver to begin with, but it harbored the scent of Rune's perfume and residual smudges of her makeup, and he couldn't bear to leave it.

His luck couldn't have been worse. That particular spy had first-hand knowledge of Rune and her friends. And, being a musician, he'd also had the perfect vantage point from the stage to watch as Thorn led each one away during the performance.

It wasn't until Erik and Thorn returned home that he realized the man ratted him out. In a tirade, Erik found the blindfold inside Thorn's jacket pocket. The Phantom held it up, initiating one of his magic tricks to spontaneously ignite the fabric. The blindfold drifted down—flickering with orange flames—then landed on the marble tiles and tapered to ashes and smoke at Thorn's feet.

Furious, Thorn had threatened to pay a visit to the drummer . . . make him regret ever double-crossing him. The man was nothing more than a marionette. It was time his strings were cut.

Erik turned his back then, assuring Thorn, should he try to leave that night, there would be deadly consequences.

But that was *last* night, when Erik was still brimming with power and life after the feeding frenzy at the club. Tonight, if he happened to catch Thorn on his way to the escape route, he would be weakened from spending all that energy in the cellar.

The elevator rattled to a stop and Thorn hesitated, his nostrils stinging from chemical and electrical scents.

He hadn't been down here for several weeks. He'd grown to dread the horrific, heartbreaking scene that awaited him each time, for it forced him to cross-examine the moral philosophies his maman had instilled in the boy he once was. Principles he lost sight of, but never forgot. He failed to voice these concerns to the man who saved his life and taught him how to survive. He'd had too much respect for Erik to crush his hopes.

Hope . . . what a tragically miscast word for what was contained within this room.

Thorn dragged his gaze to the glass chamber in the corner, where yellowish plasma discharges pulsed with the rhythm of a heartbeat. Hidden by a tarp, the fragile occupant—frozen within a syrupy mixture of glycerol and other cryoprotectants to prevent crystallization of tissue—fed off the buzzing, popping currents. The sophisticated life-support and preservation system had been built at Erik's hands, over a century before human medical standards had ever reached such technological advancements.

Thorn was struck by all the hours and days he'd spent down here, aiding his father as they kept her alive—injecting her with osmolytes drawn from winter flounder and wood frogs, small molecules that worked like antifreeze and prevented damage to her bodily fluids and vital organs so she could be suspended in time.

As he opened the gated door, Thorn allowed himself to relax slightly, grateful for the tarp blocking his view. He couldn't have stomached looking upon her tonight, regardless that she hadn't changed in the twelve years he'd lived here, and hadn't aged for more than a hundred years before that.

"Have you come to twist the knife in my back?" Erik's weary accusation greeted him from a plush chair in the adjacent corner where he often sat to recuperate after siphoning away his energy.

Thorn's shoulders sunk beneath the wounded tone of that dulcet, waning voice.

Erik's bony form shifted in the shadows to better face him. An operating table stood between them, and a dim lightbulb swung above it, reflecting off the shiny metal surface. This was the table where Erik had gently and patiently taught Thorn how to be a surgeon as a child. How to piece animals back together once they'd been broken. Later, his responsibilities changed to unnatural alterations that left him feeling at odds and out of sorts, procedures that Erik didn't have the stomach to do himself.

As if it could read his thoughts, one of the birds in the cages he held whined like a fox and a lizard hooted in response. Thorn's head bowed, heavy.

When he was young, and honing such strange skills, he could've never imagined why: That one day they would be used upon a girl who was his mirror soul. How could he possibly bring himself to slice through her beautiful skin?

A twisting agony clenched his chest. The last time he'd been here, the table was covered in dust. Over the past few weeks, Erik had prepped it for Rune's Halloween visit tomorrow night, including updating and testing the metal coils, levers, and switches that would aid in conducting the transfer. He'd even gathered strands of blond hair out of the overpriced brush Thorn had stolen from that snotty prima donna, and had them braided with nylon and threaded through sterilized needles, placed on a tray beside Thorn's scalpels. Now everything was set.

Just the thought of the heinous excision made the room spin around Thorn: wooden shelves with unrecognizable organs preserved in formaldehyde, test tubes, beakers, and distilling columns. A worn chalkboard filled with mathematical and scientific equations, and a table where encyclopedias—chemistry, physics, biology, occultism, and alchemy—were opened to pages of underlined text.

Overcome with dizziness, Thorn coaxed his boots forward, setting the animals outside the elevator then leaning against the cool, stone wall to regroup. Ange tottered over and pecked the bars with her bill, sympathizing with her caged friends.

"I have the last of my patients to free," Thorn said, pulling gloves out of his cloak's pocket to cover his trembling hands. "They're healed, and as you always taught me, shouldn't be caged a minute longer than necessary. Already, they've been waiting a month due to our neglect. And since we'll be busy the next few nights . . ."

If there was one thing in the world Erik revered above all else, it was the lives of lesser creatures. When he had Thorn use them in experiments, he ensured Thorn took the utmost care not to harm them, and watched them fervently as they healed. Even in his torture chambers, Erik chose to use wasps, scorpions, and hornets—insects that could sting repeatedly without hurting themselves. Never bees. He couldn't stomach forcing an insect to commit suicide for his cause. He would only use bees as a diversion or an intimidation in wide-open spaces, where the insects were less likely to attack.

Thorn could argue it was fitting in some way, using nature to manipulate the Phantom, as he himself had manipulated so many victims over the years.

"I would have you free them *for* me, Father." Thorn met Erik's eyes, struggling to hide the dishonesty in his heart. "But you're too weak to go to the surface."

In the dimness, the answering tremor in Erik's chin appeared more threatening than usual, shadowed as it was by the skeletal mask still covering his deformed face. He must have slept in his clothes, because he still had on the monk's robe, too, as if he hadn't bothered to change since last night. "It's obvious that it's your freedom you're seeking. You want me to release you? First, you will explain why you've proven to be the crimp in my plans. You, who vowed loyalty to me years ago. You, who said you would dedicate your life to bringing me my most quintessential need and desire. I would never have opened my home to that vagabond child had I known he was only pretending so he could have her for himself." Resting on his knee, Erik's right fingers twitched beneath his robe's sleeve. His breath broke in restrained gusts.

Thorn recoiled. The subtle flash and crackle of the electrical currents in the glass case mimicked the unease erupting along his nerves. He'd underestimated Erik's vulnerability. Even half-asleep, the master assassin could still cast a Punjab lasso. Thorn lifted his hand to the level of his eyes, an attempt to protect his throat from the lethal wire and lead ball being slowly threaded out of Erik's sleeve.

Ange flapped her wings and warbled low in her throat, sensing the mortal magnitude of the moment. She lighted atop the operating table and nested in place, situated between them.

"I was protecting our way of life, as I'm avowed to do." Thorn looked past the swan's glossy red plumage, disturbed by how closely she resembled a pool of blood on the stainless-steel surface. "I had to escort Rune's friends away before they ended up with puncture marks on their wrists and ankles. For five years, the club has managed to stay under the radar . . . considered nothing more than rumors, only because the victims are consenting adults. The police will be forced by parents to investigate should under-aged teens start sporting the telltale physical symptoms discussed on the streets and at underground clubs."

"I've nothing to fear of man's law," Erik scoffed. He wasn't being boastful. He'd spent more than a hundred years evading repercussions for the countless murders he had committed. Most of them could be justified as vigilante justice, since the victims were murderers themselves—or worse. And here in Paris, he had the added benefit of contacts in every branch of law enforcement, psychic vampires who'd mastered blending into the common populace. It was their job to keep any traces of their kind under the radar, so they would never be exposed.

Early on, Erik convinced them any murder he committed was to preserve their obscurity—that his victims in some way threatened their lifestyle—and so his contacts covered his tracks. But ultimately, he had been using those stolen years of life to extend his own . . . so he might live long enough to experience what he'd been seeking since he was treated as an abomination by not only the world, but by his very own mother: unconditional love.

"You're right," Thorn answered at last, sympathy tugging at his resolve. "There's no need to fear mankind. But our *own* kind? That's a whole other level of culpability, isn't it? Our subterranean alliances wouldn't appreciate the complications such inquiries would present. It goes against our vows to keep our kind hidden. It would pose a threat to the anonymous mass feedings made possible by your club. The club they poured all their money into, so you could make their lives cushy and comfortable. You wouldn't wish them to discover the other reason for your grand design. That you had to find a way to absorb extra energy for her." Thorn shifted his gaze to the cryogenic chamber, fighting that tinge of bitterness again. Why would Erik put everything in danger for her . . . when he already had the unconditional love of a son? "Should our investors feel threatened, they will pull the plug, and she will suffer most of all."

Erik tucked his hand into a pocket—putting away his Punjab lasso.

Thorn let out an indiscernible sigh of relief.

"Let us be clear." Erik barely spoke above a hissing whisper. "She's already suffering. How could you look at her all these years and think otherwise? And it's not that you led Rune's friends away. You led *her* away. Last night was set up to be her final downfall, so she'd be desperate to escape the torment of her conscience. It's our one chance to trick her into compliance, since somehow she's overcome her fear of the music itself." He flashed an accusatory glare at Thorn who turned his gaze to his boots, dulling any emotional reaction so his aura wouldn't give him away. "But we still have her uncontrolled appetites. That is our ace. Tell me you at least allowed her to feed. And be aware: Your answer determines more than the fate of your animals tonight, *my son*."

Thorn paused, pulling his gloves into place and working out the wrinkles in the dark leather. "I let her feed off one of her companions." Duel emotions wrestled within him each time he remembered watching Rune attack her friend so viciously: one part impressed, the other part sorrowful. "The blond boy. Just enough to taint her relationship with her friends. But I stopped her before she could kill him. She wouldn't do us any good in prison."

"Fair point." Erik stood, hand still rested in his pocket, and dragged his feet over to the glass chamber. Ange fluttered down to stand beside him. He propped his slumped frame against the metal counter, raising one corner of the tarp so he could glimpse inside. "What upsets me is you took her *before* I could provide guidance and comfort. Before I could get inside her head so that on All Hallows' Eve, she would beg to make the sacrifice. You've made ill-wrought choices over the past few weeks that are coming to light, and I am not pleased. However, I'll give you the benefit of the doubt one final time. You have served me well over the years. You've brought her this far when no one else could have."

Thorn narrowed his eyes. There was a pointed, underlying message within the mock praise that he couldn't quite grasp. But he didn't dare push. With the mood Erik was in, he'd risk never getting out tonight.

"Go free your patients," his father said. "You must be thrilled it's the last time you'll have to do it."

Every muscle tense and alert, Thorn drew up his hood and retrieved the cages. He started toward the tunnel leading to the exit route.

"Thorn . . ."

He stopped in his tracks but didn't turn around.

"Do you remember my reasoning?" Erik baited, his voice a lyrical, hypnotic menace. "When you were young and I insisted you never keep a beautiful, wild creature caged for your own purposes for too long?"

Thorn tipped his head, weary of the passive badgering. "You said the animal would either lose the ability to function in the world without their keeper, or would turn feral and attack the one who feeds and cares for them, and have to be put down."

Erik's ensuing pause felt interminable, his silence louder than the plasma's crackle. "Yes, my lovely wild-boy," he said at last. "In hindsight, I realize I've kept you caged in darkness for far too many years. Now we face the consequences, and I fear the fates that will befall us both."

A surge of impending doom raised the hairs along Thorn's arms. Squinting to suppress the burn behind his eyes, he ducked into the tunnel. He followed the phosphorescent guidelines painted along the walls. His footsteps didn't slow until the buzzing and popping of that artificial heartbeat faded to the soles of his boots scraping across pebbles on the way to his freedom—however tenuous it was.

19

CLIMBING TO
THE STARS

"A poet is a man who puts up a ladder to a star
and climbs it while playing a violin."
Edmond de Goncourt

The platform beneath me seems too small . . . too tight. I'm not one for a fear of heights, but having nowhere to turn other than the locked door in front of me and the steep, winding stairway behind, I'm less confident than usual.

Diable mewls at my feet—a grumpy, scolding sound.

"I'm trying." My tote's strap balances precariously on my shoulder as I juggle my phone so the flashlight app can spotlight the keyhole in the door. I work the key into place. The tote slides down, its weight dropping to my wrist and yanking the chain from my nervous fingers. The key clatters to the stone step beside my feline companion. He hisses in disgust.

"Yeah? Well at least I have opposable digits," I grumble. "I'd like to see you unlock something." His unimpressed green gaze blinks up at me, reflecting my phone light as I fumble for the necklace. "Oh, I forgot. You're a ghost. You'll just materialize on the other side, right?" I tease him with the dangling chain.

Diable bats at the key until it's out of his reach. He then yawns, stretches, and saunters back down the long, dark stairway we wound through minutes earlier, his jingles slowly fading away.

"Typical tomcat," I say as he turns a bend where my light can't reach. "Happy to have a paw in the mess, but always turning tail when it's time for cleanup."

Talking aloud to myself is the only way to keep my nerves in check. I've had a miserable, albeit productive, day: Turned all my friends against me, made Kat drop out of the opera, and won the diva's role in one fell swoop.

After the auditions, Sunny tried to talk to me once or twice, but I shut her down. I can't tell anyone why I did it. If I admit the truth, Jax will forget that I'm a heartless opportunist and start questioning our kiss again. And Audrey will never go along with a setup; she won't honor her understudy duties if she knows I plan to fake being too scared to perform on opening night. That role belonged to her from the very beginning; this was the only way to make sure she gets her shot.

Most of the day, I hid in my dorm, while the other students decorated the foyer, stairways, and the ballroom on the third floor for the Halloween masquerade tomorrow night. Laughter echoed outside my door along with the sound of my four friends horsing around. Hearing them, wanting to be with them, hurt more than I thought it would. I know they're safer if I avoid them. But why did they have to be so great? And why did I let them into my heart?

Dinner was just as excruciating, eating with my aunt—who was silent for the first time in . . . well, ever—as far away from the other kids as I could get. With every forkful I craved something other than the salmon, almond, and eggplant salad on my plate. All the while I wished Mom was there, or Trig and Janine. But would they even know me now?

Then again, maybe Mom already knows. She always said I was my father's daughter. Is that what she had in mind, when she told me to be something amazing? Something *better*?

I almost considered calling her today to feel her out, but changed my mind. As skeptical as she was about Dad and Grandma's talk of auras and his superstitious upbringing, there's no way she knew how deeply rooted in vampire mythology they were. It's better she doesn't. If she knew the truth, she would hate me as much as Grandma for what I did to Dad.

The edges of my eyes sting. After seeing how easy it is for me to drain people's energy, I'm even more convinced that I'm responsible for him getting sick.

How am I supposed to live with that?

Blotting my lashes with my sweater's sleeve, I take a last look at the empty stairwell, wishing Diable were still there.

I snuck from my room a few minutes after lights-out, Diable at my heels. I kept my phone off and felt my way around the dark foyer, tripping over a pumpkin and knocking Sunny's Red Death phantom cutout to the floor. As soon as I repositioned the prop and was assured no one heard me, I lowered the roof key to Diable and let him sniff the metal. With a twitch of his whiskers, he pattered over to the edge of a mirror and dug at one corner until a loud click snapped the silence and the reflective plane swung open.

Shutting us in, I followed as he wound through the secret tunnel. We passed a dozen different hidden door panels while climbing the stairs. With my phone lit up again, I could make out rooms on each floor from the other side of the two-way mirrors, and understood at last how Etalon had kept tabs of my daily schedule. On the second flight, I recognized Bouchard's workshop, Madame Fabre's sewing dorm, and Professor Tomlin's science lab. It was too dark to see much detail, but his costume for the masquerade was still hanging on his cabinet door where I saw it Friday—a gas mask of black leather shaped like a jackal's head, along with a matching jacket. Even his costume was cooler than anyone else's.

Diable and I passed a few of the burned-out storage rooms on the upper flights, and even with the glass barrier, the sight of the scorched props and singed costumes felt too close, too real. It brought back memories of that fiery Valentine's party in second grade, and Grandma's vendetta. Tucked in the corners here and there were small barrels with wires swirling out from the bases. I had to make a conscious effort not to get sidetracked by them, assuring myself I'd try to find a way into the rooms to explore later. My meeting with Etalon was too important to miss.

It took ten minutes to make that climb. Now, I can sense Etalon on the other side of the door. His emotions emanate through the wood, threatening to boil over: anxiety, anger, attraction, and dread. I can taste their vaporous sizzle, and I share every one. If I walk through, neither of us will go unscathed or be the same again. But he owes me explanations, and it's time he pays up.

Shoving the key into the hole, I click to release the lock. A gush of night air sifts across me, chilled with the scent of damp stone, greenery, and roses.

I step out, close the door, and button my shin-length sweater to cover the scar on my knee peeking through the rip in my jeans. My hair billows in unruly waves, and I scold myself for forgetting to at least wear my knit cap. I knot the strands at my nape in a loose bun that will never hold in this wind.

White pinpricks dot the black sky overhead and drape the dark shadows in lucent shrouds, like webs made of starlight. In the dimness, Etalon's signature Fire and Ice roses deck every corner of the long expanse, spilling out of giant pots. Their vines and blooms wind along the five-foot-high stone wall encompassing the roof's circumference like a guard rail.

At last, I know the origins of his supply.

He's nowhere in sight, but he discarded his gloves a few feet from the threshold. I lift one and sculpt my cheek with the black leather, remembering how I wore it weeks ago. How he took it back during our first magical dance in the theater. Placing it atop the other glove, I continue my perusal of the surroundings.

It had to have taken years to convert this place from a barren rooftop to a moonlit courtyard. How long has he lived at this opera house, haunting the corridors and passing through mirrors?

I peer over the top of the guard wall where the chapel, cemetery, and forest dot the landscape below like grayscale imprints—dark and borderless.

The stony surface is level beneath the soles of my boots as I move on, no wooden beams or shingles to trip me up. Strands of miniature greenish pearls glimmer along the auditorium's cupola where it rises like a tower on the far end of the lengthy rooftop.

At this end, overshadowing me, the fifteen-foot Apollo and Pegasus statue stands guard, lit by those same luminescent strings.

The greenish lights trail down to outline the back of a stone bench beneath the stallion's giant wing. They're like Christmas decorations, but softer and more natural, gilding everything in a misty glow, without electrical outlets or cords.

I stop at the bench and lay my tote on the seat to caress a strand. The tiny orbs feel warm and slick beneath my fingers. They brighten at my touch, and their light hums through me with a revitalizing pulse. Their glow is an aura. They're organic—living things.

"Eggs maybe . . . or worms?" I conjecture aloud.

"Firefly larvae," comes Etalon's husky answer, muffled but close.

I spin around in the direction of his voice.

"Up here," he summons, coaxing my gaze skyward. Above the bench, an empty can that looks suspiciously like one of the tins Professor Tomlin uses in his lab to store solvents hangs from a red ribbon laced through one end. The string stretches across the horse's raised foreleg and disappears around the other side of Apollo. "Take it." Etalon's instruction seems to travel from the ribbon into the tin cylinder. He's throwing his voice—a practiced ventriloquist.

In spite of my anger over his deceptions, a smile teases my mouth as I drag the can down. There must be another one tied to the ribbon he's positioned somewhere behind Apollo, out of sight. It's a replica of the homemade toy phone Mom and Dad once used to talk to me at the hospital, before I started first grade. He had to have climbed a ladder to thread the ribbon through such a high point in the statue.

To think he went to all that trouble just to re-create the comfort of sharing secrets with the two people I trusted most disarms me. I consider the fairy tale book I gave him, and the toe socks I finished today that are tucked in my bag on the bench, and at last understand why we're so determined to help each other hold onto our most safe and precious moments. We've both missed out on carefree child-hoods and lost parents we love.

I hold the open end of the can to my ear, waiting. Etalon's inti-mate gesture has left me vulnerable and without words.

"You won the role of Renata." The observation warms my temple—as if his very breath travels through the ribbon and the metal—a magical sensorial experience like when we dance in our minds.

I hold the can to my mouth. "Yes. But . . ." I return the metal cylinder to my ear, testing to see if he knows how I feel without my even saying it.

"Why did your triumph make you sad?"

Nailed it. I frown up at Pegasus's form draped in that glimmering veil of larval fireflies, grateful for the make-believe safety net, but also wanting to finally look at Etalon's face with no more guises between us—to have him explain this deep connection we share. "I used a gift that I never had to earn, to steal the role from someone else who'd worked hard for it."

"If you hate this gift so much, why did you use it?"

I'm going through the motions now, moving the can back and forth without even thinking, as if it's the most natural form of com-munication in the world. "I don't hate it." *Not anymore, thanks to you.* "I just don't feel like I deserve it. But I'd rather my friends be mad at me and still have one another, than know what a monster I am."

He sighs into the phone, and it flutters several strands of loose hair that cover my ear. "'Whose ravening monsters mighty men shall slay, not the poor singer of an empty day.'"

"I'm pouring out my heart, and you're spouting lame poetry."

"Lame?" A rough chuckle bursts through our makeshift phone line. I've only heard him laugh in childhood memories with his mother. Now that he's grown, it's a deep, broken sound, and even more affecting. "The grand Sir William Morris would roll over in his grave." Etalon's tone sounds suspiciously like teasing. "My point was you're not some ravenous, unthinking beast. You're a girl with a talent for song who happens to feed on energy to survive."

I laugh this time, but it's hollow. "Talent? I beg to differ. And we both know what I did to my friend last night in search of energy. That makes me a beast."

"Were you hungry today, at any time?"

I think of how I couldn't look at the students or teachers, even at dinnertime with a delicious salad in front of me, without seeing their auras and wondering how those emotions might taste. "Yes." My voice echoes in the can.

"And did you attack anyone and drain them of their life-force?"

"Well . . . no. But I had to make the conscious choice not to."

"Beasts are driven by savage instinct. Not conscious choice. Our kind has a unique way of relating to the physical world. We consume, transmit, and manipulate the life-forces around us."

The firefly larvae brighten as he says this, as if he's empowering them with a surge of energy, reminiscent of how I channeled the earth's pulsing nutrients into the dying roses in the garden.

"So . . . we can bring things back to life?" I ask. The possibility feels like a knife at my chest. Why couldn't I have known that when I was seven years old, saying good-bye to Dad in his casket before they closed the lid?

"Unfortunately, no. If something is dormant, we can keep it alive with a transfer of energy. But death has no reversal. Which is why we must be very careful when we feed."

The cold metal numbs my fingers as I digest the information. "Be careful, how? You saw what I did to Jax . . . and there's another guy back home—" I stall there, ashamed to give the details.

"When we're small, our bodies don't require any more energy than what the earth provides. Sunlight, plants and flowers, animals. They all offer sustenance, just by being around them. But we come to a point when we need more—an awakening. Human emotions hold the most potent forms of energy. That's what you were craving with the first boy. And you've been starving since that taste, causing an energy imbalance. Now you've addressed that at the club. You will learn to curb your appetites by supplementing between significant feedings. Usually, only a sampling of a plant or animal's life-force is enough to tide you over. And you will learn how to feed with caution. It doesn't have to hurt anyone or anything. And it doesn't have to be the end of your world as you know it. Many of us live among normal people and are never discovered."

I hold the cold metal to my mouth. "You don't. You hide inside of mirror passages . . . behind masks."

"That is *my* conscious choice." His answer rattles through the metal at my ear.

"Is it? I sense loneliness, a desire for something more, every time I'm with you." I crimp my lips, my breath balmy and hot inside the tin can. "My guess is, if you had your conscious choice, you wouldn't hide at all."

There's a pause, as if Etalon's considering my words. "Tell me, if all of this could be taken from you, would you want that?"

It's obvious he feels as miserable and hopeless at offering

the option as I do, knowing it's impossible. "The music, or the hunger?"

"Either. Both."

"Since we're playing pretend, yes. If I could go back and choose, things would be different. Then I wouldn't have killed my—" Regret steals the air from my lungs and cuts my confession short.

Resituating the can, I strain to listen for his response with tears gathering on my lashes. He's seen my childhood. He knows what I've done. *Please, please. You're my last hope. Tell me I'm wrong. Tell me there's another explanation.* The pain that I've held inside for so long expands behind my sternum as silence swells between us.

With the cold metal still cupped to my ear, I sit down on the stone bench, my legs too shaky to hold me up. The chilly night wind gusts around me, snagging my bun loose. Even when the strands stick to my tear-slicked cheeks in itchy tangles, I don't attempt to dig myself out. I want to stay hidden forever.

The phone's ribbon goes limp across the horse's leg and the other metal can hits the statue's edge. Etalon has dropped his end. It's then I know that I really am a monster, because one of my own kind can't even face my sins.

"Sweet Rune, don't cry." His voice reaches out—no longer a vibration along the ribbon, but in front of me.

I release the can and shove hair from my face.

He looms over me. His white half-mask reflects the greenish glow around us, giving him a spectral air. He offers me a rose. I take it—careful not to get pricked by any thorns—and nuzzle the duotone petals, inhaling the sweetness.

"There is no agony more acute than believing yourself responsible for the death of a parent." Wrapped within his cloak, he seems even taller and broader than I remember, almost godlike with Apollo holding vigil behind him like a stony doppelganger. Yet there's a softness in his eyes at odds with his powerful form. "It took me years to make peace with my maman's murder."

I'm reminded of the tiny toddler who watched his mother being driven away in a dark car every night to sell her body so she could care for him. And then, that little boy on the porch, the moment he realized she was never coming back after he'd finally convinced her to change her life.

The aching chasm in my chest fills with empathy. "But you weren't responsible." I wind the rose's leaves around my finger. "You were blaming yourself for something someone else did."

"As are you." His reassurance grinds like deep, sanded velvet from his throat—a tender virility that strips away the image of the boy and leaves the man in his place. "You did not kill your father, and I can prove it."

From within the hooded cloak, he brings out his other hand clutching a violin case.

Daddy's Strad. I drop the rose, eager to see the instrument again, yet dreading every painful memory woven within those strings.

"You were only a child when he died." Etalon lays the case on the bench between me and my tote bag. My nerves twitch both at his proximity and at being so close to my father's beloved violin again. As Etalon works the latch open, I study his hands—strong, with the long, skilled fingertips of a master musician. I'm transported in time, to uncountable moments when Dad opened this case, preparing for a performance with me. Etalon's cloak sweeps the tips of my boots as he kneels. "You hadn't yet had your awakening when you were seven. That didn't happen until you attacked the boy in your hometown.

So it's impossible that you could've killed your father. Although I'm starting to think this Strad played a role. Playing the instrument might have been his downfall."

I frown. "What? How?"

"I don't have that answer yet. Only a suspicion, and three puzzle pieces."

He drags his cloak from his head and shoulders, revealing a creamy thermal undershirt, its V neck dipping low enough to showcase a fine line of hair between his pecs. Tweed pants sculpt his legs like well-worn jeans, hooked to a pair of brown suspenders holding his shirt snug against his toned build. He no longer looks like an out-of-time gardener or an employee at a psychedelic rave club. He looks gentle and philosophical: a musician, a poet, and a romantic dreamer.

He leans over to arrange the cloak at my feet. Thick, dark curls flutter across his forehead and dust the nape of his neck in the wind, close enough for me to reach out and touch, if I had the courage. I catch a whiff of his shampoo—something woodsy, soothing, and spicy, like the ginger root tea I like to drink at home.

After smoothing the fabric on the roof, he seats himself, his hand at rest on the violin's case. The flawless side of his face is tempting in the soft light: one-half of a squared chin, one-half of full lips. He flips open the lid, and my eyes well up, drowning at the sight of the instrument nestled in the velvet lining. Not a scratch or a crack anywhere on the glossy surface.

"Thank you." I rub at my wet cheeks without looking up. "For taking such good care of it."

He doesn't respond, but I can feel he's honored by my gratitude.

I touch the rich, black wood. When I lift it from the case and hug it, the scent of the wood fills me like a symphony, and in that moment, I'm holding Dad's music snuggled against me. The O.G. engraved in the lower bout offers a familiar comfort as I trail it with my thumb.

Etalon crouches lower so I'll be forced to meet his dark gaze, studious behind the mask. "Do you know those initials?"

I nod, swept away by Dad's songs taking flight in my mind. "Octavius Germain. One of our ancestors from the eighteenth century. He marked it to keep it in our family."

A pensive expression crosses the left side of Etalon's face. "Yet I know it to stand for *Opera Ghost*. Someone has been lying to one of us, or both."

I'm reminded of the signature on his note when he gave me the fiber-optic dress in the chapel. He'd signed it O.G. *That's* why the initials had seemed so familiar. "I don't understand."

"Me neither . . . but I have a hypothesis." He fishes two items from a hidden panel inside the velvet lining of the case. One is a picture, the other a rolled piece of yellowing paper.

First, he hands me the picture. I settle the violin on my lap to take it. The image is faded and grainy, yet clear enough to make out a tragic young boy, standing with a burlap bag over his head—holes for his eyes and mouth cut into the brown, woven material. In his arms he cradles my Dad's Stradivarius. With the one-of-a-kind scroll at the end of the neck, there's no mistaking it. "Is this you?"

"No. Look closer." Etalon points to the photo. "This is a daguerreotype. The oldest form of photography. It's dated 1840. Hundreds of years before I was born. There were no initials engraved on the violin yet, which discounts your ancestor doing it. In fact, the Opera Ghost still had two decades before he would manifest. The boy in this picture would one day conceive of that persona, when he traded the bag over his head for a mask and an opera cape."

My mouth dries. "This is the Phantom as a child?"

Etalon nods.

"Okay. So, how is that possible?" I ask. "That he's lived all these years? I mean, I get that he's like us. I saw him channel the horror from everyone. But . . . do we reach a point and never age?"

"We have the ability to stall the aging process, to store a surplus of life energy within ourselves, but only by siphoning away all of our prey's remaining years."

"By killing them," I say, almost choking at the thought.

He tilts his head in affirmation.

My stomach turns as I contemplate how many people the Phantom must have murdered to accrue so many extra years of life. Then nausea hits full force as I realize how close I came to doing that with Ben and Jax. Thoughts of Dad aren't far behind. Did I take his remaining years? My vision blurs to even consider the possibility. But Etalon said I'm not to blame. "I still don't understand what this has to do with my father's death."

"I'm getting to that." He unfurls the rolled paper next. It's an aged, hand-drawn sketch of a man in a vintage suit playing my dad's violin—complete with the O.G. engraving on the bout—his deformed, hideous face relaxed in pure euphoria. It's dated 1864 and signed by the artist, Christine.

"*The* Christine?" I ask, eyes meeting Etalon's.

"Christina Nilsson often signed her name as *Christine* in correspondences and on her artwork. Not many people knew she was an amateur artist, but the Phantom did. He cultivated every creative outlet she had. He was her tutor, her angel of music, her muse. They had a passionate emotional affair, although sadly, she was young and immature. Contrary to what most people think, there was only twelve years' difference in their ages, not twenty or thirty. But still, upon their first meeting, she wasn't yet ready for the selfless, soul-deep level of love he required. She was little more than infatuated with his mystique and genius." Etalon's aura grows sad for an instant, then jumps back to stern determination, as if he catches himself. "Somehow, your family ended up with the Phantom's violin. The exchange had to have taken place sometime after he'd trained the woman he loved to sing alongside the instrument's voice, because that's when he engraved the initials."

My mouth sags open.

"I believe this violin had some sort of penalty attached to it when it was taken from the Phantom," he continues. "A gypsy curse. Whatever you want to call it. I believe it drained your father of his life. I'm not sure how. But my gut tells me they're connected. I think your family knows the answers. Possibly even your aunt. You should start with her."

My mind swirls in confusion. "My *aunt*? What does she have to do with any of this?"

"She never wanted you here. Your uniforms and the dead crow . . . she's responsible. I only borrowed your school clothes after the fact. She cut them up and hid them in hopes they'd be discovered. She was determined to scare you and your mother so she'd take you back home. Once your mother left, the pranks stopped. I assume your aunt gave up, since she'd failed in her efforts to drive you away."

In spite of the cold air, sweat beads at my hairline. I place the picture and violin back in the case. "Why wouldn't she want me here?"

His jaw clenches tight. An incongruous blend of unease, guilt, and loyalty tinges his aura—blue, dusted with brown and gray. "I've said all I can for now. You need to find out how your ancestors got the instrument, and how it found its way back to the Phantom. Then . . . then I'll know how to answer that question."

My throat lumps. "But you're the one with the violin. You've been playing it all these years. Not the Phantom."

Etalon stares at his hands fisted in the cloak, retreating not only behind his mask, but within himself. "He gave it to me as a gift. Someone had to return it to him first."

Grandma. I clutch my chest. A bleak darkness shadows my heart—memories of Grandma Liliana trying to kill me now intertwined with my aunt's efforts to scare me. Is there no one in my family, other than Mom, who I can trust?

Etalon raises to his knees, prying my fingers from their death grip on my sweater. He takes my hand in both of his, sheltering it. "It will be all right," he promises. "Speak to your aunt. There's more to her than you realize, and it's not all bad. If she'd planned to harm you, wouldn't she have already done it?"

His logic is sound, but it's the energy ebbing and flowing between us that calms me. Warmth and light hum through my skin, making me stronger.

"I'll have to visit my grandma in Versailles, too," I manage, though it's the last thing I ever wanted to do, and I know he senses the hesitation I'm trying to hide. "She mailed the violin here to Paris." Etalon begins to respond, but I interrupt. "Wait. For you to have started playing the instrument when you were nine, to get it as a gift, to have these personal pictures of the Phantom, you're more than just an employee at his club. You're—"

"His family."

Astonished by the confession, I turn to the sketch curled on the roof beside him. Somewhere behind the Phantom's desolate face hides the rest of Etalon's past; the parts I've never been able to see. New questions awaken inside me, but only one clutches my ribs and rattles them like a cage. I choose my words carefully, trying not to be insensitive. "Is the deformity inherent? Is that why you wear a mask?"

He squeezes my fingers. A current passes between us—sparking through my chest and bouncing along my spine, titillating and musical. He guides my hand to the covering on his face. "If you want the truth about the man behind the mask, you'll have to unveil him yourself."

There's a seductive undertone to the request that makes my skin tingle, reminds me that I'm here on the roof alone with an incubus who towers over me when he stands, who knows how to command the ancient instincts I'm struggling with, and who lives in the shadows mastering abilities that border on sorcery.

Yet I'm not scared, even when I probably should be.

I slide off the bench and kneel beside him on the cloak. He eases down from his knees, sitting so we're eye level. His gaze holds mine—an intense optical coupling that renders me immobile, anchored by the significance of what's about to take place. The aura surrounding him deepens—dark red and searing, passionate and sensual—and his scent overpowers the roses along the walls: a heady mix of musk and pheromones that kicks my pulse into overdrive.

I inch toward him until our breaths mingle in the air between us. Biting my inner cheek, I curl my left hand around the mask's brittle form. My stomach clenches, overtly aware of how close his face is to my chest as he bows so I can work the ties free from around his head. Nervous anticipation radiates to every extremity, leaving my right fingers clumsy and quivering. His hair sweeps across my palm, softer than the velour Madame Fabre chose for the nun's habits in the opera. I drop the strings in front of the mask, so it's only me holding it in place when he looks up.

I've been waiting a month for this, but now I'm hesitant. Not for me, though. Etalon's palms flatten against the cloak on either side of him—a submissive pose—while his fingers dig into the fabric, visibly tense. I'm taking away everything that makes him feel safe. How would I feel, to be stripped of all concealments, with my flaws hung out to dry?

"Are you afraid?" I ask, overcome with compassion as I study the bared side of his face.

"Are you?" He flings the question back, slapping me with the truth: I'm every bit as vulnerable in this moment as he is.

The Phantom's tragic face from last night intrudes on my mind's eye. Seeing his disfigurement didn't scare me, not like I would've expected. I pitied him and the life he must've known, but there was no fear or disgust. With Etalon, I've had weeks to prepare myself. No matter what's on the other side of his mask, there will be no fear or pity. We're linked through our music and our memories, and I'm grateful for all the years he played for me in my dreams. I don't care what he looks like. I just want the obstacles gone and the isolation to end—for both of us.

"No," I finally answer his question, then pull the cover away. A whimper snags in my throat and I drop the mask. It clatters outside of the cloak, its fragile surface cracking.

Neither of us stops to inspect the damage. We're too busy watching each other. His impenetrable gaze tracks my every feature, taking measure of my reactions.

I was right . . . he is his own foil: two polar opposites, a contrast of masculine angles and elegant curves. Every delicate feature rests symmetrically atop a strong bone structure: rugged jaw line, shapely lips, straight nose, a falcon's eyes—alert and piercing—buried in myriad lashes, and a flawless olive complexion almost celestial beneath the filmy lights.

I expected to be struck mute, but not by his beauty.

He takes my hand—that small contact colliding in a union of the senses: I feel, taste, smell, and hear only him.

"*Rune*." My name claws free from his damaged vocal cords.

"Etalon," I answer, mesmerized.

He grins at that, an arresting flash of white teeth.

"Why?" I ask. "Why the mask?"

He swallows, his Adam's apple bobbing. "It is only behind the mask where I feel I belong."

"No." I squeeze his hand. "You belong up here, out in the open, with me."

His mouth twitches. "Prove it."

"How?"

"There are no more walls between us, neither manmade, nor cosmic."

My heart pounds. "I know."

"So . . . touch me."

A wave of shyness heats my cheeks, but he's done waiting. He cups my hands around his jaw on either side, holding them in place. Electric pleasure crackles between us like lightning.

He lets go as I take over, tracing the graceful curves of sinew and bone along his face then down his neck to his collarbone. Trails of light follow my fingertips, as if carving a path through his emotions.

Arms at his sides, he closes his eyes in rapturous beauty, long lashes fanned across sculpted cheekbones.

I stop at the V of his neckline. We both catch a breath as the fine line of hair tickles my palm. I rest my hand just above his racing heartbeat, coaxing out a pulse of bright green in his chest. My heart answers with the same shimmering color.

His eyes snap open, coppery and glimmering: the eyes from my dreams.

As if he's held back long enough, he sweeps away the tangles from my temple and caresses the shell of my ear. His other hand skims down, his thumb exploring the shape of my lips. Every touch feels new and remarkable, yet at the same time, familiar—an all-consuming sense of recognition.

When I look at him like this, unmasked and bared, I can see inside him—inside *myself*—even more clearly than the day in the chapel and all the nights we've danced together since.

"I know you," I say, dreamily. "I was never able to see your face in the memories or visions. But somehow, I know you. You feel like home to me."

Growing somber, he turns me loose and stands. His clothes tighten around his flexing form as he stretches to tug the tin can off the statue. The other can drags along the roof with a metallic scrape as he pulls the ribbon free from both.

He kneels in front of me. "You know my soul. Just as I knew yours before seeing you." He curls the fingers of my left hand into a loose fist around one end of the ribbon, and brushes my knuckles along his smooth cheek, spurring jolts of sensation that wind through my arms and burrow deep into my chest. "We're twin flames. Incarnations of the same soul, parted while reentering the world . . . predestined to find each other again. Everything we've ever experienced in our separate lives has been working to reunite the mirror pieces of ourselves we left within the other. Twin souls always come full circle, as natural and ineludible as the migration of birds or the alignment of planets. All of this has been set into motion in the past by our spirit, for our bodies to discover in the present. Now, at last, we're here."

I rake a fallen lock of hair from his otherworldly eyes and repeat his words: "We're here." The explanation should strike me as unbelievable, but instead, the rightness of it is undeniable.

All those nights we climbed the stars and rearranged the planets with our songs, we were complete and invincible when we stood together.

Only in the context of predestination could those dream-visions make sense.

He lifts my fisted hand, pushes my sweater's sleeve to my elbow, and trails warm, soft lips along my inner wrist. Then he twines the length of the ribbon around the lingering imprint of his kisses, winding his own bared wrist into the loops, until we're fused as one, my now-opened palm facing his, our fingers entwined.

"We're destined to be lovers, Rune. Connected by the thread of our shared soul through space and time. Now that we're united, no matter the where or the when, or whatever circumstances come between us—that cord will stretch to accommodate it all, pliant and giving. It may tangle, but it will never snap. We will always be tethered. Always find each other again . . . because it's fated to be."

My blood burns hot, the veins bright and luminous under my skin. Etalon's veins flare in response. As if ignited by our combined surge, the ribbon catches fire on our arms. I don't even blink because the flames don't hurt, although they blaze through a rainbow of auras. Only when they fade to the purest white do they snuff away on smoky tendrils.

The ribbon's crimson stamp remains—a visible coiling tattoo on my left wrist and forearm, mirroring the image on his right—while leaving us free. As we pull our arms apart, I still feel the tug between us . . . an internalized bond that can't be broken.

I gasp and smile, looking up into his face. Returning my smile, he catches my hips and draws me to him, long legs cradling either side of my body. I move my hands along his shirt, learning the hard planes of his chest and stomach over the soft fabric. He groans and his fingers slip to my nape and clench my hair, forehead pressed to mine. His breath is scented with an elixir of emotions—smoke and honey and rose petals. I shut my eyes, drifting to the stars as I breathe him in.

His lips hover inches from mine—a torturous tease of sparking currents just out of reach—but he jerks away at the last minute. My eyes pop open, vision clouded and unfocused. In the distance, at the other end of the roof behind the auditorium's cupola, rises a cacophony of sound.

Someone or something has been watching us. My mind is too fuzzy to react, my body too swept away by sensation and awe to move. I'm a trapped rabbit, helpless against the wolf closing in.

20

UNEARTHLY ENTANGLEMENTS

"It is the dim haze of mystery that
adds enchantment to pursuit."
Antoine de Rivarol

Thorn stood—nerves abuzz—rocking from his soul-deep reunion with Rune after all these years of being apart. So close to tasting his name on her lips. But even with the frustration of that loss, he couldn't deny how potent the surge had been between them. He'd never felt such a pure electric thrill. His body stung from the inside out—alert, alive, ignited.

He helped her up and motioned toward the door. She wavered in place, absently rubbing the ribbon's burn imprinted on her arm, unable to budge. She was dewy-eyed enchantment shrouded within her white aura of innocence and wonder—lost and confused. He'd given her too much too fast. He should've stopped with the information about the violin; her mind hadn't been ready for the unity ritual this soon. But Erik had forced his hand.

Thorn kept his sights on the green-lit cupola in the distance, his body planted firmly in front of Rune, waiting either for the spy to reveal himself, or for Rune to recover enough to get back inside, where he could keep her safe for at least one more day.

He'd explored the roof when he arrived but failed to check the cupola's secret passage. By then, he could think only of making everything perfect, of winning back Rune's trust and feeling her in his arms without time or space between them, of her breath catching on his face—both of them bared of masks and lies.

Most of the lies.

He hadn't outed Erik's plan yet. He couldn't, not until he'd confirmed or negated what he'd come to suspect after that cryptic discussion with Erik in the lab a few hours earlier.

Thorn had always believed the universe lined up every event that brought Rune into his path. But now, it was starting to appear that the universe had help. That Erik had been using Thorn's connection to Rune from the very beginning to summon her to this place, in this time.

You have served me well over the years. His father's melodious taunt writhed and pricked inside Thorn's brain, an earworm with a serpent's bite. *You've brought her this far when no one else could have.*

Was that why he gave Thorn the violin to begin with, all those years ago? When he told him to play it every chance he could? Because Erik knew it had been tied to her father somehow? Some kind of magical tether?

Thorn would never forgive himself if it were true, especially now, if his role had put Rune in even more danger. It was one thing, if she wanted to escape her voice like Erik had always said she would. But Thorn had come to realize she needed the chance to embrace the gift, free of pain, before making that decision. He of all people understood what it was like to have such a talent stripped away.

None of it mattered, though, if the spy behind the cupola was the Phantom. Everything would be over tonight.

Already things were spinning out of control. Law enforcement was out of the question. Erik had trip wires and land mines set in place on the upper floors, and would trigger them all without hesitation should he sense someone closing in. Everyone in the academy was a sitting duck unless Thorn could sabotage the pitfalls himself, covertly. He was the only one who could, since he had helped Erik plant most of them, two years earlier.

He'd already disarmed the ones he knew of over the past few weeks, but there would be some Erick had set up in secret. Thorn had searched all the floors except the top two. He needed at least another day. One more day of committing treason against the man who'd raised and nurtured him.

Thorn's chest ached. "Show yourself!" He shouted to their stalker, straining his voice.

A rush of rustles and growls stirred behind the cupola, but nothing came into view. He would've suspected Tomlin, had he not already checked in on Erik's puppet before coming to the roof tonight. The drummer still hadn't returned from the city.

That left only the Phantom. But how? When Thorn last saw him, he was barely able to stand. It usually took him all night to recuperate from pouring his energy into the cryogenic chamber.

Thorn's feet shifted as Rune's body slumped against him. He wrapped an arm around her. "Come on. Snap out of it. Rune—"

Snarling hisses and tingling bells preempted a flurry of movement from the shadows. A sprinkle of red feathers tufted on the wind in the wake. Thorn almost laughed, so relieved to see the swan and the cat. Both animals had the habit of behaving like dignified emissaries in the presence of the Phantom. They'd never lower themselves to this level of playfulness were he here.

But there was still the chance he might be close behind.

Scooting everything to one end of the bench, Thorn eased Rune down and lifted her legs so she could lie on her side. He patted her face until she roused.

"W-wha's happening?" She slurred, her eyes wide as Ange fluttered past, squawking, with Diable happily prancing in jingly pursuit. "Wait . . . Diable, no!" She rolled off the bench, diving to grab Diable but missing when the cat ducked and slapped a paw across the swan's tail feathers.

Thorn caught Rune before she face-planted next to his boots. She looked up, blinking, not fully cognizant.

"H-how'd Diable get up here?" She rubbed her eyes as he settled her to sit back on the bench. "Oh, yeah. Ghost kitty."

Thorn frowned. It was taking her longer than he'd anticipated to come down from the drunken crest of energy they'd shared. How was she going to manage the trek downstairs?

She leaned forward, elbows on knees, so low her hair hid her face.

He could scoop her up and carry her. He'd prefer that, with her warmth nestled against him—as close as possible to the citrusy vanilla clinging to those glossy strands wound about her head.

Diable darted past, Ange chasing him this time. Her wings splayed low as she waddle-hopped behind. She stretched her neck and chomped the cat's tail. Diable let out a nerve-wracking yowl.

Rune sat up straighter, though still wobbly. She peered through her hair. "Why aren't you doing something? They're going to kill each other!"

Thorn steadied her. "They're fine. Tag is their favorite game. They were playing it that day we first met in the chapel. Ange doesn't need our help any more than Diable needed yours then."

"But . . . he was drowning."

Thorn rolled his eyes. "That was a ruse on his part to get your attention. He was sweet on you from the beginning. Cats are naturally afraid of water but can overcome it. I made sure Diable could swim ever since he was a tiny kitten, because of where we live." Thorn winced. The less Rune knew about the Phantom's lair, the safer she was. He must be energy-drunk himself to let that slip.

One glance at her face and the ribbon marks on his arm sizzled with hot friction as if in confirmation.

"*Where you live* . . . under the opera house, with the Phantom," she reasoned, knotting her unruly waves at the back of her head. Her mind was getting clearer by the second. "That's what you mean, isn't it?"

"Enough chatter." He cupped her elbow and helped her stand. "It's time."

Misreading his intentions, she snuggled close. "Finally," she mumbled, her head against his chest, all of her curves pressed to him—softness and trembling expectations. "I was wondering when we were going to dance." Her fingertips slid up his back, igniting a voltaic charge through his entire body. The force of their bond took even him off guard. Their link had coalesced faster than he expected.

"No." He pushed her away. She was steady on her feet now, so his tone harshened. "Time for you to *go*."

She flashed him a bewildered pout that flung him back into the moment he'd traced her lips. His thumb twitched, craving that sensual perusal again.

"What do you mean, go? After everything you told me about me and my family? After what just happened between *us*?" She dragged her sweater's cuff down to cover her ribbon tattoo. "You don't drop life-altering things like that on someone and send them on their way!"

"You're not safe up here." He shoved her tote into her hands, hating that his roughness rocked her back a step.

Her eyes scanned the rooftop. "From what?"

He shook his head, feeling each second slice through him like a scalpel. He had to get home and assure the Phantom was where he had left him. Time was already short enough without Erik looking over his shoulder. "Go get some rest."

She frowned as Ange and Diable darted by in their periphery. "Like that's a possibility. My friends all hate me. My aunt despises me as much as my grandma. And now I have to find some way to cut school and visit the prison." She held the bag against her chest like a breastplate of armor as she studied her father's violin case. "You're coming to the vent, aren't you?"

Imploring eyes turned up to him, wide, green, and edged with filigrees of gold—an enticing testament to their spiritual fusion. They would sparkle like jewels for hours. He wished he could be there to watch them fade, so he could light them up again.

"Please," she continued to torment. "I don't want to be alone tonight. I need you to stay with me . . . to play a song for me. It's the only way I'll fall asleep."

Longing clawed through his chest. She might have the sense to be scared, if she knew how much he wanted to stay with her, and not on the other side of some damned wall with a violin filling his arms, coaxing out fantasy serenades. No. He wanted to hold her while tangled in the covers on her bed, flesh to flesh—coaxing out the beast she was so frightened to become.

He wanted to end the evening on that note, with a promise she'd never spend another night alone. But the masquerade would be here too soon, and there were traps to be discovered, loose ends to tie up, and a harrowing secret still between them.

"I can't stay with you." His response was designed to cut with its spiky edges and sharp apathy. "I have things to do."

"Ah." Her voice cracked. "Things to do." With only a grunt to warn him, she kicked the mask on the roof between their feet. It slammed his heel with such force, the crack in the forehead fissured like a busted eggshell. He was impressed by the power behind the angry gesture, knowing their merge had given her that burst of strength. But the hurt looking back at him crushed any satisfaction. "FYI," she snarled. "Having some magical thread between us that can stretch across the universe doesn't take the place of being *physically* there when I need you."

She kept him pinned with a glare and backed toward the door, her posture stiff and ready to snap. He couldn't have her lumbering down the stairs like a raging bull. She'd fall and break her neck.

He caught up to her and drew her close enough that her breasts grazed his rib cage. Her expression softened, all that tension draining away in an instant. It was daunting, how quickly she responded to his touch now.

"Etalon . . ."

"That's better." He spun her around and aimed her for the door once more. "Get those answers for me—as early as possible. Morning, preferably."

She glanced back, her tough façade continuing to crumble. Her chin trembled.

He schooled his features to an expression as blank as his busted mask, in hopes she couldn't see how she affected him.

She opened the door, but stopped midstep. "Oh, I—I have something to give you. In my bag—"

"It will have to wait."

Sniffing, she sealed herself inside. He watched her white aura filter through the space at the doorjamb, watched as it faded to a miserable bluish gray.

Her emotions lingered, torturing him. He'd sampled the heartbreak of years long gone, each time Erik grew reminiscent of Christine. It was a stale flavor . . . flat and dusty, with the slightest hint of decaying lilies. But fresh heartache was an entirely different sensation—like overripe peaches scattered too long in the sun, a fermented sticky sweetness that left his teeth sore and his tongue parched.

One thing Erik had been honest about: finding your twin flame could be hell if the time wasn't right. Thorn touched his forearm, his fingertips prickling as they followed the ribbon's imprinted coils.

Diable mewled.

Thorn rolled down his sleeve. He frowned at the animals seated next to his feet and panting. "Well, you two have a lot to make up for."

After a yawn that showcased a full cast of needle-sharp teeth, Diable pattered to the door and scratched at the base, his crooked tail twitching expectantly.

"That's a start." Thorn opened it, peering inside to see that Rune had already disappeared around the first turn of the corkscrew stairs. Diable sauntered in and shot Thorn a slitted, glimmer-green glance. "See that she gets down the steps safely. And don't leave her side tonight. *Comfort her.* Be there for her, since I can't."

In less than a blink, the cat vanished around the bend, svelte as a shadow.

Upon shutting the door, Thorn turned to Ange who was preening her ruffled feathers. "As for you, vixen-angel . . ." Her elegant neck curved so her clouded eyes could focus on him. "Where exactly is your master?"

❈·I·❈

Having Diable join me on my journey down the dark stairwell is the only thing that keeps me from falling apart. The thought of lying down in my room, with only the dismal burble of my lava lamp for company, threatens to drag my loneliness to new depths.

I'm so happy when I notice the cat slinking down beside me. I consider offering him the gift of Etalon's toe socks—for a scratching post.

"Your master is a jerk. You know that, Ghost Kitty?"

The cat glares up at me. If he had eyebrows, I'm pretty sure one would be raised in derision.

"Okay, he's not your master, *per se.* And I guess he's not a jerk, *completely.*"

Not if I stop nursing my wounded ego long enough to be honest. I'm assuming he's the reason Diable is here now. On the roof, I watched Etalon's aura fluctuate between his longing to stay with me, and the battle he waged to push me away. He was trying to protect me from something. Something shadowing him so closely, he's in

316

danger himself—a paralyzing thought that revives those uncomfortable, stinging tickles in my throat.

Doesn't he get it? He needs to let me in. There's no place for secrets, not after everything we've shared. That's why I wanted him to spend the night. To keep us both protected. There's safety in numbers. I should've told him that. In fact, I should've told him the truth I was hiding . . . that I didn't want him to sleep on the other side of the wall at all. That I wanted him in my room next to me.

A flush of heat works its way across my face. I guide my flashlight app to light my footsteps. "He senses my emotions, so I thought . . ." My free hand runs along the two-way mirrors. "I don't know what I thought. I acted like a diva."

Diable responds with a profound sneeze.

I attempt a smirk and play with the roof's key where it hangs from my neck. "You're right. Renata's role must be going to my head."

The cat's tinkling collar offers the only comment on our continued descent. I lift the key and hold the metal to my mouth, thinking of Etalon's soft lips. He almost kissed me. A real kiss, from someone I don't have to worry about killing, from someone who makes me feel extraordinary yet grounded, just by pressing a fingertip to my temple.

With a touch that potent, I wonder what his kiss will be like?

Diable and I pass room after room on the other side of the mirrored walls, but I don't bother looking in this time. I'm too preoccupied, too confused, too . . . resonant.

There's no other way to describe how my body feels—pulsing, glowing, an ember of flame wrapped in song. The moment Etalon joined our hands with that ribbon, we became harmony personified—musical notes that could not only be heard, but seen, smelled, felt, and tasted. At first, I'd been drunk on it. With so many sensations to absorb at once, my nervous system dulled to cushion me.

But now, wide-awake and sober, everything is radiant and vivid and thunderous. Our shared life-force rocks like a lightning storm of melody: reverberating inside my chest, vibrating through the tributaries of my veins, echoing in depths I never knew were silent . . . flooding hollows I never knew existed.

We're destined to be lovers, Rune.

The power of that truth levels me, unbalances me. That he's been trying to find me, just like I have him, although I never knew what I was looking for, or how much I missed him until this moment. Yet he's missed me for so long. And now, for us to finally be here together, he has to be just as leveled and unbalanced as I am. It's that knowledge that quiets my racing heart and calms my trembling hands, in spite of the monumental weight his words carry.

Everything he said is a fact. I believe it. Not just because of the red, winding imprint scintillating and secure on my wrist and arm, or the green electrical sparks that bridge our hearts when we touch. I believe it because looking at Etalon and seeing into his soul is like looking into my own. And I'm positive it's the same for him.

I don't have experience with romantic love, but this stretches beyond that. What I feel for him penetrates deeper than emotions or desire, deeper than tissue, bone, or marrow—an astounding, wondrous, and terrifying consumption of my entire being that is also somehow the summation of who I am.

Twin flames.

I settle the key atop my sweater as Diable and I reach the stairs' end, ready to leave behind the hidden passage, along with my self-pity. I need to brainstorm how to get myself to Versailles in the morning. It's time to end this curse that has darkened every corridor of my existence up till now, so I can make peace with who and what I truly am, and walk the halls of something new and bright— hand-in-hand with Etalon.

Cautious, I ease open the secret door. Diable and I creep into the grand foyer. In the deafening silence, the squeak of the mirror's hinges seems to reach all the way to the spiraling ceiling, sending nervous shudders down my spine. I hold my breath. Hearing nothing in response, I shut the mirrored panel and tiptoe toward my dorm room with Diable jingling at my heels.

Moonlight traces the floor and bounces off the reflective walls— silvery-blue luminaries that paint my skin as I reach the Red Death phantom cutout standing beside the stairs. I stop there, remembering Etalon's warning: *You're not safe up here.* And his reaction at the rave club in the elevator . . . when he told me the Phantom couldn't know I was gone, that his wrath would follow.

A chill drizzles down my spine. It's the Phantom who's a threat to us both. That's what Etalon is afraid to say aloud. But why is he in danger, too, if they're family? Maybe the same reason I've been in danger from mine. And somehow, it's all tied to Dad's violin.

The reminder of my trip to Versailles sets my nerves on edge even more.

In the recesses of my mind, the Phantom's mesmerizing operatic performance at the club reawakens and unfurls, elemental and sylphlike. With Etalon's guidance, I'd suppressed that bewitching song, but I didn't kill it. Now, the heavenly notes compel me to reach toward the cutout's deathly white, skeletal mask. At the instant of contact, an icy splash of dread begins at my fingertips and frosts my body, threatening to freeze the symphonic flames Etalon so masterfully stoked in my blood.

I jerk back. The Phantom's voice fades, but I still feel it lingering at the back of my skull . . . cold, coiled, and waiting to strike again.

A sudden rustle alerts me to someone hidden in the shadows on the stairway behind the cutout. My heart pounds when Diable hisses at my feet. I'm afraid to budge, the hair on my neck stiffening.

An icy grip on my shoulder from behind makes me drop my tote and sends me twirling around to face a snake's gaping mouth only inches from my nose. I yelp as Diable leaps up, claws digging into the olive scales. He knocks the serpent to the floor and a delicate clatter of metal pins follows.

"*Fichu* cat!" Madame Bouchard's pinched and made-up face leans into the moonlight, ghastly as a specter. "What are you standing there for?" She snarls my direction. "Help me salvage Franco!"

I expel a relieved breath to find Diable's victim is Bouchard's latest dead-pet project. Serves her right for waving *Franco* in front of me. My guardian kitty will be getting an extra bowl of cream tomorrow.

I kneel beside the music teacher, hands shaking as I concentrate on gathering the pins she dropped.

"*Oiseau chanteur*," she snips. "Imagine my surprise, to find you wandering the foyer an hour after lights-out. This should be enough to disqualify you from the role you won today." There's no missing the glee in her voice.

Dropping the pins into a plastic container, I debate saying something snarky to ensure I'm booted out now that Audrey has the part of understudy. But it's possible the lead role would buoy back to Kat since auditions were less than twelve hours ago. I have to tough it out until dress rehearsals in the late spring, so Kat has no chance of reprisal.

"I—I was feeling nauseous. I just came back from the bathroom." I drag my tote back into place on my shoulder, keeping my eyes averted, concerned they might still be aglow like Etalon's were when I left the roof.

Bouchard folds her limp, partially stuffed snake over her arm. "Hmmm. There is something decidedly flushed about your complexion tonight. Come here, into the moonlight." She yanks me toward the windows. Diable follows, spitting at the snake's dragging tail. "*Faire taire*, rancid feline," she scolds.

Diable claws at her ankles until she drops the snake. It glides to the floor—a bone-curdling whisper of scales on marble. The cat attacks the dead reptile, leaving me to my face-off with the music teacher who no longer seems to care about her precious Franco.

Her clammy hand cups my chin and forces my gaze up. Already powder-sheen pale, she drains to almost transparent. "*Non, non, non.* I've seen these eyes before." Her aura shifts from a stubborn brown to the grayish yellow of trepidation. "She's going to want to know about this." Her last statement carries a sour whiff of the coffee she must've been drinking while in her workshop.

I try to break free. Bouchard struggles against me, fingernails digging into my skin through the weave of my sweater's collar. Her thumb catches on the roof key's chain, breaking it. It drops to my feet. Before I can retrieve it, there's a rustle again on the stairs, close to the second flight.

Bouchard trains a glare toward the noise. Panic lines her forehead. Shooing Diable aside with her pointy shoes, she snarls. "Come, wretched child. You should've listened to me from the beginning. You're endangering others as much as yourself by being here."

We head toward the teachers' dorms and understanding slams into me. Aunt Charlotte's the one whose glimmering eyes Bouchard has seen. Somehow, she's been hiding them. *She's* the one who'll want to know about my awakening because I'm like her now.

The Bride of Frankenstein has been working with my aunt all along, to chase me away. They both want me gone, maybe as much as Grandma did.

Other than dropping my tote like a lonely, pitiful bread crumb for someone to find should I go missing, I don't even attempt to escape as Bouchard jerks me behind her. Where would I go?

Diable falls into step close at my heels—my knight in woolen armor.

In a matter of minutes, I'll have those answers Etalon needed. But there's a brand-new question scratching at my psyche that I would've never thought to ask when I first arrived at RoseBlood six weeks ago:

Will I live to relay everything I'm about to find out?

21

BOOK OF BLOOD

"Everybody is a book of blood . . ."
Clive Barker, Books of Blood, Volumes One to Three

I'm strangely calm by the time we reach Aunt Charlotte's room and Bouchard knocks almost reluctantly on her door. I've remembered what Etalon said about my aunt not being "all bad."

He wouldn't have sent me her way unless he knew I'd be safe. He knows her secrets, and that she's one of us. I suspected it for an instant once I realized the deviation originated on Dad's side of the family, but it seemed so far-fetched.

The door cracks open and Aunt Charlotte peers out with one arm behind her back, white braids piled high on her head and a terrycloth robe wrapped around her dancer's frame. Taking one look at my eyes, she ushers me and Bouchard across the threshold before shutting us all in.

I cast a quick glance around the room. It's designed just like mine—spiraling mini-stairway and loft, antechamber bed with a vent in the wall, zero windows. Instead of violet light, the soft amber glow of a floor lamp casts long shadows across her décor: black-and-white posters of stage productions and hooks holding ballerina shoes of various sizes from different times in her life—details that seem carefully staged, knowing what I know now.

After that glimpse, I stare directly at my aunt, on the chance Etalon's wrong. If so, she's going to have to hurt me with my mom's and her brother's likenesses staring back—damning her.

Sighing, she draws out her hidden arm and gestures with an e-cig toward the chaise lounge. I relax my shoulders a fraction as I plop down and Diable leaps up into my lap.

"Françoise." Aunt Charlotte aims a grimace at Bouchard. Her voice is tinny, as if she's speaking through a metal pipe. "How did this come about? Did you catch her feeding?"

Bouchard snatches the cigarette and leans against an armoire to sip the vapor. The scent of cloves drifts over to me. "She was meandering around the foyer, already looking like that. Most likely she siphoned off one of the boys as they slept."

"I would never," I say, surprised by my security in that knowledge. Not just because I'm no longer hungry after being with Etalon, but because I'm aware of what I'm capable of now, and that I control it, which has nothing to do with our twin flame connection. It's because I make my own conscious choices. I can live with this and learn to blend in. My aunt is proof of that.

"Whatever the case," Bouchard responds to my denial but keeps her gaze trained on Aunt Charlotte. "She's a danger to the other students now, and to our secrets. She's cured, yes? So we should put her on the next plane back to the States."

My aunt tightens the belt at her waist. "There are things she needs to understand first. Now that—"

"*Now that what?*" I screech, causing Diable to growl my direction; it's mostly for show, because his weight continues to warm my thighs. "Now that I know I'm a vampire like you?"

Bouchard slants her gaze to the vent over my aunt's bed then shushes me, releasing a pouf of scented white fog.

I calm myself by plaiting my hair to a side braid. I'm not sure how the rage bubbled up so fast. But it's long overdue. "Why did you go to such lengths to scare me away?" I ask, careful to keep my voice low.

Aunt Charlotte and Bouchard exchange glances.

"I didn't agree with your *grand-mère's* decision to bring you to RoseBlood," my aunt answers. "But I'd made a promise to at least try. Still . . . I wasn't convinced her strategy would have the desired results. I was worried it was a trap."

Bouchard clears her throat.

My aunt rolls her eyes. "We were *both* worried of that."

I crinkle my forehead. "So . . . you tore my clothes and killed that poor bird to save me from another of Grandma's psycho vendettas?" My stomach turns, remembering the crow's greasy, clumped feathers.

"Not exactly." Aunt Charlotte moves closer to the lamp. Her eyes come to vivid clarity in the light, glimmering like Etalon's when energy is brewing beneath the surface. Does she absorb it from the cigarettes somehow? Her irises are brown but fringed in gold. They've always been normal behind her glasses . . . hazel like Dad's.

Sunny mentioned my aunt having boxes of contacts stashed with her cigarettes. I glance over where Bouchard studies her e-cig from end to end, far too comfortable propped next to the armoire.

The armoire where my aunt stores everything.

I jump up and Diable grumbles as he's spilled onto the floor. I rush to the other end of the room. Bouchard tries to block me, but I slap the cigarette from her hand, throwing her off balance.

I force open the doors, and there they are. Disposable colored contacts: *hazel brown*. Aunt Charlotte's camouflage.

It appears we each have to wear some form of mask to fit into this world. Just like Etalon and the Phantom.

"It's good that you know at last. You won't feel so alone now." Aunt Charlotte's warm hand clasps my shoulder gently. "I've wanted to tell you for years. But your *grand-mère* wouldn't allow it. She feared it would endanger your mother, and she'd made a promise to your father to protect both of you at all costs. I didn't realize you'd had your awakening, or I would've told you, regardless." I start to shake her off, but her gentle touch reminds me of Mom's, and I surrender to the sensation. "Sweet child, please be assured: Where your *grand-mère* is concerned, there's never been a vendetta. It's always been a rescue attempt. However warped."

I turn to her then. "What . . . drowning . . . catching fire to—how's . . . *rescue*? Bird killer!" I bark the accusation to mock her like her patronizing explanation has mocked me.

Aunt Charlotte shakes her head sadly. "I didn't kill that bird. I simply used its corpse. Françoise . . . she's Death's handyman."

Bouchard huffs as she picks up the e-cig glowing at her feet. "A crow that has the voice of a kitten is an abomination. As is a viperine snake with a growl like a wolf. I was trying to save those creatures."

My chin drops.

"Pssshhh." Aunt Charlotte waves a hand. "I've heard it all before. Each fresh animal hanging in your museum of atrocities. All of them an abomination that needed redemption at your scalpel's blade. Perhaps, had you not dropped out of vet school, you would've learned how to operate successfully."

"So . . . the rumors are true?" I ask with a stiff tongue. "About the animals in the forest?" But I don't get an answer. Bouchard and my aunt are too engrossed in their bickering. The more I listen, the more it's apparent how long they've known each other, and how Bouchard seems to be accountable to my aunt. Or at the very least, an ally.

"No way," I say. "She's your familiar. People can be familiars, right?"

They both stop talking at once.

"Oh, look, our newly awakened *ingénue* thinks she's figured it all out." Bouchard narrows her beady blue eyes, deepening the web of wrinkles around them. "You're only halfway there, tripe." She points the e-cig my direction. "I'm not a familiar. I'm family. A second cousin twice removed, one generation older than you."

An unexpected snort bursts from my mouth. "Make that three or four generations, Lady Methuselah." I'm not intimidated anymore. After everything she's put me through while I've been here, I'm ready for a fight. And now that we're on familial ground, I have nothing holding me back.

Bouchard curses in French and starts toward me. I step up to meet her halfway. Diable hisses from the chaise across the room as Aunt Charlotte steps between us.

"*C'est assez!*" She grabs her cigarette from Bouchard and pokes a finger into her chest. "I'm over being patient with you. Yes, yours is a recessive gene; yes, the power passed you by. Stop taking your jealousy out on Rune. Remember what I can do to you, should I decide I no longer care to tolerate your negative energy." She opens the door to show our bony second cousin out.

Bouchard twists around and shoves her pointed toe over the threshold, preventing Aunt Charlotte from closing it.

"Oh, you don't believe I'll do it?" my aunt asks her on a sinister murmur. She looks to the left of the door, where a clock hangs on the wall. "Hmmm. A quarter to eleven. I suppose I could have my midnight snack early. Cynicism tastes like flat ginger ale and cold peppermint tea, two of my favorite flavors. Rune, you'll join me, won't you? *Bon appétit*." She licks her lips and her eyes flash.

Bouchard shrinks back and her foot slips free.

"Off to bed then. And sweet dreams, dear cousin." Aunt Charlotte closes the door.

I stand there in awe of the energy-sucking aunt I'm only starting to know, too tense and confused to move.

"Sit." She commands.

An ember of rebellion flashes to life, but she inferred she wants to give me answers. I'm not about to jinx that.

I take my seat. Diable has forgiven me for dropping him, and curls into my lap again. In all these weeks he's been my companion, he hasn't let me pet him, but he's been more attentive tonight than ever. I'm guessing Etalon gave him very strict instructions. Testing my theory, I stroke his back. He arches his spine toward my palm, a request for more. Despite looking like an abrasive steel-wool cleaning pad, he's plush, thick, and so warm.

As I continue to caress his fur, he purrs and squeezes his eyes to blissful slits, his peaceful energy soothing me enough that I find my voice again. "Dad's violin," I say to my aunt, massaging the downy skin between the cat's bat-like ears. His front claws knead my thighs. "Everything is tied to it."

"Who told you that?" Aunt Charlotte asks, frowning. She sets her e-cig aside, waiting.

I don't answer. Etalon is *my* secret. One I'm not willing to expose. I have to keep him safe, just as he's doing for me.

Aunt Charlotte makes a frustrated grunt before turning her back. She shoves aside e-cigs and disposable contacts to clear a space at the bottom of her armoire. There, she exposes a hidden compartment from which she drags a shoe box.

"I apologize for allowing Françoise such liberties the past few weeks." Taking a seat next to me, she places the box between us. "When you began to show signs the music no longer controlled you, I had to let her test you to be sure. She took too much glee, tormenting you. But as you're about to see, it was all in hopes of helping."

I frown. "Right. Just like Grandma's homicidal boat ride and the Valentine's fire parade?"

Aunt Charlotte's mouth tightens. "We each have different ideas of how to help, *clairement*."

"Clearly," I repeat, scoffing. "I need to see her. I want answers for what she did . . . and I want to know about Dad's Strad."

Aunt Charlotte opens the box between us, revealing old newspaper clippings, a folded stack of aging letters with the name "Christine" scrawled underneath a string holding them together, a playbill spotlighting the famous Swedish soprano, and a black journal with the words *Livre Ancestrale de Sang* embossed across the front in shimmery red text.

Ancestral Book of Blood. In spite of the morbid curiosity spurred by that title, I reach for the letters first, drawn by Etalon's brief insight into the affair between the prima donna and her opera ghost. My aunt stops my hand.

"Patience, Rune. An opera is best viewed in the sequence the composer intended. And know this: your *grand-mère* has been paying for what she did while locked in prison. Now she will die there, alone. She is too weak to answer questions. So I will answer for her."

Before I can respond, my aunt flips through the journal pages then brings it closer, brushing Diable's tail with her wrist. He leaps down and settles on the other side of my feet to lick himself clean.

Aunt Charlotte moves her hand so I can see the diagram spanning both sides . . . a family tree, with names partitioned off on countless branches. Her fingertip trails to the line at the top, a script I can barely read for the faded ink.

"Comte Saint-Germain," she reads the name aloud. "You were researching him yesterday at the library?"

I let my silence answer.

"I'm not sure how much information there is online . . ."

"The last thing I read was that he died, but there were rumors of sightings years after."

Her finger taps the page. "It was his death that was the rumor. He faked dying, then took his leave of society to travel with a caravan of gypsies with whom he shared all things alchemy, herbs, magic, and holistic. He grew powerful feeding off their superstitions and lively music. He even bargained an instrument of his own from an artisan witch—a Stradivarius violin made of enchanted black heartwood. Saint-Germain became the Romani Roi of the group—their gypsy king. He took a wife, and had children. Some fifty-three years later, a masked boy stumbled upon that very gypsy camp after escaping his abusive mother. Saint pitied him, and took him in. He recognized that he was one of his kind. A young incubus, although disfigured and emaciated."

The photograph Etalon showed me of the childhood Phantom surfaces in my mind's eye. "So, Saint-Germain gave him the violin?"

Aunt Charlotte shuts the *Book of Blood*. "Not in the beginning. Our predecessor was growing old by then. He no longer wished to accrue any extra life. There is such a thing as outliving your soul. And he was wise enough to know he had. He wanted Erik—the mysterious incubus child—to take his place as Romani Roi, for he could see the genius in him, even at such a young age. Not only because he could play any instrument put before him, not only because he could sing and enrapture even the most cynical audience. But because he had the ability to absorb knowledge and talent at an unprecedented rate. Saint schooled him as his apprentice. Taught him all his tricks and wisdom. Told him all his secrets. Things he hadn't told his own children, like where he'd hidden his jewels— here, in the bowels of the Liminaire, in a secret labyrinth of tunnels. When Saint died a few months later, he bequeathed his grown children and young grandchildren his beloved Stradivarius violin. But that wasn't enough for them. They turned on Erik, locked him in a cage, stripped him of his clothes and dignity, and forced him to perform like an animal with that very instrument, because he refused to confess where Saint-Germain's treasure was hidden. Erik at last escaped, and took Saint's violin with him. He knew nothing of its rumored magic, but it was all that was left of the only father he'd ever known, and he deemed our ancestors unworthy of it."

My stomach turns. I never thought I'd empathize with a stranger over my family. But after the way they treated him, they were unworthy. "We got the violin back. When?"

Aunt Charlotte lays the newspaper clippings in my lap. "You know of Leroux, the author of the fictionalized account."

I tilt my head.

"As it happened, in 1909, while researching a piece on the Palais Garnier, Leroux stumbled upon Christine's letters wrapped up with a delicate necklace threaded through a ruby wedding ring. They were tucked beneath architectural blueprints in a box marked O.G. and hidden inside one of the opera house's crawlspaces. The letters were actually loose-leaf journal entries, dated forty-five years prior, and were Christine's account of her time with the opera ghost. Leroux tracked down the only soprano by the name 'Christine' who would've been performing around that date under the stage name: Christina Nilsson. She was sixty-six by then, an old widowed woman who became distraught when confronted with the letters and ring. She claimed they weren't hers . . . how could they be, she insisted, when she'd never performed at the Palais Garnier? Perhaps it was partly for show, since her maid was in the room, but she demanded Leroux take the letters and the ring out of her sight and never return. Since there was no last name, Leroux published the letters, embellishing versions of the story, in bits and pieces as a serialization, keeping the only two names that were in the original papers: Erik and Christine. The rest of the cast he made up. He hoped by doing this publicly, he might draw out their true author."

I sort through the newspaper clippings from *Le Gaulois*, my gaze passing over the text and eerie illustrations of a ghastly phantom creeping through the underground labyrinth of the opera house. The scent of ink stings my nose and black smudges my fingers.

"No one ever came forward for them," my aunt continues. "However, the letters and necklace were stolen out of his office shortly after the final serialization in 1910. It didn't matter to Leroux. He went on to write the tale as a book, building upon the scant details gleaned from his articles."

"So . . . the Phantom stole the letters," I mumble, wiping my hands on my jeans.

"Actually, our own Octavius Germain did that. He was one of Saint's ungrateful grandchildren, close to Erik's age. He'd lived in the gypsy camp when Erik escaped. Octavius read the paper, saw the similarities between the story's villain and the masked boy who had absconded with our family's violin and fortune over sixty years earlier. Having something of Erik's to bargain with at last, he posted an announcement in another newspaper."

She slips out an article and holds it up.

O.G. to O.G.

Found: 1 necklace attached to ruby ring. 1 stack of lovelorn letters. Willing to trade for 1 family fortune.

Contact me via post.

The address is blurred, as if the clipping suffered water damage.

"Every week, for *ten years,* Octavius posted an identical ad. Then at last, in 1921, shortly after Christina Nilsson's obituary ran"— Aunt Charlotte gathers up the clippings and drops them in the shoe box—"he received a response from 'Opera Ghost.' Octavius and Erik arranged to meet here in this very opera house for the trade. By that time, the Liminaire had fallen into disrepair, and Erik had charmed the deed away from the royal family it once belonged to.

Octavius came armed, with no intention of making a trade until the money was in his hands. But he underestimated the Phantom's cunning. Using ventriloquism, Erik lured Octavius to a room on the fifth floor. Seeing the violin within, Octavius stepped inside. The door slammed shut, imprisoning him. Within minutes, Erik triggered fire traps across the top three flights. He provided an escape route for Octavius that could be accessed only by inserting the ring into a groove carved in the door . . . a keyhole that would fit only one unique ruby stone. Once inserted, the door opened, but the ring was stuck, and could not be relinquished. Octavius stumbled through the passage to escape with his life, none the richer. However, he carried the violin and Christine's letters. Erik cared nothing for the letters. No doubt to read them would have broken his heart. But the violin . . . he'd not only played it to give birth to a musical virtuoso, but he played it for her on her deathbed, coaxing one last duet between them before she closed her eyes forever. Still, he let it go. In his mind, he was honoring Saint-Germain by returning what the man had intended his family to have. All debts were paid, and Erik kept the fortune for himself free of guilt." She sighs. "I almost feel sorry for him. Knowing that he didn't recognize at the time the precious cargo contained within that instrument."

My mind twists in knots, struggling to reconcile that shattered, lovesick man with the dangerous and compelling Phantom I saw at the rave club. "Precious cargo in the violin? What does that mean?"

"Well, that has to do with Christine." Aunt Charlotte offers me the stack of Christine's letters. My fingers practically itch to open them. "Before you read them, there's something you need to understand about yourself. All of us, of otherworldly leanings, are incarnations."

Her claim is reminiscent of Etalon's: *We're twin flames. Incarnations of the same soul, parted while reentering the world . . . predestined to find each other again . . .* The ribbon imprinted around my wrist and forearm tingles under my sweater.

"But the vampiric gene in the Germain bloodline is so far removed"—Aunt Charlotte's voice pulls me back—"it's recessive for many of us. Françoise, for instance. For me, it was dominant. For your father and *grand-mère*, recessive. I have an uncle and a great aunt who are like me. There's no rhyme or reason, really. But then, for a rare few like you, you're incarnated from another vampire, of another era, of another bloodline. In those instances, the gene is neither recessive nor dominant. It is, rather, *dormant*. Waiting for something miraculous to bring it to surface. In your case, it was the musical essence of your preincarnate self, held at bay for years inside a very special violin rumored to have the power to capture a person's most quintessential life-spark within, if played at the moment of their death."

My heart pounds as the profoundness of what she's saying hits me. My palm finds my throat. "I—I have Christine's voice."

"Yes. And your father, *bénissez-le*, was the bridge. The voice was waiting to be reunited with Christine, the moment she was reborn as another person. *You*. All it took was your father choosing to play the right kind of music . . . opera. That was the key. Once those familiar notes wailed forth from the violin's strings, her voice found its way back. But being that bridge drained him of his life-force. Had he been like you or me, it wouldn't have harmed him. He could've recharged by feeding off any living thing. If only I'd known . . ." Her graceful figure curls to a slouch, like a candle melting. "So often I've mourned that. Not knowing in time to stop it. When I realized, it was too late, and I—"

"You couldn't face Mom or me." I wipe tears from my cheeks. "That's why you didn't come when he got sick, or for his funeral."

"Forgive me, Rune." She pats my hand, blotting moisture from her eyes with her robe's sleeve.

I nod, sniffling. Diable leaps up between us, scowling at her, as if blaming her for my change in mood. I place a hand on his back and he lies down, but doesn't stop glaring. "That's why Grandma hated me . . ."

"No. You were a vessel. *Maman* knew that. But she also knew that if Erik ever learned of what he'd forfeited by giving up his violin, his wrath would come down on our family. So she tried to scare the voice out. Submerging you until your screams turned to bubbles that burst with Christine's song . . . starting a fire that would singe Christine's harmonious notes to smoke. She wasn't trying to harm you. She was trying to kill the voice . . . hoping to free you. *Maman* was half-mad with grief and determination. Losing a beloved child can make even the sanest person crack, and she was never sane. She even mailed the violin to me, demanded I bring it here to this opera house and leave it in box five, with an anonymous note requesting the Phantom lift whatever curse had been brought upon you in exchange for the instrument, yet not specifying what that curse entailed. So much time went by, and you never improved. But then, out of the blue, he tracked Maman down. Showed up at the prison three years ago, offering his aid. Desperate, she confessed the truth about your voice. He took it in stride, almost as if he already knew somehow. He proposed we open a school of arts in his opera house. Proposed establishing its legitimacy by inviting the Nilsson girl . . . Katerina . . . so we'd have the support of the Royal Swedish Academy of Music. He said if we brought you here, he could train your voice himself in secret as you slept, using the violin as your father had. He instructed we not tell you anything. He said it was best if he cured you via your subconscious." She inhales a deep breath, then all her somberness melts away to an expression of pure joy. "And he did it. You won the role of Renata earlier without any pain! And your voice, oh, Rune. I've never heard anything so pure and powerful." Her smile is dreamy. "Your *grand-mére* was right. It was worth the risk after all." She laughs, a liberated silvery sound that rivals the bells on Diable's collar as he jumps at the outburst.

Unlike my aunt, I don't feel any contentment, because it hasn't been the Phantom training my voice. How does Etalon fit into this?

"I'm just so relieved you can go home now and live a normal life at last. Well, as normal as any of us do." Aunt Charlotte winks at me, then stands and puts the remaining items in the shoe box. "You wouldn't believe the crazy theory going through Françoise's head. That somehow the Phantom was planning to take back his true love's voice—surgically. It's because of her paranoia I tried to frighten you and you mother away in the beginning. She had me convinced that the students' rumors were true. That the forest creatures were modified for practice or some such folly, although I've never seen any evidence myself." Strolling to the armoire, she tucks away the family treasures and slides the wood into place, hiding them. "But then, when you started to improve, I realized the flaw in her rationale. Erik is renowned for his affinity with animals. He could never bring himself to imprison them for experiments, much less take a knife to them for his own selfish motives. Even the all-powerful Opera Ghost would need aid for something so adverse to his nature. And I can't imagine anyone brave enough, or deviant enough, to be the Phantom's apprentice. *Risible.*" She chuckles again, moving the boxes back into place over the secret panel.

Ridiculous indeed, to imagine anyone brave or deviant enough . . .

Anyone other than family.

The air gushes out of me, as the realization punches holes in my lungs.

That night, when Etalon and I spoke through the vent and I asked what his hobby was. And his gentle, broken voice answering: "*I tend the animals of the forest. I suppose you could say I'm their . . . doctor.*"

The blood rushes to my head, and the bottom drops out of my world.

22

THE IMITATION
OF LIFE

"Art is always and everywhere the secret confession . . .
The immortal movement of its time."
Karl Marx

I stumble into the moonlit foyer in search of my tote bag. It's ten after twelve, and I'm so wired I don't think I'll sleep tonight. Maybe never again.

I didn't read Christine's notes. And I haven't told Aunt Charlotte anything about Etalon. Every time I try to say his name, the tattoo around my wrist and arm stings as if electrified, a sensation that spears like a high-voltage burst into my throat and across my tongue so I can't speak. Maybe the cord that would never break is snapping after all, and unraveling everything inside of me along with it. Or worse, maybe Etalon tricked me and our so-called bond was some vampiric ploy to make it impossible for me to turn against him.

He's been lying to me about everything else. Why not that, too?

Since I can't confess anything to my aunt, I asked her if I could spend the night in her room. I want to feel safe, and I finally know she only wants what's best for me.

What hurts is I thought that was true of Etalon, too. Did I misread his auras on the rooftop? Wasn't he worried for me?

Then again, he led me to the rave club where I almost killed Jax.

The hospital wristband and IV tube used to lure me there take on a whole new twisted meaning now. How can cutting out my voice be done without killing me? My welfare's probably not even a consideration. It's hard to believe that the guy who was so careful not to pull my hair when he was tying my blindfold could be so detached about helping the Phantom carve Christine's songs from my body.

A lead weight rests in the pit of my stomach. The thought that Etalon doesn't care, after all the nights he inspired me to love music again, gave me fantasy dances, and shared intimate secrets, gores deeper than anything he could do with a scalpel.

I can't imagine what they're planning for my voice once they have it. Put it in a jar like a trapped bug? House it inside a field mouse for my second cousin to capture, mount, and slap on the wall, like one of those stupid singing fish plaques?

I sniffle. It's crazy, horrific, and demented.

Diable scampers around in the shadows as I search for my bag. Even thinking of how affectionate he was earlier doesn't comfort me. Maybe he's never been my guardian at all; maybe he's actually my jailer.

It's dead silent in the school. The cat's collar is the only sound, which for some reason disturbs me more than the rustles I heard behind the phantom cutout earlier. My aunt had offered to come with me to get my pajamas, but I turned her down. Now I'm regretting that.

I was trying not to be a complete coward. Aunt Charlotte said she'll arrange everything—my transfer back to my school in the States, limo ride to the airport and a ticket for the first available flight tomorrow, and a made-up excuse for Mom. I hate to run away like this. I don't want to leave my friends with all of them thinking I'm a jerk. I don't want to leave them *period*.

I've actually come to like this place: the rehearsals, the kooky teachers, the weekend trips to Paris. Even my time in the garden.

The chapel flits through my thoughts. A knot swells in my esophagus—a burning sob I refuse to release. I grip my throat as dread creeps across my mind, taking the shape of that heartbroken water-goblin princess, Rusalka, from Antonín Dvořák's fairy tale opera, as she sings her final song to the moon, a sacrifice she's willing to make for a chance at happy ever after.

Not me.

I finally know the truth . . . all of my family history, everything about the violin . . . and I don't want to relinquish my gift. It is mine. I *did* earn it. I realize that now. I earned it because Dad gave up his life to give it to me, unintentionally or not. I lost the person I loved most in this world. If that's not earning everything that came of that sacrifice, nothing is.

Dad wanted me to have this talent, this voice. It made him happy. And it's an integral part of me. Enough that I'll fight for it till my final breath.

I'm not weak. I know who I am now and why this happened, at last. I'm stronger than when I first got here. Like Etalon said,

I'm a psychic vampire with the power to "consume, transmit, and manipulate life-forces."

But so are he and Erik . . . and they've had a lot more practice at it.

That sob I'm fighting breaks loose.

I squint in Diable's direction. He's found my bag in a splay of moonlight, next to the hall leading to the theater. I didn't drop it over there, yet it's open, and everything has spilled out.

Eyes and ears alerted, I crouch to toss things back in. I pick up the last two items: a pack of gum and a wooden knitting needle. Everything's accounted for, all but my cell phone and the toe socks—balled up, wrapped in tissue paper, and tied with ribbon. I glance around to find Diable batting the socks down the corridor. With a groan, I drag my tote onto my shoulder and follow with the knitting needle still in hand.

The cat leads me to the theater door and I freeze in place, surprised to see it open. Jippetto usually locks it up at night after he's done working on the sets. All the lights are off, and the pitch-dark depths stretch wide. Diable gives the ball a final cuff, and it rolls inside, the tissue paper crinkling.

My fingers grip the knitting needle tighter. I consider turning around. I don't care about the stupid socks anymore. Even though a tiny part of me still wants to give them to Etalon, to see if there's any good left in him: if that little child who wanted to buy his mother all the candied fruit in the world just to see her smile, and the young boy who saved me in my dreams every night, survived in spite of the Phantom's influence. That's what terrifies me most of all, that I still want to have faith in him, even knowing his part in this vile plan.

A few feet inside the door, a rectangular glow catches my eye. It's my phone, with the flashlight app activated. My pulse skips . . .

This is an obvious setup. I should go get my aunt.

Just as I take a step back, Diable's shadow saunters across the phone, Franco's scaly tail flopping in his mouth.

Bouchard.

That witch. I'm so done letting her bully me. Snarling, I step inside, the knitting needle poised like a miniature spear in my hand. "Seriously, *Françoise*. I'm really tired of your—"

The door sweeps shut and the phone blinks off, leaving me cloaked in heavy darkness. Diable's jingles trail off in the distance, close to the stage, but I sense a living presence nearby. Weapon raised, I swing around blindly. Someone grabs me from behind with a hand clamped over my mouth, pulling me back against a rock-hard body. I know him by the current that sparks between us. The succubus inside wants to betray me, melting into his muscles where they twitch along my spine.

I should've never let him seduce me on the rooftop. It's a battle to resist his touch now. The energy that pulses between us in even a graze of our skin gives me the same jolt of rejuvenation that I got from kissing Ben and Jax.

A sweet, solvent odor radiates from Etalon's clothes— medicinal. *Doctor.* That thought revives my fighting spirit. I struggle as his free hand captures my fingers where I clench my knitting needle.

"I heard everything between you and your aunt." His hoarse whisper ruffles my hair as he holds me tight.

Of course he was listening at the vent. Here I thought he was busy. Should've known that's just incubus code for eavesdropping.

"If you promise not to scream," he continues, "I'll let you go." His grip over my lips loosens slightly.

I bare my teeth to bite him, but that imprint on my wrist flares, leaving me unable to. "What did you do to me?" I growl under his fingers and wrestle his hold on my hand, wishing I could stab him with the knitting needle.

"I did what I had to, to protect you," he growls back. He pries at my fingers in an attempt to steal my sad excuse for a weapon. I make a fist around it, resisting. The moment my knuckles start cramping from the force of his digging fingernails, his own ribbon imprint brightens under his sleeve. He curses and drops my hand as if he's been stung, leaving me armed and moderately dangerous.

"See that?" he asks, head lowered so his shaved chin cradles my temple. "I'm no more able to harm you than you are me." He rakes his arm along his thigh to push up his sleeve and showcase his blistering-hot tattoo. Even in the dark, it looks worse than mine felt when I tried to rat him out to Aunt Charlotte. "This is why I rushed our unity ritual tonight. I don't want him to be able to force me to hurt you . . . not with hypnotism, not with threats, not with guilt. I've made it physically impossible for you to go under my knife. So . . . I ask again. Will you promise not to scream?"

Numb, I nod and relax my body in his embrace. His hand falls from my mouth. He turns me around.

I can't make out his face, but his eyes glimmer like embers— flecks of coppery light softened with shadows of brown. "I know you're afraid, but if you leave now, you'll endanger everyone here. He'll burn RoseBlood to the ground with all of the students and teachers locked inside if he fails in his mission. There's only one way we can stop him: by working together." Diable's bells bounce around the theater, as if he's scoping things out. Etalon shifts nervously.

"Are you afraid he's watching us?" I whisper, nerves alerted and prickled.

"He was in his coffin when I checked on him minutes ago."

"Coffin?" I squeak, sounding more wobbly than I'd like.

"He sleeps there. Listen, I want to take you somewhere where we can talk safely. Somewhere I know he won't follow. Will you let me?"

With my friends and teachers in the line of fire, there's only one right answer. I drop my arm to my side, releasing the knitting needle so it clatters to the floor. Then I take his hand in mine.

❋·I·❋

While Etalon helped me gather my things and drop them in my tote, he told me he'd filtered an inhalation anesthetic through my aunt's vent to put her to sleep so she wouldn't miss me tonight. That's why his hands and clothes smelled medicinal. He assured me it wouldn't hurt her, and since he was honest about the injections he gave my friends at the club, I chose to trust him.

Next, he led me through the secret passage in the orchestra pit where he'd hidden Dad's violin, and sailed us across an underground river. In any other circumstance it might've been hauntingly romantic. But it was too similar to the canals leading to the secluded lair I'd always heard about in the stories: the Phantom's house of horrors.

Even worse, I was surrounded by water—the stagnant and threatening scent of it, the currents like laughing, taunting tongues, inky depths made even more endless by the blackness of the cave surrounding us.

Sensing my panic, Etalon awoke the firefly larvae along the roof of the cave to give us some light. We banked on an underground dock and took another secret tunnel on foot up into the forest. A

345

quick moonlight jog along a path through some trees, well-worn by Jippetto's wheelbarrow wheels—with only the sighting of a fox and an owl, each speaking their own natural languages—and now we've arrived.

From the outside, the caretaker's cottage is smaller than I expected. It borders the bank of the river in back, and looks more like a shed, shadowing another shed. A soft light greets us from the sole window on the top half of the front door. Etalon, having held my hand the entire way here, leads me inside without even knocking.

The cottage's one room serves as both a kitchen and sleeping quarters. It's tidy. There are two sconces on the wall aglow from bulbs giving off a soft yellow light. A small antechamber with a sink and toilet is off to the side, where plaid curtains pull across for privacy. Framed watercolor paintings deck the walls around the bed, each one a likeness of a different French shop with displays featuring Jippetto's mannequins. The artwork is signed by him.

"He painted all these?" I ask.

Etalon nods. "There's more to him than most people think."

The caretaker must be expecting us, because there's a kettle of tea steaming on a potholder at the table. Its smoky, caramelized scent fills the room with warmth. Then I realize the hospitality is probably for the mannequins stationed in chairs around empty teacups.

Apparently, the guys' rumors at school were right about a lot of things.

I shiver in contrast to the cozy surroundings.

Standing over me, Etalon places his cloak around my shoulders so I can absorb his body heat. He cups my face with both hands, soothing my nerves with that ability he has, then skims his fingertips along my braid before moving away, leaving me tantalized in his wake. "Jippetto won't be joining us until we're finished up here. He's waiting in the aviary, on the lower level."

"Lower level?" I survey the area again, seeing nothing that indicates stairs or a basement. "How can there be room for a bird run in such a small space with a river out back?"

"You'll see soon. But first . . . tea?" He places the violin case on the floor between the mannequins' chairs, wraps a potholder around the kettle, and pours a cup.

I thank him and grip the handle as he cautions me not to get burned. "Why are we here?" With a sip of hot, caramel-flavored caffeine sinking into my throat, I finally have the courage to ask.

"To make a plan," Etalon says between blowing on his tea. "The Phantom avoids coming here, just as he avoids strolls through the forest." He sets his cup aside. I watch how he moves, flowing grace and sensuality in spite of his height and build, and wonder if it comes naturally to him, or if it's part of being an incubus. Aunt Charlotte is graceful, too. I always thought it was the dancer in her, but maybe it's inherent.

Etalon leans over one of the male mannequins and surprises me by unbuttoning its shirt. There's a black heart in the center of its polished torso, carved of ebony and embedded into the white pine of the chest.

"Recognize the wood?" Etalon asks as he backs toward the chair holding the female to make room for me.

With my free hand, I touch the male's sleek heart, shimmery like an ink spill. "It's like the Stradivarius."

Etalon buttons the shirt back, as if to respect the mannequin's privacy. "Until two days ago, I didn't know it was my violin that your father played for you. And now I see he formed a bridge with his love so Christine's song could find its way into your body. I always thought you were simply born with the voice. Erik made it sound like he'd had the violin since he stole it from the gypsies. Like it had never been out of his hands."

I study him, confused.

He frowns. "Remember the artisan witch your aunt mentioned? The one who sold Saint-Germain the enchanted Strad?"

I nod.

"Jippetto is the last of that clan. They were known in otherworldly circles for working with a special wood that could trap the essence of a spirit. But the black heartwood they used was rare, and grew only in one place. Deforestation decimated their supply along with their craft. Erik's violin was the last instrument they made. Jippetto preserved his family with what little wood he had left. Within these three mannequins are his mother, Adella, and his two twin brothers, Kendric and Kestrel, who died of pneumonia."

I glance from each painted face to the next, seeing new depth to their eyes. I almost expect them to move. Suppressing a shiver, I rest my hands beside a gray cloth napkin, the teacup cradled between them. Steam rises up like a spectral omen. "Poor Jippetto. But what does this have to do with—"

"I came here right after I heard you talking to your aunt," Etalon interrupts. "I asked Jippetto to be honest . . . to tell me all he knew about Erik's history with the Strad. Just like what your aunt said— Erik thought he could let the violin go." Etalon motions me to the empty chair. The one reserved for the caretaker. I sit with my hands on my knees, my body tense. "For three decades, he tried to find a replacement, but nothing could match the purity and resonance of the original instrument. In the 1950s he launched the search for the craftsman, in hopes he could have another made. When it led him to Adella, who was on her deathbed, he learned the truth about the enchanted wood's capabilities. He explained how he'd played for Christine as she died. How she'd sang for him. Adella told him that Christine's voice was trapped within, and that she could be revived one day via the instrument. That when her soul was reincarnated, it could be reunited with her voice. He knew then that the violin was irreplaceable."

I rub my sweater where it covers the scar on my knee. "So why didn't he steal it back from us? I would've thought he'd move heaven and earth . . ."

Etalon props his hands on the table. "Even someone as brilliant and unrelenting as Erik can't outthink destiny. Adella cautioned him that since a duet of love had trapped the voice, it would take the same purity of emotion to release it. So he was powerless, for he couldn't predict who would have Christine's soul, much less make himself love them. The only thing he could do was keep tabs on your family and violin from afar, and wait for any sign of her rebirth. When he heard about me as a child, about my angelic singing, he assumed I was her, reborn. He was partly right. Since you and I are twin flames, I'm one part of her soul, and you're the other. But that never occurred to him as a possibility. He almost turned his back when he saw I was a boy and that I could no longer sing at all—" Etalon's tremulous voice cracks.

My chest aches on the memory of his nightmare experiences in the human-trafficking world. I cup my palm over his hand. "I'm so sorry for what those bastards stole from you."

His fingers fist beneath mine. "Yet we were going to do the same to you."

"Were . . ." I whisper, to comfort him and assure myself.

His fingers relax. "How could we be so blind? Had we followed through . . . we would've deserved the same end as my jailors."

The confession triggers a profound realization. "That's how Erik found you. That's how you became his son. He saved you from them, didn't he?"

"Yes. He killed them all and absorbed their cumulative life years. Then he brought me here. Took me in. Cared for me. I owe him . . . everything." He slumps his broad shoulders. The suspenders draw his shirt tight so the knit conforms to every muscle. "He has another side to him. One that wants nothing more than to be a good father. And he *is* a good father."

My heart breaks to hear him try to convince me. Or is he convincing himself?

"I had my awakening when I was fourteen. Erik knew it was time, he sensed it, and led me to a whorehouse so I could feed off a woman's energy. She was older . . . in her twenties. I crept into her bed and her dreams, and had my fill of both. After I recovered from the energy surge, I couldn't stop remembering that another creature had done that to my own mother, spawning me, leaving her to face it all alone. The guilt became too great, and I told Erik I would never feed again. Not like that. That I'd rather starve and die. He came up with the idea for the rave club to save me, once again. A heartless beast wouldn't do something so accommodating for a child who wasn't even his by blood, would he?"

I want to agree with him. But Erik's sinister plan glues my lips shut. I squeeze Etalon's hand, hoping to transmit the same calming support his touch offers me. Our ribbon imprints flare, synchronized. His deep-brown gaze finds mine, tortured and seeking. The pull between us intensifies, but he breaks our hands apart and moves to the sink to dump out what's left in his cup.

I stand, prepared to give him my cup, too.

His back stays turned. "Erik has a conscience about things, you see. He can't bring himself to visit Jippetto, because he feels guilty. He can't walk through the forest for fear of encountering the animals we've altered. That makes him reachable, on some level."

I grip the handle on my teacup, forcing myself to ask a question I'm not sure I want answered. "Why does he feel guilty about the groundskeeper?"

Etalon sighs, running a hand through the dark curls on his head, leaving them disheveled. "Jippetto was twenty when his mother died, with his magic used up and nowhere to go. Being a mute, his options were limited. Erik used his underground connections and arranged for him to make mannequins for shops. He also put him up in a house in the city—a kindness in return for the information Adella had shared. When Jippetto retired four years ago, Erik invited him here, to live out the rest of his days in peace. But he had an ulterior motive, for by then Erik was formulating a plan to reunite Christine's voice with a new body." Etalon's profile tenses. "Jippetto was my first, and only, human experiment to prepare my skills for the transfer. The bird whistle around his neck is hollow. It makes no sound. And the handkerchiefs he wears, they cover the scars."

His words funnel around me—violent gusts tearing at my fortitude. My sympathy for the caretaker is shadowed by fear for my own fate. "That means . . . there's someone else Erik wants to put my voice in. Christine's body . . . he still has it! How's that possible?

She's dead. She died an old woman . . . almost a hundred years ago. We are her *soul* . . ." My hand trembles and tea sloshes between my thumb and forefinger. I yelp.

"The *hows* are not your concern." Etalon takes the cup away, setting it at the sink. "Because it won't come down to you being on that steel table." His voice is gentle as he takes my hand and blots the tea with a napkin to check my burn. Hard as I try, I can't stop envisioning those long, caring fingers using a scalpel, tearing away muscle and cartilage. Slicked in blood. I jerk free, in spite of how much I crave the contact between us.

He winces and slings the napkin to the table. "Of course you fear me. I've done monstrous things." Regret chokes his voice as he strides to the violin case and lifts it. "But please, know this . . . I tried not to *become* a monster. No animal has died under my watch. The donors are simply left mute, like Jippetto once was. And as for him? I decided if I had to commit this gruesome atrocity to give my father the happiness he's never had, I would offer the caretaker something to make him happy, too. To soften his loneliness. So I gave him a way to talk to the birds he loved to watch from afar, and now they come seeking him, to keep him company."

I can't react, trying to process it all.

Etalon's jaw muscles spasm as he grinds his teeth. "My choices have been as reprehensible as Erik's deeds. But the difference between us is I lived long enough with a mother who loved me, to know light from darkness. Erik had only darkness from the moment he was born. To live a life with him, I learned to walk in the gray. And to be the father I needed, he learned to do the same. But gradually, Erik lost his way once more. I closed my eyes to it. Until you came, and unraveled all of my pretending. You reminded me of light, of peace and comfort. Of things I've not had since I stepped into the Phantom's world. And I'm so grateful for that. I love my father. But there is no gray with him now. There is only the deepest, most harrowing black. To find him in those depths, to pull him back to the in-between, I'll have to reach for his humanity—whatever he has left. Music and guilt. They're the only two weapons I possess. But I need your help to wield them."

Carrying the Strad toward the bed, Etalon turns to see if I'm following.

I tremble beneath his cloak, unable to budge. It feels like I'm sinking into the floor, as if my legs are made of ice and slowly melting to puddles.

"Forgive me." A slant of light from the sconces casts shadows of Etalon's long lashes, smudging his high cheekbones and carving his lovely features to an expression that's pleading. "I never intended to bring you to RoseBlood. Not *you*. But I will protect you with my life, now that you're here. I'm going to lose Erik. I have made peace with that. But I can never lose you, my mirror soul. The only way to find the path to wholeness, to the man I'm meant to be, is to see myself reflected in you."

My pulse pounds at the magnitude of his words. Uncountable emotions tangle through me.

He pulls a latch behind one of the paintings. The bed folds up and fits securely into an indention in the wall, revealing a trapdoor in the floor. He lifts it open. A scent of greenery and feathers drifts up.

"Please, come." Even with his back turned, his deep gravelly request is a sweet enticement. "I want to give you at least one beautiful memory, before we face Erik." With the violin case clamped under an arm, he climbs down the rungs of a ladder, his head disappearing.

The sound of fluttering wings and trilling birdsongs makes me curious enough to place his cloak and my tote on the empty chair, taking time to put his unopened toe socks in my sweater pocket before I follow. Etalon's waiting at the bottom of the ladder. He catches my waist and lifts me down when I almost lose my footing trying to take it all in.

The aviary is an underwater greenhouse, at least three times the size of Jippetto's cottage. Overhead, a tall glass roof reveals the river's currents sweeping over us. The walls flash with fluid reflections. Assorted pots of fragrant flowers and greenery, even small trees, hedge a grassy path. Silhouettes of birds flutter through the leaves and branches, responding to Jippetto's voice somewhere in the distance.

Crickets chirp in the shadows, and tiny glowing balls—smaller than a candle's flame—slide through the moonlight on a gentle breeze stirred by fans in the walls. The sparkles take me back to my childhood, evenings spent in the dark with Mom and Dad catching—

"Fireflies," I whisper, entranced.

"You see, I do eventually set them free to grow and fly." Etalon's voice borders on flirty, and his hand finds my lower back. A thrill races through me at his touch.

I glance upward at the currents swirling across the roof again. A small school of fish swims across—graceful, sleek silhouettes. I turn to him. "It's the first time I've ever been surrounded by water without feeling suffocated."

He tilts his head in response. "This was built back when the opera house was first constructed centuries ago, before the river flooded to cause the island effect. But they used such thick panels of glass for the roof, even once it became submerged, it withstood. And the depths are only three feet overhead. So it still allows for sunlight during the day and moonbeams at night. I come here a lot to compose. During many of our dream-visions, I was in this place. So, I wanted the first time I played for you—face-to-face—to be under the water-drenched moon."

Before I can even react to the beautiful sentiment, Jippetto appears from behind a bush. I say "hi," and he nods to me, stroking his beard. He points to the violin case and shrugs.

"*Oui*, I'm going to play," Etalon answers.

Jippetto shakes his head, scolding, then tugs at his flannel shirt and kicks up his dirty boots before shaking a finger in Etalon's direction.

Etalon smiles. "Of course. I'll leave my shirt and shoes on this time. I'm in the presence of a lady, after all."

I smile. "What's that supposed to mean?"

"I'll show you one day," Etalon teases—although there's a faint aura of desire around him that when paired with the huskiness of his voice offers a promise of something scandalous and somber.

I have to drag my eyes from his or be swept away by my racing heartbeat.

Jippetto winks, then mimes drinking from a cup. He climbs the ladder, vanishes into his cottage, and lowers the trapdoor. There's a handle in the middle, for when we're ready to leave.

I've never seen the caretaker so settled. So . . . normal. And happy.

It's this place. It has to be, because it's making me feel the same. The life-force brims to overflowing here. If I try hard enough, I can almost see the pink and white auras around the flowers, insects, and birds. Pure, positive energy.

That's why Etalon brought me down. To give me a chance to breathe before the nightmare of facing his father begins.

Etalon leads me to a bench beneath a fragrant cove of lilac—flowers that should be out of season, yet are alive and thriving here in this glass sanctuary where the outside elements hold no sway. My escort takes a seat first, laying the violin at his feet to leave room for me beside him.

Instead, I kneel between his legs. My sweater rides up on my thighs and the grass tickles my knees through the rips in my jeans. I look up into his face—the one he's always hidden behind a mask; the one that I knew even before I saw it. "You asked me to forgive you. And I do. Erik has manipulated you since you were a child. And I know how much that hurts because he's family. But you have me now. I promise not to take you for granted, or use you."

Etalon touches my cheek. The vulnerability and gratitude looking back at me almost makes me leap up and hug him. Instead, I take his hand and flip it over.

"The monstrous things you've done don't make you a monster. You made a conscious choice tonight, to rise above it. To help everyone at your own expense. So, you earned these." I place the tissue-paper-wrapped gift on his palm and close his fingers around it. Furrowing his dark eyebrows, he tears open the paper. Moonlight streams through the water to gloss his hair with moving, silvery shadows as he spreads out the knitted footwear next to him on the bench. He looks up at me, questions in his eyes.

"Monsters don't wear toe socks." I point to the emoticons, hoping to see him smile, hoping he won't think I'm a child for making them. "And now you have your piggy puppets back, see?"

His answering grin is boyish astonishment. "Best of all, these won't wash away," he adds.

I laugh and he joins in—the spontaneous outburst as exhilarating and uninhibited as a song. But I sober immediately when he props his elbows on his knees so our heads are level, and tilts my chin toward him.

"Say my name," he murmurs, serious and low.

"Etalo—" I can't finish, because his warm lips cover mine.

At first, he takes his time with it, guiding my face with his calloused fingertips, teasing me—feather-soft contact with just enough spark to electrify my mouth and send tingles through my teeth. We're one for an instant, lips sealed, then sipping hungry breaths before clinging again. The moment his gentle ministrations coax a whimper of pleasure from my throat, he drops to his knees and drags my body against him, gripping my lower back in a seductive bid for more.

His lips part and our tongues meet, lighting up my insides with voltaic pulses of emotions, auras that burst in my mind on explosions of color flavored with caramel, midnight flowers, and singed spices—dark, tempestuous, and succulent. I tighten my arms around his nape, fingers curled in his silken hair, lost to the magic of us.

He moans and lowers me to my back, breaking our kiss so his lips can traverse my cheek, my ear, my jaw, my neck—discovering me, tasting me—igniting the spiritual music that only he inspires. A jarring jangle of stimulation rushes through every sensory receptor, a string of songs, ringing and humming like tiny bells set loose beneath my skin.

And I hope against all odds this night never ends.

23

MASKS

"Vice, in its true light, is so deformed, that it shocks
us at first sight; and would hardly ever seduce us, if
it did not at first wear the mask of some virtue."
Philip Stanhope, fourth earl of Chesterfield

It's fourth period, and my stomach reminds me that lunch is just a
few minutes away.

Even though my time with Etalon left the psychic vampire in
me satiated, my physical needs haven't been met today. I couldn't eat
breakfast due to my fear of what's coming tonight . . . of the traps
the Phantom has lying in wait on the floors of this opera house—the
ones Etalon couldn't find. Add to that the strain of trying to go to
classes and pretend that nothing has changed in my heart or in my
life, when both have been altered forever.

"Follow the routines, appear oblivious." Those were Etalon's
instructions when he left me inside the orchestra pit at three a.m.

with one last scintillating kiss burning on my lips. *"We can't let Erik get any more suspicious than he already is."*

Erik, as in the Phantom. As in, Etalon's father. And to think, that was the least shocking thing I found out last night.

I also learned that Professor Tomlin was the drummer at the rave club who I thought looked familiar. He's not one of our kind, but he is in the Phantom's pocket. Etalon warned me to be most cautious around him.

Luckily, I haven't seen him. Being at the head of the masquerade committee, he dismissed his classes for the day. First-period science became a study hall monitored by Madame Harris in the library, so Tomlin could make last-minute additions to the ballroom. I can only hope those *additions* aren't under the advisement of Erik.

I tamp down the unease in my gut to keep myself in the moment.

Bouchard's sharply angled back faces the class as she scrawls some vocabulary words across her dry-erase board: *Intermezzo, Afterpiece, Ballet héroïque, Romantische Oper, Tragédie lyrique.*

Fifteen sets of pens scratch on notebooks.

"You ain't seriously giving us homework on Halloween," Sunny grumbles from her seat behind me. Every other student is thinking it; she's the only one bold enough to say it. I nibble the end of my pen, surprised by the longing her voice inspires, wishing I had my friend to talk to. But what would I tell her if I did?

Hey, bestie! Last night I made out with my incubus twin flame in a greenhouse beneath the river. Gave new meaning to the word steamy. And tonight, we're going to fight a centuries-old phantom before he can steal away my voice and bring the school to the ground with everyone in it.

That would get her Halloween festivities off to a rip-roaring start. I know it has mine.

Bouchard stops writing and shifts on her pointy heels to show-case her equally pointy profile. Her cheek matches the dyed ends of her hair. "'Ain't' is not proper English, *Mademoiselle* Summers. Assuming that's the indigenous language of your species."

Sunny huffs, followed by a snort from Jax and several chuckles around the room. I scowl, being the only one privy to the innuendo behind her criticism.

"Each of these terms," Bouchard continues, "has to do with masques, pantomimes, exotic heroes and heroines, or the super-natural and mythological. That would be 'Halloween'-themed homework, for the symbolism impaired. If any of you have an issue with it, we could take a pop quiz instead."

She slants a glare across the class as everyone returns to scrib-bling. She's careful to avoid eye contact with me. Aunt Charlotte's threats are keeping her at bay.

Although, since I'm wearing sunglasses, she really doesn't have much choice to avoid my gaze. An eye infection—that's what Aunt Charlotte told everyone to cover up that I'm still radiating the energy Etalon and I exchanged last night. My aunt's already planning to get me some green contacts ASAP.

The minute I got back this morning, I went to my aunt's room, Diable in tow, and using the key she'd let me borrow, crashed on her chaise lounge until it was time to get ready for breakfast and classes. I wanted to be there to make sure she slept off the sleeping gas.

She was fine upon waking, but I wasn't. I've only known I'm descended from ancient vampires for two days. And now, I'm about to be in a fight for the very gift I once wanted to throw away. I'm reeling internally, yet I don't have time to stop and absorb it all.

I told Aunt Charlotte I've decided to stay at RoseBlood. That I couldn't leave now that I finally found myself and my voice. I had to lie to her about my eyes . . . I used the excuse of snacking on a rose's life-force. Pretty sure she didn't buy it. But I'm planning to tell her the truth later today, about everything.

Etalon encouraged me to let her in on the plan. Even Bouchard. He says we can use all the help we can get tonight at the masquerade. And I agree . . .

Now that I'm not betraying him, I'll be able to talk about him. To make them understand he's an ally.

I lift my braid to chew on the ends of my hair. Maybe the dry-erase marker fumes are getting to me, because I'm no longer hungry. I'm nauseous.

Of course the real reason behind my kinked-up insides is my concern about the masquerade and the part I have to play. Even more, I'm scared out of my mind about Etalon's. His part is more dangerous than anyone's, because he's betraying the man he lives with, the man he swore his loyalty to as a broken seven-year-old child. The man who was an assassin in Persia over a century ago. The Phantom is not famous for forgiveness.

The dismissal bell rings, and I gather my pen, notebook, and bag then tumble through the door before I have to face Sunny or Jax. I'm sure they think what everybody else does: that the real reason I'm wearing sunglasses is to flaunt that I won Renata's role. That my superstar complex is growing by the hour.

They're really going to think that tonight, when I have to give a solitary impromptu performance. But if everything goes as planned only the Phantom will be my audience.

Shivers join my nausea as I wind through the bodies darkened to silhouettes by my glasses. Ignoring their auras, I make my way downstairs to my dorm room. Aunt Charlotte offered to bring my food since it's an extended lunch today, so I wouldn't have to hide my eyes during the hour break. I'm hoping she'll stay and we can talk; maybe read Christine's letters together. Anything to get my mind off tonight. I have to wait until after school to discuss the plan with her. Etalon insisted we go to the forest so there's no risk of the Phantom overhearing.

At least it's promising to be a cloudless day so we won't be stuck in the rain.

Diable is already in my room by the time I arrive, and I'm so happy to see his adorable grumpy face, I don't even question how he gets in anymore. He's seated on my bed like he owns it, his wooly fur taking on a different violet shade with each burble from the lava lamp.

After unclipping the tie at my neck, I drop my sunglasses, bag, and books on the floor. Then I pick up the stack of Christine's letters I brought over this morning when I came to put on my uniform. Diable doesn't grouse as I drop beside him on the bed. Instead, he snuggles into my side with a gentle tingle of bells. I rub between his ears until he purrs.

"You know I'm sorry I doubted you, right?" I tease. "As if you could be anything but honorable, with a name like Devil."

His eyes squeeze to happy slits. I put the letters on my pillow, turning my head toward the wall's vent, and trace the ribbon tattoo under my shirt sleeve. My ears ache for the sound of a violin's serenade. I wish I knew he was safe.

Last night when we were kissing, our pent-up emotions and suppressed appetites overcame us. Things got intense, but we stopped ourselves. That kind of intimacy should never be rushed.

Even though both of us admitted it might be our only chance to be together.

Etalon helped me to my feet and we danced instead, face-to-face in reality, for the first time. He told me, in that grinding voice that incites my succubus to ravening heights, that when all the bad is behind us, he'll lay me down on a bed covered in rose petals and kiss every inch of skin until my body is aflame with song.

I didn't answer, because I was too busy blushing, but I'm going to hold him to that.

We talked as we danced to the sound of crickets and buzzing bugs. I asked him all the things I've been wanting to learn: his birthday, his favorite color, his favorite foods and books, how it felt the first time he helped an animal, and how long Diable has been his companion . . . details that might seem insignificant to other people, but for me and Etalon, we already know each other's deepest soul-secrets. Now, I want to know the little things that make him tick. Unfortunately, even that was cut short, because we had plans to make.

I shut my eyes, humming the melody he taught me on the violin. It was incredible, performing with him in reality, side by side. It was like our dream-visions. Joined together in triumph to align the planets and rule the universe.

That's what inspired his scheme, in fact. He believes those visions were the stars intervening, telling us how to defeat the Phantom.

Many of the operatic arias that have possessed me throughout my life were songs Christine learned via Erik's tutelage with the Stradivarius. And there's one song they sang together that Etalon's convinced can break the Phantom: the duet they shared when she was dying.

It's a ballad. The same sweet, gentle melody that Etalon has played for me through the vent these past weeks to help me sleep. He knows it from his childhood, having heard Erik hum it subconsciously anytime he was busy doing something that made him nostalgic for Christine.

Etalon taught me the lyrics. They tell a story about a tree that's ugly and withered, losing all its leaves. But the leaves lift to the sky and become shimmering, glittery stars. Decay becoming new life; disfigurement becoming beauty. So poignant, knowing the Phantom's history as I do now.

Tonight, everything will go according to the Phantom's original plan, in the beginning. Tomlin is going to sneak out to a party in the city so Erik can use his gas mask/jackal costume and take his place at the masquerade. Erik is a master at mimicry, and has already perfected Tomlin's voice. He'll lure me into the hallway away from the party with the excuse of discussing a missing grade. Once we're out of everyone's sight, Erik's plan is to kidnap me through a secret passage . . . to take me to his labyrinth where Etalon will help him perform the transfer.

But things will never come to that with Etalon's revised strategy.

I'm going to dress like Christina Nilsson for the party. It's a far cry from the zombie banshee I was planning to be, but Etalon's observation—that the only thing that ever made the Phantom aspire to be human was Christine—makes this our one and only shot.

The goal is to throw the Phantom off his game when he sees me. He has a portrait hanging on his wall where she's dressed as Pandora. All I need is a dark golden wig to reflect her Swedish coloring, a long white column dress, a gold-leaf tiara, and a panel of sage fabric to use as a wrap. There are endless costumes and hairpieces behind the locked doors of the opera house. Etalon assured me we have everything to complete the look. He's putting it together today, using the portrait as a guide. He'll place the articles in a bag in the orchestra pit this afternoon, since rehearsals were canceled to allow everyone time to get ready for the masquerade at six.

When the Phantom arrives, it's up to me to make him vulnerable. Shake him back to reality and the ugliness of his obsession. We expect him to move past his initial shock. He's too determined to be stopped that easily. So I'll pretend I believe he's Tomlin, but as soon as we step out of the party, I'll make a run for the stairs . . . lead him to Bouchard's workshop on the second floor. Jippetto will already be waiting inside to force Erik to face the quiet, gentle man he used so callously and the animals he inadvertently slaughtered.

If that's not enough, I'll serenade him with the deathbed ballad.

Etalon's job, while the Phantom is preoccupied with us, is to dismantle the machine in the cellar lab that aids in the transfer . . . in case we fail and the Phantom still manages to drag me down.

If that happens, or if anything else goes wrong, Aunt Charlotte and Bouchard will be charged with everyone else's safety. Etalon will supply them with smoke bombs to set off the alarms and sprinklers, so all the teachers and students will run outside, away from Erik's undiscovered pitfalls.

It would be easier if we weren't trying to hide the secret vampire society, and if the Phantom wasn't a mad genius with traps around every corner. This is the only way to protect everyone.

My gut twists again at the dangerous conspiring. I'm just about to sift through Christine's letters for a distraction when I hear a knock. More eager to see Aunt Charlotte than my food, I swing my door open to find Sunny's freckled face looking back, lunch tray in hand and book bag hanging over her shoulder.

A groan escapes my lips. With all of the secret spy tunnels and mirror windows in this place, you'd think someone would've thought to install peepholes in the dorm room doors.

The scent of roasted cod drifts between us, making my stomach growl.

"Exactly as I thought," Sunny says. "When I saw your eyes last night, I knew you must've taken a page from my playbook and stolen them from your aunt." She leans in close. "Coolest zombie contacts ever. How'd you get her to forgive you and let you wear them today?"

A few students walk through the foyer on their way to the stairs and glance over their shoulders at us. It's too late to hide from Sunny, but no one else needs to see me. I usher her in and go along with her creepy contacts theory. If she only knew the irony of it all.

As I shut the door and lean against it, she sets the tray on my nightstand and plops onto my bed. Diable jumps down, taking a jingly, dignified stroll to the chaise.

"I'm surprised you're here," I say to my unexpected guest. What I want to say is: *How did you see my eyes last night?*

Sunny frowns and drags her book bag off her shoulder. "I swiped your lunch tray before your aunt saw it. I wanted to tell you that I know what you're up to. It's honorable and all that, but there's gotta be another way."

I struggle to stay standing. She can't possibly know my plans for the party. "What do you mean?"

"What you said yesterday, before you went out for Renata's part. That isn't like you. You had an ulterior motive . . . you're planning to roll over so Audrey can have the lead. Am I right?"

I sigh. As many secrets as I'm hiding, I can't resist sharing at least one with Sunny. "Yeah. And it's working. Jax hates me, and Audrey's not mad at him anymore."

Sunny shakes her head. "He don't hate you. Neither does she. All of us—well, everyone but me—are just confused, that's all."

I make my way over to the bed to take a seat at the other end, playing with the ruffled cuffs of my dress shirt. "Well, I'm a confusing person."

"And secretive." A weird expression crosses her face as she sees the pile of letters from Christine on my pillow behind her. She grabs them before I can. Her bluish-purple eyes turn to me. "*The* Christine?"

I scramble for an excuse. "I—I found them."

"Oh yeah? In the chapel, or on the *roof*?" Her eyebrows shoot up accusingly on the last word.

The sick nausea pools in my stomach again, and the cod no longer smells appetizing except to Diable, who's seated himself at the base of the nightstand and is staring up, sniffing the air.

Sunny leans down to open her book bag, the letters snug in her lap. She drags out two familiar tin cans with holes in the bottoms, and a cracked white half-mask. "At first I thought this belonged to Professor Tomlin, since these are the tins he uses in our labs to store solvents and stuff. But why would you be meeting him up there? And why the mask?"

The room tilts topsy-turvy. Etalon must've been in such a hurry last night that he left some things behind. But how did Sunny find the secret passage? And how did she unlock the door? "I . . . I don't know what you're talking about."

"Right." Sunny's smug glare stands out against the purple-lit walls, brighter than her red hair. "You were so busy arguing with the Bride of Frankenstein about stealing your aunt's disposable contacts, you forgot you dropped this, huh?" She places the rooftop key on the bed beside the other items.

My tongue freezes. I piece together the events of my encounter with Bouchard last night, her words to me before she snapped off the necklace: *I've seen these eyes before. She's going to want to know about this.* Sunny construed that as Bouchard accusing me of stealing contacts. But where would she have been, to see and hear everything?

Then I remember. "You. You were the rustling I heard behind the phantom cutout . . . you were on the stairs—"

"Yep. I'd come out to go to the bathroom and saw the mirror door opening, with you sneaking through. I decided to retrace your steps after you dropped the key." Sunny unties the string from the letters.

I grapple for them but she jerks away. The papers go flying, sending Diable darting up the spiraling staircase to the mini-loft. I crouch to gather the letters before Sunny can. My brain flips through uncountable scenarios, trying to find one that will explain all of this.

"Whoa. That's creepy as hell," Sunny says from where she's picking up behind me.

My shoulders stiffen as I turn.

Her face is so pale her freckles stand out like specks of mud on a whitewashed fence. She holds up a sketch of the disfigured Phantom similar to the one Etalon showed me on the rooftop. It must've been stuffed inside the stack of letters. Brownish-red spatters fleck the background, like aged blood. Sunny's trembling finger points to the bottom, beside the signature, where Christine scripted the words: *Guard your throats and hide your eyes. He's not dead, you fools. Legends never die.*

❖ · 1 · ❖

Seated on his bed, Thorn slipped his feet into his new socks and wiggled them. The colorful faces on the toes appeared to dance in

368

the hazy blue light of his aquarium. He smiled, then shoved his feet into his boots, tying the laces up to his calves, his mind on those moments spent with Rune in the aviary.

He'd read the insecurity in her aura—sensed she was worried he'd think her gift was childish. It was such an intimate and kind gesture. One that made him feel treasured and gave him hope. He'd wanted to share that hope, share that energy she inspired in him.

Holding her in his arms, tasting his name on her lips, had been even sweeter than he'd ever imagined it could be. As were her whimpers asking for more.

And her voice when he played for her? Seraphic, just as Erik always said. Thorn knew they were taking a chance dressing her as Christine. It could backfire, presenting her as the object of Erik's desire. That's why Bouchard and Rune's aunt were there. As backup. He hated putting Rune in danger, but she was stronger than she realized. She would discover that tonight.

He hadn't told her everything about the ballad. He wanted to spare her the knowledge that Erik often sang it, with tears in his eyes, to the body in the cryo-chamber. Some images were too morbid and tragic for anyone to have to live with. It was enough Thorn would never stop seeing it himself.

He smoothed the hems of his black scrub pants into place over his boots before pulling on the matching top, saturated with the scent of rubbing alcohol. He had to look the part of the surgeon. He'd wear the lab jacket, too, to cover up the ribbon imprint on his arm. That's the last thing Erik needed to know about.

Thorn stood, checking his room, assuring everything was in place. He'd already emptied the aquarium of the fish. Freed them in the river from where he caught them; though he'd left the aquarium filled with water and the light on, to keep Erik from noticing the change. All of Thorn's animal patients were free, and he'd never have to alter another voice. In the chapel was a suitcase holding his scant possessions: clothes, a few half-masks, a hairbrush, a toothbrush, some soap, the fairy tale book Rune gave him, and the Stradivarius.

If he escaped alive tonight, Erik would disown him, or, worst case, chase him down until he'd had his revenge.

The thought not only filled Thorn with dread, it also made his heart sink. Yet, one thing buoyed it: imagining a life that was above ground, with no masks or cellar labs or deadly traps. A life among people who had jobs, who went to dinner and attended the opera houses as guests . . . not eternal ghosts haunting the performers within.

He wanted to take Rune to Paris every morning with sunshine warm on their faces, and let her shop to her heart's content, or duck into an antique bookstore during a rainstorm and read together all afternoon. Or walk alongside cafés and elegant gardens—holding hands until the sun disappeared, then sit with her in front of the Eiffel Tower all lit up like a beacon—and kiss her face in the glow of yellow light.

To be a real couple. To have real friends. To blend in, except when they were alone and could let their inner beasts out to play.

That telling moment in the sewer twelve years ago kept surfacing like an omen: *"You could still have a normal life,"* Erik had said. *"Your perfect face, flawless features . . . they'll earn you a place of respect and power in that world. You can blend in, even rule, where I never could."* And Thorn's naïve, childish answer: *"I don't want to blend. I want to belong."*

He didn't belong. Not here. Not anymore. He didn't belong up there, either. The only place he belonged was with Rune. But since that meant living up there, well, he'd warmed to the idea of blending.

He just wasn't sure a phantom's son could have a normal life, with nothing to offer but dark talents and blood on his hands.

A part of him wanted to go back to last night, endlessly relive that quiet, perfect moment in the moonlight garden with Rune, drinking in her delicious white aura, tasting her soft skin, while giving her all the pleasures he'd promised. Because here in the present, a cloud of gloom closed in. Something primal hung on the air—scented with a mix of burned flesh and compost. Regret and death.

The plan he'd made was good, but it wasn't fail proof. If he knew anything of the man who had raised him, he knew the Phantom was always one step ahead.

Always.

Thorn had put blinders on the day Rune came, too blissfully happy at their reunion to pay attention. But now, looking back, he saw the signs. All along, Father Erik had been aware that Thorn was secretly helping Rune break free from her musical demons. Yet he'd pretended not to notice and let it continue. Now, in these final hours of her freedom, Thorn realized there must've been an underlying reason.

Erik had insisted from the beginning that the girl who harbored Christine's voice would have to want to sacrifice it for the transfer to work. So why would he allow Thorn to help her learn to appreciate and cherish her talent, unless it somehow furthered his cause? It surely wasn't a virtuous gesture, a change of heart brought about by watching his only son fall in love.

One way or another, Thorn would find out tonight—a knowledge that sent knifelike jabs through his chest.

The elevator's motor triggered Ange's answering squawk. Erik was on his way up from the cellar. He'd been in costume for hours, impatient to go. Now that it was time, he would expect Thorn to see him off.

Struggling to steady his raging pulse, Thorn stood and slipped into the lab jacket. He took a shaky breath, raked his fingers through his hair, and looked in the mirror. He thought upon the coverings he'd created to hide behind over the years: clay, porcelain, satin, and copper. Then he schooled his features to a guise of obedient compliance, because tonight, his face was the most important mask he would ever wear.

24

FIRE AND ICE

"Some say the world will end in fire, some say in ice. From what I've tasted of desire, I hold with those who favor fire."
Robert Frost

The ballroom is abuzz with activity. The colorful auras of fifty students and six teachers mix and mingle, clash and conflict, even more distracting to my eye than the bright and extravagant costumes that range from modern culture to mythological, fairy tale, and classical.

Seated at a table, I nibble on hors d'oeuvres—grilled zucchini rolls with herbed goat cheese, tomato-and-bacon-topped marmalade on bruschetta—in an effort to look nonchalant while keeping the entrance in sight.

The Phantom is late.

Either that or he's behind the mirrored wall, observing and strategizing. I'm shocked that I'd prefer the latter. Otherwise, something's gone wrong with Etalon, and that's unbearable to even imagine. The ribbon tattoo on my arm keeps stinging, as if to validate that fear. It was feeling like this even before Sunny touched it upon my arrival and commented on how well I'd drawn it, and that it was an interesting addition to my Pandora theme, and also, why did I change themes anyway, and where's the glowing contacts?

If it weren't against vampiric law, I'd tell her everything. It's exhausting fabricating cover stories for such an inquisitive mind. And it would be nice to have girlfriend talks about Etalon.

The red coil on my arm burns again at the thought of him.

I glance down where Diable bats at the hem of my white flowing dress, exposing my bare feet—a result of not having the right sandals to go with my costume.

"Hey, Ghost Kitty." The cat pauses and blinks up at me. "Go find your master. Make sure he's okay." I half expect him to refuse, considering his pride and that no one is his master, but he seems to sense the tension in my voice.

Wiggling his whiskers, he stretches, yawns, and jingles away, darting between students and through the double doors.

Maybe I'm worried over nothing. This is still so new to me. All I know is the sooner I get the Phantom to Bouchard's workshop and incapacitate him with the song that breaks his heart, the sooner I can look for Etalon myself.

The aroma of melting wax, spiced cider, and smoky-savory finger foods offers an olfactory-parallel to the rich décor. Considering Tomlin's creepy alliance with Erik, I expected gothic, but he chose elegance over eeriness.

Building on the glittery gold floor, he stationed round black tables and matching chairs along the edges of the room, adorned with "spider" webs made of delicate gold chains in place of tablecloths. Black-and-gold-damask plastic plates, gold silverware, miniature pumpkins rolled in glitter, and fall bouquets of orange mums, ivory roses, and sage greenery in crystal vases complete the settings. Ivory tapers in wrought-iron candlestands add a touch of illumination between tables. Black-shimmer organza drapes the side walls in sweeping arcs that reach up to the domed center of the ceiling. Each panel is tied to a chandelier almost the size of the theater's. Glistening gold streamers drizzle down from the crystal fixture, making me think of the "octopus" at the rave, leaving my stomach queasier than it already is. I reach for my pumpkin cider, lifting the plastic stemware to my lips. The brown sugar-and-nutmeg coating on the rim adds a comforting dimension to the flavor.

Lining the back mirrored wall is a row of ivory trees with twisted branches, seated in matching pots and varying from four to six feet in height. Black leaves, wired to the scraggly ends, add a haunted quality, while some branches are left bare. Behind, panels of sheer gold organza drape across the mirrors from the ceiling to the floor, with individual black leaves pinned in place to simulate the wind's movement. Loose leaves speckle the floor in intervals and bring the motif full circle. The chandelier's electric bulbs are turned off, leaving only the candles to cast gentle, warm light and long shadows over everything. It's sparkly and mystical, with only a subtle hint of Halloween.

The opulent serenity is at odds with how I feel.

Appear oblivious. Etalon's instruction keeps looping through my brain, making me second guess everything. How do I appear oblivious while knowing the danger hidden beneath this opera house for over a hundred years is about to lurk into full view? Two worlds colliding, and my four accomplices and I have to ensure there are no casualties.

My heartbeat knocks in rapid rhythm against my sternum. I can actually see its movement beneath my dress where the one-strapped bodice hugs my curves like a second skin. The sage panel of fabric I'm trying to use as a wrap keeps sliding off my shoulders. Sighing, I rub my temples. The gold-leaf metal headband is too tight atop the golden-brown wig I've swept into a high bun. Under the wig cap, my thick hair bulges and takes up too much space. I consider removing the headband, but there's too much riding on getting this role right. So I choose to ignore the dull throbbing headache, although the stress isn't making it any easier.

Over at the dessert buffet, my friends gather to fill their plates with bite-size ganache truffles and assorted candies. Quan and Sunny came as the Corpse Bride and her prospective groom—complete with bluish-gray complexions. He helps her with her plate since she has only one working arm. The other is hidden inside her tattered gown to make room for the skeletal limb covertly sewn into the bodice. Jax is a butterfly collector with round owlish glasses that magnify his blue eyes, and a handlebar moustache that looks like a fat brown caterpillar. Tiny artificial monarchs cling to his safari hat, shirt, and pants. He's tucked his giant net under his arm to help Audrey resituate her angel-size set of monarch wings across the black leotard and spandex polka-dot skirt that cling to her dainty form. After the wings are in place, Jax thumps one of her springy antennae, causing the sparkly bulb to bob back and forth on her head. She gives him a playful scowl before reaching for the cookie cups and dropping two on her plate. She probably wouldn't have agreed to the matched costumes had they not purchased them before I sucked his face and his energy; but at least it's giving them something to bond over now. Seeing them happy and teasing is my one bright spot. I'm determined they'll get the chance for many more memories like these.

As if sensing me watching, Jax casts a glance over his shoulder in my direction. I look away, focusing instead on Kat and Roxie off in a corner. Roxie's glistening pewter-statue makeup and skintight costume, complete with cracks in the stone, is stunning with the matching gray contacts that fog her irises and the metallic silver glaze in her hair. Kat's half-skeleton, half-human makeup and costume are just as creative and gorgeous. They both have a chance at winning the artistry portion of the contests later, but with the way their gazes keep flitting over, that's the last thing on their minds. They're conspiring payback. Little do they realize their petty revenge is the least of my worries tonight.

Most students stand around talking, others are on the dance floor, rocking out to the dark, electronic indie-pop playlist streaming through the speakers. Tomlin put it together. Hard to believe he had time with teaching every day and moonlighting for the dark side. A few small groups occupy the tables around me. One couple dressed as silent-movie characters—in black and white from head to toe—hold up signs with clever dialogue to answer their friends' questions. They all bust out laughing, oblivious to who's on the guest list.

Aunt Charlotte and Bouchard are on the other side of the room, watching me. They've come as Red Riding Hood—in a long red cape and dress—and Grandma in a wolf costume, complete with nightgown and cap. No surprise Bouchard chose to be the furry, snarling half of the duo.

They're keeping their distance, although Bouchard didn't even like handing her key over to Jippetto. Predictably, it has more to do with her aversion to anyone going into her sacred shrine of dead animals than watching over me.

I touch the necklace hanging at the dress's deep V above my cleavage. The ruby ring pendant is only costume jewelry. Etalon put it in with the Pandora pieces to be worn as the final nail in Erik's sentimental coffin. And I understand the significance now. The true meaning of the ring.

During lunch, I convinced Sunny that Christine's letters were another prank, along with the broken mask, and that Professor Tomlin was going to help me catch my creeper tonight. I told her if she saw me leave with him not to follow, because she could mess up the plan. It was as close to the truth as I could get to protect her without blowing her mind.

After she left for fifth period, I chose to skip theater, which was to be another study hall, and read Christine's journal entries, in case I could find anything to use. Instead, I found the heartbreaking ending to the Phantom and his love's star-crossed saga.

Shortly after Christine's husband died, Erik faked that he, too, was dying. Years earlier, he and Christine had made a pact that neither one would let the other die alone. When she found him, he confessed he still loved her. He hadn't aged a day in the ten years since they'd last seen each other, but Christine was in her early forties, and had at last matured beyond her fear. She gave in to her heart after years of denying, and they had a night of passion that resulted in an unexpected conception. Terrified of how a baby would react to his face, Erik holed himself up underground and locked Christine out of his life. It took him five months to conceptualize a mask so real he could wear it and look "human" enough not scare his child. He went to Christine. She'd been concealing the pregnancy to perform, as she'd signed a contract with a French opera house two years earlier. He told her his plan, but she said she didn't want him to hide from their baby, that the child would grow seeing him each day. That their child would be the one person in the world who would never think him repulsive or different. Overcome with happiness, the Phantom asked her to marry him, offering the ruby ring. She said yes, and for a week they hid away, blissfully happy in his underground apartment. But there Christine went into premature labor, giving birth to a perfectly formed beautiful little girl—weighing less than a pound and lacking the ability to take a breath—too fragile to survive outside her mother's body. Christine was devastated and bedridden, unable to even name her, so Erik buried the infant while composing the ballad her tiny ears would never hear.

There was no more to the entry. After reading it, I checked the cemetery. The unnamed infant's headstone—which cradled my roses and led me to the chapel a month ago—had the same birth/death year as Erik's poor, tragic baby: 1883.

He'd almost had everything, then was left with less than nothing—with a heart so battered and beaten, it turned to stone as dense and immovable as his daughter's nameless grave.

The ballad Etalon taught me, the one Erik sang with Christine, belonged to that child. It's undeniably the most powerful weapon I could wield, but I dread using it.

As if feeding off my morbid thoughts, the music overhead changes to a throbbing, angry song, snapping me back to the present. All around the room, the candles flicker, as if blown by a breeze. Yet there's no wind anywhere. I turn my attention to the entrance just as he steps in—black pants and shoes, black leather jacket and gloves, black rubber gas mask molded to look like a jackal with a pointed muzzle and ears, yet somehow still human and undeniably male. In spite of his monochrome ensemble, everything else seems to drain of color and life, paling to his feral dominance and those yellow eyes glittering in the depths of his mask.

I hunch my shoulders to make myself small, long enough to nod to my aunt who's talking to a group of junior dancers she's been tutoring. She nods back, the worry on her face glaring. Although my instincts tell me to crawl under the table, I stand.

His eyes lock on mine, and the shock wave of recognition snaps through my legs and arms, sapping me of my strength. The wrap falls off my shoulders as I grip the table to hold my balance. At the same time he wavers and backs up four steps in a daze, bumping into Headmaster Fabre, who's speaking to Principal Norrington and Madame Harris. They all three turn to him and laugh, then welcome him into their group, chatting, oblivious.

His eyes keep flashing in my direction, his wits gathering again like a lightning storm radiating through his frame and coloring his aura brick red: controlled anger, simmering resolve.

My heart rate spikes. Sunny and the others head my way with full plates in their hands. "Okay, Rune," she says. "We're going to share our desserts with you. You're looking way too lonely over here. Time for bygones to be bygones, right?"

Sensing the Phantom's gaze on us, I shudder. I can't let him come to me. I can't risk them getting in the middle.

I shake my head at Sunny, a signal just for her. I mime "the plan," then turn, leaving my friends gaping as I head for the door.

I pass the Phantom. Even with the distance between us, I feel the energy pulsing around him. His voice bewitches the teachers—the perfect imitation of Tomlin with an underlying musical command so subtle they're helpless to stop it, so heart-wrenchingly lovely it nudges that song he planted inside me at the rave, and wakes it up.

Pushing through a cluster of students, I step into the abandoned corridor where the glossy floor reflects the shimmering candlelight from the ballroom. The marble is cold to my feet, but it's my breath that freezes, my lungs that feel heavy and glacial. I force the air in and out. Then I head for the stairs.

Bouchard's workroom. All I have to do is make it there. Jippetto's waiting with the animals, and I won't have to sing that haunted ballad.

I sense Erik's ominous presence following. Not rushed. Cat-footed and quiet. That celestial song he planted in the back of my mind is guiding him, twisting and twining . . . restless.

My legs shake as I take the steps, winding as fast as I can go without sliding on my bare soles. At last, I'm on the second flight and the door is just at the end of the hallway, ajar and slanting light onto the floor like a beacon.

He's close enough now to hear his breath inside the gas mask, a grinding, mechanical sound that worms its way into my brain, causing me to stumble over my dress and bang my scarred knee on the marble. Wincing, I glance over my shoulder. He's just coming down the last step, yet his grisly breath rattles in my ears, a ventriloquist's trick.

Gritting my teeth, I limp the rest of the way, then push Bouchard's door open.

Jippetto lifts his white eyebrows with a question and I nod, backing up to the far wall underneath the stuffed crow that greeted me with a cat's meow the first day I arrived . . . what seems a lifetime ago.

The Phantom steps in. His eyes graze me but fix on Jippetto as the caretaker releases his trilling whistles. Erik's head darts left to right, taking it all in, and I see it . . . the clarity, the guilt, the change. A melting of ice and frost. His vulnerability gives me the strength I lack. He needs one more push, so I unleash the ballad. My voice lifts, soars above him, angelic and accusatory. He drops to his knees and joins in—a sobbing duet—pure, beautiful, remorseful. His body trembles, his eyes wet with tears inside their shadowy depths.

It's working. I raise the volume of my voice, channeling the ghost of his dead love with new confidence.

He slumps forward, the jackal's muzzle almost touching the floor. His gloved hands grip the ears of his mask. "Forgive me, Christine"—his voice a potent, symphonic wail as he looks up at me—"I *had* to keep her alive. Please, please, let me do what's left. I've waited so long." Heaving sobs roll out of him, shaking his entire body.

Still humming the ballad's notes, I inch closer, trying to make sense of his confession, when I catch movement in the corridor and lose the melody.

Bouchard stalls at the threshold in her wolf costume, a few inches behind the Phantom's prostrate form, waving a length of rope in her furry paws. "Hurry, let's tie his hands!"

He's on his feet before I can blink, shaking off whatever trance Jippetto and I managed to evoke. In a controlled blur of black leather and rage, he shoves Bouchard into the hall after snatching the rope. "Don't move." He casts the command like a silken net. She obeys, flat on her rump and not budging. "You, too. Sit." He motions with his jackal head, directing the caretaker to Bouchard's worktable. Like a robot, Jippetto takes a seat in the chair and becomes still as stone.

Witnessing the hypnotic mastery of his voice is awful and awe-inspiring—a fictional legend brought to life.

The Phantom's eyes flare inside the mask. I tremble, backing up to my spot against the wall. "Come, pigeon." He holds out a gloved palm, the other fisted around Bouchard's rope. "You won't want to be here for this."

I fight the urge to obey, but his seductive voice shakes the caged song in my head as if it were a wild animal, stirring it to primal heights. The only way I can soothe the beast is to reach for him.

He pulls me close and ties my wrists together before working off my metal headband, wig, and cap. My black hair springs free, wild and tangled. He lifts my chin to study me, as if assuring himself I'm not Christine.

Then wrapping one arm around me, he lifts his free hand in a wave directed at the stuffed trophies on the wall. A loud buzz grumbles from the animals' throats. I swallow a scream as swarms of bees burst from the muzzles and snouts—clouds of stingers and wings polluting the air.

Sunny and her allergy springs into my mind, followed by everyone else I'm supposed to be protecting.

I struggle, but the Phantom loops my tied arms around his neck so I'm facing his chest. With his heel, he nudges a ridge in the baseboard, opens a secret panel, and yanks me in with him, before shoving it closed and leaving the confused insects on the other side.

Darkness surrounds us. He drags me up some stairs. I clutch at the edges of each step with my bare feet, boring with my toenails until they bleed. He overpowers me and we reach the upper level. The instant we step into the narrow passage, he picks me up. His scents of formaldehyde and leather sting my nose, making me woozy. That embedded song claws deeper into my cranium, incapacitating me.

"Take her." This time, his words aren't directed to me. They're for Professor Tomlin, who's waiting in the shadows.

"It will be over soon, Rune. Then you can have your life back." My body is too limp to react to the betrayal slithering through my veins as Tomlin slides my tied wrists from around the Phantom's head and scoops me into his arms, his beard brushing my temple.

I'm only half-aware when my captors stop on the other side of the ballroom's mirrored wall. The sheer gold fabric paints a hazy scene within: staff and peers oblivious to the swarming bees on their way up. I try to find my friends or my aunt in the crowd, but my vision blurs. With a twitch of his fingers, the Phantom conjures another trick, stirring life into the black leaves on the trees and the floor. They burst into flight like bats, lifting the cobweb chains lining the tables and dive-bombing the now-screaming students and teachers. The bats drop their nets, trapping everyone. My mind is muddled . . . I can't decide if they've really morphed into bats, or if I'm totally unconscious now, having a nightmare.

Tomlin moves us out of the way. The Phantom pulls a lever on the wall that instantly shuts the ballroom's double doors, locking everyone inside, then releases the enormous chandelier. It plummets to the floor on a high-pitched whistle, raising the chaos to another level as people struggle to scramble out of danger while tangled in the nets. I must be dreaming, because a statue comes to life to shove one of the students out of the way, and ends up getting crushed itself beneath a bone-jolting crash of glass and metal. The fabric tied to the crystal fixture catches fire as it makes contact with the candles around the room. In an instant, the trees against the wall erupt like kindling, cutting off my view with a wall of smoke and flame.

I barely hear the screams inside. I barely hear anything but the Phantom's lyrical voice, filtered through his mask. "So, so clever . . . using her song, dressing like her, wearing her chains." He jerks the ring necklace from my neck. "But you broke the tether of illusion just a moment too soon." He traces the coiled ribbon marks on my wrist that show between spaces of rope, sending a chill through me. "My son should've taught you better. The devil's in the details." The Phantom takes me back from Tomlin, securing my wrists around his neck again, and cradling my body in his arms. My foggy head lolls against the cool leather of his jacket. "You, stay and see that everything goes as planned," he directs Tomlin. "Miss Germain and I have an appointment with fate."

25

SWAN SONG

"The timing of death, like the ending of a story,
Gives a changed meaning to what preceded it."
Mary Catherine Bateson

The asp bared its fangs and struck. Thorn stiffened, adrenaline pumping through his body, setting all his nerves on high alert. An instinctual response. He reminded himself that the clear panel separating him from his death wouldn't slide open to allow the five serpents from their lower compartment into the glass case surrounding him, unless Erik was here to activate it.

Another asp struck, leaving behind droplets of clear, deadly venom on the glass surface beneath him. A pheromone filtering into their section of the case had provoked the reptiles to a raging state. Their auras were bright, frenzied. Thorn's feet shifted, but he suppressed the urge to move his hands. It wouldn't do any good to try with the iron bands holding him pinned to the wall.

"You almost had it that time." Thorn lifted his shoulder as high as it could go to give Diable leverage. He knew Rune had sent him; she was his guardian angel. If she hadn't, he'd be alone and useless, contemplating worst-case scenarios for the masquerade going on hundreds of feet above him and unable to do anything constructive to help.

Now, he could possibly climb out and make a difference.

The cat's body stretched, hind feet settled on Thorn's right shoulder while one front foot planked his forearm and the other dug with extended claws at the keyhole in the locking mechanism.

Thorn's glass case was flush to the wall and a few feet from the operating table, to give him a bird's-eye view of Rune's torment, and her a bird's-eye view of his fatal predicament. His stomach knotted. Erik had knocked him out with gas before he left. A tribute to his deviant sense of humor, since he'd been wearing a gas mask himself. When Thorn roused, he was strung up in only his scrubs, feet stripped of his boots, although Erik left him his socks. That, too, was a strategy to play on Rune's sentimentalities.

All along, this had been his plan. To use Thorn as the bait that would convince her to give up her voice. That's why he'd allowed Thorn to woo the music in her, to bond with her. She might've chosen Thorn's life over the music even before they had the unity ritual. But now, it would be physically impossible for her to let him die. By trying to protect her, Thorn had damned her.

But there were three things Erik hadn't counted on: One, he was walking into a trap himself; two, he'd left Thorn within reach of the lever that would release the dams and flood the apartment—Erik's very own trap. It was on the wall, level with Thorn's head, no more than two feet away. And since the glass case only came to his chest, if he could free his right arm, he could stretch far enough to trigger the self-destruction sequence. And three, although the cord between twin flames would never snap, it could be severed if one of them died. Thorn was willing to meet a drowning death, for Rune's freedom.

Erik had lost sight of that detail, since he'd never shared the ritual with Christine. Since she left him forever after she found out he didn't bury their daughter at all . . . after she wandered into the lab a few nights postbirth, and saw her half-dead, premature infant being treated like a science experiment. Erik had been so desperate to keep their child alive he never considered he might lose the love of his life in the process.

Thorn averted his gaze from the cryogenic chamber and its pulsing yellow light on the other side of the room. Even now, he couldn't look at her perfect, tiny form. The nameless baby that would've been his sister. He hated what destroying this lab would do to her. What it would do to Erik. Total obliteration of his dream for a family and unconditional love.

Why? Why could Erik never see he already had that? It was the very reason Thorn had looked away from the depravity for so long, to bring some measure of happiness to his father's broken soul. Had Rune's arrival here not forced Thorn's eyes open, who knows what he might've done . . .

If Rune could manage the same awakening for Erik, she could sway his dark side and reach his humanity. She had the power. As long as nothing or no one intervened.

The ribbon tattoo beneath Thorn's iron cuff stung at just the thought of her, alluding that something had gone wrong. He'd do anything to be up there with her now.

Clenching his teeth against the cat's sharp barbs digging into his bicep, Thorn kept his arm still. Diable had already left trails of bleeding claw marks across his left cheek, neck, and shoulder, having leaped from one of the wooden shelves on the wall to get to him. It had been the only way for contact, with the glass between them.

While Diable shifted positions, still digging at the keyhole, Thorn's head sagged, trying to ease the tension from his neck. Hearing a small click in the iron band, he looked up. Before he could test his wrist, the elevator motor rattled to life and Ange trumpeted from within.

Ears back, Diable dropped to the ground and scrambled for a hiding spot. His jingles silenced upon finding one.

Thorn's pulse raced as he waited, hoping against all hope that Erik was coming to confess the error of his ways. The minute the gated door opened, his heart fell, seeing Rune unconscious in Erik's arms. This was no longer his father. This was the Phantom—in all his dark and depraved glory. Every spark of light had been snuffed out.

The Phantom's yellow gaze met Thorn's as he passed him to lay her on the table. Ange tottered behind, grunting, obviously vexed by their guest's motionless state.

Rune moaned without opening her eyes—toes spotted with dried blood; hair bedraggled; clothes dusty, rumpled, and scented with smoke. She'd been through a hell of a fight. That could only mean one thing: the Phantom hadn't fallen for their ploy, he held Rune inside a musical thrall, and the opera house was burning down.

Thorn took one look at her tied wrists, and his entire frame shifted and compacted—muscle and bones bracing together like tectonic plates against the explosion he felt inside of himself, a final detonation that killed every last ounce of the compassion he'd been struggling with for years. No more hesitation. The moment the opportunity presented itself, he would destroy this lair and everything in it. He'd sooner see their home demolished and lives ended than Rune pay the price for their deviant choices.

The cuff on his right wrist felt looser. Diable had managed to unlock it. With just one tug, it would pop open. But his left hand was still locked in place; he couldn't pull the lever until Rune was able to swim out of here herself.

The Phantom turned his back and lifted off the bulky gas mask, replacing it with a flesh-colored one that stopped at the bottom of his upper lip. It was always his choice for meticulous work: form-fitted with larger eye holes, leaving him unhindered while still covered. He mumbled under his breath like a madman as he shucked off his jacket onto the floor.

Curious if the key to the handcuffs might be inside one of the pockets, Thorn sent a silent command to Diable to check it out. The cat slinked from his hiding spot, not even ringing one bell, and wound around the edges of the room toward the jacket. Ange's long neck arched gracefully as she watched her feline friend, considering whether it was a game she wanted to play.

"What have you done, Erik?" Thorn tossed out the question as a diversion.

"Christine will forgive me. She has to. I'm giving her voice to our daughter." Erik replaced his leather gloves with latex, snapping them tight over quaking hands.

Thorn had never seen Erik so shaken. His gaze fell to Rune's sleeping face—hope sparking anew. It had worked. She'd chiseled away enough of the Phantom's protective shell to give Thorn a tender spot to gnaw on.

"She won't forgive you," Thorn baited, ignoring how his arm muscles were aching from their position. "You went to her on her death bed and swore you'd abandoned this madness. You sang with her in a final tribute to your child who was at last released to the dirt. Christine can't forgive you, unless you follow through. Unless you make it true."

Waddling around Erik's feet, Ange fluttered up to the table and perched on Rune's stomach where her hands were tied. The swan nudged the ropes with her bill and honked at Erik, scolding.

"Enough from the both of you." Erik's shaky fingers sorted through scalpels and instruments, arranging preferences on a silver tray with wheels. He also added the needle threaded with Katarina's hair—planning to stitch the baby's incision with Nilsson DNA, his own superstitious precaution. "Rune offered her consent, on the way here . . . upon hearing your plight. So no more guilt. She will live, just as Jippetto did."

Thorn watched his father tremble. Rune would never survive the surgery under such quavering hands. Erik would slice her carotid artery and she'd bleed to death.

"She has this one small sacrifice to make, then you can be together," Erik continued. "So ironic." His gaze snagged Thorn's with otherworldly potency. "I never expected to find you first. One-half of the *flamme jumelle*."

Thorn's jaw dropped. "What? How—"

"Adella told me, before either of you were even born. That since Christine and I were twin flames who never ritually united,

Christine's soul would be divided. A boy and a girl. You proved you were the other half when you followed me into the depths of that catacomb all those years ago. You had her fire. And when you touched my hand and stole away my energy, I felt her. I knew then that the prediction would come true: Unite the souls and the song will be reborn. A willing sacrifice to end all pain. All I had to do was find the girl, and make it so she could never say no."

Thorn almost choked on the bile climbing his throat. Not once had Erik mentioned twin souls as part of the foretelling. That's why he brought Thorn home with him as a child, even after his voice was taken away. That's why he gave him the violin after Rune's grandmother left it in box five. It was to connect Thorn to Rune early enough in their lives to make all of this inevitability come about on Erik's timetable. He had known they were destined to be together even before Thorn did. And he arranged to make it happen here in this place, on this night.

"You . . ." Thorn's voice was nothing more than a gritty moan, his eyes stinging with angry tears.

"Sometimes fate needs a little push." Erik turned on the transfer machine. Lights flashed to life and reflected along the walls in time with a barrage of metallic clicks. "I've learned not to trust the universe to get things right on its own." He resituated his mask, underscoring the statement. He wheeled the tray over to the opposite side of the operating table, facing Thorn with his patient between them. "Now, here we are on All Hallows' Eve, the night of liminality. The four of us together . . . and Christine's music will live again."

"Are you sure?" Thorn asked, composing himself. The snakes under his feet had grown more agitated, striking at the glass with vicious tenacity. Thorn absorbed their combined life-force, sipping it through his feet. A pull of energy so minute, it felt like needles prickling his skin, so subtle Erik wouldn't notice. Thorn siphoned the energized pulses to Rune through their shared imprints. A fiery sensation ignited along the coils of his wrist, real enough to heat the iron clamped over his skin. Rune's coils responded, and a threadlike trail of smoke rose from the ropes binding her, burning away the fibers . . .

Ange stretched, spreading her wings wide across Rune's body, hiding the phenomenon.

"What do you mean, am I sure?" Oblivious, Erik planted one hand on the edge of the steel table to steady it, and leaned across Rune, his shadow creeping over the skin bared above the bodice of her white dress. In his other quivering hand, he held a scalpel, studying her throat intently. "I heard her voice tonight. It was—"

"Seraphic?" Thorn offered, biting back a surge of panic. Rune's long, dark lashes fluttered, then the eye closest to him opened a slit, peering his direction. She was awake and aware, biding her time, listening. *Good girl. Don't move until he turns his back to you.*

"Yes, seraphic. Precisely." Erik pulled down the overhead bulb to spotlight Rune's head. He tilted his chin and laid the metal flat to her neck, planning the incision, though his hand still jittered. "I can't seem to remember. Where is it you make the first cu—?"

"Haven't you considered," Thorn interrupted upon seeing Rune grow tense—a miniscule twitch of her cheekbones that only he would catch. "That the prediction's already been fulfilled? And that you're the one who has to make the sacrifice for us all to be at peace?"

Erik drew back, glaring at him. Scalpel in hand, he walked around the table to Thorn's side, his back to Rune. Her face muscles relaxed.

"How do you mean?" Erik asked, his lovely, menacing voice more of a dare than a question.

"My and Rune's souls are united, as you know." Thorn held his gaze, catching Ange's movement in his peripheral view. She fluttered to the floor with Rune's frayed and scorched ropes in her bill and waddled into a corner, out of Erik's range. "The music lives in her, and together we tamed it. Now, Christine's voice thrives in Rune. She can use it and grow it, and glorify it. But were you to take it out and put it in a—"

"Your sister is not a corpse!" Erik lifted the scalpel to Thorn's throat from the other side of the glass, his hand quaking. Thorn stretched his neck, felt the twitching indention at his tendon—skin still intact, but cold from the metal bite. He swallowed and his Adam's apple rolled under the pressure of the blade. Rune had managed to sit up, a little unsteady, but cognizant enough to escape.

Thorn kept his father's attention on him, baiting him again. "There's no guarantee the incubator you've made will grow her a pair of lungs. This is all an idealistic design that's never been tested. You could be killing Christine's essence forev—"

"Silence!" Erik seethed, accidentally cutting Thorn's neck in his rage. Thorn felt the drizzle of blood. It was only superficial, but it stung far deeper than his skin.

Eyes widening behind his mask, Erik stepped back and dropped the scalpel to the floor with a metallic ping. "I'm sorry." The apology seemed strange—so vague and hollow—considering he had Thorn standing over a nest of asps. Erik drew a handkerchief from his pocket and reached over the glass to blot Thorn's neck with a gentle hand. "I'm so sorry, my son."

"I've never been your son. I was just a means to an end."

"No, I grew to love you." Erik squeezed his eyes shut and pressed his sunken forehead to the glass case inches from Thorn's chest. "I *do* love you."

Rune dropped to the floor on the other side of the table while Ange fluttered her wings to camouflage the sound of rustling clothes. Gripping the table for balance, Rune turned tear-sparkling eyes to Thorn, an unspoken inquiry for how she could help. He shook his head. Erik was too unstable, fluctuating between the monster and the man.

"You and I," Erik moaned, hands gripping the glass's edge, eyes still closed. "We have our family together at last. Please tell me you can see that, as she never could . . ."

"Yes," Thorn answered, dismal and dark. "I see it. We'll live as a family, you and I. Or we'll die as a family, the three of us." He yanked his right wrist free of the loosened cuff and slammed down the lever. "You choose. That's the sacrifice." The roar of gushing water tumbled upstairs in the apartment, instantaneous.

Erik's head popped up. His mouth gaped at the bottom of his mask. Horrified perception crept across his bright eyes, hazing them like storm clouds, as water flooded in from the elevator chamber and filled the cellar, scented of fish, mud, and algae. Within seconds it rose to Erik's knees and Rune's thighs.

With an agonized cry, Erik spun, wallowing toward the pulsing glow of the cryogenic chamber. When he reached the glass case, he wrestled with cords and tubes, wailing as he fought to free the tiny body.

"Etalon . . ." Rune's voice, little more than a squeak across the room beneath the thunder of water.

"Go now," Thorn insisted. "Diable will show you the way. It's irreversible. There are only forty seconds left."

The water pulled at her white dress, rising up to her neck. "No," she whispered. "I won't leave you!" She stood there, stubborn even while her aura was desperate, a thousand emotions in her teary eyes.

Her heartache ripped through his own heart, leaving his tongue soured with the flavor of hopelessness. Thorn tugged at his left wrist still clamped to the wall as water started sloshing into his glass case, upsetting the snakes under his feet. "I'll find a way out." A lie. The only one who could save him was mourning the child he never even had, oblivious to the one he did—a cruel truth that bled like a gaping wound in the core of his being. "Your friends, your aunt . . . they need you."

Rune's delicate features shifted to pained resolution. Diable paddled atop the water, spinning circles around her. Sobbing, she gave Thorn one final, imploring glance and dove in—braving her fear of water and disappearing with the cat into the passage that led to the chapel.

The first place he touched her face . . . and the last place she would see his.

26

LEGENDS

"Legends die hard. They survive as truth rarely does."
Helen Hayes

After Diable and I climbed free from the airtight chamber that opened into the baptismal, the rest of Halloween night played out in agonized slow motion.

I stumbled upon Etalon's suitcase in the chapel and opened it . . . I cried over the violin, fairy tale book, and clothes inside. But when I found the half-masks, perfect copies of his beautiful face, I broke down completely. Then I heard sirens and smelled smoke, and remembered the other side of my life. I slammed the suitcase shut and left it all behind, racing through the dark cemetery in soaked clothes and bloody bare feet with Diable at my ankles—making a point not to look at the baby's grave—across the footbridge, through the garden, and to the opera house.

Someone had used the landline to call for help, and the flashing lights of ambulances and fire trucks greeted me. I was surprised by that . . . The Phantom could've disabled the lines, had he wanted to. He would never have forgotten a detail like that. He left us a way to save ourselves. Which gave me hope for Etalon.

Almost everyone was in the parking lot. Aunt Charlotte and Bouchard, included. Besides Tomlin, every teacher was accounted for. Same with the students, other than Sunny and my friends, who Aunt Charlotte saw leave shortly after "Tomlin" followed me out of the ballroom.

She couldn't find Bouchard to help, so she went after my friends herself, to make sure they didn't get involved. She lost them by the time she hit the second floor and saw the swarms of bees surrounding Bouchard and Jippetto. Because neither of them was moving, the insects hadn't attacked. Another unexpected detail that gave me hope . . . The Phantom had commanded them to stay still for their safety—I saw that with my own eyes. Or maybe it was to protect the insects, so they wouldn't sting and die.

Aunt Charlotte released her smoke bombs to daze the bees. Then she woke Jippetto and Bouchard out of their trances right before the screams started in the ballroom. The doors had slammed shut just as the three of them got back up the stairs. Together, they were able to remove the hinges and get everyone out before the flames engulfed the room. The overhead sprinkler system had been disabled.

The Phantom was nothing if not mercurial.

When I realized that they'd also had to remove the hinges from the front door to get outside, it wasn't hard to piece together where

Sunny and the others went once they spotted the bees that would be deadly to her. I hadn't even thought about my roof key being missing again until that moment. Since all of the second and third floors were up in flames at that point, and the secret passages were also consumed by fire, I turned to Diable for help, remembering how he and Ange had stormed the roof the night before, during my rendezvous with Etalon.

Bells jingling, the cat led me to a secret passage behind some shrubbery—a flap similar to a large doggie-door—on the back of the building. It led all the way up to the cupola on the roof, so I was able to guide my friends to safety and won the title of hero.

But I knew who the real hero was, and my heart ripped a little more every time I thought of him.

I found out, as I walked with my friends to the parking lot, all of us arm in arm, that after I left the ballroom, Sunny told them about Tomlin "helping me" find my creeper. Quan, Jax, and Audrey debated for twenty minutes before deciding that Tomlin might actually be the one stalking me. That's why they followed me, to have my back, like they always did. Like real friends do.

When the cars arrived to take us to the city—those of us not riding in ambulances—I realized Diable was gone. And I whispered a prayer on the smoky, floral-scented wind that he'd found his master and they were somewhere safe.

A day later, my mom arrived in Paris to stay for a week . . . to make sure I didn't want to come home. I told her Paris was where I belonged now.

As they searched the academy, the police discovered Tomlin's corpse behind the mirror wall, which had shattered during the fire to reveal the secret passage. The science teacher was burned and sliced with glass shards, but not beyond recognition. They suspected he was behind everything. The elaborate setup in the ballroom—complete with hallucinogen-laced food and punch—and the bees filtered through pipes he'd installed in Bouchard's wall behind her plaques. He was also responsible for my torn uniforms, the dead crow on my chair, the broken white half-mask, the "fake" letters, the roses in the chapel, and the wristband and tubing—although me and my rave partners never dared admit that those led us to a club; what difference would it make, since we couldn't remember where it was or what happened there anyway?

A part of me regretted him taking all the blame. I myself saw how easily Erik could manipulate people. Tomlin wasn't all bad. He was just . . . misled. I did, however, have to admit he kidnapped me and held me in the secret passages where I saw him flipping gadgets and switches for the nightmare in the ballroom. The police also combed the chapel for evidence, but found nothing there, other than a red swan that fluttered out the moment they opened the door and flew into the cover of the forest before she could be captured. Yet nothing was mentioned about luggage filled with clothes, masks, and a violin.

At the end of the day, the police decided it was an open-and-shut case: a teacher whose bright mind had been damaged in a motorcycle accident years before. Who'd never been the same since. Who harbored a sick obsession with The Phantom of the Opera, and decided to live out his fantasy via the academy's up-and-coming opera star, Rune Germain. The girl once possessed by song.

The girl who was cured by the Phantom's son.

※ · I · ※

The first few weeks of November pass quickly, in spite of my aching heart. The fact that my ribbon imprint—or henna tattoo, as far as everyone other than Aunt Charlotte and Bouchard are concerned—feels warm, yet doesn't sting or hurt, gives me a small fraction of hope. But why hasn't he tried to reach me, at least in my dreams?

Every time I sing, I think of him, along with that poster on my wall back home of the bleeding rose: white petals, red liquid oozing from its heart. Only I'm the little girl fearlessly reaching into the thorns, not caring if I'm pierced and bloody; because those wings are so worth every ounce of the pain.

I've learned to control my appetites with daily samplings of energy, though I know that I'll need bigger feedings at times. Without Etalon to guide me, I rely on Aunt Charlotte and follow her routines. She's been keeping her secret since the age of fifteen, after all. She found the perfect shade of contacts for my eyes and I'm already used to wearing them when Mom and Ned fly in to spend Thanksgiving with us, bearing news about Ben—he's out of the hospital and doing great, though the doctors say he'll probably never regain memory of that night—an early Christmas gift even brighter than the cards from Trig and Janine.

Our school has continued with the support of all the parents. The classes, rehearsals, and dorms have been moved temporarily to an apartment building we're renting in Paris—Headmaster Fabre has a friend in the real-estate business—until the repairs to the opera house are completed. Since the anonymous benefactor can't be found, the deed now belongs to the investors, as per the contract. These include Aunt Charlotte and Madame Bouchard, who are both determined that RoseBlood will be up and running again, in all its old-world splendor, in plenty of time for our summer production of *The Fiery Angel*.

However, there's a new Renata. I was too "traumatized" from the kidnapping for such a taxing role, and have taken one of the smaller parts that opened up, although I've already signed up to audition for La Schola Cantorum Conservatory where Audrey is hoping to get a scholarship. And now that she's playing Renata again, she has a real chance. It's a shock to all of us that Kat didn't even bat her pretty eyes at losing the part. She's too preoccupied toting Roxie's books to classes, helping her up the stairs, and carrying her food trays to the table for meals. She hasn't left her friend's side since Roxie broke her leg while pushing Kat out of the way of the chandelier on Halloween night. It seems Kat has learned there's more to life than the pursuit of stardom and a hot guy with twinkling blue eyes and blond hair.

As for Jax and me? We've decided what happened between us at the rave club was drug-induced, no more real or mysterious than the delusions everyone had on Halloween night. Audrey's forgiven us both, and has told Jax how she really feels about him. They're dating now, and supercouple status is on the horizon. After almost dying, they're not wasting any more time.

The Friday after Thanksgiving, Ned takes Mom to see the palace in Versailles, and I go with Aunt Charlotte to visit Grandma Lil. I learn something while looking at my grandma's lifetime of wrinkles, and her nose and eyes so like Dad's: forgiveness is much easier than holding a grudge. She isn't expected to live through the end of the year, but at least now we've made peace.

After the visit, my aunt asks if I want to go with her to check on the renovation's progress at RoseBlood. It's the first time I've returned since Halloween. I don't waste one second following her into the opera house, just like she doesn't ask a single question as we part ways. The only thing she says is to be back in an hour.

The sun shines bright, but the wind is brisk with the scent of greenery and soil. I pull my cap over my head and snuggle deeper into my multicolor embroidered jacket and knit scarf. Today I wore my jeans with the patches, so no air can seep through the rips and chill me. I follow the trail through the garden, giving passing glances to the flowers and plants—some wilted and dormant, others still holding their shape and color while glistening with the first touch of frost. Come spring, I'll visit them every day.

My cheeks grow warm at the thought of carrying on Dad's love for gardening here, on his side of the ocean. At last I can honor his memory free of guilt.

There's a smile on my face by the time I cross the footbridge, no longer leery of the water underneath. My mood changes the moment I spot the baby's grave. When I saw her in that chamber, enveloped in liquid, hooked up to tubes that pulsed light and life into her empty body, there was a second that I hesitated—that I almost considered surrendering my gift—until Etalon's logic broke through. It wouldn't have grown her a set of lungs, or a beating heart. I've been blessed with both, so it's up to me to keep Christine's voice alive.

Noticing something different about the epitaph, I move closer to the cradle. Someone has etched *October 31* beside the year 1883, along with the name: *Hope*. The dirt around the grave is freshly dug.

It's confirmation. Erik chose his son, and Etalon's alive. Tears scald the edges of my eyes, a burst of relief.

He's alive.

But . . . that means the Phantom is alive, too.

What was it Christine said on her drawing? Legends never die.

That knowledge doesn't seem as intimidating now. He'll never hurt me again. Etalon will see to that.

I blot my eyes with my jacket's cuff and turn to the chapel. That ache begins once more in my heart . . . such a deep longing I can hardly breathe. I didn't plan to go inside; I didn't think I was ready. But a magnetized, tugging sensation winds through my tattoo, making it impossible for me to walk away.

My hands hover over the serpent door handle, spurring a gut-twisting memory of Etalon inside that glass case with snakes under his feet. I shut down the fear, because he made it out okay. I can find peace in that, even if I never see him again.

Just please, wherever you are, be happy, Etalon. Don't hide anymore. Live.

He deserves that, after the childhood he endured, and after all he did to save me and the school despite it.

A knot builds in my throat, belying my brave front. I'm selfish, because I don't want him to be anywhere else. He's part of me. I want him here. Now and always.

I shove the door open, painting the dirty stone floor with a slash of yellow sunlight. The soft illumination continues in colorful patches along the walls, stamped in place via the stained glass. I close the door and silence engulfs me, other than the whispers of wind seeping through jagged cracks in the windows. The scent of damp stone tinges the air, overpowered by the aroma of roses.

I move forward, taking cautious steps across the gritty surface as my eyes begin to adjust to the filmy yellowish light gilding the room. My breath locks in my lungs when I see the baptismal and my dad's violin propped at its base. Beside it, a blanket cushions the stone, dusted with a layer of duotone rose petals.

"I know I promised a bed, but I couldn't fit the box springs through the baptismal."

A sob catches in my throat at the sound of that broken French accent. I turn and he steps out from the shadows on the other end of the chapel—tall, strong, and gentle. *My maestro.*

He holds Diable in his arms. The cat scowls, disgusted by the confinement. As Etalon and I stare at one another in silence, Diable twists around, his collar jingling, until his "master" finally sets him down.

The cat bounds my way in a flurry of bells and wooly fur, stops long enough to wrap my ankles in greeting, then races into the shadows behind the baptismal. His jingling stops, a sure sign he found a way out.

Etalon hasn't budged from his spot, other than to take off his shoes. His dark wavy hair has been trimmed and swept into some semblance of order. He's wearing a lightweight navy sweater, dark-blue blazer, and ribbed navy pants, and stands beside his discarded shoes, showcasing my toe socks.

I clasp a hand over my mouth, caught between laughing and crying. My legs jitter, ready to run to him, my arms ache to embrace him. I'm hungry to kiss those lips and mess up his silky hair with my fingers. I've wanted it for a month. But I can't move. "You look . . . so normal," I mutter between my fingers.

A chuckle rumbles from his chest. "Well, there's a first time for everything, yes? I had a job interview in Paris today. Veterinary assistant. At last, I can use my talents once more to *heal* instead of alter. Erik pulled some strings."

To see Etalon so content, to know that he can start to atone for what he's done—it should unkink the twist in my gut. But the image of Erik pulling strings on any level sends shivers through me. I still remember how he held the scalpel to my throat, then did the same to Etalon, actually cutting him.

And I remember how I thought I'd left Etalon for dead.

"No." I drop my hand and struggle to contain the current of mixed emotions rising in me. "We're not doing this. Having a typical conversation like neither of us went through hell and back. You could've at least sent me a note! Something! Anything to let me know—"

He's towering over me before I can finish, a graceful slash of deep blue through the sunlight dappling the walls. "I thought you *did* know." He catches my palm and pushes my jacket's sleeve to my elbow, tracing the ribbon's band along my wrist and igniting the coils with delicious fire. "This should've told you." He lifts my knuckles to his soft lips then shakes his head. "I forget sometimes. The concept is foreign to you still. One day you'll learn to trust your intuitions."

I pound his chest, just once, with my free hand. "Even if I did sense it, that's not good enough! When you didn't come to me in my dreams, I was afraid you didn't want to find me."

His dark gaze intensifies and he backs me toward the baptismal, stopping when my hips hit the coolness of the bricks' edges. He slips off my cap and tosses it into the pile of rose petals, then winds his fingers through my hair and tilts my face so I can see the sincerity etched in every perfect feature. "I will always want to find you." His deep voice grinds through me, imploring me to believe. "Sometimes we can't be together. But even then, I'll be tied to you. I was giving you time to find *yourself*, to get your footing, while I found mine. But never doubt that I would cross the universe for you, *flamme jumelle.*"

Twin flame—the most disorienting and exhilarating juxtaposition I've ever encountered: adrift and independent, yet at the same time, rooted deep and bound to another.

His knuckle grazes my temple. "Now, all better?"

I lean into his body heat, holding him tight with one arm while basking in his woodsy, spicy scent. "Yes." I sigh. This is what I've been missing. This is what I've been waiting for. Peace, comfort, and completeness.

Home.

Both of his arms wrap around me, fingers trailing my vertebrae underneath my jacket as he nuzzles the top of my head. I press my ear to his sternum and open my hand on his chest, so I can hear and feel his heartbeat.

"Where were you?" I ask at last, snuggling closer to share his energy.

"After we escaped the flood"—balmy warmth dusts my scalp as he breathes the answer—"Erik and I stayed at Jippetto's for a few days, until the police thinned out. Then we went to the club in Paris for two weeks, arranging for others to take over its running. Erik had masks and clothes there, so once he was well enough to travel, we took a plane to Canada. We wrapped his face in bandages, as if he'd been in an accident. Ange and Diable accompanied us in the cabin. There's a mirrored underground city where I have . . . family."

I pull free to look up at him. "Mirrored and underground. So, our kind of family?"

"Yes. I'll take you one day, if you'd like to see it. But Erik needs to be there now. Somewhere safe, where he'll be accepted. He's still so fragile. I wanted him away from—" He cuts himself short.

"Me."

Etalon narrows his eyes in thought. "This place and all its memories, at the very least."

He's trying to downplay it, but even if he has forgiven Erik to some extent, there's still a part of him that doesn't trust his father anywhere near me. And I'm okay with that. I'll feel a lot safer here at RoseBlood knowing the Phantom is in Canada and that no one— other than a cranky cat—is lurking in the shadows.

"So," Etalon presses. "Your turn. Tell me about you."

I snort. "My details pale in comparison. You really want to hear about school? Boring, everyday things?"

"Always." His hands drop to the basin's edge on either side of my hips so he can hunch down, his forehead inches from mine. "But for now, I was thinking along the lines of something more *intimate*." The way he growls the word sparks my insides with anticipation, yet instead of the passionate kiss I'm expecting, he nuzzles my nose, sending electric tingles up the bridge. "When's your birthday . . . what's your favorite breakfast . . . how did it feel the first time you knitted a scarf? How many pets you've had. Oh, and what your favorite color is—"

"That's easy," I interrupt his teasing, noticing his chest aglow with that greenish light where my hand's still touching him. "It's green."

He laughs.

I laugh, too, until it registers what his job interview today must mean. "Wait. You're going to live in Paris?"

"I already have an apartment. I'll show it to you as soon as I'm moved in."

I bite my lip, trying not to give away how happy that makes me. Although I know he can read it in my aura. "Hmmm. You've made a lot of commitments to show me things. The mirrored city . . . your apartment . . . the rose-petal-covered *bed*."

He raises one dark eyebrow. "That one's my favorite."

"Mine, too." The admission warms my cheeks. "And maybe you can also show me how to play the violin?"

"*Bien sûr.* However, you know I like to play half-dressed." He grins—a seductive tease of teeth and lips.

"I'm all for learning my maestro's techniques," I respond without missing a beat.

"Just the answer I was hoping for." He's preoccupied with my hair again, winding the waves around his fingertips as if it's the most natural thing in the world. There's an easy rapport between us now . . . a pleasant contrast to all the heavy emotions and drama that brought us together. It's going to be nice to finally live in the moment, after so many years of being trapped in the past.

I smooth the lapels of his blazer. "You know, I'm liking this new look. It'll make things easier when you meet my family and friends if you appear reasonably human."

"Meet them—" The color drains from his face, mirroring his aura as it fades to pure gray terror.

I bark a laugh. "Oh, come on. *That* scares you? After everything we've been through, that's what leaves your blood cold? You have to meet them . . . it's one of the unwritten rules of dating."

"There are rules for a boy wooing a girl?" Tugging gently on my hair, he brings my face close enough to taste his warm, sweet breath. "I'm afraid you're going to have to write them down for me. I'm new to all this."

A smile curves my mouth, to imagine an incubus asking for dating tips. "There are only three others you should know. First, never say the word *woo*. Second, don't spout lame poetry, unless the occasion calls for a little extra romance." I push a fallen curl from his forehead, amazed and awed by how lucky we are to have found each other at this moment in time. Something I might be grateful to Erik for one day, many years from now. "And third, just be yourself. Guaranteed, you'll have all the girls falling at your feet."

I've no sooner said it than he scoops me into his arms, cradling me as if I weigh no more than one of Ange's feathers. "I have only one girl in mind," he says, close to my lips. "And I'll never let her fall. Too poetic?"

I trace the sculpted lines of his chin and jaw, breathless. "No," I whisper once I finally manage a response. "The occasion called for it."

Eyes copper-bright with the energy pulsing between us, his features grow somber. I hold his face as he bows his head for a kiss—a teasing crackle of sensation through my lips, tongue, and throat—flavored of spun sugar melted by a smoky flame. Carrying me to the rose petals, he lays me down. Then he lowers himself over me, and his mouth finds my skin, lighting up my body with song.

AUTHOR'S NOTE

AUTHOR'S NOTE

Caution: *RoseBlood* Spoilers

One of my favorite undertakings as an author is research. Inevitably, I learn something new, but nothing is as exciting as when I stumble upon facts from my everyday world—historical details or unique ideologies—that not only fortify the foundations of my fictional worlds but also enrich my real life, adding colorful layers that wouldn't have been there otherwise.

I first discovered Gaston Leroux's *The Phantom of the Opera* in high school, and was captivated from that moment on by the tragic, dangerous, and often sardonically humorous antihero, Erik. Over time, I evolved to a true-blue phan (Phantom fan), always eager to experience the story's many incarnations, be it as a musical, movie, or book adaptation. A few years ago, while surfing the web for information on Erik, I stumbled upon a phan forum that hypothesized he might've been a psychic vampire (also known in some circles as an incubus)—a supernatural subterranean creature who lives off of energy instead of blood.

Once that idea was in my head, I couldn't stop thinking about the possibilities. If the Phantom was an otherworldly creature, he could be immortal. After all, what would produce more energy for him to feed upon than the rapture of music or terror? (Both of which he inspired in spades.) Maybe he didn't die at the end of the original book. Maybe he made the ultimate sacrifice and faked his death to go underground again so Christine might have the normal life he could never give her. I wondered what—if anything—would ever be powerful enough to lure him to resurface in modern-day Paris over a hundred years later. Only two things I could think of: to rescue a mistreated child (Erik himself was physically and emotionally abused by so many, including his own mother), and the possibility of resurrecting his love for Christine somehow. These speculations gave birth to *RoseBlood*.

The idea for this novel percolated in my mind for several years while I wrote *Splintered*, but I didn't start researching *RoseBlood* until Abrams bought the book on proposal after I'd finished the Splintered series. Once I began, I took a page from my Wonderland retelling and opted to include Leroux's real-life inspiration for Christine, rumored by many to be the world-famous Swedish operatic soprano who went by the stage name Christina Nilsson (birth name: Kristina Jonasdotter, born to Jonas Nilsson and Cajsa Månsdotter).

There were some facts I stumbled upon along the way that gave credence to Christina Nilsson being the "real" Christine:

- Christina used to sign her name as "Christine" during written correspondences.
- Christina had blondish-brown hair—a much closer match to Leroux's original description of a blond Christine than the dark brunette version inspired by Hollywood and Broadway.
- Christina's talent flourished at a young age, and a civil servant became her patron, enabling her to have vocal training despite her peasant background. Leroux's heroine was also lower class and beneath Raul's station in the story; her patron, who appeared out of nowhere and offered the vocal guidance she needed to rise to her full potential, was a mysterious and elusive voice from behind the mirrors and walls—aka her Angel of Music, the Phantom.
- Christine's father played a violin in the novel; in real life Ms. Nilsson herself was a violinist.

As I began looking into Christina Nilsson's timeline from birth to death, I found it can easily run parallel with Leroux's Phantom, with only a couple of minor discrepancies. Her birth was in 1843, and Erik's is calculated to be somewhere in 1831, according to his age in *The Phantom of the Opera*. That would make Ms. Nilsson only twelve years younger than the Phantom, as opposed to twenty-some years younger like Leroux's Christine. Also, some phans have estimated that the bulk of the book, when the Phantom and Christine meet and interact at the opera house, took place between 1863 and 1864. Since Ms. Nilsson did in fact have her debut in 1864, that's the ideal span of time for them to meet and for her to receive his musical guidance. However, the renowned soprano never once performed at the Palais Garnier—the opera house said to have inspired Leroux's Opéra Populaire. Her debut took place in another Parisian opera house called Théâtre Lyrique. Furthermore, if Erik indeed "died" in 1882, as some have estimated, that would be the perfect time for him to fake his death and lure Christine to his side (which was pivotal to *RoseBlood*'s plot)—especially considering Christina Nilsson's first husband died that same year, so she was between the only two marriages recorded in her personal history.

Upon learning all of this, I knew I had my "real-life" Christine Daaé counterpart. I simply needed a way to explain the discrepancies and weave the Swedish soprano into Erik's history. That's where Leroux's original serialization of the Phantom tale in a French newspaper—prior to his writing and publishing the novel—comes into play, as you've seen in my story.

To give the incubus/succubus element even more depth, I found another historical figure to tie into Rune's family. Any online search for Comte de Saint-Germain will turn up fascinating and unsettling rumors from the 1700s of a man suspected of being a vampire and having great talents and intellect, along with a knack for alchemy and black magic.

While trying to uncover a more mystical and powerful term than *soulmate*, because what Erik and Christine shared was beyond anything cliché or traditional, I stumbled upon the concept of twin flames. It's inspired by Aristotle's philosophy of love: one soul inhabiting two bodies. The concept is beautiful and empowering, yet in some ways tragic and overwhelming—the perfect summation of their relationship. As I researched twin flames, auras and chakras kept surfacing, which gave me the idea to weave them into my succubus and incubus canon.

Of course, as a writer, I exaggerated and embellished the details to fit my story line. So, if any of these concepts or histories captured your imagination while reading *RoseBlood*, be sure to do your own research and seek the truth behind the fiction. The only thing better than visiting fictional worlds is realizing how interesting and colorful the one you already live in actually is.

ACKNOWLEDGMENTS

ACKNOWLEDGMENTS

Gratitude to my husband and children: Vince, Nicole, and Ryan. It takes special people to coexist with a writer. Your patience over the years each time I've had deadlines and you're left eating TV dinners in a dusty house while wearing the "least" dirty of your neglected laundry has gone above and beyond. Let there be no doubt: You are the heroes of my life story. Also, thank you to other family members who offer constant support from the sidelines.

Grateful hugs to my #goatposse for their uplifting witticisms, heartfelt posts, and unwavering devotion to "the herd." And to my critique partners: Jennifer Archer, Linda Castillo, April Redmon, Marcy McKay,

Jessica Nelson, and Bethany Crandell. Without your writerly wisdom, business savvy, and faith in my work, I would still be writing under a rock somewhere, afraid to show my words to anyone.

The sincerest appreciation to my resourceful and knowledgeable agent, Jenny Bent; to my gracious and insightful editor, Anne Heltzel, whose valuable suggestions inspired me to take the scenes and characters to a new level; and to my fabulous publicists, Caitlin Miller and Tina Mories. Also, my gratitude to copyeditors, proofreaders, and all the unsung heroes behind the making of every beautiful book at Abrams. On that note, thank you once again to Maria Middleton and Nathália Suellen for being the most imaginative and artful book design team.

SMUGS to the best beta reader and online supporter any author could hope for: Stacee (aka @book_junkee). And hugs to Heather Love King, my Pinterest buddy who is as addicted to eye candy as I am. No one could ask for better cheerleaders than the two of you! Also, a special thanks to Jaime Arnold and Rachel Clarke of Rockstar Book Tours for their outstanding work on my virtual book tours.

To my Facebook Splintered Series Fan Page moderators: Katie Clifton, Diane Marie Hinds, Natalia Godik, and Autumn Fae Evans, and to my RoseBlood fan page mods: Amanda Colin, Adriana Colin, and Chara Sullivan. I value you so much. The effort you put into maintenance and interactions keeps the pages afloat when I'm working to meet deadlines. Also, *waves* to all of the fan page followers. Hanging out with you is one of my favorite pastimes!

A depth of gratitude to my Twitter, Tumblr, Pinterest, blog, GoodReads, and Facebook followers, along with book bloggers, fellow authors/writers, and readers. Writing can feel like a solitary endeavor at times. Having your online support reminds me that I'm never really alone at all. Also, a deep bow to Gaston Leroux for writing the gothic and tragic masterpiece that has lit the imaginations of so many and inspired movies, musicals, and countless retellings.

And last but not least, my thanks to God for giving me this passion for storytelling, and for keeping my well of inspiration filled.